HEART OF THE WORLDS
BOOK 2

FAERIES DON'T FORGIVE

TF BURKE

SYLVAN SWORD PRESS

WILLIAMSPORT, PA

Book Cover by Cristina Tanase

First edition 2025

ISBN: 979-8-9903741-5-7

Library of Congress Control Number: 9798990374133

To sign up for TF Burke's Wyrd & the Wisp newsletter, visit https://BookHip.com/PMWQAPV

Or visit her website at https://tfburkeauthor.com/

—To Eli, my first superfan and sword-sibling.

CONTENTS

South Eastern

N
W E
S

Dawn's Way

Worley Province

Wythrindle River

Whisp River

Hauser Tower

Worley

Plardonway

the forgotten Way

Spatelly

Catherine's Cottage

East-West Trade Route

Zig Road

Zig Road

Komstaay?

Vraely River

Vrael Ma

Vrael road

Scorched Earth

The Fork Woods

Hall
Ea

Wraithmere
Sea Marsh

Map of Tamore

Vrael's Duchy

Grashbear Mts

Dead Lands

Froidelac
Marchlands Baxter's Way
Stewing Gateway

Britchway

Bernal

Eddac Tower

Vrael's fork

trade spar
Dalin

Alevis

Dalin Marchlands

Swordspur Way

Stanz Tower

Dunmaris Earldom

Linden River

Caelthorne Earldom

Baxter's horn

Idenweigh

East-West Trade Route

...ere
...dom

Elswyth Duchy

Varundu Forest

the fort

Adarian Sea

20 miles

CHAPTER ONE

THE BRAINHEDGE TREE

All of life will circle back, becoming what we once knew and we will learn it will never be the same again. — Nyrissa Rieson, flyer of Lydinairre, daughter of Dar Zeller Rieson

Being thrown high into the sky to one's death was not an easy thing to forgive. Aunia stiffened with the memory of free fall . . . where wererat people, ant-sized at first on the Grashbear's tan-colored slopes, grew with alarming speed.

It was only a few hours ago that Hebsolum, the marble giant, had helped her to imprison Edvaras' storm cloud of magic within her mother's amulet. It was the only thing they could do to prevent the Boggleman from using that magical Nymer to destroy the human world but it came with a price. Aunia tapped her collarbone. That amulet had been the only thing she had of her mother . . . and now it was gone. The marble giant had taken it while she had been pinned by a veil tendril through her gut. And not only that. He had tried to take Mygul, her magical globefire from her as well. But, she had fought him, and he had tried to kill her.

Aunia pressed her shoulders into Mathias' chest and he wrapped his arms around her while Tafiriel's broad blue wings lulled a portion of her heart from her throat. They soared so high over her mother's lands, irregular shapes of greens and browns, on a pegasus' back through a cloud-dotted sky. A beautiful view if only the land below would stop spinning.

I won't let you fall, Tafiriel sent telepathically.

Hebsolum shouldn't have thrown me. She bit her lip. She had no idea that the marble giant would retaliate when she refused to give up Mygul, but she had no choice. Her globefire wasn't a part of Edvaras. It was a part of her.

Hebsolum . . . he has his own code, Tafiriel sent.

His own code? Aunia dropped her hands from her collarbones and gripped Mathias' arms. What would happen to Mygul if she would have died?

You didn't die, Tafiriel sent. *And you're safe.*

Aunia closed her eyes. She didn't die, all thanks to Basil. His magic had allowed her to float like thistledown to the wererat people.

Forgive me. Mathias pulled his arm from her to gather her long blond hair. He tucked its length into the back of her tunic. *Your hair's tickling my nose.*

Aunia shivered against Mathias' fingertips on the nape of her neck . . . a curious sensation of liquid fever and quiet. She relaxed into his touch while the land spread out before her . . . tens of thousands of Naoma Sacella fields on all sides, and the receding Grashbear Mountain range behind them.

She frowned, straightened, and laced her fingers through Tafiriel's blue mane. *He's drooping.*

Keston, maybe a mile ahead in the afternoon sky, sunk heavily in the saddle. His head injury from the wyvern's tail needed healing attention. It made the soles of her feet ache, imagining what would happen if he lost consciousness and slipped.

I see. Mathias straightened too.

How long till we're there?

We're close, Mathias sent. *See that ribbon of gray-white and brown up ahead?*

With that line of shadow running beside it?

Yes. The ribbon is Baxter's Way. It's a highway that connects the northern part of my country to the southern border and to our Adarian neighbors. The shadowy line . . . that would be the brainhedge.

Aunia looked over her shoulder. *No tree is that long.*

Mathias, dark wavy hair blowing in the wind, smiled. *That is a living fence of trees. It keeps the Marchlands of Dalin and Froidelune separated.*

Marchlands?

Think of them like mini kingdoms, Mathias sent. *And these two do not have good relations. That hedge keeps them from warring over water.*

Why would they—

There's a stream that runs from a tethered blade-cave in-between the two hedgerows on Froidelune lands. And Dalin . . . well, they think the water has magical properties and want to cart it off for their sword making operations.

Tafiriel lowered in the sky. The land's green patches transformed into crops with wavy green tops and pockets of brambly wilderness.

The rover caravan is near the Brainhedge gate on Froidelune lands, Mathias sent. *Just a few minutes more, but there is something I need to warn you of.*

Warn me? About what?

Mathias' sigh tickled the back of her head. *Rovers can't be trusted.*

Aunia frowned. *What do you mean, can't be trusted? Basil helped us. Saved me from—*

They do what they can to curry favor, Mathias interrupted. *And they have their uses, yes. They're good at healing. Trading in magic potions and hard to get items. Telling fortunes. But they steal and they lie and they feel no guilt for it. All Tamorians know, you watch your money and your children around them.*

They drew near to the double hedgerow of trees, and Keston started his descent toward the road.

Basil knows things about my parents, Aunia sent. Not only that, but Jennium, her garden faery friend, trusted Basil and the man's powder blue glow felt incredibly familiar.

He could have just been saying that.

No, he knew them. She crushed the fabric of her sky-blue cloak with her fist. Mathias had been wrong about wererats being monsters when they encountered them on the Grashbear. He was wrong about this, too. She'd seek Basil out as soon as she saw that Keston was mended.

Mathias is right to be wary, Tafiriel sent. *But I will be here, if you need.*

They flew over the first hedgerow with its globular yellow-green clusters of fluffy-looking flowers and over the space between, a lush narrow strip of land with a stream running through it.

"Aunia," Mathias spoke into her ear.

I'll be careful, she sent.

"And no talking to faeries."

"But Tafiriel's—"

No getting caught talking to faeries. Mathias' arm tightened around her middle. *And no magic. It's dangerous here.*

They flew over the second hedge with one tree, presumably the Brainhedge Tree, towering over all others by a house-height.

They dove. Not the steep-you're-going-to-die type but a gentle decline over the white-gray road, and looped back to face eight colorfully painted wagons—reds, oranges, yellows and blues. The people, traipsing between their roofed wagons or huddled in small groups, wore bright colors as well.

Aunia bit her lip against the empty sky in the direction they had come. *Where's Fallo? He's bringing Basil, isn't he?*

Fly him? Mathias jerked away, leaving a space between them. *Fallo wouldn't give a rover a ride.*

But how will he—

He's a Mystic. He'll skip.

Skip. Magically transport from one place to another. Aunia had learned of that when she and Tafiriel used the Boggleman's veil tendril as a catalyst to use that magic. *I see Keston. Middle campfire.*

They veered toward a rope-fashioned corral between some wagons and hedge-wood and landed. A blue wagon with painted black knotwork partially blocked the sight of Keston sitting on a high-back chair being attended to by two rovers, an old man with a pipe and a girl dressed in blue. She was peeling away Keston's head bandaging.

"Leave it to him to find a girl." Mathias dismounted.

Aunia plucked her canvas knapsack from the bucket seat saddle horn and dumped it on the ground out of her way. She dismounted and ran past Revellie, who stood within the enclosure, sipping at a bucket of water near beautiful horses with long tails and feathered legs.

She wriggled through the corral's ropes and darted between the colorful roofed wagons to the stone-ringed campfire to Keston.

Keston greeted her with a smile and dilated eyes. "There you all are."

Aunia slowed on the pebbled grass. He had a potion in him. She wasn't sure what kind but Mathias said they were good healers. She shrugged off her cloak. "I can care for him."

Sitting by the fire, an old man looked up from his short stool. He held a long wooden dowel across his lap and his sage-green and amber glow swirled.

The girl also turned. This child was younger than Aunia thought, maybe twelve years old. Under her pair of dark brows, she gazed out with deep-set defiant eyes. Eyes like Limi's after her mother, Nehla, had died. Too much like . . . except this girl's irises were dark blue, like Aunia's own, not deep brown like Limi's.

A nearby knot of girl-children playing with cloth dolls under the bright yellow wagon — they were easier to look at.

"Are you a flyer like Keston, the sculptor's son?" the rover girl said.

"Sculptor?" asked Aunia.

Keston slurred with a nod. "My dad's one of the best."

"I'm not a flyer." Aunia said.

How could she make this rover girl with her purplish-gray glow step away? It hurt Aunia's heart to see someone else with Limi's glow. A glow that stuck after Limi swore she'd not become the village's next Eldest Daughter. But this girl wasn't Limi. She was too young and too fancy with her tiny embroidered flowers edging a blue circle skirt and bodice. And the girl had twin thick braids for her dark hair, not Limi's many.

"I've most of the wyvern scale splinters out," the girl said. "I'm Taya, by the way, and this is my grandda, Niall."

CHAPTER TWO

HORSEBREAD

When people talk about you, they typically don't want you there — Basil Mensani of the Mensani caravan

Mathias scooped Aunia's knapsack from the ground and looped it back on the saddle horn. Leaving it unguarded . . . not a smart idea, though other than a book, what did she have? Probably only a small bundle of clothing.

Where was Fallo? Not even a black dot graced the sky. There was so much to talk about now that they were in Tamore and everything had turned complicated. Too many things needed answers. Near the top of the list: how to answer Cat's threat to bring them to trial for abandoning their post.

Mathias ran a hand through his hair and sucked in a breath to settle himself. It was only an illusion that the nearby ridged bark trees pressed in too close. That their thorns sought to pierce his flesh. He couldn't face another trial.

We didn't abandon our post, Taf sent.

Well, technically? They just followed wererats over the Grashbear. But they had cause. Wererats had attacked and burned Britchway. And they had bitten Jules.

Mathias took several steps to get a clear angle of Aunia working on mending Keston's head. Or rather, Aunia watching over a rover girl doing the healing. What a scare Keston had given him during the wyvern battle. A wyvern had nailed Keston with its tail and Aunia had screamed with the wyvern's fireball. It could have been far worse. He was grateful Keston would pull through fine.

Jules, on the other hand . . . where could he be? He had disappeared with or without his pegasus, Brinsaber, who was hiding somewhere on the Grashbear Mountains. Another riddle to figure out. One that had to be solved.

Is Aunia okay there? Mathias sent to Tafiriel.

They don't mean her harm and Revellie's relaxed, Taf sent back.

Revellie. Keston's pegasus. She had the best sense of spotting danger, not that it helped during the festival when—

She gave me warning at Britchway, Taf reminded him.

Warning would have been nicer sooner. It could have prevented Jules from being bitten. Or the town from being burned down. Then they wouldn't have gone over the Grashbear. He wouldn't have met Aunia either. Mathias swallowed hard. And then, he wouldn't have ruined her life. He scanned the heavens again. *What's keeping Fallo?*

Paderro sends they're on their way, Taf sent. *You could get all this gear off me while you wait.*

Mathias rapped his thigh with a fist. They were relatively safe here. And Taf had worn riding gear since they left Aunia's village. *Of course.*

He unbuckled the reins, pulled the nose bridle gently over Taf's ears, and draped the leather straps over one of the camp stools.

Finding Jules was key. For his friend's sake, yes, but they could also provide proof that wererats had attacked. Taf and the other pegasi's word should be good enough, but they had been inside the stable, not the attack site.

They could also find the healer at Dalin, who had treated Jules. Mathias unfastened the girth and removed the saddle. He placed the saddle on the stool and whistled for Revellie. Best to get her gear off, too.

Some of the wererats provided aid on the Grashbear, Taf reminded.

I wasn't bespeaking you. Mathias walked over to Revellie. But Taf was right. That was another riddle. Why had wererats helped? Because they had a Mystic in their midst? That certainly wouldn't make any difference in the Tatian Court nor in the House of Nobles. They'd always remain suspicious of Mystics. They were, after all, the ones blamed for the Blood Ball, which had nearly annihilated the royal family over a decade and a half ago.

Keston believes Basil to be a good guy.

Mathias frowned. *Well, Fallo knows him.*

He pulled off Revellie's gear, found a rag under a camp stool, and dunked it into a water bucket. The gold pegasus had green wyvern ichor around her mouth and it was best to get that gone. Groom both pegasi and Fallo would be here before he was done. And after his dressing down, he needed to talk Fallo into going to Dalin to find out what happened to Jules.

What if those wererats are under the marble giant's protection?

Taf, just stop. Mathias pulled the green stained rag from Revellie's face. *It was likely Fallo would complain about the marble giant when he showed up. And with a crater where a mountain once stood . . . that gave credence to the giant's appearance. But none of that was relevant. The problem was . . . would Fallo agree with him?*

He needed to be sure that Fallo focused on finding Jules, clearing their names, and letting Nyrissa and the Queen know that knowledge of a faery repellant was coming. That last thought sent Mathias' stomach to twist. Going back to Tatia was going to be a problem.

Mathias grabbed a handful of straw from a broken bail and rubbed Revellie down.

"Flyer?" A tall semi-bald rover man approached and patted a seven-pointed star that was pinned to his red vest. Behind him, followed a woman with cinnamon-colored hair and high cheek bones.

"That's a royal star," Mathias accused.

"It is," the man said. "Mine came to me through my wife's grandmother in 953."

"Tharon," said the woman. "Just tell him it was a gift by Queen Silvani to Prince Elris on the eve of his wedding and he can check the star's history at the exchequer's office when he visits the capital next."

"Prince Elris?" Mathias straightened. He heard the stories of a royal-born marrying a rover lass. A peasant tale he had thought. "You're kin to the Maid of Idenweigh?"

"We are," Tharon said. "We're still awaiting aid to rescue our Olivia from the Boggleman."

Mathias stiffened. While they had flown to the caravan, Aunia had told him some of the things she had seen in Nonderu, including seeing Olivia imprisoned in Chand ice. An incredible story to believe. She also said she thought her mother had been a Chandarion. "That was over seventy years ago."

"Time in Faery moves differently. And what should it matter? She saved Tamore during the Mockmen Wars," the woman said.

"Let the young man catch his breath." Tharon extended his hand. "I'm leader here and this is my sister-in-law, Lena."

"Mathias." He kept his hands at his sides. "I need another bucket of water for my pegasus."

Tharon whistled, and a moment later, a lad of about fourteen years scurried forward, sloshing water from a large bucket.

He set the pail in front of Taf, turned, and shoved a chunk of bread checkered with peas and beans at Mathias. "You've a beautiful companion. She yours?"

Mathias let the unappealing food crumble between his fingers. "We don't own people."

"The horsebread was meant for your pegasus, flyer," Tharon said. "We're planning on offering you what we have from our stewpot. If that's all right with you, of course."

Heat radiated from Mathias' face.

Do you plan on being leader here? Tafiriel sent.

What? No. Mathias got Tafiriel's meaning. Ingratiate yourself. Remain cordially aloof. Leave or fight. Those were the acceptable choices one made within a new group. "My apologies," he said slowly. "There was . . ."

Pandemonium on top of the Grashbear. Did these Rovers know that? Could they have seen the dust clouds rising from the Grashbear when Hebsolum burst through the mountainside? Even from this distance? But then that forty-some-high hedge . . . it could have obscured their sight. And if they didn't know . . . the last thing Mathias wanted was questions, which he had no answers for. He turned his palms over. "It's been a long couple of days."

"It has at that." Tharon crossed his arms.

"Do you know how Keston is doing?"

The rover boy perked up. "The girls are sewing 'im up and he's a healing potion in. Took a nasty gouge to the head. Was it from one of the wyverns? We saw them flying about."

"Besnik, leave it," Tharon growled.

"Da." Basil strolled between two blue vardos wagons to them and pointed over the hedge. "That would be the flyer we need to talk with."

Fallo, on his black stallion pegasus, flew over the brainhedge and over the rover caravan.

"Lagging a bit, eh?" Tharon said.

Basil shrugged. "Said he had a matter to handle."

Mathias' breath caught. Had Fallo taken a moment to see if he could find Brinsaber?

I think not. Taf stomped a foot.

Fallo and Paderro landed in the corral close to Tafiriel and the commander dismounted with a furrowed brow. "Hope you have a brandy on hand."

"Of course I have," Tharon said.

Basil pulled his orange bandana from his black-haired head. "And we've much to discuss."

"About Hebsolum? Or Jules?" Mathias stepped closer to Fallo, wondering why ruorks had stung up the commander's face. Those faeries didn't often sting. But Fallo and Keston had been in a cave before the Grashbear incident. "Or maybe wererats?"

Fallo clapped Mathias on the shoulder and pointed to the fire. "Keep those two out of trouble."

Mathias jerked back. "I should come, too."

Fallo's grip refastened on Mathias' shoulder and he squeezed. "You'll do as I say."

Clenching his jaw against the pain, Mathias refused to nod. He had every right to know what was happening.

Taf swished his tail. *He isn't in the mood—*

I still haven't learned what happened in that secret meeting in Aunia's village. Bespeak Fallo. Tell him you and Rev can keep an eye on Aunia and Keston.

Fallo released him without any further acknowledgment and followed Tharon, Basil, and Lena through the corral's opening to the rover wagons.

Fallo bespeaks you are to follow orders. And he...sends something about wondering if you're capable. He plans on talking with you later, Taf sent back.

"Would you like a tour of the caravan?" the rover lad, Besnik, asked.

Great. A simple rover lad watched him be dismissed. Mathias pushed past the boy and out of the corral. He leaned against the nearest vardo and idly traced over the painted evil eye pattern. Keston looked like he was dozing in the chair while Aunia, pot of steaming water at her feet, worked on his head. It didn't look like there'd be trouble even with the girl in blue hovering over them. Seemed more of an issue of the commander and rovers wanting to keep him from their conversation, but why?

If he was Keston, he'd sneak behind and eavesdrop. Aunia would too, probably. Why not him? How hard could it be?

CHAPTER THREE

WARNINGS AND QUESTIONS

We believe what we think, whether it's true or not. Won't you pause and consider? — Gaitha, Eldest Daughter of Naoma Sacella

"Here, I'll take care of this." The rover girl pushed Aunia aside. "Grandda, get that needle ready."

Aunia bristled until Keston shot Aunia a painful smile and re-closed his eyes. He was pale sitting in the dark-wood rover chair, but not as pale as when the wererats had brought him out on the Grashbear. Wererats were dangerous, Mathias had said. But they had tended to Keston. And Rovers?

She needed to dismiss the similarities that Taya had with her foster-sister. Even if Limi had betrayed her. Taya was not Limi. Aunia stepped closer toward the pungent, savory-sweet smelling bowl. "What are you using to clean his wound?"

"Apple-cider vinegar with thyme and lavender." Taya waved bloody fingers at Niall, her gray-bearded grandda.

Niall had retrieved his wooden dowel and plunged it into the small red-brown cauldron, which hung over the fire from a black metal tripod.

A light breeze cooled Aunia's cheeks. Keston's puckered laceration—a mingling of crusted and fresh blood brought memories from caring for her village's wounded only a few short days ago. Her hands spasmed with a deep ache. A bone ache from the hours tending to green-streaked limbs, missing flesh, and so much blood. "You sure all the wyvern scales are out?"

"Every last one. Now it's wash the ill-humor away so there's no festering. Don't want any ooze between the stitching."

Taya wrung more healing wash over Keston's wound while Niall turned his wrist as if he were hooking a fish. He pulled the wooden dowel from the boiling water and a pair of scissors dangled from its end.

Taya squatted and dropped her linen cloth into a wooden bowl at her feet. Another waft of vinegar rose. "Grandda, my hands."

"Here. Don't touch the metal till ya washed yer hands." Niall foisted scissors and dowel onto Aunia.

She took them, blinking. She had been Gaitha's apprentice. She knew how to dress a wound.

He picked up a bucket by the fire and poured water over Taya's hands, rinsing away blood. She then scooped a soft cake of soap—pale yellow streaked with dark green—from a chipped flower-patterned plate. "You never mentioned your name."

"Aunia. And I know what I'm doing."

Gaitha, Eldest Daughter and medicine woman, of Naoma Sacella easily could have used a similar treatment.

Taya shook water from her hands. "That's obvious with your field dressing. Fine work. But you didn't have supplies at hand. The bandaging. It was from a shirt."

Aunia scowled. She couldn't argue with that.

Taya glanced toward the Grashbear Mountains. "Does the flyers' healer want to do the stitching?"

"I'm not the . . . no. I'll watch."

The girl's gaze raked Aunia from sandaled feet to tangled hair before she pulled the scissors off the dowel's end. "Quite unusual. Flyers don't take on passengers. Where are you from?"

Keston opened his eyes. His pupils nearly took up most of his amber irises.

"The other side of the Grashbear Mountains," Aunia replied. "What did you give him?"

"The other side?" Taya's eyes grew wide. "I've wondered what's past the Dead Lands."

"What did you give him?" Aunia repeated.

"Only a sleeping potion." Taya clipped the light brown, blood-soaked hair at the edge of the wound. "Stitching sort of hurts otherwise. Grandda, thread me a length?"

"Think I can get more wine?" Keston slurred.

"I think you've had enough, flyer," Taya said.

Niall reclaimed the wooden dowel from Aunia and used it to lift a strand of thread from the pot's boiling water. Handing the dowel off again, he pulled a metal needle from the inside of his red-brown vest and dunked the tip into the boiling water.

His glow, except for the pink flickering at its edges, nearly matched the pot, and Aunia's heart squeezed painfully. Like Taya reminded her of her foster sister, this man reminded her of her village's chief and storyteller. A man who had been more fatherly to her than her own.

"Healing heat before we sew . . . into living flesh we go. Feverless, the wound doth close," Niall intoned as he threaded the needle.

"Stitching me like cloth?" Keston slurred.

"Yes, my sculptor's son. For it to heal faster." Taya poked at the wound's puckering. "Probably won't even leave a scar."

"Leave a . . ." Keston trailed off and his eyes closed.

Sleeping potion. Herbal, Aunia reminded herself. Not magical. Pegasi guarded against magic affecting their flyers. It was the only reason that Keston survived the wyvern fireball after it had struck with its tail.

"Here." Niall held out the threaded needle.

"Aunia, can you wash up?" Taya asked. "I could use you holding the wound together so I can stitch this up good."

Aunia lathered up with the rosemary and mint squishy soap. Gaitha would always wash out a gaping wound, but she often used a healing word of power before she packed it with medicine. Gaitha had even whispered power words over Mathias's shoulder bite from the heeble. Stupid that she never took the time or had the curiosity to learn what those power words were.

Shaking the water from her hands, Aunia stepped in place as directed, and pushed the wound closed with her finger pads.

"Excellent." Taya pierced the flesh, drawing the thread through skin. Keston didn't even flinch.

"So, on the other side of the Grashbear, are there cities there or—"

"A village . . ." Aunia bit her lip. Mathias had confessed his part in Fallo's plan to annex her village. The plan had failed and the villagers spelled the village into invisibility with the shrouding flower. However, how could she be sure no one else would try to harm her people?

"Gabin, you set that down right now," a voice barked from Aunia's left. A woman a few yards away scooped up a wriggly toddler and walked back to a secondary cook fire which crackled near the last wagon in the caravan. It was a red one with a curved roof. All of the eight wagons did, except one. The woman, child in arms, took a seat beside two other women. On the other side of the fire, a lanky man stirred a large pot.

"So, a village," Taya murmured. She jabbed through Keston's flesh again. "Why did you leave? Was it for the handsome flyer?"

"They didn't want me," Aunia snapped.

"Didn't want you?" Taya's glow flickered with deep blue and cloud-white. "You have known sorrows. I understand. But you did make quite an entrance, didn't you? What with the wyverns and—"

Aunia's fingers slid on Keston's blood. She bit her lip and concentrated on keeping the wound closed. "I had nothing to do with that."

But she did have something to do with it. It was because the Boggleman, in wyvern form, had chased them through the Dead Lands and when they reached the Grashbear Mountains, he had called the other wyverns.

"Lots of wyverns have been flying over the mountains these days," Niall said. His glow, brown like a flooded river, turned honey-amber.

"And the marble giant exploding forth!" Taya shuddered. She glanced back at Aunia. "But they didn't want you? Not enough husband material, so they sent—"

"Husband?"

A beaded mate, Tafiriel sent from the corral.

Aunia flushed. "No, I just . . . I wanted to see my mother's lands."

"You have family here? I wouldn't have guessed flyers could be so charitable."

Aunia frowned.

She means that they would do something only for the good of doing a good deed, Tafiriel sent.

What an odd thing for Taya to say. Aunia turned her attention to the children playing under a yellow and black wagon. One little girl, maybe six years old with dirty blonde hair, stomped off to the blue wagon with the curious painted knotwork and paned windows. She sat heavily on the bottommost step at the wagon's back.

"Reina," Taya said.

Aunia frowned. "What?"

"The little one with the storm cloud face." Taya pulled another stitch tight. "So, your mother's lands. What part of Tamore will you be heading to?"

Aunia shrugged.

"Well, what's the name of your mother's town?"

Aunia looked at her feet. How would she know that? Tamore was a wide-open land, stretching between two mountain ranges. She never had anyone to ask that question to.

Taya's voice turned soft, soothing. "You don't know."

Keston leaned heavily against Aunia's arm.

"Think he fell asleep and I have the last of this if you can keep his head up," Taya said.

A hauntingly rich resonance drifted on the breeze as if a faery or a sunset sang of longing and hope.

Aunia perked up. "What is that sound?"

Taya smiled. "Yasko Coates. Lena's younger brother. He's quite good with the violin. He'll play for us after supper during music hour. Do you sing, Aunia?"

"Me? A little," Aunia said. "In the evenings after Caedmon would tell stories about Tamore being a land of music everyday. Big cities and—"

"Is that where you're going? Big cities?" Taya's glow grew fuzzy like a thundercloud spreading for the rain.

"I don't know where I'm going."

"Well, big cities you have to be careful. I know that. You need to know that, too. But if you know the name of the place, they'd be maps or if you have her family's name, there's always a domesday."

"Domesday?"

"A written record that gives all the people and where they live. Or at least all the highborns. You'd have an easier time there than I would."

Aunia frowned. So many things she didn't know. She had not realized that she'd have to know but . . . everything earlier had been too rushed. Too dangerous. But now that she was in Tamore, what would she do?

Look for her mother .

Rescue her father.

The Boggleman's gone, yes . . . but there were still Mockmen trolls. If she entered Nonderu to get her dad, she would need help. That meant talking to Mathias. Could she get his aid to go back to a betwixting tunnel to rescue her dad? Could she get him to go with her alone so Fallo wouldn't try using a betwixting tunnel to get back to her village? She had no idea how long the Leiaphae flower shrouding would work and when her village would be in danger. Even though they exiled her, she didn't want anything bad to happen to them.

"Well, I hope these flyers treat you right," Taya said.

Aunia startled. "Why wouldn't they?"

"Well . . ." Taya's glow turned darker with a blood-red current flickering around her heart. "They probably are the souls of well-meaning but . . . Aunia, sometimes those in power believe manners are beneath them."

"Taya." Niall's tone sounded like a warning.

"Basil said we're to treat her like family and she deserves to know what dangers may face her." Taya knotted the last stitch in place and wrinkled her nose. "And I'm not saying the flyers would mistreat you. But you must know those who come from noble-birth—"

"You have known sorrow." The words slipped from Aunia's mouth without thought.

"Not her," Niall said. "Her parents. And not by flyers."

"They didn't help, though, did they?" Taya snapped.

Aunia straightened. These people didn't trust others either. And it sounded like they had cause.

The sorrowful lilt to the distant violin changed, becoming sass and spring and powder blue. There were answers to get. "Where's Basil?"

Taya pulled a canvas bag out from under the camp chair, one that Aunia hadn't noticed before, and pulled out strips of crisp, white linens. "He wanted to talk to the flyer commander when he arrived."

"Basil can skip, can't he?" Aunia said. She shivered a bit, remembering the strange sensation of being in two places at once. It was like sliding in and out of your skin. She had felt that when they traveled through the Boggleman's veil tendrils, those wafts of translucent material fashioned from the betwixt of the worlds. If she could do something like that on her own, she could return to the Grashbear where Mathias told her a betwixting tunnel was at.

"Yes," Taya murmured, "But watch who you say that to. That kind of magic can get a person hung."

Aunia stayed silent as Taya finished wrapping Keston's head with the fresh bandaging. When she finished, Niall gave a sharp whistle and two tousled-haired teen boys approached. They wore orange-red tunics with thick black and yellow trim.

"Besnik and Camlo." Niall rose from his stool. "Carry our young guest to my vardo, if you please."

"Course," the taller of the boys said, giving Aunia a wide grin. "You were there to see the wyverns fly, weren't you?"

"There were so many," said the shorter boy, "And then Ag-Haggy exploding and—"

"Ag-Haggy?" Aunia asked.

The taller boy pointed to the top of the tree hedge. "The mountain that looked like the wide tooth in a giant's mouth."

"Yes, boom!" the other boy said. "Big dust cloud and it crumbled into nothing."

"How could you see that?" Aunia held Keston by the sides of his face to keep his chin from falling against his chest.

"Don't matter how we saw," the shorter boy said. "You'll tell us what you know, won't cha?"

"Besnik," Niall said, "stop interrogating Rune's daughter."

Aunia jumped. "You know me?"

"Come take the flyer, you idgits," Taya said.

The boys hurried forward and took Keston in their arms.

"Your parents stayed with us for a bit." Taya pulled Aunia back. "Before I was born."

"They stayed here?" Aunia said then clutched her fists. Was Taya distracting her deliberately? "Where are you taking Keston?"

"Niall's vardo. Last one there. He'll sleep off the potion." Taya jabbed a finger at the slow-moving boys. "Get on with you."

Aunia watched until the rover boys and Keston entered the wagon then she turned her attention to Niall. "Did you know my parents?"

"Basil says you defeated the Boggleman," Niall said. "You would have made a friend out of Basil just for that."

"Because of Wendalin," Taya said. "The Boggleman always gave her nightmares."

"Wenda . . ." Aunia shook her head. She was not going to allow them to distract her.

"Basil means to talk to you . . . soon as he's available." Niall pulled a pipe from his pocket, bowed, and fled.

Back at the corral, Paderro had joined Tafiriel and Revellie but Mathias wasn't anywhere to be seen. He was probably where Fallo was.

Aunia hugged herself. The violinist still played as did the children under the yellow wagon but the sulky six-year-old on the wagon steps was gone.

Chapter Four
UNDER THE VARDO

Beware the words from liquid learnings. They may start with silliness but oft they break your heart — A Cold Festival adage

Mathias returned to the corral seconds after the rover boy left but he didn't remain there. Instead, staying close to the rover wagons, he darted toward the front of the caravan. Eavesdropping wasn't honorable but what choice did he have? Fallo, Basil, Tharon, and Lena strolled in the same direction on the road-facing side, less than two wagon-lengths ahead of him, their voices a tantalizing murmur.

He had an idea of what Fallo might want to discuss with the rovers. The marble giant. After all, Basil had burst through the mountain riding the marble giant's hand with a pack of wererats. But what could the rovers want with Fallo? For him to be silent about it? Is that why Fallo didn't want anyone else listening?

The marble giant . . . a living creature. It still seemed so surreal along with Edvaras' crackling thundercloud-shaped magic, and Aunia nearly stepping off of Tafiriel while they were in the air.

Fallo may simply be mad at you, Tafiriel sent.

He wasn't mad at me at Aunia's village when he discovered Rune. Mathias hit the edge of the make-shift corral and shimmied under the taut hemp ropes attached to a cornflower blue vardo. It still rankled that he was excluded when Fallo had met with some of the village heads and Rune after Fallo had threatened Aunia's dad with a sword. That was only a week ago. *I need to find out what's hidden.*

Maybe Fallo was looking to see what information the rovers had. These people, thieves and liars, weren't only known for healing abilities. They were procurers of hard-to-find baubles, people, and gossip.

Could it be about Aunia's parents? Basil had said on the Grashbear that he knew both of them. But why would Fallo care? Mathias shook his head. It couldn't be about Aunia herself . . . unless it was about what Cat was planning. But having Dar-Elect Nyrissa bring Fallo and the rest of them up on charges for abandoning their post wasn't something the rovers would have interest in. Except for maybe selling that information.

Mathias' jaw tightened. Nyrissa already blamed him for the death of Zeller, her father. Would she blame him for the heebles that attacked Dalin too? Or rather, the deaths that happened while they were away in Aunia's lands?

"You're supposed to go round the other way," a voice said from under the cornflower blue wagon.

Gripping the rim of the waist-high wagon-wheel, Mathias ducked for a look. Four children sat beneath with a scattering of rag dolls and one child with a cat-cradle string laced between her fingers. "Apologies. I'll go round."

They giggled.

A line of itchy sweat ran along his skin as he straightened. What he wouldn't do for a bath, but Keston always said to act casual—like you belong. It's how he's never caught, Mathias told himself.

If you want to convince Fallo not to take Aunia back to her village, Taf replied, *Do you really want to do this?*

Mathias brushed against the gold-painted corner of the next vardo and looked over his shoulder. Paderro had taken position beside Tafiriel near the water buckets. *He's listening in on you, isn't he?*

Taf stomped the grass once, then turned his hindquarters at Mathias. Revellie nickered and walked by Taf and Pad. A signal to proceed cautiously? Rev often provided a distraction for Keston when suspicious eyes needed to be diverted. She whinnied at him. Then again, it could be her way of asking to check on Keston.

Tell Rev I'll head for the fire soon. Mathias made himself droop his shoulders before slipping into the gap between the vardos as if he were returning to the fire where Keston and Aunia were. *Stupid . . . sneaking under the eyes of the commander's pegasus.*

He stepped out onto the road-side view of the caravan. Fallo and the rovers were more than two wagon lengths away and Aunia was talking to the girl in blue at the fire. Mathias frowned. Where was Keston?

Rovers took him to lie down, Taf sent. *They should be able to get you water.*

A ghost of a smile touched Mathias' lips. This was the closest Taf could get to lying if Paderro was listening in. The rovers, after all, probably could fetch him water should he ask. *Lying down where?*

Inside a vardo.

Mathias tightened a fist. He didn't like the idea of Keston being stashed inside a rover's home. But Rev would know if anything askew was happening. She'd fly to Keston's rescue faster than Mathias could. He sucked in a breath and continued gliding toward Fallo, sticking as close as he could to a yellowish amber vardo with black and burgundy accents. Fallo and the rovers' murmuring voices became almost clear.

Because the rover party stopped. Mathias ducked between the amber and the orange vardos.

"First," Tharon declared, "I've no dealings with wererats and I do not condone any of my people speaking with them."

"Fortunately, I and they were there," Basil said. "Otherwise, our flyers wouldn't have escaped the Grashbear. You know this band is different, Da. They've been keeping—"

"Enough," Tharon barked. "There are things I've agreed this flyer needs to know. And we'll tell. And Fallo . . . afterward, I will be no longer in your debt."

Basil was right about his band of wererats being different, though Mathias didn't understand why. What were they angling for by helping?

Fallo's tone turned angry. "You think a bit of gossip will pay off that—"

"Peace, commander," Lena said. "We've grave news but needful before you fly into Dalin."

"Who said I was going to Dalin?" Fallo asked.

Tharon cleared his throat. "I assume you'll go after—"

"Tharon. This is a conversation best told with mugs of ale, or stronger," Lena said.

"I will know how these wererats formed an alliance with . . ." Fallo's voice drifted off as the party moved again. They paused at the back of the lead vardo, a rich crimson red.

Moments later, Tharon's voice drifted back. "So, is she behaving herself?"

"Da," Basil protested.

Mathias peeped from behind an orange vardo, the second lead in the caravan. How did Tharon know of Aunia? Had Basil ratted her out about her magic on the Grashbear Mountains? His stomach turned queasy. With one of the mountain peaks pulverized, what should he expect? They probably heard the explosion from here. But Fallo could explain it away, should he choose. Just a simple explanation that it was all Edvaras' magic. And oh, the talk when people realized that the rogue Chandarion's magic was in the world without Edvaras. All the augury stories would be dusted off and retold. Doomsayers and quest finders. People would tell tales of seeing the marble giant from afar. They'd whisper in corners saying this is the time of the choosing.

"She does her duty," Fallo said, "And the Queen relies on her when she isn't in with Syrick."

Mathias' foot staggered and he almost lost his balance. Not Aunia. But who? He paused as a door creaked open along with the squeak-thump of someone stepping onto the vardo's attached steps.

Mathias snuck another peek. Lena had already gone inside and Fallo was on the steps.

"I'd wager most of the court forgets where she comes from." Fallo ducked inside.

"Da," Basil muttered. "Don't be asking him for help with Ella's—"

"I'm genuinely asking about my daughter," Tharon said. "I'd know if at least one of my children walks the path of the Augurites."

Basil looked over his shoulder and spotted Mathias. "The Augurite path twists, Da."

Ducking back, Mathias' heart raced. He pressed himself against the orange-painted wood and tried to think of a reasonable excuse.

More creaking footsteps entered the vardo and then . . . nothing. Had Basil not called him out? Maybe he recognized a fellow augurite, one that followed the augury. Or maybe Basil hadn't really seen him. Mathias tapped at his thigh. There was a rover inside the Queen's court?

You know the girl, Taf sent.

Do I? Who?

The red dar's apprentice. You've spoken to her many times.

Wendalin? Mathias ran a hand through his hair. She had the same olive-tinged skin and dark hair like Basil, the same high cheekbones. A nice enough girl. Helpful with keeping her royal highness from any true scandals. *I'll have to find out when we get back to Tatia how a rover got to be a dar apprentice.*

Does it matter? Taf sent back. *She might become friends with Aunia.*

Icy anxiety stabbed at the bottom of his ribcage. What exactly would he do now that he and Aunia were back in Tamore? He wanted to be with her but where could they go? Not his home. Not the capital. An answer for later.

Mathias soft-stepped to the hedge side of the vardo line. He sank onto his haunches by the back wagon wheel and an open window. From within whispered voices drifted out, unintelligible until Fallo's gravelly voice rang out. "The moons don't add."

"I tell you, she is," Basil said.

"Just a doppleganger's spell on a poor innocent," Fallo said. "Who knows what she really was. I tell you Runoldi would've returned otherwise."

Runoldi? Mathias swallowed hard. As in Ferris Runoldi? That was the name of the Mystic who was responsible for the Blood Ball.

"Enough," Tharon said over a wooden thump. "What we need to discuss is what to tell her."

"You daft?" Fallo said. "I may not believe but I won't see her hung as a murderer's daughter."

Who are they talking about? Mathias sent to Taf.

I do not hear them.

Mathias closed his eyes. It was likely that Taf had spent his magical energy for this day. *Get some rest.*

You should too.

"Runoldi is no murderer," Basil said, "Aeryk had—"

"You cannae be pinning any of this on Aeryk," Fallo said. "The man was betrothed to the heir. What purpose would it serve?"

Mathias leaned forward, his fingers brushing the grass. What information did the rovers think they had on the traitor king-consort? And did it matter? Aeyrk da Wyvert had been executed years ago.

"Basil, enough." Lena said. A hissing rush of pouring liquid followed. "How about you tell us what happened on the Grashbear instead?"

"The red marks on my face. Right." Fallo said. "I encountered ruork faeries in a blade-cave."

"Wouldn't have gotten stung up if you stopped consorting with faeries," Tharon growled.

"Tharon," Lena protested.

"Consorting?" Fallo said. "I came to the aid of one of my men. He was being attacked by wyverns."

"Attacked," Tharon repeated. "What are you doing in the mountains that's provoking them?"

"I think Tharon is asking," Lena said. "Is why you were on Grashbear in the first place?"

Fallo snorted. "A flyers business is his own."

Annoyance crept into Lena's voice. "Don't you get it? Talk is spreading about the harm that flyers do. Is that what you're—"

"Harm?" Fallo barked. "We protect the people. If we hadn't sent the wyverns packing—"

"And the flyers were chasing a wererat over the Grashbear," Basil interrupted. "One of their unit had been bit at a Besmarion festival."

"Yes, you should know about wererats," Fallo growled.

"I told you my band is different," Basil said.

"Your band?" Tharon's pitch went up.

"Stop it," Lena said and a chair leg scraped. "Fallo. The border spell fell, didn't it?"

"Why," Fallo asked, "would you say such a—"

"Because," Basil interrupted, "the walking mouths wouldn't have attacked if—"

"Firelings," said Fallo. "It had to be because of firelings."

Mathias blinked. Firelings? He hadn't heard of that Adarian cult since he was little. They had, he'd been told, been the reason why Dar Syrick placed the border spell around Tamore in the first place.

"No. It was the Boggleman," Basil said. "Why make that face? You've seen him. Why deny, here of all places, what your eyes have witnessed?"

"Fallo," said Lena. "We're afraid. As we and everyone else in this country should be. We need to know where these walking mouths have come from and better . . . how do we be rid of them?"

"You want to be rid of them?" asked Fallo. "Help me find a bit of marble from that giant. Basil rode on its hand. Surely, him or one of you can get me a scraping."

A rhythmic wooden tapping punctuated a long silence.

"Exactly how would a . . . scraping . . . from Hebsolum, guardian of the Eaburrai Court, help?" Basil asked.

"It's probably nothing more than a rock giant. Stop giving it mythical proportions. I need it to cure—" Fallo coughed before he continued. "Make our Queen strong and by doing that it helps all of us."

Cure the Queen? There wasn't anything physically wrong with her. Mathias released his handful of grass and rubbed his fingers against the knee of his trousers. But there were whispers she was descending into madness like the infamous Queen Didianne. Dethroning Didianne in favor of her heir had kept war from springing between Tamore and the neighboring kingdom of Adar. It was possible that Fallo was lying. After all, he told Aunia's village that the marble would be used to get rid of wererats.

"We support her majesty," Lena said, "we always have but we're heading inland. Further out from these mountains."

"Cowards," said Fallo.

"Fallo," Basil said. "Hebsolum wouldn't leave a part of himself behind and we must figure out how to be rid of these walking mouths."

"These so-called farmers that visited told us that Dalin's storm disintegrated the beasts," Lena said. "But I know of no legal means to call up a handy storm for when they come back. These things we should all be afraid of. They don't care if you're low-born or noble. Flyer or rover."

Mathias' breath froze in his chest.

"Why don't you believe they were farmers?" Basil asked.

"Their hands and their bearing were too soft," said Lena.

"Well, my cup's empty," Fallo said with a scraping of chair legs, "And this has been a waste of my time."

Mathias shifted to stand before he was discovered.

"There's reason why no one cushions a blow for you," Tharon said.

"Indeed," added Lena. "Sit. We've bad news for you." More liquid poured.

Mathias gripped another handful of grass.

"There's no way to soften this but," Lena said. "One of your men went headfirst over the wall into those walking mouths."

Mathias slid from haunches to backside. Jules?

I can still sense Brinsaber, Taf sent.

Breath seeped back into Mathias' lungs. When a pegasus' flyer died first, the pegasus would return to the wind, whatever that meant. They simply disappeared like Startengo, Zeller's pegasus, when Zeller breathed his last. Mathias shook himself. But for Brinsaber to still be in the mortal world . . . Jules had to be alive. That meant the dead flyer had to be one of the knight-sons, one of Fallo's kin.

"How?" Fallo croaked.

Taf, can you hear the knight-sons' pegasi?

"Some say it was Lord Emmet," Lena said.

"Or faebloods," said Tharon.

"There's nothing a faeblood would gain by attacking flyers," Basil muttered.

"Basil. We're simply repeating what we heard from these farmers," Lena said. "They had escaped Dalin."

"So was—" Basil stopped mid-sentence. "Where are these farmers now?"

I'm not hearing either of them, Taf sent back.

"They went northwest," Lena said. "In the direction of Vraelsfork."

"Well, we've given you the news," Tharon said. "Dreadful news. What do you plan to do with it?"

A thud hit, like a fist hitting wood. "If someone's killed one of mine," said Fallo, "He'll pay, even if he's a lord."

Mathias' shoulder eased. He was speaking like a true commanding flyer. The lingering animosity Mathias felt for Fallo drained out but a bit of sorrow filled its place. Mathias never liked either of Fallo's kin, sons born from Vraelsfork knights, but they were still flyers. The only balm they could offer would be justice. Any flyer deserved that much. And there was hope of finding Jules.

"What of the girl, Aunia?" Tharon asked.

Mathias pulled himself back onto his knees. Taking Aunia into Dalin, a potentially hostile territory, and with her proclivity of bringing un-wanted magic or faery creatures . . . it would be like adding black powder to a fire.

"We'll return her to her village after this is over," Fallo replied.

Mathias' attention snapped to the window shutter and its soft sway-ing. He would not be sending Aunia back.

Tell Fallo of the faery repellent, Taf sent. *Tell him she's needed here.*

"You can't," Basil said. "The Boggleman's after her."

"Boggleman," sneered Fallo. "She said that to sweet talk her way over the Grashbear. And Mathias was fool enough to believe her."

Mathias throttled the grass beneath his fingers. The Boggleman absolutely had been after Aunia. Thankfully, he had plummeted to his death. Surely Basil had seen that as well. But. . . Fallo knew about Jaia from the time the villagers spread the repellent on the village wall. And, Fallo had seen heebles attacking Glevis. Telling Fallo that bringing Jaia salve to the Queen would be a royal gift, might do the trick. Might be enough to get them out of trouble as well for when Cat's men and women came to arrest them.

"We'll keep her safe here with us until you are done in Dalin," said Tharon.

"Safe?" Fallo said. "Well, I don't see a better choice. But I'm not paying for her."

Mathias vibrated with a mix of anger and dread and then a light titter drew his attention. It was coming from under the vardo wagon. Being caught on top of all of this? Mathias leaned down to look. Underneath, elbows digging in the grass, hands under her chin, and her small feet kicking the air, lay a dirty blonde-haired little girl.

"Of course not," Basil said. "We would consider her family."

Chapter Five

A Change of View

The Maid of Idenweigh is a cautionary tale to remember. Even if you find hope springing forth, it's important to prepare yourself for black despair. If you'd risk your heart, you'll find yourself looking foolish. — Aeryk de Wyvert of New Berlin, king-consort

"They'll get your friend settled," said Taya.

Aunia bit her lip, uncertain if she should join the two rover boys who had hauled an unconscious Keston to the last vardo wagon, a dusty purple—almost the color of lilacs— or if she should remain and wait for Mathias so she could tell him where Keston was.

I am watching over him, Keston's pegasus, Revellie, sent with her high silvery voice.

"Would you like to sit?" Taya said.

"I sat enough on the way here." Aunia twisted mid-waist to face the corral. Revellie stood at the ropes between the two blue vardo wagons while Tafiriel and Paderro stood a couple of yards back. The two stallions were grazing at a hay bale in the growing shadow of the tree hedge row. *Tafiriel, where's Mathias?*

Tafiriel raised his head and nickered. *He'll return shortly.*

The black pegasus flattened his ears and crowded against Tafiriel.

Aunia frowned. Was Paderro annoyed she was talking to Mathias' pegasus? She mostly avoided Paderro because he was Fallo's. But he was a faery creature, too. She could try befriending him but . . . Aunia crossed her arms. *Mathias is with Fallo, isn't he?*

A burst of high-pitched laughter drew Aunia's attention to the children at play. Giggling littles like those at her village. She smiled and then she wrapped her arms over the hole inside her chest.

There's talking going on, Tafiriel sent.

Talking. Of course. Aunia turned toward the road to hide her face from Taya. And probably about her. Fallo certainly hadn't been happy to see her when they landed on the Grashbear Mountains. He wanted to take her back to Naoma Sacella. And he certainly wouldn't care if she wasn't welcome there. Fallo was less trustworthy than these rovers.

"Do you need some water? Or wine perhaps?" Taya asked. "I might be able to nick you a bit of cheese or—"

"I'm okay." She rocked back and forth on her feet. The important thing was knowing Mathias stood with her. He had told Fallo that she would stay in Tamore and he didn't care what Fallo tried to do. It was possible Mathias was telling Fallo now about the village being shrouded, magically invisible to all outsiders.

"It's Aunia, yes?" said a young male voice.

Aunia jumped before facing the two rover boys.

"And you were on the Grashbear," said the wiry-framed younger boy. He looked to be about fourteen years of age. He had a blue-gray bandana wrapped around his head, thick dark brows and hazel eyes. "How'd you escape the wyverns?"

Aunia stepped backwards, ready to tell them she didn't make the wyverns attack but instead she glanced at the row of brainhedge trees. It wasn't possible that they could have witnessed any fine detail from over twenty miles away. And most of the mountain peaks couldn't be seen over the tops of the trees. She relaxed her shoulders. "Where did you hear that?"

"She don't think we saw the battle over the brainhedge," said the taller boy. The irises in his eyes were black. He extended a hand, patterned striped sleeve pulling back past his wrist. "I'm Camlo."

Aunia remained still.

"We could see." The first boy pointed to a dull red vardo with green-painted vines curling around its windows and twisting beside a metal ladder which ran up the wagon's side. This vardo stood in front of Niall's dusky purple one but unlike all the other vardos, the dull red one had a flat roof surrounded by brown-gold metal railing. "Atop there."

"We'll show you," Camlo said.

Aunia frowned. Height always gave a greater perspective, like the platforms atop her village's protective wall or flying on Tafiriel's back. But a vardo roof . . . what could they see from twenty miles away?

"Climb up with us," said the first boy.

"Camlo and Besnik love stories," Taya said. "And they know a few themselves. I'm here if you need."

"Besnik?"

"That's me." The first boy adjusted the strap to a tan satchel which hung crossbody along his chest. He held out a thin hand. "Come on. And tell us the story!"

Aunia bit her lip against the memory of the Boggleman in wyvern form . . . large triangular orange head and one whirling eye. He nearly had ripped away her sense of self but she had fought and he had pierced her with one of his veil tendrils. Fire and sharpness. Her belly feeling scooped away . . . and then Hebsolum mindspeaking to her. "Fine. Show me."

Aunia strode to the flat-roofed wagon and climbed up with the rover boys following her. She knew from aloft she could make out more of the Grashbear mountain peaks but she'd . . . they'd . . . have no way of knowing if a wyvern flew there.

The boys thumped onto the roof behind her.

"You can see with this." Besnik reached into his satchel and pulled out a foot-long tube made of reddish-brown wood and brass fixtures either end. The boy shook them at her. "Take it. Put it up to your eye."

"It's a far-viewer and charmed with legal magic, you know components," Camlo said. "Not leylines or fae stuff so . . . legal."

Aunia snatched the far-viewer, faced the distant mountains peeking from behind the tall trees, and put it up to her eye. The dirt-tanned peaks expanded instantly as if she had skipped to their feet and stared at them through curled hands. She swayed and hands supported her shoulders.

"Careful," Camlo said.

Aunia lowered the far-seer. "How—"

"Spelled." Camlo dropped his hand from her and crossed his arms.

"Spelled?"

"By Taya," Besnik fidgeted with his fingernails. "We saw wyverns this morning and a glowing blue cloud and pegasi flying, and then Hebsolum. And somebody knows the story. Somebody who was there. Like you."

Aunia turned back to the Grashbear peaks. Hebsolum. Both an enormous marble giant before her eyes and a dwarf with red-brown hair before her minds-eye. Only the dwarf part of him spoke and it was a mindspeak like her faery friend, Jennium. But how could one being be two separate things? She could tell the boys that he had helped her with reboxing Edvaras' light and defeating the Boggleman but it twisted in her belly to have to admit that he had thrown her to her death. If not for Basil . . . "You know about Hebsolum?"

"Of course we do," Besnik said. "There are plenty of stories about the guardian of the Eaburrai Court. Showed up to our world when Yasendra did."

"But he mostly stays hidden," Camlo said. "The last time he was spotted was during the Mockmen battles with Olivia."

"Yes." Besnik clapped his hands. "And Idenweigh had taken extensive casualties, and the survivors had retreated to the Bearpaws—"

"Bearpaws?" Aunia asked.

"A pair of tall hills a few miles of Idenweigh and near the Grash-bear," said Camlo. "Thousands of Mockmen were traveling through the Grashbear tunnels to destroy the survivors—"

"And take Olivia," Besnik interrupted. "But she outwitted them. She called on Hebsolum and he collapsed the tunnels on them."

"Yes, but the Boggleman still got her." Camlo locked his dark eyes on Aunia's face as if he could pull information from her mind. "And the Boggleman was after you. Are you like our Olivia?"

Aunia's stomach curled up at the memory of Olivia in the Boggle-man's ice columns. "What do you mean?"

"A Chandarion. Not as powerful as Edvaras. He did something, but she was the first to appear after the rogue made blade-caves," Camlo said.

"I . . . I think my mother might have been one. She had created an amulet that could . . ." Aunia frowned. "... could store Nymer energy."

"Your mom?" Besnik said. "But the Boggleman was after you."

"He took my dad. And I saw . . ." Aunia bit her lip uncertain if she should tell them she had had visions about the Boggleman when she was in the birchwoods. "I know the Boggleman tried to take my mom, too. Only, she's dead."

Camlo lowered himself to sitting on the vardo's roof. "I hadn't heard of another Chandarion in Tamore. She must have kept out of sight and had been killed early—"

"Camlo, losing a mom isn't easy." Besnik chastised and turned back to Aunia. "You've our sympathies. How long ago?"

"I never met her. Or at least I don't remember her. I'd like to know who she was but I don't even know her name." Aunia frowned. Fallo did. "Fallo blamed my dad on her death. He wanted to take my dad's head off."

"She has to be highborn then," Camlo said. "There are domesdays in the cities and in Tatia."

Aunia frowned. "Taya mentioned a Domesday."

Besnik spread his arms wide. "All-encompassing list of names and titles and relationships of who's who in the nobility circle. And the low-born, if they're lucky get included in the number of lands' people. Being traveling folk, we don't even have that."

"But cities are dangerous," Camlo said.

"Taya said that, too," said Aunia.

"She'd know," Besnik said. "Her parents were killed in a city."

Aunia clutched the hem of her blue tunic. That explained the sleeping rage in Taya's eyes. Why she reminded her of Limi.

"But Aunia," Besnik said, "Can you please tell us the story... about how you escaped the wyverns?"

Aunia sucked in a deep breath of afternoon air, nodded, and took a seat on the roof as well. "I can."

She launched into story, first telling them about how she and Mathias had accidentally released Edvaras' magic and how the Boggleman intended to use it to destroy the human world if they couldn't rebox it first.

"But how to rebox it?" Besnik leaned forward, elbows on his knees and chin in his hands.

"My mother's amulet. I found it and realized it was made of Chand ice."

"Truly?" Besnik breathed, "That stuff is very rare."

"It is," Aunia said, "and without it—"

"No," interrupted Camlo. "In order. Please."

"Of course." Aunia set the far-seer beside her and slipped back into the tale from encountering the Boggleman in the Birchwoods to Hebsolum throwing her high into the sky. She did, however, omit some of the details about the heebles attacking her village, her time in Nonderu, and her interaction with faeries.

Besnik scratched his chin. "And Hebsolum truly helped you change the Boggleman back into humanoid form and he . . ."

"Plummeted to his death? Yes." Aunia crossed her arms. The Boggleman was dead. And that meant his cloak wouldn't be eating any more faeries.

Camlo tapped at his knees. "Wendalin will be pleased to hear that. Maybe even Tharon too even if he won't—?"

"Who is Wendalin?"

"Basil's sister," Camlo said. "She's in Tatia serving the Queen."

"It's not that odd," added Besnik. "We're distantly related to the royals."

The wagon side shook and a small blonde head popped into view. "They got Chand ice in the Darra Chamber, too."

Camlo rose to his knees, his glow flickering pale blue and sickly green while Besnik scooped up the far-seer, shoving it into his satchel. "Reina, go away."

The little girl clung to the ladder. "I'm an augurite, same as you."

"Olivia's caravan, course we are." Besnik's glow flickered with gray and dark-yellow.

Why were they upset with this storm-faced little girl? Aunia blinked. And they were part of Olivia's family? She chewed on her lip. Mathias told her that Olivia had been taken 70 years earlier by the Boggleman. .

. and this was her family. They'd want to know what happened to her. Wouldn't they?

Camlo got to his feet. "You should see if Lena needs help with—"

Reina climbed another rung, her glow shimmering as if it was made of thousands of fireflies. "Lena's talking with that flyer in Tharon's—"

"Oy," Mathias yelled up.

Aunia half-crawled to the edge of the vardo and Mathias' eyes widened. He took in the two boys and his graying spring-green glow flickered with red.

"What are you doing up there?" he demanded.

"Telling a little girl she can listen to my stories, too," she said.

"You are not chaperoned. Do you know what this looks like?"

Aunia slid closer to the ladder. Mathias' mood had to be because of his worry for Keston. Reina climbed down and Aunia followed.

Her feet touched ground, and Mathias reached over to grab her hand. "You shouldn't be alone with them. They're not to be trusted. They take advantage—"

"They're nice. And we were just talking." Aunia pulled her hands back. They were more than nice. They made her feel accepted. They wanted her story and they didn't act like they were afraid of her.

"That's what they want. Put you at ease so they can rob you blind."

Aunia plucked at her dirty tunic. "Exactly what will they steal?"

Then she bit her lip. She had her father's book and Edvaras' astrolabe in her rutsack.

I'm watching over your things, Tafiriel sent.

"She was just telling us the story of what happened that brought you here," Camlo said. Both boys had climbed down from the vardo. "We saw how Ag-Haggy blew and—"

"I wasn't talking to you," Mathias said.

"You're being rude," said Aunia.

"Oh, and you're just flirting like Keira does. No concern about consequences."

"Keira? Who's Keira?"

Mathias glow shrunk against his skin. "I don't have time for this."

He walked briskly away.

Aunia shifted her weight to chase after him and Taya jumped in her way.

"Let him cool off," the rover girl said.

"Move," Aunia snapped.

"He just found out a friend of his is dead. Give him space."

"A friend?" Aunia's anger drained into the pit of her stomach. "Jules."

"Someone from his unit. Reina said no names were mentioned."

Mathias continued his angry walk to Niall's vardo—probably to check on Keston. And he did not want her comfort. Aunia clenched her fists. She didn't do anything wrong. Why did he compare her to this . . . Keira?

"I've a deck of cards my mom left me," Taya said. "Let me read your future."

"Cards?" Aunia bit her lip. She had a lot of uncertainty about her future. Rescue her dad. Find out about her mom. Figure out what she and Mathias were going to do. He wouldn't stay mad at her. Leave her behind. Could he? "Who is Keira?"

"The heir princess," Besnik's voice sounded behind her. "She's flirting, I'd assume, because the suitor games are taking place."

Aunia turned toward the rover boy. "Suitor games?"

"She must choose a husband and every unmarried lord's son is in the capital hoping to be king-consort." Besnik readjusted his blue-gray bandana on his head like Basil did with his orange one.

Aunia crossed her arms. She didn't like being compared to another girl...someone she didn't even know. And she'd ask Mathias about it later. But right now, she needed answers. And that meant Basil.

"Come on." Taya pointed to the smaller blue vardo with the black knotwork design. "You probably want to know more about the Darra Chamber."

Aunia shook her head. "Not now."

Chapter Six

MEMORIES AND RAGE

When ghouls arrive to eat us all. You know the time has come.
The seven will merge to save us all. But Olivia will succumb.
— Lovari caravan traveling song

How stupid could he be? Aunia was just like Keira with attracting all the boys and holding a version of court. And Aunia had only been within the rover caravan for how long? An hour or two? Mathias' body vibrated with every pounding step. She'd do just fine here when they traveled to Dalin. She was probably just like them.

Dalin. Mathias slowed his pace and rubbed at his burning eyes. To find which flyer had been thrown over the wall. He could ask Taf if he could reach out again but... it would make no difference. After dozens of attempts to have Taf contact Jules... If anything changed, his pegasus would let him know.

Mathias picked up the pace again. Better if he saw how Keston fared.

Your kind like mine and horses don't do well when the herd rejects them, Taf sent.

"My kind?" Mathias slowed again. *You're talking about Aunia, aren't you?*

Do you not remember how she was treated in her village?

Mathias ran a hand through his dark hair. He was probably the first one who ever treated her decently, except for Caedmon and maybe Gaitha and Limi. Of course she would gravitate to him. Gravitate to anyone who paid her a kind word. Was that what this . . . love . . . he felt was based on? Her gratitude? And she probably wasn't even feeling that with how he had just behaved.

"Love is overrated," his father had told him. It was an excuse his father gave when Mathias learned, courtesy of a pair of visiting rover children, that his father had a mistress. Shocked and angry, he confronted his father. He'd hoped that would prevent him from returning to his Heavensfeet mistress. It didn't. Instead, his father laid guilt upon him. "You worry about your own duty. You've one chance to make up for all your horrific mistakes. You hear me, boy?"

Mathias shook the image of his father's broad face with his shaved and freshly nicked chin. Duty. Always duty. But his father hadn't caused a death. Even an accidental one. But Mathias had.

Up ahead beside the last wagon and on a stool sat the old man who had helped the rover girl and Aunia tend to Keston.

"Hey," Mathias called out. "The other flyer. Where is he?"

The old man looked up from his whittling, gave him a crinkled smile, and pointed to the dusky purple wagon. "Best healing happens when our spirit roams the dreamlands and he's sleeping soundly." The rover stiffly got to his feet and extended a knobby hand. "Niall's the name. And you are?"

"I'm going in." Mathias headed for the back of the wagon.

"By all means, oh strange-named one. What has you all riled up?"

"Riled?" Mathias came to a halt and refaced the man. "We've heebles in our lands. Demons who'll devour everyone to their bones. They've attacked Glevis. Dalin."

"Yes, we've heard too. Thankfully, they die in water, but it makes me wonder. Perhaps these are the ghouls that are foretold. You and Dar Zeller—"

"Don't talk to me about Dar Zeller," Mathias snapped. He stamped to the vardo, calling over a shoulder. "And heebles are not ghouls."

"They serve the same function." Niall followed behind. "And more beasties are coming from the Grashbear just as Olivia had warned."

Mathias pinched the bridge of his nose. The time of the augury. Yes, he believed in it, but there was nothing he could do to fix it. He had tried with Aunia and all they did was release Edvaras' Nymer. Fortunately, they had been able to recapture it with the help of the marble giant and a bit of Chand ice. But Edvaras' Nymer was now gone and perhaps any chance of restarting the augury was also gone.

"Olivia warned of this," Niall said softly, "and Mollie Mae . . . she confirms more—"

"That's one of the wererat names." Mathias turned again to face the rover. "Are you in league with them?"

Niall crossed his arms. "Mollie Mae was Tharon's wife before she was bitten. And not all of them turn to bad."

"I've heard different." Mathias stomped to the wagon door and yanked it open. He stepped inside the dim interior where a dark wood table and four chairs were pushed up along one side. Shallow drawers marched down the other side. And at the back of the wagon lay a double-wide bed covered in plushy blankets and small pillows. Keston, knotted up on his side with his ribcage softly rising and falling, slept.

The rovers gave him a sleeping potion and Revellie said he's resting easy, Taf sent.

Mathias sucked in a relieved breath just as Niall stepped into the wagon.

"I've heard the rumor about Arch Vicar Bibb being at the Bellows when Zeller died."

Mathias turned to face this upstart rover. "I told you . . . don't speak of Zeller."

"I am not your enemy. Zeller was a dar for all of us. But what I say is to warn you. Arch Vicar Bibb is in Dalin. Has been before these walking mouths attacked." Niall turned for the door. "Take your time with visiting your friend."

The rover left, leaving Mathias standing in the center of the wagon, seething and feeling lost. Arch Vicar Bibb in Dalin? When Mathias was still in Aunia's village, Jules had bespoke that Da Vennen soldiers were there for recruitment. But for the leader of their order to arrive at a border city . . . that made no sense. Mathias balled his fists. The Arch Vicar was responsible for Zeller's death—even though there was no proof other than his own fuzzy memory. He knew Bibb had been on the Bellows. Remembered the feel of Bibb's nose giving under his knuckles.

The problem was it was only his word and Mathias had huge gaps in his memory. Nyrissa, after hearing the bits and pieces he did remember, commanded other flyers to seek Bibb out. Only, when they visited Bibb's grotto, they discovered not a mark on Bibb's face and he had others vouch for his whereabouts.

Bibb received an apology and Mathias received a six-month banishment to get him out of Nyrissa's sight.

His memories had to have been tampered with from those little blue flowers he had spotted in Taf's feed that next morning. Scorched petals of that flower had been inside the wererats' fire ring in the blade-cave, too. Navenra. He had only learned its name and that Edvaras had created it after visiting Naoma Sacella.

Just this morning, during the wyvern battle, wererats had burned it on the Grashbear. The smoke had made him dizzy, but it made Aunia try to dismount while they were hundreds of feet up. Where was this plant coming from? He needed to find out . . . but not at this moment.

Mathias stepped closer to Keston. Barely any seepage leaked through the bandaging around his friend's head. The question was whether Keston would be fit to fly into Dalin because Fallo surely wouldn't wait. And it would be foolish for the commander to go alone. With the marble giant gone and his men needing him, Fallo would stop behaving so erratically. He'd give Fallo a chance to reveal what was said in Tharon's wagon. And if the commander didn't, he'd follow Fallo anyway. But Aunia . . .

Mathias closed his eyes. Aunia had looked so hurt and angry. Tafiriel was right to remind him how her villagers had treated her. Exiled her. She wasn't anything like Princess Keira. He needed to apologize to her.

Mathias touched Keston's shoulder and his friend rolled onto his back.

Rev is working on healing him. It's easier anyway with him sleeping, Taf sent.

Mathias nodded and left the vardo. He passed the cooking fires where small, plucked birds, doves more than likely, cooked inside iron roasters which dangled on metal tripods. He also passed a large bubbling cauldron with its delectable smell of rich mutton and potatoes, ignoring both his rumbling belly and the stares from the rover women.

He didn't see Aunia. Where could she be? Both she and those rover boys were missing. And so was the rover girl dressed in blue. Mathias kept walking toward the front of the caravan.

"What do you think you're doing?" Fallo's voice rang out from the top of the caravan's line.

Aunia is with him, Taf sent.

Mathias slipped to the tree hedge side of the wagons and ran toward the voices.

"You have no say with what I do," Aunia yelled.

"They've water a plenty," replied Fallo. "And you won't be getting through."

Aunia and Fallo stood nose-to-nose at the Brainhedge Tree's brass and living wood gate, Fallo commanding and Aunia not bending. Mathias had told her that the marches of Froidelune and Dalin were like battling mini kingdoms but she probably didn't understand the strict truce. Only a select few were given keys for the gates to collect water. No one else was to pass through.

"Commander," Mathias called out.

"Move her away from here," Fallo growled.

"Basil went in there," Aunia said, "and I want to talk to him."

Mathias turned to Aunia, his stomach feeling as if it had been kicked when her angry expression turned bleak.

She crossed her arms.

"Supper is almost ready to be served. I'll escort you," Mathias said, intentionally making his voice light. "We'll both feel better after food and—"

"You're lucky my faery friends aren't here to see." Aunia reached out, tracing her fingertips along the gate's ornately twisted metal. "But you don't have any here, do you?"

Mathias ached to pull her near. Wrap his arms around her. Chase the stiff unhappiness from her body.

"I . . . owe you." Mathias swallowed hard and all the guilt, worry, and anger over Jules and the rest of his unit flared. Clenching his teeth, he reached out and tugged on her wrist. "Come on. We both need food and rest."

CHAPTER SEVEN
WIGGLE ME DO LOVE

Yasendra watched through the window anytime Uriah stayed in Tatia's Grove, until of course, that entire room disappeared. — Taya of the Mensani caravan

Aunia sat quietly beside Mathias on the clover and blue sheep fescue grasses while the sun lowered on the western part of the sky. Lowered in the realm of Tamore, her mother's lands. She was so close to learning everything she wanted to know but Basil had ventured past that iron gate and disappeared through the hedge. Fallo had no right preventing her from following.

She bit her lip and side-eyed Mathias. Should she ask about this heir princess? Should she ask about his friend? Should she tell him he needed to help her? She felt abandoned and alone but he was mourning a friend. And he hadn't even told her yet.

A woman dressed in a tight-fitting bodice and a wide circle skirt approached and handed both Mathias and Aunia pale wooden bowls full of chunky stew. She left and returned moments later with wooden cups and flatbread.

Mathias dug into the food immediately, but Aunia, despite knowing she should eat, wasn't hungry. That weighted ache in her belly came from not knowing what to do next. She stuck her spoon in her bowl and stirred. Her father remained imprisoned in Nonderu. The Boggleman was dead, yes . . . but Dad would still be surrounded by Mockmen trolls. To save him was to go back into Nonderu and that meant returning to the betwixting caves to the east. But she'd have a hard time returning there without Mathias' help.

There was also a domesday in some of the cities and in Tatia. A book that would tell her all about her mother, like where in Tamore she lived. And maybe find out if she had other family here in these lands, too. She only needed her mother's name. A name that Basil would know.

"Don't you like it?" Mathias asked. His bowl was nearly empty.

Aunia tapped the tip of her wooden spoon into the stew. "It's . . . fine."

He lowered his bowl. "Aunia. You need to eat. With everything we've been through—"

"I want to talk to Basil." She frowned, wishing the other rovers weren't giving them wide berth. Taya sat a quarter-circle away from them with Besnik, Camo and Reina while Niall sat a half circle away with Tharon—and with Fallo.

Mathias ran a hand through his hair. "Look. I'm sorry I yelled earlier. I shouldn't have. You've been through so much."

"We both have." Aunia sucked in a breath and set her bowl down. "Mathias . . . tell me about this Keira."

With his glow graying, he picked up his wooden cup. "She will be Queen. Probably sooner than later."

"Besnik said there's a suitor game happening? And the winner gets picked as her husband?"

Mathias nodded but didn't look at her. "It'll be for the most strategic connection. Someone who can rule adequately and her highness can manipulate best."

"That does not sound like love."

"No. It certainly doesn't," said Mathias.

Some of the tension drained from her body and she nibbled at her flatbread while rovers spoke in low tones around them. When the bread was gone, she ladled up a spoonful of stew and paused. It was nearly twilight. "I'm sorry about your friend and everything but Mathias . . . I do need to save my dad. Even if I'm not happy with him. I mean . . . the Boggleman's dead but there are Mockmen trolls still there. And, well, he's family. Maybe all I have. We're leaving the Grashbear with the Betwixting tunnel—"

"We have to get space between us and those mountains." Mathias' glow flared with silvery-gray light. "Fallo will try to send you back to your village otherwise."

"He wouldn't find it."

"Doesn't mean he wouldn't try."

Aunia dug her heels against the ground. "What if I want to go to Tatia? See this Darra Chamber."

Mathias sputtered and the wine in his cup sloshed. "Where did you hear about the Darra Chamber?"

"Taya. She said—"

"That place doesn't exist anymore."

"How can it not exist?"

Across the fire, a rover tuned his fiddle.

"How do I explain this?" Mathias pinched the bridge of his nose. "Tatia. It stands on the doorway between the worlds but close to our side."

"Like the Birchwoods?"

Mathias frowned. "Until a few days ago, I had never heard of that place . . . but yes, I guess."

"Well, it's there sometimes. Like a betwixting tunnel. And sometimes not. I need to go to Tatia for the domesday."

"Domesday?" Mathias frowned and leaned back from her.

"Yes. There's this book that lists all the . . . what are they called . . . nobleborn and where they live or lived. Basil knows about my parents so as soon as I get a name I could see if she's in it. So, yes. Tatia. I'll find out about my mother and put together a rescue team to save my dad. She said there's a window inside the Darra Chamber that will take you where you want."

"The Queen would split your head open rather than grant a frivolous fancy," Fallo said from behind them.

Aunia whirled around. "What is it with you and heads?"

"Something you needn't worry. We'll have you back to your village soon." Fallo kicked Mathias' leg with the side of his boot. "On your feet, laddie. We're due that talk."

Mathias gave her a pained smile—almost Keston-like—and rose, hands flipping over in a shrug and apology. He glanced at her nearly untouched bowl then back at her face before he walked away with Fallo.

Taya dropped into the space where Mathias had been. The plunking of singular notes on the fiddle ended and rhythmic tones like distant thunder and quicksilver whispers came from a drum.

Aunia folded her arms around her knees. Part of her wanted to crawl out of the deepening ache in her chest, sit up and listen to the music. The other part wanted to run away and hide in the dark.

"Lots of music to come. Do you dance?" Taya asked.

Aunia held up the cup with sour wine. "You don't have plain water, do you?"

Taya turned and caught the attention of one of the children running along the grasses. She slid her hand in open air as if mimicking creek water and then made a pouring gesture. "That particular vintage is a favorite of Basil's. But I've a little coming with fresh water. Anyway, you never said how you became friends with the flyers—particularly Keston's friend. He's certainly jealous of your time."

"His name is Mathias," Aunia rocked slightly and then her arms eased from around her knees. Mathias was making claiming actions. Limi would have told her to be happy, or would if she approved of the match. Breanne would have told her well-done. But Breanne was dead. And Limi had refused to say goodbye. An ache rose in her throat. Aunia would never see Naoma Sacella again. Not that she wanted to.

"Casmia me darling," one of the rover men from across the fire called through cupped hands, "Give us a dance?"

The woman who had served them earlier in the full skirt and bare midriff rose and sauntered by the fire. She struck a pose of haughty confidence for a full three seconds, and then her arms and body glided through circles and twists.

"There will be stories after the dancing," Taya said. "And you have some intriguing ones. The wyvern battle. Seeing Hebsolum. Your journey here."

"I don't want to talk about it," Aunia responded.

"Why? Talking about your experiences is the best way to get others to talk about theirs. And we might be able to help you."

Aunia frowned, then nodded. "We escaped my village to rebox Edvaras' light. He had it stored in the ruins."

Taya's eyes went wide. "Edvaras' light? That was the magic on the Grashbear?"

"Yes. Hebsolum helped me recapture it so the Boggleman wouldn't have it. And then he threw me into the sky." Aunia rested her chin on her knees. "I know what I'm supposed to do. I just don't know how to do it. And I need to talk to Basil but he's disappeared."

"You're the one to restart the augury."

"What?" Aunia straightened. "No. Mathias was searching for Edvaras' starcharts . . . to get an answer for how to undo whatever the holy one did. But the starcharts are gone."

A niggling uncertainty gripped Aunia's belly. Was discovering a star-chart really the only way to restart an augury? It didn't seem to bear good fruit. And then there was Olivia, who some say was a Chandarion. She was born long after Edvaras. Aunia swiveled toward Taya. "Tell me about Olivia."

"She was our foremother. Daughter of a rover and a Tamorian prince. She saved us from the Mockmen trolls during the war and the Boggle-man came and took her. We haven't seen her since. That was seventy years ago. What else do you want to know?"

"I've seen her," Aunia murmured.

Taya straightened. "What?"

"I was in Nonderu. Not in my physical body, but I saw her. She's imprisoned within a column of Chand ice. Edvaras and Naoma are, too."

Besnik arrived with water. Taya took it and shooed him away.

"Your dad—"

"What do you know of my dad?"

"I know that he was questing to save Olivia. To save the augury."

"My father never mentioned Olivia." Aunia riveted her focus on the fiddle player who had joined the drummer. If her father had been trying to save Olivia, he got to see her every day now.

"You need to talk to Basil." Taya pulled on her dark braid. "He'll tell you more. I don't really know what your bloodline is—"

"That's what I was trying to do but Fallo blocked me from going through the hedgerow."

"You were trying to . . ." Taya broke into a laugh. "You certainly are more brazen than I. He'll be back tomorrow and then you can ask."

"Tomorrow?"

Taya pointed to the six-year-old with dirty-blonde hair. "Truth for truth to show I trust you. You met my sister Reina, but she's not kin by blood. She's a rescue. A faeblood. We took her in because these nobles would kill her if they found her."

Aunia jerked, spilling water on the ground. "Why?"

"Folk hate faes more than us." Taya pulled her fists against her chest. "It isn't right. But it is and you must understand that if you're to stay safe in these lands. You can't use magic. Not unless it comes from a tangible source. An ingredient. Or if you get royal permission because you are Chandarion or something similar. But we can help you. We always help our own."

Aunia leaned away. "Your own?"

"I think you and I have far more in common than you think. But the hour's getting late. They will be dancing and you'll get asked for stories, but if you'd like, I could take you to my vardo. Read your cards."

"What does that even mean?"

Logs in the fire snapped while the dancing woman's skirts moved like windblown flames and then the drums halted. Lena sang as she rose.

Wriggle me do love
Wriggle you might
In all the town's windows
Dressed in starlight

Taya bit her lip. "To tell you your future. So, you're better prepared for whatever comes."

Above them, stars blossomed across the night's canvas. Who knew how long Mathias would take. But his advice, not to trust these people, seemed wrong. Aunia sucked in a breath and nodded.

Chapter Eight

THE COST OF KINDNESS

You pray for opportunity too much. Either you make your own bread, settle, or starve but either way, I think we'll eat good at Besmarion. — Arch Vicar Bibb of the Da Vennen order

Mathias straightened his shoulders and followed Fallo to the back of the caravan, past the vardos with their hanging bronze lanterns. He was ready to face the consequences of his actions, bringing Aunia to Tamore. It surprised him he felt no anxiousness. If anything, it was gratitude that Fallo had pulled him away from that uncomfortable conversation.

She wants to go to Tatia. To find the Darra Chamber. But that chamber had disappeared from the castle generations ago with the mad Queen Didianne.

You should take her. Tafiriel paused at the edge of the corral's perimeter pace closer to the front of the caravan and several yards from Mathias. Revellie stood near Taf, unfurling her wings.

Fallo unfastened the rope gate and headed for Paderro, who stood near the large camp stool. Several of the nearby rover horses dozed, heads drooping on their standing bodies. One lay, legs folded under her.

She wouldn't be safe there and I . . . Mathias ran a hand through his hair while Fallo stopped beside Paderro. The commander hadn't taken any of Paderro's gear off while Mathias had unsaddled both Tafiriel and Revellie. He had neatly stacked the gear on a wide camp stool with Aunia's rutsack on top. Had Fallo expected him to care for Paderro while he had met with the rovers? Was Fallo going to chastise him for that, too?

Fallo's gaze flickered to both Taf and Rev before he pulled open his saddlebag. "We cannot bring that girl to the capital."

Prickled heat ran along Mathias' limbs. "I wasn't asking to bring Aunia—"

"She was. What were you thinking dragging her here?"

"The villagers exiled her. I had to. She'd be alone if I—"

"Exiled?" Fallo dug deeper into the saddlebag.

"Yes. After the Boggleman took her dad and the—"

"Yes, yes." Fallo brought a hand up in command to stop. "I heard the girl on the Grashbear."

"How did you . . ." Mathias deliberately slid his gaze from the sting marks on Fallo's face. He wanted more of the details about what happened when Fallo and Keston were under the mountain but he doubted he'd be able to get more than a few answers for everything. It made no sense wasting opportunity when he could find out more from Keston later. He straightened. "An honorable flyer couldn't have left her. And, well, she has knowledge on how to make faery repellent. We'll need that with heebles attacking our towns."

Fallo scowled and continued to rummage. "You've confirmation on that?"

"I do."

Long seconds went by and Fallo kept rummaging. Mathias dug his fingernails into his palm. The Queen surely would want to know about a faery repellent. But Aunia in Tatia . . . how awkward it would be? Not that he was planning on competing any longer in the suitor games but if his father showed up . . .

A tight band stretched over Mathias' ribcage. His father would disown him if Mathias did not compete. And Mathias owed his family. He curled his fists. It was his father who should have kept his own first betrothal, but he threw it away for his mother. A whirlwind romance they had had. It was still talked about at balls, but now? They hated each other. His own mother would tell him better to marry for connections and power. At least they would last after love died.

Mathias had never wanted to be king-consort. And who knew if Keira would even turn her head his way.

Mathias closed his eyes.

The Queen will step down, Taf sent. *And an heir will step forward.*
You're not helping.

"A pickle you are in, yes?" Fallo asked. "She is quite lovely. But there's an easy fix. You find out how she makes this faery repellent and then send her back."

"We can't send her back."

Paderro pinned his black ears back and sidestepped from Fallo.

"Then what, bucko?" Fallo gripped the dark leather shank attached to Pad's noseband. "We stash her with some lordling? Get her married off. Leave her here with these rovers? Don't you have a duty to your family? Or do you plan on giving your pegasus up?"

Mathias swayed. Unlike the other pegasi born into Tamore, Tafiriel was a wild one. Zeller's Dar medallion wouldn't work to sever their pairing. And Zeller's medallion had been stolen besides. But the threat of being severed from Tatia's court . . . never to make amends with Zeller's daughter, Nyrissa. To be cast out. He needed to think.

"I don't know," Mathias waffled. "Maybe Worley. Lord Lyle has the greenhouses and the key ingredient is in seed."

Paderro stamped as Fallo pulled a small, linen sack, curved with its contents, from his saddlebag. "That takes her too far into Tamore. But it's a starting point. Better to give her up."

Mathias' heart thudded in his throat. In his belly. But he forced himself to suck in a long slow breath. "Will we go to Dalin to look for our unit?"

"I am." Fallo re-buckled his saddlebag one-handed and then released Pad. "You'll stay here with Keston and—"

"No." The word forced its way out of Mathias' mouth and he stepped backwards in surprise. "Keston will be fine come morning. It would be better if all of us go. After all, Cat said Dalin had been attacked. I can't reach any of our unit. Can you?"

"Miss Cat Calculations needs to mind her own unit. Not mine."

Pad trotted away from Fallo and stopped by the edge of the corral facing the caravan's tail.

"Commander," Mathias tried again. "It's better for all of us to find out what happened."

"Enough. I pulled you out here to explain why you felt it was necessary to drag the girl along with you."

"I followed you when you went into the vardo," Mathias revealed. "We need to know who went over the wall and if someone pushed them."

"Eavesdropping?" Fallo faced him with a seething glare. "This is, what, disobedience number three?"

"Jules was my friend."

Fallo palm-smacked him in the chest and Mathias staggered back breathless.

"You think I abandoned him?" Fallo asked. "Think I was wrong, do you? Was I wrong for sticking my neck out for you? Have you ever considered in the tiniest sense what my kindness to you has cost me? I could be basking in the title of Dar-Elect instead of Zeller's daughter and where would you be?"

Mathias pushed aside the disjointed imagery from the Bellows and swallowed hard. "You did it because Zeller was your friend."

"Friend? A friend doesn't keep secrets and confide in foreigners. Not about finding . . ." Fallo turned away. "Enough. You will obey my orders."

"Finding what? Edvaras' village? Yasendra be blessed, you knew? Did you tell the Queen?"

"What I tell the Queen is no concern of yours." Fallo held the bulky linen sack against his chest. "You'll have a punishment. I'll decide what later. Get yourself to the fire. Stay there because if you don't . . ."

Mathias took a step backwards and Fallo exited out of the make-shift corral, turning left toward the front of the caravan. He couldn't go back to the fire yet. How would he tell Aunia that he couldn't take her to Tatia? She was right about wanting to save her dad. If he lived. Like he needed to do something for Jules. And it wasn't remaining in a rover caravan while Fallo flew off to Dalin. He wasn't even sure what Fallo would do when he got there.

Mathias curled his fists. It was entirely possible Fallo would still be focused on the marble from the marble giant.

He moved out of the corral and followed Fallo, skirting the warm glows from the brass lanterns hanging from the vardos. He had to make Fallo see reason. Convince him to take them.

If you haven't yet, Mathias sent to Taf, *tell Paderro that we've heard Brinsaber. We don't know where Jules is.*

You're trying to get Paderro on our side?

I'm hoping that Paderro will tell Fallo. That it'll make a difference.

Would Paderro be able to sway Fallo? The black pegasus didn't seem too happy with his flyer. It was possible that Paderro was angry because Fallo was only focusing on marble when members of the pegasi herd were

in need. Mathias paused beside the yellow vardo while Fallo continued on, his thick boots thumping through the ankle-high grass.

Mathias clenched his fist against another wave of heated frustration. He didn't want to disobey orders again but he had no choice.
It had to be confront Fallo or fly out to Dalin by themselves. That
could be the answer. But the consequences . . .

Fallo probably was heading for Tharon's vardo. Maybe with something tradeable in the woven sack. But what could the rovers have
that Fallo wanted? A bit of marble? Information?

Mathias followed and frowned when Fallo turned for the Brainhedge gate and pulled open the twist metal and living wood. Mathias
didn't realize that Fallo had a key. Or had Paderro cast an unlocking
spell? It could be as easy as Tharon leaving it unlocked for Fallo.
Hiding in darkness . . . that seemed to point toward contraband.
An illegal magic perhaps. But that made no sense. Flyers needed no
magic. Not with their pegasi.

Sometimes information comes when we pursue it, Taf sent, *even
when we shouldn't.*

You want *me to eavesdrop this time?* Mathias reached the gate and
pulled it open slowly, cringing at the soft squeal. He stepped inside.
Worry about consequences later, he told himself, he needed to know
what happened to his friend, whether he needed to rescue or avenge
. . . and if he could trust Fallo.

Thick, gnarled branches twisted on either side of the narrow cor-
ridor and with another two steps black darkness descended. The
hedgerow wasn't exceedingly thick, though there were some gaps
where one could hide. Would Fallo meet with Tharon within the
press of trees or inside the Brainmere where the Mere Creek flowed?
He had to be ready for either scenario.

Creeping forward, the earthy scent of decaying leaves and rich soil enveloped Mathias, reminding him of boyhood days hiding from his brother. He stiffened and then his foot came down on fallen twigs. Wooden snaps ignited thundering in his chest and he froze. Silently, he stood for a long moment with starlight filtering through crevices in the canopy. Ahead cascading water gurgled. But no voices.

Can you sense what direction Fallo went in? Mathias sent.

Paderro is shielding him.

Shielding. That confirmed Fallo wanted this meeting to be quite private. Mathias continued further for the creek. Paying as much attention behind him as in front. He had no idea if Tharon was already here or if he needed to hide before the rover came.

The murmuring of water grew louder as Mathias soft-stepped forward, attention fixed on the wooded ground until he could spot the Brain Mere through the hedgerow. He halted. A tall shadowy form stood ten feet away in the glen. One form, not two. Mathias ducked behind a stand of snaky vines and thorns. Forced his breath to slow. To be quiet.

A series of metallic clinks, probably a steel striker hitting flint, filtered over the water music from the silvery stream several yards away. A flame ignited—a candle—illuminating Fallo's bristled and ruork-stung face. That bit of tallow and light stood in the center of an irregularly shaped bowl.

Unease slid through Mathias' entire body and his fists uncurled. His mother had a similar bowl in her possession. A whisperer bowl. She had been infuriated when he had discovered it stuffed inside a small niche within her bedroom's fireplace. Ashwood. Lined with Chand crystal. One she said she had confiscated from a traitor and hid when she worked for the former queen. But Fallo wouldn't . . . couldn't be calling a whisperer.

The pungent smell of burning reached Mathias' nose. Coldness dug deeper into his chest, into his throat. This was the same smell from Naoma Sacella when he and Keston had been in the dorm room after Keston had disrupted a joining ceremony.

"It's about time," said a high and thin voice. Bits and pieces of a bone-white and finger-length skeleton emerged from the bowl. The rest of the creature, Mathias knew, was wrapped by a thick puff of smoke.

"Channel him," requested Fallo.

How could . . . why would . . . a flyer had no reason to need long-distance communication. Their pegasi could talk to other pegasi, bespeak each other's flyers. Relay messages. But Fallo must be talking to someone who was not a flyer. And someone unethical.

"I owe no screech-a-scry an apology." Fallo lowered the bowl. "And yes, I can get back. I told you. I have this stone from Edvaras. But the marble—"

The whisperer murmured something else.

"Yes, I can talk to Lord Emmet. But it's not going to be easy."

The whisperer rotated around Fallo's head, saying something but Mathias couldn't hear the words.

"I told you," Fallo said. "The statue is alive, and it dove back under the bloody mountains. I can offer Chand crystal to Emmet if he believes what I found. If I can't—"

The whisperer rushed to Fallo's face and hovered inches from the commander's nose.

Mathias set a hand to steady himself as he sat on his haunches.

"Yes, I know," Fallo said in a hoarse voice. "But the Da Vennen are there. And Arch Vicar Bibb."

Did Fallo know why the Arch Vicar was there? A twig snapped under Mathias' hand and he froze.

"Who's there?" Fallo blew out the candle and walked to the Brain-hedge. "I can hear you breathe."

Mathias launched himself to his feet and ran for the gate.

Chapter Nine

THREE CARDS

High in the clouds and far from her foes, to Tatia,
our Queen, and all that we know. — Dar-Elect Nyrissa
Rieson, flyer of Lydinairre

I nside the light blue vardo with its dark knotted patterns, Taya
sat cross-legged on her built-in bed, cradling a small wooden
box while Reina—little sister and foundling—sulked behind her,
watching Aunia with suspicious eyes.

Learning that Reina was half faery explained her unusual aura
with its thick gray-yellow and iridescent sparkles—a perfect blend
between unhappy child and mischievous faery. Maybe that was why
Aunia felt uneasy in the girl's presence. Maybe it was because of what
Taya had said at the fire. Did the little girl know there were other
Tamorians who wanted her to die? Such an unforgivable position.
How could anyone feel that way?

"Sit." Taya ran an index finger over three metal stars embossed on
top of the box. "These were my mother's."

Aunia bit her lip. There were some interesting things inside Taya's
wagon home. Small bottles and carved figures lining shallow cabinet

shelves along the interior walls. It reminded her a bit of a corner from Gaitha's apothecary room. But she didn't see any books. "Were?"

"She's dead," Reina replied.

Taya frowned. "Yes. I think Aunia heard that already."

"I did." Aunia stepped past a hanging lantern and sat at the edge of the high bed. "But I never heard what happened."

"Wrong place. Wrong time." Taya tapped her mouth with her index knuckle before dropping her hand back to the box. "She was in a city. Cities are dangerous, I told you—especially for attractive women. There was a lord. He wanted . . . he wanted something he couldn't have."

"What was that?"

"It was a long time ago." Taya shook her head, sucked in a breath, and leaned forward. "But better to think of. . . I want to help you figure out how to best find your parents. They lived here once upon a time."

"How will reading this deck of cards help?"

Taya dumped a blue silk-wrapped packet, nearly the dimension of her palm but thicker, maybe half an index finger, from the box. She then pulled what looked like loose-leaf painted pages from the fabric. "They help guide us to answers and help us with understanding."

The cards made a dry creak as she shuffled them. Taya then handed her the deck. "Draw out three cards."

The cards, a mesmerizing design swirling on their surface, felt heavy in Aunia's hand. "Three?"

"Yes. To represent your past, your present, and your future."

Aunia pulled one out, a gritty surface, and turned it over. It was a pale, silvery card.

Taya snatched it away. "Not that one. It . . . it shouldn't even be in there. Pull three others. Don't flip them over."

Frowning, Aunia complied and handed Taya three cards.

Taya laid the first card down and Aunia leaned forward taking in the painted full moon hanging over a silvery stream. On either side of the banks, wildflowers grew—pale lavenders, blues, and yellows—and barefoot in the creek's center stood a hooded figure, hands out, and cradling a pale pink multi-petaled flower.

"Mystery. Secrets." Taya frowned. "Not that this one isn't expected."

"What do you mean?"

"Well, I mean . . . Aunia, it's how you got here. Arriving with flyers from over the Grashbear. I mean that's a mystery right there but . . ." Taya heaved a breath. "This isn't my reading. I'd say there's much you've never been told. Secrets that you're trying to figure out. But were they kept from you for good reason or was it to hide a betrayal?"

"Does this card say which one?"

"Well, let's see what the other cards say."

Taya flipped over the next card and it showed a broad path carving its way through a hardwood leafy forest. Riding along its cobbled stones in a white wagon pulled by a unicorn and a bird-headed muscular animal with wings was a flowing-haired girl. Aunia touched what looked like will-of-the-wisps hovering within the tree branches.

"You are on an important path," Taya said. "Maybe the most important."

"What do you mean?"

"Well, I'd imagine Olivia would have gotten this card. She, well, she wasn't a full Chandarion, but she had more ability than a Queen's dar. She was what people are calling a potential . . . with a re-used Nymer."

Aunia squirmed a bit, remembering Olivia inside the Boggleman's ice column in Nonderu. "What exactly is a dar?"

"Well, I mentioned the Darra Chamber and—"

"Yes, and Besnik told me more," Aunia said with a frown. The rover boy had run after her when Aunia spotted Basil at the Brainhedge gate.

Had distracted her with stories about how Uriah and Yasendra had created a magical room and that it boasted a window that could take you anywhere you wanted. But Mathias said the place had disappeared. How could an entire chamber simply disappear?

"How to explain this . . ." Taya leaned back, tapping Aunia's last card against her cheek. "A Chandarion's nymer, their magic, is stored inside there. In Chand ice balls a top marble pedestals. That magic is stored up for the time of the choice but the Queen's dars are able to tap into some of that magic. Not everyone would be able to tap into it even if they're granted a commission from her majesty. But the ones who are able can conjure up some pretty powerful magic. They need it, it's said because they also stand in as advisors for the Queen. But the Queen also has her generals and the council of nobility."

Aunia leaned back trying to process what was said.

"Ready for the next card?"

Aunia nodded and Taya slapped the last card against the yellow blanket. This one showed a red bird surrounded in flames midair as if it had launched itself from a rolling hill and headed for the sun. Below, humans and faery kind looked upwards, watching.

"I knew it." Taya tapped the card. "I bet you are meant to take on your father's mission."

Aunia straightened. "Mission?"

"Yes. I mentioned it before. He came to us because he was looking to free Olivia from the Boggleman. And didn't you tell Basil that the Boggleman was after you? You and your dad have to be like Olivia. And if the Boggleman took your dad . . . well, you can free not only him but our Olivia as well."

Aunia jumped to her feet. She did not need a rover girl telling her what she had to do. She knew what she wanted to do—find a place to live with Mathias. Free her father. Learn about her mom. These cards did absolutely nothing to give her anything she didn't already know. What she needed was to talk to Mathias. To get him to agree to take her to Tatia. But he was with Fallo.

"You have a big destiny," Taya said softly. "What you do will be of benefit or detriment to us all."

"I don't know how to save the worlds. That was Mathias, not me, looking for the starcharts."

"Starcharts. What would starcharts do?"

"To figure out where and when the choice comes. Mathias said it was important to know . . ." Aunia trailed off. It was probable that the starcharts would have been as helpful as this card reading.

"Basil could help you get to Tatia," Taya said. "The Queen—"

"Stop." Aunia held both hands out. "Where is Basil? I need to talk with him."

Taya scooped the cards and wrapped them in the silk handkerchief.

"He's on a family mission to see his wererat mom," Reina said.

Aunia startled. She had forgotten about the little girl.

"Reina," Taya growled.

Running footfalls thundered beside the vardo on the roadside and Aunia bolted for the door.

"Wait." Taya caught Aunia's wrist, craning her neck toward the window. "Fallo's chasing someone."

Aunia paused, frowning. Fallo wouldn't be chasing Basil.

"You can't repeat what Reina said about Basil's mom. Please," Taya said.

Tafiriel, Aunia cast her thoughts to the blue pegasus. *Who is Fallo chasing?*

Mathias, Tafiriel sent back. *Stay where you are.*

CHAPTER TEN

KNUCKLEBONES

Convenient for Lord Emmet to rid himself of any with truth-telling ability. He may find that deed not to his liking.
— Cody Lambert of Lambert's Vineyards

B arely anyone sat at the campfire as Mathias ran past it. He needed to hide before Fallo caught up. But where? He was reaching the last vardo, Niall's vardo, where Keston was. Could he play off that he was there the entire time?

Mathias raced to the door and threw himself inside.

"You got a ghost on your tail?" a deep voice rumbled.

Four rovers sat around a small table which was pushed up against the roadside window. They were playing dice.

"I . . ." Mathias took one step in, glanced at the table and back to the door.

Niall reached for a stool on the other side of the small space and dragged it to the table. "Sit. Jarl, hand him the knucklebones."

"I was on a winning sprint," said a man with long black hair and a mustache. He held out the dice.

Mathias hesitated until he got thumped in the ribs with an elbow. As the door opened, he dropped the dice on the table.

Niall groaned. "Can you believe this flyer? Five rounds in a row rolling a seven."

Niall scooped the dice up before Fallo, who stood in the doorway, could see the double twos. He turned his head to the commander. "You come to play knucklebones with us, too?"

"You might have a hard time dicing with this one," Jarl said, pointing a thumb at Mathias.

Fallo growled and exited with a firm door slam.

Perhaps these people aren't so bad, Taf sent.

They have to want something after this. Mathias forced himself to look up. "Thank you."

Niall shrugged. "We know trouble when we see it."

"What do I owe you?"

"That's right, flyers pay their debts, don't they," said a lanky man on Mathias' right. "What do we want? Money? Power?"

"A story," Jarl said. He looked to Niall. "How about the one with what happened to Dar Zeller? Rumors have it you were with him when he died."

Mathias clenched his jaw and swallowed hard. "What do you care about Dar Zeller?"

"Flyers were viewed better when he lived. And many of us here are Augurites. We'd know who is trying to hurt our country."

Augurites. Those who believed in the Chandarion augury. That faith remained in pockets through society. Rich. Poor. Lords, peasants, and rovers. Zeller had been an Augurite. And Mathias had been, too. Until no hope remained of fixing the augury. Mathias whispered, "When seven stones fall apart . . . merging, remaking the broken heart . . ."

"And such renown for them who brave. Through sacrifice, both worlds are saved," Niall finished.

Mathias rapped his fist against his thigh. What harm was it to tell them? The truth had to be less harmful than some of the rumors he had heard. Rumors like Zeller had been killed by the former king-consort's band of traitors. That the Queen had ordered Zeller executed. And that Mathias himself had killed his own mentor.

"Zeller was looking for Edvaras' missing village." Mathias ran a hand through his hair. "He wanted to find the starcharts that showed when and where the choice would be made. It would also show when a Chandarion would be born. We could study what he created. Figure out a way to get all seven of them together. Maybe they're already in the world but their magic is stifled somehow. Boxed up in places that are not where the Darra Chamber used to be.

"We were at the Blue Onion awaiting a bladecaver to help navigate to this village. What I remember . . ." Mathias leaned his forehead into his hand.

"Jarl," said Niall. "Get up and get this lad a drink."

Jarl rose and, from a shallow cabinet along the opposite wall, plucked a water jug and a wooden cup. He poured water and set the cup in front of Mathias. Mathias frowned as he nodded his head, then took a gulp.

"One came," he continued. "Told Zeller that the right cave through could be found along the Grashbear near Britchway. That passageway would probably be open for the next moon or two."

Mathias leaned forward, squeezing his eyes shut. But what happened then? How did they get to the Bellows? This was the part he could never remember. He finally shrugged miserably. "I don't know how we got on the Bellows but we did. There's so much I just can't—"

He shook his head. "Maybe I was drugged. Drunk. Hit my head. I don't know. All I remember is pulling myself off the sands in front of a robed figure. Wererats were running and Dar Zeller was dead."

The image of his mentor surfaced in his head. Drooped over his bonds. Tied to a pole. Bloody. Mathias swallowed hard.

"You said a robed figure?" Niall asked.

Mathias nodded. "I thought . . . I thought it was Arch Vicar Bibb. But it couldn't be."

"Why not?" asked Jarl.

"Because I punched the man in the face. Broke his nose. Other flyers went to go check a couple days later. There wasn't a mark on him." Mathias took another drink of water while Jarl and Niall passed a glance between themselves.

"Well," Niall said. "Arch Vicar Bibb is in Dalin right now."

Mathias sputtered on his water and set his cup down. "Yes, I've heard."

"Supposedly recruiting," Niall added. "There's been a lot of that lately. And as for the when, that's a problem. The man seems to get to places far too quickly for traditional means."

"Particularly someone who won't use magic." Jarl scooped up the dice. "Another round? Don't want to lose my winning streak completely."

"Nah, I'm out," said the man on Mathias' right.

"Wylie," Niall said, "Keep your mouth shut about—"

"Of course," the man said, and he exited the vardo.

The remaining man, hood hiding his face, said. "Better Da Vennen than lords."

"Besnik," Niall growled.

"What?" Besnik lowered his hood and fluffed out his tousled hair. "You'd disagree after what they did to Carr and Taya's mom."

"There's good nobles, too," Niall said.

Jarl tapped the dice on the table. "There are. But there's plenty of talk. Last town we were in said Arch Vicar Bibb was making wererats."

Mathias pulled his thoughts from trying to piece together his missing memory. "Wait. What? Da Vennen would not be making wererats."

"Some think it," said Niall. "Said it would explain the missing people."

Mathias shifted his weight on the stool. Any missing people had always been attributed to rovers. For rovers to blame the Da Vennen . . . "I would have a hard time believing that. I don't like them. And I certainly don't trust them."

He stood. Keston still snored softly on the bed at the back of the vardo.

"He'll be right as a summer's day come morning," Niall said.

Mathias nodded tightly. "And Aunia?"

CHAPTER ELEVEN
FROM BLUE TO RED

Momma, Mathias says I can't hear the story about the El-darghast and the Sacred Grove. — Paulo Habrett

*B*ut why is Fallo chasing Mathias? Aunia sent to Tafiriel. She stood with her hand on the vardo door latch.

He's safe, and it's his story to tell, Taf sent. *Just stay for now.*

Aunia scowled. Obviously, he didn't want to answer.

Behind her, Taya stood between a small cast-iron stove along the left wall and a chest of drawers with a seating cushion on top. "Aunia. Stay. You can talk to Basil come morning."

Basil. Aunia's shoulders drooped. She turned, almost ready to ask how Basil's mother became a wererat as Reina had said. But she didn't. She had plenty of other answers she craved. And if Mathias was busy hiding...

Is Basil out there?

Yes. By the fire.

"I'll put you for the trundle bed," Taya said. "Reina can bunk with me."

"That's my bed." Reina dropped to the floor with a thump, her glow turning a darker shade of dried blood. Like the Boggleman's before he had changed into a wyvern.

Aunia knew she was staring. She couldn't help herself. Similar glow but Reina was just a little girl. Another thought hit. Taya . . . did she just lie to her? Basil was just outside.

She bolted from the vardo and rushed into the shadow behind the second blue wagon. Why would Reina's glow look like that? Unless it was . . . hatred. That had to be the color of hatred.

"Will you be looking for Olivia like your father?" a woman's voice said.

Aunia jumped.

Lena stepped from her vardo's rear wooden steps. The lantern's flickering light behind the woman threw shadow on her face.

"My father?" Aunia clutched at the neckline of her tunic. "You knew him. And my mother?"

"I didn't. Basil did." Lena pointed to the dwindling campfire two vardo lengths down near the flat-roofed wagon where a lone figure sat on a camp stool.

Basil. Aunia sucked in a breath and padded over to the orange bandana-wearing rover with his dark hair and patch worked vest. "Tell me about my parents."

Basil dropped a chunk of bread back into a wooden bowl in his lap and looked up. "Ah, the young miss I wanted to speak with. Have a seat."

Aunia collected a nearby stool and set it down by Basil. "Your answer?"

Basil chuckled. "Aren't you as imperious as your mother."

Her heart fluttered against her sternum. "You knew them."

"I did. We found them wandering in the woods near Vraelsfork when you were a babe. It certainly wouldn't have been polite leaving a young family alone with no supplies, so we offered our home to them. In fact, they stayed in the same vardo where Taya lives now."

Aunia drew her fists against her chest. "What were they like? Why were they there? Where were they from?"

"They were . . . well, they were like a young couple in love. In love with each other and their baby girl." Basil tore a bit of bread from the bowl and tossed it across the fire. "Your mother, well, she saw beauty almost everywhere. Take a look at the knotwork painted on Taya's vardo. That came from your mother. Or, at least, the beginnings of it did."

Aunia swallowed hard. In the darkness, Taya's vardo was just a shape illuminated by lantern lights.

"She . . . loved listening to birds," Basil continued. "And reciting silly poetry. And your da . . . all he wanted to do was protect you both. Now, why were they wandering the woods alone? Never gave a real explanation. Not unusual with your da being a Mystic."

"Mystic?" Aunia's attention snapped back to Basil's face. "Like you? What . . . what really is a Mystic?"

"That's a topic all by itself. Suffice to say that Augurites—"

"What's an Augurite?"

Basil held up a palm and chuckled. "Mystics. They believe in the augury. That when all seven Chandarions come into the world that they'll refashion the shattered heart and both our worlds, mortal and faery, will live. But there's a hex which has broken the augury—"

"Hex?"

"A dark powerful magic and nothing to be spoken of at night. What I can say is that Mystics helped to pull enough energy to create a potential Chandarion which was our Olivia. A bridge after Edvaras left. But the Boggleman—"

"The Boggleman is dead and I want to hear about my parents."

Basil lifted his palm again. "I understand that but this is about your da. The Boggleman took Olivia from our world and until she's saved, no other Chandarion . . . potential or full, can be."

Aunia shoved back images of Olivia and her orange-red hair, along with Edvaras and Naoma who were all captured inside Chand ice columns in Nonderu.

Basil touched her arm. "You're remembering something. What is it?"

Aunia shook her head. "It's nothing."

Basil shrugged. "Anyway, your da . . . he was born and raised in Bellatine, where the Mystic Court hales. And he came to Tatia with an objective: free Olivia. That meant he needed to find the Darra Chamber in Tatia and go through the window. The problem was—"

"The Boggleman pursued them," Aunia interrupted. In her minds-eye, she could see the vision of her mother and father running through the birchwoods . . . burying her mother's amulet with the moss-gnomes.

"He did," replied Basil. "But can I ask . . . when did the Boggleman start chasing you?"

"Only a few days ago." Aunia bit her lip. But that wasn't true, was it? Gaitha had told her before heebles had broken their way into the apothecary room that her father had always tried hiding her from the Boggleman. It was why he had leiaphae, Edvaras' shrouding flowers, hanging inside their home. And she held magic. The question was what kind. Mygul, her globefire, was a much darker blue than Edvaras' light—like the difference between Taya's and Lena's vardos. "But I'm not sure why . . ."

"Daughter of a Mystic. And with your mother's line, being magical—"

"And he seeks to capture magic. Use it and . . . wait. My mother's line. What could she do? What was her name?"

Basil rubbed his jaw while crickets sang in the distance. "Your da called her Leia as did all of us."

"Leia," Aunia whispered.

He pulled another finger-piece of bread and tossed it across the fire. "The long and the short of the Boggleman is he wants humankind to end. Has since Didianne's time."

"I know that already."

"Do you now? Then you put it together why he seeks you."

"Because I have unexplained magic. Is it a combination between my mother and father?"

"He wants you because, like your da, you can stop him."

"Stop him?" Aunia curled her fists into her sky-blue linen pants. "My dad? I don't understand. He just drinks, and copies books, and . . . fishes."

"Copies books, eh?" Basil shot her a smirk and tossed more bread over the fire. "From a place where a Chandarion lived? You need to get better at putting things together."

"Putting things together? I need answers for that," Aunia snapped. She had to make answers, too. Like how she would get her father back. Grashbear or Tatia. Would she be alone or have help? And when her father was safely rescued . . . where would she live? Mathias' home?

She wrapped her arms around herself. At least, she wouldn't need to confront the Boggleman when she found a way to Nonderu. He had fallen to his death from above the Grashbear Mountains. She had almost plunged to her death, too—only magic had saved her.

Aunia hugged herself tighter. "How did my mother die?"

The wooden bowl nearly dumped from Basil's lap but he caught it. He sucked in a long breath. "Her heart was broken."

"You can die from a broken heart?"

He set the bowl down. "Aunia, there's something else you need to know. To keep you safe. And it won't be easy to hear. After you leave this caravan, you cannot speak your da's name. Under any circumstances. It's dangerous."

Aunia sat up taller. "Why?"

"Because he stands accused of . . . regicide." Basil pinched the bridge of his nose. "This was the Summer Solstice ball before you were born. Most of the royal family was murdered. The belief, pressed and spread by our former king-consort, was that Mystics committed the act. Committed it because the heir refused to honor . . . well, a tradition. And your da being there and being a Mystic . . ."

Aunia stiffened. "The blood ball. Fallo said . . . but, no. That's impossible. My father can't kill anything. Not even a bug. He's . . . he's let people die . . . my foster mother . . . because he can't kill."

"I don't think he did it either but that won't matter. It's what is believed. Some will blame you if they learn you're kin. They'll do you great harm."

In the distance a vardo door opened and shut.

"How can I ask the Queen to show me the Darra Chamber if I can't tell her why I need it?" Aunia leaned over her knees. That was what her dad and Fallo meant when she had overheard them when Mathias had been bit. Her father was accused of an unforgivable act. One he did not do. "So, you want me to lie. For a perception?"

Basil threw yet another bit of bread. It arched over the snapping fire and landed in a bit of taller grass beside a small dark-haired faery with dragonfly wings—purples, blues, and yellow.

Aunia straightened. "Jennium?"

"Faery-sighted?" Basil said. "Good. Very good. But that's another thing you'll need to hide."

"How?" Aunia stood. "How do you know her?"

Jennium sprung from the grass and flew over, landing on Basil's knee.

"Mystics, well, they have a faery familiar," he said. "Someone from the other world who'll share their magic for the betterment of both worlds.

Jennium was your da's familiar. And after he . . . disappeared, she came to me."

Jennium jingled and pushed a mental image into Aunia's mind. That of a marble-white castle, maybe seven stories tall, with round turrets and intricate spires sitting on a bright-white puffy cloud. Tatia.

Aunia blinked. Obviously, Jennium had seen the castle before. Been with her father when he had been there. She bit her lip, uncertain how to ask by mind picture whether Jennium could help her find the Darra Chamber. She returned the image of the castle and what she imagined Chand ice balls sitting on marble pedestals inside a small room would look like.

Jennium rose from Basil's trousered knee and blinked out of sight.

Aunia rested her fist against her mouth. Tatia was days, weeks away—if she could find it. Unless Mathias agreed to take her. She didn't like his glow during supper. He seemed a bit distant but then again, he was mourning a friend.

Jennium re-emerged hugging a small silver hand that gripped a round cherry-sized crystal. Her mother's amulet.

The faery held out the orb to her with its silver chain, maybe five faery lengths dangling past her tiny feet. Aunia hesitated.

How did Jennium get it? And full of Edvaras light. She swallowed hard.

Yes, Jennium was a friend, or at least Aunia thought so, but faeries always demanded something for a gift. But refusing was never a good idea either.

Jennium dropped the amulet into her lap, robbing her of choice. But Aunia did want it. Her mother's amulet. She never thought she'd see it again.

In slow motion, Aunia slid her fingers across the crystal, bracing for quaking, or pain, or something from Edvaras' imprisoned magic. There was nothing.

Frowning, she picked up the amulet, letting the silver chain slide through her fingers. Such a delicate silver-wrought hand which clasped the orb. Aunia held the amulet closer to the dim light of the fire. The tiny jewels that represented fingernails . . . they looked more red than blue. Still, her mother's necklace . . . she threw Jennium an appreciative unspoken thanks, and the faery buzzed noisily, blinking from sight.

"Familiar too with their antics, I see," said Basil. His swarthy complexion had turned pale.

"I've been around them my whole life. My mother's amulet. I didn't think I'd see this again."

"No. This one isn't faery-wrought," Basil said, "It belonged to your da. It's another thing you'll need to keep hidden."

Aunia straightened. "My father's? No. I saw my parents bury this. It's my mother's."

"Your mother said she had one. Manifested from faery itself but it was based on this. Some will be upset with you having it but perhaps it's better it comes to you."

Chapter Twelve
A Prod to Leave

Beware those who welcome you in. They may well steal your heart or your means. — Wendalin Mensani, apprentice dar to Dar Syrick

Yards away, Aunia sat at the fire with Basil, her posture a bit hunched and her hands gesturing broadly. She had made friends with that Mystic. And she seemed at home with these people.

Mathias rubbed his face. Why couldn't she understand that they could be treacherous?

And they can be kind, Taf sent.

When it suits them. Mathias rapped the side of his thigh. They had covered for him with Fallo and the cost while unpleasant had lessened the tightness in his chest, giving him a clearer head. And he needed it. Particularly because he still had to decide what to do with what he had discovered in the Brainmere. *Where is Fallo now?*

Inside the leader's vardo. He was demanding to know what rover followed him through the brainhedge gate.

Mathias stiffened with commingled relief and guilt. Fallo didn't know it was him. But the commander had a whisperer. Malicious things. Did Fallo not know that? Whisperers stole a bit of essence from a man with every message they passed until all that was good faded away. And Paderro knew. Mathias was sure of it. Why else would the black pegasus sidestep away from Fallo.

He counted his fist taps against his thigh. He ought to report this to Dar-Elect Nyrissa. But with Nyrissa's distrust of him, compounded with Cat's probable report, what could he do? He'd be done for either way.

A good sleep could clear your mind, Taf sent.

A good sleep? I can't. Not with Aunia . . . Not with Aunia with the Mystic. Those people weren't to be trusted. But how did Basil—a rover's son —take fealty to that Bellatine order, the Mystic Court, far to the south, past Adar, and to those islands?

Mathias shifted deeper into the shadows behind the flat-roofed vardo. Basil, at least, kept a seemlier distance than those rover boys had. They had practically been in Aunia's lap and she had been utterly oblivious. But oblivious was just a part of her. Could he make her understand that her naivety could cause as much danger to herself as her magic? Her magic. It was probably illegal or maybe worse. And he brought her to this place.

They'll keep her secrets, Taf sent.

With a price.

She misses her home.

Mathias's shoulders sank. Her not having a home was his fault. He should be the one comforting her, not this rover-Mystic. But he had abandoned her. His heart felt too raw with worry for Jules, the fury for tomorrow's journey to Dalin, and concern for his future. No. It was better waiting nearby in case he needed to swoop in—swoop in like Keston—with a girl in every village.

Skulking in the dark isn't what Revellie's rider would do, Taf sent.

Mathias stiffened. *Right. Keston would stride right out there and charm her from that rover.*

Aunia lifted her hands to her collarbones. And Basil leaned over her, hands at the nape of her neck. Mathias gritted his teeth against the heat pouring into his fists. That Mystic was clasping a necklace on her. Behind him, laughter drifted from Niall's vardo, filling Mathias' anger with pain. She didn't need him to swoop in. She seemed at home here.

A part of him wanted to stalk away . . . but whether or not she needed him at this moment, he wasn't going away. At least not yet.

He would be going to Dalin. Whether Fallo allowed it or not, Mathias would be flying there come morning—he had to. Both for Jules and to learn Fallo's plot with Lord Emmet Dalin. And Aunia. Would she be safer here? The rovers . . . they wouldn't do anything terrible to her in a day. And they'd be back before the dark hours again.

Aunia's attention was on her new necklace, making him clench his teeth. And then, he blinked several times against the tiny white light hovering over her chest.

Did he give her a magic trinket? Mathias sent.

I'm not sure, Taf sent. *We'll find out soon enough.*

A few more long moments passed before Basil got to his feet, extended a hand to Aunia, and pulled her up. Mathias only unclenched his fists when Basil released her hand. He was taking her somewhere, leading her toward the front of the caravan line. Oh, Mathias was not going to permit this rover to walk with Aunia unescorted. He followed them from the shadows, zipping past the circles of light from the hanging lanterns.

They stopped at the back of Taya's vardo and Basil opened the door. Aunia went inside. Alone. Mathias inhaled, and that breath caught in his chest when Basil turned and winked in his direction. That Yasendra-cursed Mystic knew he had been there the entire time.

He seems to be protective of the girl, Tafiriel sent.

Perhaps.

Basil continued his walk toward the front of the caravan, probably to Tharon's vardo where Fallo was, and Mathias stamped toward the corral and the wide camp stool. Best to have his bedroll set up before Fallo returned. He stiffened when he got there.

Where is Aunia's knapsack?

Tafiriel walked over from the front facing line of rope. *No rover got past me.*

Did you see Aunia get it? It was a possibility during the time he was in the hedgewood spying on Fallo.

I did not.

Tafiriel. Mathias rubbed his forehead. *Okay. We'll assume Aunia has it and we'll ask her . . . when we see her next.*

But it might not be morning. Mathias grabbed his bedroll and walked back to Taya's wagon. And would Aunia yell about being left behind when he returned? Perhaps that would be the tell on how much she liked these people. How much she might miss him.

He unrolled his blankets beside Taya's vardo and lay down.

Who knew how long before the occasional laughter from Niall's wagon died down and all grew quiet except for distant snores. Mathias flipped over a third time, dragging his blanket over his shoulder. Jules. Zeller. Aunia. Fallo and the whisperer. Fallo might not know it was Mathias who had spied on him. Or he might suspect. Was Fallo even trustworthy anymore? But the commander still had the loyalty of his pegasus, even if Paderro looked displeased.

Mathias rolled to face the corral. Tafiriel stood near the camp stool with Revellie. Had she eaten anything with worry about Keston? That was one thing he could do. Take care of his friend's pegasus.

Mathias went to her and patted her neck. "It'll be fine, girl. Keston will be up probably before the sun is."

Revellie bespeaks his head will be on fire, Tafiriel sent.

"Probably. A headache will mend though."

Revellie snuffled at Mathias' hair and walked to the feed bucket. After a few minutes, Mathias returned to his bedroll and breathed in the night air with its damp green smell. At some point consciousness slid away, and he was dreaming of Aunia sitting beside him and they were pointing at the stars.

A boot skimmed Mathias' calf, jarring him awake to the assault of bird song. He blinked against the grainy predawn light and Fallo standing beside him.

"We breakfast at Dalin," Fallo said. "Saddle up."

Relief . . . surprise flooded Mathias, even more so when he spotted Keston by the second blue vardo talking quietly with the cinnamon-haired woman. He wasn't sure what caused Fallo to decide to take both himself and Keston, but it meant he didn't need to disobey another order. "Yes, sir."

Mathias slipped away briefly and then entered the corral. Keston, near the camp stool, was putting on Revellie's gear with the woman at his side. He said something to make her laugh before she reached up and caressed Keston's cheek. She winked at Mathias and sauntered away. Mathias frowned.

"Not what you're thinking." Keston walked over and handed Mathias a horse brush. He tapped at his new knit hat. "Lena re-wrapped my noggin and sold me this. Said my head would fall off if I didn't. Course that could have been an exaggeration."

Nearby, Fallo checked Paderro's straps. "Less gum rattling. I want to be in Dalin before its bells."

Mathias gave Taf a quick groom to guarantee the tack would sit well for the journey. "Is Aunia still abed?"

"She's staying here," Fallo said. "And hurry up if you're planning on coming."

Mathias' fingers fumbled on Tafiriel's noseband. "We're almost done."

"Good."

Minutes later the three of them on their pegasi lifted into the sky and as eager as Mathias was to find out about Jules, he rocked anxiously in his saddle.

She'll be alright here, Taf sent.

I hope so.

The trip to Dalin would have, on most days, been idyllic with the contrast of rocky mountains against lush fields and meadows. Not today, however. Mathias's mind was too busy racing. So much had happened in such a small space of time. Wererats and wyverns. An exploding mountain. Hebsolum. Not a myth but all too real. And the Arch Vicar Bibb inside Dalin's walls.

Mathias reminded himself he was a flyer. He did not need to fear some cult leader. But it seemed awfully ironic that Bibb was here when they couldn't find their unit. When Mathias knew Bibb had been at the Bellows. All he lacked was hard proof and a complete memory.

They flew over Baxter's Way to the Trade Route—a highway to transport goods between Bellatine and Tamore—while shadows shortened over the too-quiet landscape. No farmers in the field nor caravans on the road. That was odd in itself; however, it wasn't until they cut diagonally, bypassing much of the poorly maintained road spur, that Mathias spotted ravished animal carcasses.

He swallowed hard. Nearly fifteen hundred souls lived outside of Dalin's thick, rough city wall. Walls made to protect the population from

Mockmen trolls and forest fae. He hoped the people had made it to safety. Most probably had. After all, Dalin, lay centrally located to all the nearby villages even though it sat twenty miles from the main Bellatinian trade route. Its fame of ore mining and sword forging had gained it a semi-maintained road for retinues of merchants and farmers to travel.

They continued on for what seemed like forever before a dark-smoke plume and the taste of burning announced that Dalin's forges were still operational. And then the circular city appeared through smoky fog. Mathias pushed his scabbard back with an elbow and leaned forward.

Behind the city, workers dug an enormous mass grave. Mathias clenched his jaw. There had been many deaths at Naoma Sacella and it made his stomach turn, threatening to upend last night's supper. This attack on Dalin, with its greater population . . . it had suffered higher casualties. Yes, it was happy news that the storm had dissolved all the heebles. But what if more came? They had to create that faery repellent.

Keston, flying alongside Tafiriel, had gone ash-pale. Fallo and Paderro sped toward the city. Averting his eyes from the soon-to-be occupants of the pit, Mathias focused on a smattering of carts queued in line before the gate while a half dozen town guards, dressed in red wool, pawed through their inventory.

The merchant guild building fell, Tafiriel announced as they flew over Dalin, circling high.

Mathias took a tally of the buildings which had collapsed inside the town's tightly packed and crooked footprint. Several, though not surprising with how Dalin's upper stories overflowed its taxable ground level footage. So many buildings leaned and had to be bolstered by poles or by its neighbors.

The guild building, however, was as sturdily built as his father's keep.

The rovers said faebloods conjured a storm to be rid of heebles, Mathias sent. *It must have been a whirlwind.*

They circled back to the town's eastern gate and landed. Caravan merchants gazed at them with a strange mixture of hope and with disgust. Three town guardsmen, dressed in red wool, also looked at them with surprise, pausing in their inventory search.

"Dalin's lord has denied all flyers entry," said one of the guardsmen, who had a pale yellow dress over his shoulder. He stood at the back of a box-shaped wagon where the canvas covering had been flipped up exposing barrels and crates. "Fly back to your tower."

"Is there a problem?" Fallo asked, lifting in his saddle.

"I'll say," said the largest guard. He stopped rummaging one-handed through a barrel of grain and pulled his left hand, which held a square wooden box, out of sight. "Our Lord, the Marquis of Dalin orders all flyers to stay well away."

"He don't want more mishaps," said the dress-stealing guard, grimacing a bit.

"Mishap?" Fallo raised a brow.

"You musta heard, flyer," said a more portly guard. "One of yours tumbled from the wall after the faebloods dropped a twister on us."

Fallo lowered his left hand, out of sight of the guardsmen, in a gesture to stay. "Pawing through the inventory and taking a cut. Does your lord know?"

"We've the right to search for faebloods."

Taf flattened his ears. *And the lord will paw through those faebloods like his men pawing through inventory.*

Mathias slid his hand toward his sword. To his left, blood streaks ran from the top of the gray and tan stone wall. Heeble blood or human? Probably both. "Where are the other flyers?"

Fallo bespeaks silence, Taf sent, tossing his head. *Keston bespeaks we could have landed inside already.*

And against protocol, too. Mathias patted the side of Tafiriel's neck while the stench of decay and metallic sulfur breathed on the wind. In front of them, the guardsmen also straightened with pale complexions.

"Indeed," said Fallo. "As her majesty's commander of Eddac Tower, I'm here in an official capacity to investigate."

"And we're following our lord's commands," the large guard said. "Fly back to your tower."

Fallo's sting marks reddened on his face. "I'm a flyer of her majesty's pegasi army. You have no right to deny her majesty—"

"We ain't denying you anything." The dress-stealing guard barreled forward. "But we've archers to encourage you leave."

Chapter Thirteen
Nightmare

Oh, some may think the Holy One touched you, but I know you're nothing more than a Dagel demon in human skin.
— Sigmus from Naoma Sacella

Aunia floated over pink fluffy clouds while sylphs glided by her. It was peaceful. Pleasant. If only the sylphs stopped telling her 'It's the solitary current you must fly. You're the only one who truly sees.'

But it wasn't difficult to see rich green land peaking between the poofy clouds. She lowered in the sky, alone. Without wings. Without a pegasus. Or magical assistance and flew past rolling hills with carved-out terraces. Each level flourished with short, gnarled trees which were covered in silvery-green leaves and small flowers of creamy white and pale yellow. The hills faded back and dramatic mountain peaks rose with craggy ridges and steep slopes.

Then they melted away, and she stood in the shadows before a wooden room divider with narrow, evenly spaced slats. Morning light spilled through a spacious room with high ceilings. Pale gossamer curtains on tall windows swayed with a light breeze, as if they breathed in harmony with the very air. Sounded like it too as they brushed the edges of some of the pale wood tables lining the room. Glass tubes, leather-bound books, and wooden bowls filled several of the tabletops.

Aunia stiffened. Someone covered in blankets slept atop a large bed which stood in a shadowy corner. Someone the size of a man.

A door squeaked to Aunia's immediate right and then crisp footfalls. She crouched deeper behind the divider, nearly holding her breath as a woman with mahogany-brown hair walked into the space bringing with her the smell of sizzling grease. Some sort of meat was on the pale wooden tray she held. The woman walked to a low, circular table near the bed and set the tray down . . . looking for a moment as if she'd spill out of her low-cut green gown. She straightened and moved to a table shoved between two windows. As morning light painted copper highlights in her hair, she scooped up a long-tubed glass hanging from a brass chain.

Aunia leaned closer to the divider's wood slats. Light flickered inside that tube.

On the bed, the figure stirred and said in a high-pitched musical voice, "Those are mine."

Aunia's heart froze, the coldness spreading out to the ends of her fingers. It couldn't be.

"Good morning, Master." The woman turned. "We make these for good cause. Let me explain and you'll approve, I'm sure."

The figure in the bed pushed blankets aside and sat up. The Boggleman threw his twisted legs over the side of the bed.

Aunia had seen him fall. How could he live? But then again, she had taken that same plunge to the ground.

"Master, don't." The woman set the glass tube aside, glided over to the tray, and brought it to the Boggleman. She even sat ever so demurely at his side, tray in her lap. The woman smoothed his long white hair back. "It's just a matter of time before you are strong."

The Boggleman knocked the woman's hand aside. "I choose their captivity, Gabryella. When and if."

"Choosing their captivity may be difficult. And we're doing this for you." Gabryella pulled a purple napkin from the tray. "I've fried pork here. Sweet bread. Your favorite cheeses."

"Release them."

"Master." The woman held up a pastry. "There is market for trade. After we gain enough faebloods, how easy it will be to spell you back to Nonderu, if that is your wish."

The Boggleman grabbed the woman by the throat and his high-pitched voice turned to grit. "What I wish is my cloak."

"We haven't found it yet," Gabryella said hoarsely. "Too many wererats poking around but, we're looking."

The Boggleman couldn't reach Nonderu yet? Aunia's chest eased slightly. And he didn't have his cloak.

Something brushed against her leg. Aunia jerked, slapping a hand over her mouth. It was Narvis, and he was shaking.

"Nia," the fire salamander whispered. The pupils in his slitted red eyes were wide, and he looked far rougher than in Nonderu, more gray mottling his yellow lizard skin. He stepped closer on thick bipedal thighs, coming up to her shoulder from her crouched form. "Nia come to help? Send shadow faes away?"

"Help?" Aunia breathed. "Where am I?"

"Fireling keep."

Across the room, the Boggleman backhanded the woman and pulled the tray from her lap.

"What is a fireling?"

Narvis pointed at the table where the woman had returned to. "Fire salamander enemy. She put kin in glass tubes. Will put all kin there. Narvis, too."

"For . . . for trade?"

Narvis nodded. "Faebloods for lights. Cromis Boggleman keep calling for Narvis but Narvis knows. Glass tube or eaten by cape. Poor, poor Narvis."

Aunia pressed her knuckles against her mouth remembering her mushroom sprite friend, Teezo Popkins. Just a few days ago his small, lanky form sailed to the Boggleman's cape, and it consumed him. The Boggleman had done this because her faery friend had warned her—as had the moss-gnomes from the Birchwoods.

"He doesn't have it right now," Aunia whispered.

Across the room, the Boggleman ate his breakfast, dropping some of the food disdainfully onto the floor.

"He will. Unless..." Narvis touched her shoulder and it felt as if a hundred bees walked across her skin. "Wererats have cape. Get from wererats. Destroy."

The Boggleman flicked meat from his fingers and his face turned toward the room divider. And then he stood up.

Aunia flung herself awake, clinging to the trundle bed's edge while the world careened and creaked, and laughter rang.

"You jump funny," Reina said.

"That's impolite, Reina," said Taya, barely suppressing her own grin. "Come on. We've been waiting for you to wake. Breakfast is on the run."

Taya walked through the moving vardo with items clattering together rhythmically. She opened the door and stepped down easily. Reina joined her, though a bit more clumsily.

Aunia rose, fingertips along the carved shelves as she maneuvered through the wagon. She nearly lost her footing twice before she braced herself in the vardo's door frame. The blur of broken limestone pebbles mixed with dirt and bits of grass challenged her. She was meant to leave a moving wagon?

Taya waved at her from alongside the road, and then they disappeared behind the next vardo where Besnik and Camlo sat at the driving board. Aunia sucked in a breath and dropped to the ground, scurrying to the side of the path like Taya and Reina did. She waited for Lena's vardo to go by.

It did, and through its open door, Taya waved at her from the bed. Reina sat beside her, along with Lena, who sat on a nearby chair and mended a shirt. Aunia ungracefully vaulted inside.

"Sleep yourself out?" Lena secured a last stitch and set her sewing aside.

Aunia braced herself against carved cupboards while pans on hooks swung.

"She had a startle dream." Reina grabbed a fistful of cheese from a ceramic bowl which sat on a small sideboard between bed and wall.

"Oh, come over here and tuck in. Let's hear all about it," Lena said.

Aunia blinked. No one ever asked to hear her dreams. Had it been a dream? A nightmare? It felt so real. More real than the nightmare she had about running before heebles. And that horror had come true shortly after.

"A nightmare, I'm guessing." Taya lowered a half-eaten hand-size pie. "But shared will lessen its grip."

Aunia walked hesitantly through the moving vardo. "Are there such things as firelings?"

Lena straightened. "You dreamed of firelings?"

Aunia situated herself on the bed while Taya pulled the large bowl from Reina and held it out.

"Meat pastries and cheese."

Aunia took a pastry. Cold, its bottom a bit soft, but it had a satisfying heft. "Maybe. And the Boggleman."

Reina slid closer to Taya. "My mama says he steals children and turns them into toads."

"He could at that," Lena said, and traced a star on her forehead.

"He wouldn't for you." Taya squeezed Reina's hand. "You're part fae."

"Taya," Lena murmured.

"Aunia already knows about Reina," Taya said. "And I trust her."

"A fireling is trading fire salamander lights for faebloods," Aunia said.

Taya sat up straighter. "They're what?"

"Where did you hear that," Lena asked. "Your dream?"

Aunia nodded.

"Well. Dreams . . ." Lena started. "They're mostly caged-up worry and the wrong thing you ate."

"No. I think this one was real. I need to tell Mathias."

Lena and Taya exchanged a glance.

"I didn't think he was dead," Taya said.

"You knew the Boggleman fell?" asked Aunia.

Taya nodded. "Basil said. But it's been a long time since the Boggleman worked with firelings."

"Founded them is more like it. Those Cragborns . . . they're our opposite. The enemy," Lena said.

"Cragborns?" Aunia asked. She reached for another pastry.

"Mountain folk," Taya said.

"They use any magic. Light. Dark. Legal. Illegal," Lena said. "And they don't believe in the augury."

"They've attacked our country before as well," Taya said. "It's why Dar Syrick created our border spell and why Basil is working with the wererats. To keep these wyverns that the firelings called from eating our defense."

Lena pulled a black-laced shawl from the back of the chair and wrapped it about her shoulders. "But you actually dreamed of the Boggleman?"

The wagon jostled with a thump and a shadow passed by the curtained window.

Aunia scooted back and wrapped her fingers into Lena's wool blanket. "I know it was more than a dream. I know he's convalescing on top of a mountain in a fireling's home. And I know he's looking for his cloak."

"Cloak?" Taya said.

Aunia turned her attention to Taya's wide blue eyes. "His cloak eats faeries. I've seen it. Sucks them in and they're gone."

Reina dropped a handful of cheese in her lap. "And humans?"

Aunia shrugged. "I don't know."

"Well, my sister gave me a copy of Olivia's journal." Lena slid to the chair edge and pulled a low chest from beneath the bed. "Let's look at the story she wrote about him."

From the chest, she extracted three thin books wrapped with red and gold cords. She untied the cord, leaned back into her seat, and shuffled through pages from the middle volume "Here we go. Pogonias Cromis."

"Pogonias?"

"It's written here. His name before he was the Boggleman. My Nona told me a tale from when Rhugante still stood," Lena said. "It was about a strange child who had both gills and a tail. He washed up on the Adarian beach in eyesight of Bellatine. And there was a fish widow, Ladonia who adopted him."

Chapter Fourteen

Healer Where Is Your Patient

One can only hope that two enemies come for you, you can ally with one. — Dar Zeller Rieson of Tatia, late Dar general of her Majesty's Pegasi Fleet, flyer of Startengo

*B**espeak Keston. We need to be ready with a shielding spell.* Mathias gripped his sword.

Pegasi always protect, Taf sent back.

"Faebloods." Fallo held his hand parallel to the ground, the signal to wait. "What can you tell us about them?"

The box-holding guardsman glanced at the archer window slits, third and fourth story up on the closest watch tower. "Can say the lord has 'em in custody."

"Because of the storm spell?" Mathias said and persisted further despite Fallo's glare. "Who was on duty during the attack?"

"Don't matter names," another large and bulky guard said. He walked forward from behind a different wagon. "They're dead."

"Then we'll leave you to your inspections." Fallo's words dripped with disdain. He motioned, forefinger flicking, to return to the sky.

The large guard stepped in front of them impeding the run they needed before launching. "Fly around the wall. Not over."

"You will move," Fallo ordered.

"And you'll not be entering our town by our lord's orders. Try us, and like you've been warned, our archers will shoot you down."

"You dare threaten a flyer?" Fallo snapped his fingers. "I am the Queen's representative."

The dress-stealing guard stepped forward. "What Willard is saying is if you're looking for your men, fly to the west gate. You'll find them where that grave's being dug."

"They're helping to dig?" Keston asked. His complexion had gone pale and his hand too was on his sword.

"They ain't doing nothing," Willard said. "When you called those walking mouths—"

"All three of them are dead?" Mathias whispered.

"See, you don't deny calling them forth," the dress-stealing guard said.

Iciness filled Mathias' stomach.

They tell an untruth, Taf sent. *I hear Brinsaber. His flyer is alive.*

"Mathias, snap out of it," Fallo growled. "We've concern for our own and we will learn what happened."

"Flyers protect." Mathias barely could contain himself from drawing his sword. "They don't call on evil. Now answer. You saw our unit members killed?"

"Perhaps we should send a message to our lord." The portly guard yanked the canvas back in place over the merchant's wagon.

"And perhaps your mates should stay out of a flyer's way." Fallo shook out Paderro's reins, and they stormed at the guardsmen.

The men jumped out of the way. Mathias, cursing, followed after the commander. All three of them lifted into the sky. At least three arrows were shot from the wall-walk as they sailed atop the town. They bounced off a shield spell—Fallo's perhaps, maybe even Keston's.

It was mine, Taf sent.

A deep bell rung, a warning Mathias was sure, as they flew over the town's main artery.

Shooting off the wider road, pigs scattered through narrow alleyways. Waste splashed raucously from upper-story windows into the streets. And urchins splashed in color-slick puddles. Dalin stunk with its narrow, tunnel-like side streets where upper stories spilled over their foundations.

Movement caught Mathias' eye. A dozen townspeople in dirty clothes and leather caps, jogged toward the gate while bulky men in kettle-hat helmets flanked them. The helmeted ones wore leather armor. Bits of metal. One had a breastplate. Another, a set of greaves for his lower legs. These were mercenaries.

Reinforcements, Mathias sent.

I think not, Taf sent. *Hobbling them is unnecessary.*

Hobbling? Mathias looked again. Leather caps and pickaxes were identifying tells for miners. Miners with mercenaries to protect them and . . . Tafiriel was right. A young woman and a nondescript old man, chains on their wrists and ankles, staggered within the center of that crowd.

Faebloods, Mathias sent back miserably. *Precautionary to bind their magic.* But were these the same faebloods who had conjured a whirlwind to destroy the invading heebles?

Without any pause, a few of that unit looked up and watched them as they soared to the merchant square, where the sewage and unwashed bodies mixed with the savory smells of meat pies.

I hear Brinsaber, Taf sent. *He said to beware of Dalin. And do not drink.*

Mathias straightened. Had the wells gone bad? *Ask him where he is.*

They approached the main square.

He is not answering. But I think I can find him.

Then bespeak Fallo and . . . Mathias clutched the reins. Fallo couldn't be trusted. *Wait. Where on the Grashbear? How long to get there and back?*

The sun would be past its zenith and then some.

They landed in the open-aired market where haggling merchants and customers normally jostled each other within a small sea of merchandise: blades, armor bits, leather, jewelry, dried herbs, pastries, spring vegetables, and other sundry items. Some people were out shopping, a pittance of the usual number. More disconcerting was the handful of bear-fur cloaked soldiers clustered at the square's southern edge. Da Vennen.

So about mid afternoon? Mathias sent.

Paderro's hooves clip-clopped against the cobblestones by Mathias' left.

"Think they can shoot a flyer from the sky?" Fallo shook a fist and his broad shoulders bowed briefly. "I'll have them all up on charges."

"I was afraid we'd have to sleep all of them at the gate," Keston muttered from Mathias' right.

Fallo threw Keston a 'shut-up' look at the same time Mathias told Taf to bespeak the same message. They couldn't risk a non-flyer hearing that.

"What's the plan, commander?" Mathias asked. "There's Da Vennen watching us."

"Give them no heed." Fallo pointed southwest toward the town corner closest in direction to the Grashbear and the road leading to Adar. "We're getting company."

Tafiriel pivoted toward a small gathering of women Mathias' mother's age. Knotted buns. Tan-colored clothing. Baskets hanging from the crook of their elbows. But then, a man, clean-shaven with a mop of gray and brown hair, ran through the women's midst causing them to scatter.

Fallo waved at the runner, who sprinted faster before he stopped three pegasus lengths away from them. He staggered forward, hands on his knees, and panted.

"Did his lordship send you, Gregwin?" Fallo asked.

The man took another couple of breaths and straightened. His well-worn tunic stretched over an ample belly and partially hid his sturdy belt. But it was Gregwin's pendant, round with a mortar and pestle carved into it, that grabbed Mathias' attention. This had to be Jules' healer . . . the one who sent out for wine to celebrate Jules recovery from a wererat bite.

"Jules," Mathias said, surprised at the fire in Fallo's eyes. "What happened to him? And to Patrick and Garret?"

Gregwin closed his eyes and panted twice more. "Brave individual he was. Bravest. Only just recovered from grave injury and he came rushing to our aid against the walking mouths. Those you never want to—"

"They're called heebles," Mathias murmured.

Gregwin's mouth went slack, and he gave himself a little shake. "I doubt anyone here will call them different. But be it as it is . . . my news is not pleasant. He . . . he fell off the wall. And there was nothing anyone could do—except afterwards to name him a hero."

Mathias' stomach dropped to his intestines.

He's lying, Taf sent. *Brinsaber says different.*

"And the other two?" Fallo asked.

Gregwin knocked twice against his pendant. "I didn't see, but the talk is, they fled."

At the eastern end of the square a few red cloaked guardsmen ran toward them and the group of Da Vennen on the southern edge stepped forward.

"Fled?" Fallo barked.

I cannot feel either of their pegasi at all, Taf sent.

"We're getting company," Mathias said in a low mutter.

Fallo glanced at both guardsmen, then Da Vennen, and finally Gregwin as the healer reached into the front of his tunic.

He pulled out a damp scroll. "I'll warn you, too, that the Stanz Tower commander knows about your men. She arrived to help beat the . . . what did you call them? Heebles? She helped for a bit but then fled as well."

The guards were only a few yards away when Gregwin raised the scroll and waved it. "They're here with me. The lord signed off on it if you want to see."

The guardsmen scowled, but they went back the way they came. The Da Vennen returned to the bakery front.

"I'm off to see Lord Emmet," said Fallo. "Get yourself some breakfast then make your rounds. I want any and all information about what happened."

"Give the Da Vennen wide berth if you can," Gregwin said. "They're not impressed with flyers right now."

Fallo and Paderro followed Gregwin across the square and back up the southwestern road, the lord's road which led to Emmet's bleak fortress.

"Probably should stable our pegasi if we want people to talk," Keston said.

Mathias dismounted. "I'm having Taf fly to Grashbear."

"What? Why?"

Mathias explained to Keston about Tafiriel being able to sense Brinsaber in the Grashbear. "Taf says Jules is alive."

"Then where is he?"

"Brinsaber isn't saying."

Keston tilted his head. "And you didn't tell Fallo?"

Mathias stepped closer to his friend and lowered his voice. "We can't trust the commander. I saw him using a whisperer."

Keston's eyes widened. He opened his mouth, closed it again, and then swallowed. "So he was the one that the villagers suspected. I just thought maybe one followed us through the blade-cave."

Keston dismounted. "Well, Revellie says she wants to go, too."

"I don't think it's smart for both of them to go but . . ." Mathias scowled. He never asked Taf if he could sleep or shield from such a distance. But Brinsaber might need their help.

Mathias and Keston collected stashed weapons from their gear and Tafiriel and Revellie winged into the sky, distracting mostly anybody from noticing them tucking blades inside their clothing.

Keston shoved his smallest dagger in his boot. "Let's hope we don't have too much trouble with those mudcloaks."

CHAPTER FIFTEEN
UNWANTED

Miserly hums a funny tune while walking to the fair.
And dreams of satin and wine-lace kisses. But Miserly's
going no where. — a Spatelly drinking song

Aunia tapped at her knees. She generally liked stories but Lena's voice droned without reflection. "So, the Boggleman has always delighted delving inside the skins of others."

"I would say." Lena looked up from the thin, dark leather-bound book. "But I'm not finding any mention of any cloak."

"Well, that cloak is as scary as that scar on his face."

"Scar?" Taya sat up. "That's right. You've actually seen him."

Lena flipped another page. "I see where the fish-widow's village told her to be rid of him."

"I'd be mean too if people wanted to be rid of me," Reina said. "It's not nice."

Aunia cringed with the memory of her own exile while Reina bit into another meat pastry with wide brown eyes locked on her. Aunia cleared her throat. "Did the fish-widow put him out?"

Lena sat up straighter, holding the book closer to her nose. "And in the time before the cragborns fashioned strongholds inside the Tatian Mountains—"

"Lena, please," Aunia interrupted. "Don't read. Tell me it."

Lena lowered the book and glanced at Reina. "What can I say. The villagers there were afraid of Pogonias. And why wouldn't they be? He slaughtered their farm animals not for meat but to learn how they worked within. And it was said he tried to do the same with faery kind as well and that brought evil luck with it."

Reina shuffled to the bed's corner and leaned against the wall. "The fish-widow. Did she say begone foul crows?"

Taya frowned. "She said no."

"Yes, but the villagers persisted," Lena said. "What's truly sad is they killed her and all the magic that had lay semi-dormant inside that foul creature exploded. The next thing everyone and everything save for Pogonias Cromis lay dead."

Aunia clasped her knees, pulling her legs in close. Pogonias Cromis to Cromis Boggleman as Narvis called him. "And then he became the Boggleman?"

"Not immediately but yes." Taya swung her legs, her heels tapping the wooden storage drawers beneath the bed. "He ventured into Adar and founded the Fire Keep and the firelings. He was hoping to also get to Tatia and see the Darra Chamber."

"Why?"

Lena closed Olivia's journal though she kept a forefinger inside its pages. "Who knows? Somehow I doubt he wanted to find the entrance to the Eaburrai court."

"The Eaburrai . . . didn't Uriah travel there, and he met Yasendra and they fell in love?" Aunia asked.

"Yes," Taya said. "It's the origin story of how Chandarions came into the worlds. How they were supposed to save us . . . only something happened to stop them from being born and if they're not here when the time of the choosing comes . . ."

"A world dies," Aunia said.

"Yes," Taya and Lena said at the same time.

A poem-song that Caedmon used to sing wafted into Aunia's memory and she hummed the tune.

Reina pulled her fingers out of the breakfast bowl. "What is that song?"

It was Taya who answered Reina.

"People of the caravans, a floating
castle and its trees.
Wishing groves and thousand souls
crammed into cities.
Riders of the Winged Horses, armies
full of force.
Yasendra bred, augury led, and blind
to who's its source."

"What does that even mean?" asked Aunia.

Taya frowned. "There are many thoughts on it but no one knows for sure."

"I need to go find Mathias." Aunia slid to the edge of the bed. She enjoyed the time with the rovers but she wanted to see him. See him smile at her and know that they were no longer irritated with each other. "Do you know if he's riding or is he in a vardo?"

Taya paled. "You should wait till we stop."

"And don't you want to look cleaned up when you talk to him next?" Lena pointed at one of the blood stains on Aunia's tunic.

Aunia absently felt her tangled hair and there was dirt under her fingernails. "Mathias has my knapsack."

"Bath in a bowl. And you could borrow something of mine." Lena leaned forward again and pulled a second chest from under the bed. "That is, if you don't mind being garbed like a Mensani."

Aunia eyed Lena's shawl with its lace scalloping and tiny blue fabric flowers. "Why would I mind? Your clothes are beautiful."

"We're not one for status." Lena dug through the clothing, "but we do watch out for our own."

She shook out a green and orange skirt.

"Tharon won't like seeing all that green," Taya said.

"I've extra things only because no one told me about Wenda—" Lena stiffened. "Well, my birth caravan didn't have such thoughts."

"What's wrong with green?" Aunia asked.

"Faery color." Lena lay a matching blouse with an embroidered house-cat pattern along its sleeve cuffs. "Taya, the jug. And clean rags. Reina could use a bath, too."

"I don't wanna bath," Reina protested.

"You'll be getting one, stinky child," Lena said. "Or I'll be making you bean porridge for your breakfast."

Taya swayed almost effortlessly through the vardo and filled a large wooden bowl from a child-size metal jug near the vardo's floral-painted door. She returned with a filled bowl, a sliver of soap and a handful of clean rags.

Lena set a board on the clothes chest and motioned Taya to set the bowl there. "Here we be. Bath in a bowl."

Aunia made use of the soapy water as did Reina, though she complained for the entire time. Afterward, Lena combed and braided Aunia's wet hair.

It felt nice to be pampered. It was almost like having a mother, like Nehla . . . Aunia swallowed, remembering Nehla's sweet smile.

But here she was a stranger to these rovers, and they treated her with such kindness. Mathias had been wrong to call Rovers thieves and liars. He said they stole children, but Reina, clean and belly full, leaned against Taya who ruffled the child's hair. These people had rescued a child. Treated her like their own. Maybe Mathias didn't know. But she could tell him. And she had to get him to agree to take her to Tatia.

Aunia blinked with sudden realization. "Basil's mom."

Taya straightened and looked to Lena.

"What about Mollie Mae?" Lena tied the end of Aunia's braid with a ribbon.

"I was thinking about the Boggleman's cloak. If it got lost on the Grashbear . . . maybe the wererats might have it. But I should go find Mathias and—"

"Have you ever wondered how the Mensani make potions?" Taya interrupted and waved to a narrow cabinet, along the wall beside the door. "We've a range of samplings.

"Maybe after I talk with Mathias." Aunia staggered to her feet, bracing herself from the vardo's movements. She had plenty of things to ask him from taking her to Tatia to seeing if wererats could find the Boggleman's cape. "I should check on Keston, too."

"I saw him earlier this morning. Awake and doing just fine." Taya said. "Anyway, potions for healing, for luck, for—"

"Love," Reina said with a drawl.

Taya pinched the girl.

"Ow," Reina cried out. "Why don't you just tell her he left?"

Aunia felt flattened as if a house fell on her. "What do you mean he left?"

Taya held her palms out, smile tight. "They thought it was too dangerous for you in Dalin and people don't travel with flyers. It's improper and—"

Aunia lost her balance and sat heavily on the bed. "Where is Dalin?"

"To the south and west."

Aunia looked out the window where a shadow from the hedgewood fell. That sight should have been on the other side. "We're heading in the opposite direction."

Taya reached out to pat Aunia's hand. "It's too dangerous there."

"Fallo and Basil both agreed your place should be here," Lena said, "until—"

"They've no right to say where I go," Aunia yelled. How could she have believed Basil to be a friend?

"Sometimes you have to do what you're told," Lena said. "Fallo wanted—"

"No." Aunia stood again, this time keeping her feet.

"Please," Taya said. "Calm down. It won't be long—"

"No." And with that Aunia flung herself to the vardo door. Angry, yes she was. But it was the panic making her feel as if she'd rip in two that propelled her forward. How could Mathias leave her with strangers? She yanked open the vardo door and fell against the ground.

Burning skinned her knees.

Secrets, always secrets. And then hands were lifting her up. Voices asking if she was alright. But she wasn't. She filled her lungs with breath to scream and the world slid through her body. And then everything was gone.

CHAPTER SIXTEEN
FRUSTRATED QUESTIONS

Mind what you reveal. There's plenty here that others don't wish to know. — Fallo Vrael, Commander of Eddac Tower, flyer of Paderro

*K*eep *in contact,* Mathias sent.

Most of the people—plainly dressed townsfolk, more colorfully dressed travelers and vendors, and a pair of urchins wearing patch worked tunics—watched Tafiriel and Revellie disappear in the azure sky. The Da Vennen soldiers, however, continued to stare at Mathias and at Keston. As long as they kept their distance, it would have to do. The more important thing was deciding where to start their investigation.

Revellie will be staying behind but hidden, Taf sent, telepathic voice still vibrant and silvery inside Mathias' mind. *To extend protection should you need.*

Mathias inhaled with surprise and Keston looked to the ground.

"Didn't want to stable her alone," Keston said. "And she'll be safer out there. Us too."

"I hope that part's not necessary."

"Breakfast at the bakery would've been nice."

"They'll probably move later." Mathias turned his back to the Da Vennen who blocked most of the golden baked goods inside the bakery's window. "For now, we ask questions."

He pivoted toward the square's stone well. The benches around the decorative space— basin carved in sword motif and iron helms laced with red ribbons hanging from the well's roof iron hooks—was empty of people. A sad irony that the townfolk decorated the well in a sign of victory when the destruction across from it said something entirely different.

Untouched stood a redbrick shop with a swinging jeweler's sign. Also untouched was the Constabulary Hall with its large arched doorway and small iron-barred windows. However, the merchant guild hall which used to stand between them lay like a giant's broken black tooth.

"We'll start there," Mathias said.

A dozen men worked through the rubble. They scooped chunks of black-fired bricks, broken glass, and other debris with broad shovels, and dumped them into wheelbarrows.

"Good morrow." Keston nodded to a tall worker who stood in the center of the operation with his arms crossed over his chest. "Can you tell us what happened?"

The man threw an arm wide to highlight the damage. "Their Lord Chance brought an ill wind. It decimated the walking mouths, yes, but then it wheeled round and attacked us."

"Lord Chance?" Mathias said sharply, thinking of Jules' Lord Mimsy book. "This wasn't some fopdoddle adventure, surely."

"They don't read and I don't think they're talking about Mimsy," Keston murmured. He stepped forward, projecting his voice. "Where's this Lord Chance now?"

"In an iron collar at the Lord's keep." A second man paused in his shoveling. He stood a few feet from the tall man. "Probably be made an example of if they're lucky."

"Lucky?" Mathias shook his head. "Can you tell us the whole story?"

"What's to tell?" the first man replied. "Day started normal til the countryside rushed the gates crying about these walking mouths. Never seen nothing like them. Small. And nothing to their faces but o' mouthful of knife chompers."

"And squealing like rats," added the second man.

Mathias' stomach squeezed painfully at the memory of heebles attacking Aunia's village. "And the ill wind?"

"Whirlwind it be. Rain pouring down, dissolving the whole koboddle of them like a child's chalk markings."

"This Lord Chance conjured it?" Mathias asked.

"Aye," said the first man. "But never trust a faeblood. Soon as the walking mouths got gone they tell us they're subja . . . subjuga—something . . .

"Subjugation?" Mathias suggested.

"Aye. That. Then it's all whoosh with the wind howling . . . and the merchant guild hall falls."

"You're daft," said an older man who stood on a pile of rubble on the building's east side. "Twister showed up at the gate. Pelted me sideways."

"Quit your gumming," the first man said. "You think this building got tired o' standing?"

"But Ganger," said a boy who popped up beside the older man with a fist full of debris. "A mudcloak said after the twister hit guildhall it bounced over to the wall."

"Careful you." Ganger, the first man, peeked a glance to the bakery where the Da Vennen soldiers still stood.

"Did any of you actually see any of this?" Mathias said with a frown.

"Aye," said the older man. He pointed the boy to another section of the tumbled building. "I saw the flyers on the wall shooting arrows til they started fighting among themselves. Next thing one flyer's down and the other two are flying away."

Mathias gripped his sword hilt. "You're saying flyers attacked flyers?"

"Maybe a simple argument." A third man set his shovel against a wheelbarrow and walked over. "I heard about the flyer that went over but I heard the twister threw him off."

"Threw?" said Ganger. "They bloody flew off before the walking mouths came over and ripped into the Shambles. Me wife lost kin."

"Begging your pardon, Ganger," said the second man, "but my brother was on the wall and said he saw one o' those flyers take a tumble. He thinks it was the lord hisself."

"The lord hisself," said Ganger. "That's a bunch of drivel-tosh. What lord wouldn't be hiding during such an attack. Be what it is, flyer, we're honest men living a hard life. Nothing bad to say 'bout the Eaburrai, may they be forever wise, but his Excellency needs this finished right quick."

Mathias felt another rush of ice flood his veins. "Lord Emmet isn't addressed as his Excellency."

The older man further in the rubble straightened. "You be right. We speak of the Arch Vicar who—"

"Shut up," Ganger shouted. "Look, flyers, we can't tell you more but you're free to ask about. Now, if you please, we've work to do."

Keston placed a hand on Mathias' shoulder and leaned close. "Mathias, take a breath. I think they've told us all they know."

Mathias yanked back, clenching his teeth to keep curses and accusations from pouring out. These workmen worked for the Da Vennen. They could even be corvus novices though that was doubtful if Arch Vicar Bibb meant to pay them. But if he was, they might even get a few pennies more for handing out wild stories.

Keston bespeaks you'll do no good starting a fight, Taf sent, his silvery voice less vibrant. He was getting further away on his way to Brinsaber.

Mathias straightened, turning from the stares of the workmen. Keston stood before him, concern on his face and his light brown hair mushed under a rover's knit hat. Mathias loosened his fists. There was no point indulging in the fiery gratification he'd feel with his knuckles against the foreman, Granger's face.

Mathias walked back to the well, counting his steps. How could flyers be fighting each other? That had to be a lie.

"A drink of water to cool off?" Keston pointed at several clayfired pitchers sitting on a table between two benches.

"I wish people wouldn't bring up that dang faeblooded Lord Chance."

Keston shrugged. "That little book of Jules might have grown in popularity. But as I said, I doubt any of them have read it."

Mathias growled under his breath. "The Queen needs to know about this infestation of Da Vennen."

"She's probably already aware," Keston said. "Probably knows about the heeble attack, too. The problem will be when we get summoned back to the capital."

Mathias drew in a deep breath. "She might not be quite so angry when we tell her we have faery repellent."

Keston's eyes widened. "You . . . you brought it. Does it work?"

"I assume so," said Mathias. "I was gifted a seed pouch for the flowers. It will take a bit to grow."

"Dar Syrick could shorten the growing cycle."

"I'm thinking more Lord Lyle and Worley." Mathias rapped his knuckles against the well's stone lip.

"These faebloods . . ." Keston took a seat on a bench. "They seem to have gotten stuck with the bitter end."

"What do you mean?"

Keston cocked his head. "Don't you get the meaning behind Jules' little book? There's bad in any group but to paint an entire canvas as such, that isn't quite fair."

"Well . . . my father always said sometimes the assumption is what keeps us safe."

"Matty—"

"Don't. We don't know who we can trust. Faeblood. Not faeblood. Taf can hear Brinsaber but not the knight-sons' pegasi. I don't care for them but Fallo doesn't seem to much care either and they're his kin. Something just isn't right."

Keston rose from the bench. "Well, I've an idea. Let's head over to the Whistling Teapot and catch a pint. It'll be the best place to find us some blather-mouths."

"You just want ale."

Keston shot him a grin. "There are women, too."

"Is everything a joke?" Mathias snapped. "Jules is missing. Who knows if the knight-sons have betrayed us. And some backwards blather-mouth isn't going to do a thing to help."

"Matty. If I don't make the occasional joke . . ." Keston stiffened. "Look, all of this is hard. But, if you'd understand, old salts hide among fools 'specially after bad things go down. Then, they drown their sorrows. It's an opportunity to find out what really happened. And get a bite."

Mathias crossed his arms. "I'm not interested in whiling away time with a bunch of drunkards.

"Fine." Keston walked to the stalls, wobbling a bit. "We'll talk to the vendors then."

Mathias closed his eyes. His friend was newly healed. The sun was near midday. They hadn't eaten yet. He had been too caught up in his own anguished frustrations and worries. Across the way, the Da Vennen had moved. Where they went, he didn't know.

Mathias swallowed hard and ran to catch up with his friend. "Hey Keston, you notice what's missing from in front of the bakery?"

Chapter Seventeen

CLURICHAUNS

What makes a man something worth admiring and when will you doubt his worth? — Queen Didianne, during the reign of her madness

A buzzing brushed Aunia's skin like a hive of bees as she lurched in a mad attempt to keep her footing. The smell of woods, perfumes, and herbs had disappeared and in its place was the stench of waste, unfamiliar food, and burning metal.

A village-full of voices swirled within the buzzing . . . one pulled at her plaintively, though she couldn't make out the words. Dust skated over Aunia's feet as she appeared in a long boxed-in area surrounded by bulging timber buildings covered in faded paint and smeared pitch. And pressed within this area were more people than she had seen in her entire life.

"I said let the child go," a gruff voice said from behind her.

Aunia swiveled.

An older man with a broken-nose, well-muscled and tall, like Oskan from her village, stood in front of two men in red cloaks.

"We don't take orders from you, Mason," the shorter of the two red-cloaked men said. He yanked a small boy towards him by the arm and the child's sandy-haired head bounced off his chest.

"He's hungry is all," the broken-nose man said. "I'll pay for him."

"Bugger off," the red cloak said.

Aunia stepped forward. "You can't let a child go hungry."

Several of the people glared at her.

"Shut your mouth, rover," said a pillar-built woman with a messy bun, brown hair streaked in gray. She stood in front of a building with large windows and a swinging sign, which read 'Forged Tankard.' "Ain't no food he stole."

"Brana," the broken-nosed man growled.

The woman rolled her eyes and pushed past him, holding up a small ring with two finger-length keys. "Missing these?"

The larger of the two red-cloaked men reached under his cloak patted his side, and his face turned red. "It's the stocks for ye, boy."

The boy dropped to the cobblestones and the shorter, red-cloaked man yanked him back one-handed. Held his other hand high to strike.

"Stop it," Aunia yelled.

The larger of the red-cloaked men turned in her direction.

"Not the stocks." A bearded man in a long-sleeved patchwork tunic, white powder streaks along his sleeves, stepped forward. "You've the boy's mother in custody already. She was an unbraceleted faeblood. He'd be the same. You know it. It's prison he should go."

Faces pressed against the glass windows of the Forged Tankard's tavern. Some folk stepped forward. Others melted back, including the broken-nosed man.

Aunia shook. Taya was indeed right of cities being dangerous. If this was how they treated small children . . . but what could she do? She was only one in a crowd.

"Stop," she slid back, beseeching the broken-nose man. "You have to help. He's just a boy."

But the man slid into a narrow alleyway between the tavern and another building, and past a pig rooting in a pile of broken barrels, jugs, food scraps, and rags.

"She ain't my mom," the child screamed. "Not my real one. She picked me out of the garbage. I was just a slave to her."

The taller, red-cloaked man yanked the child's sleeve up. "Unbraceleted. You. Run to Yanna's forge. Grab a cuff. Now."

"Don't be thinking of calling on any magic," the shorter, red-cloaked man said, bending to sneer those words in the child's face.

"I'm . . . not a faeblood." The child stopped his struggling and with his wrist in the guard's grip, pointed in Aunia's direction. "That's the one you want. A real faeblood. Didn't you see? She just skipped out of nowhere."

The larger man straightened. "You. Rover."

Aunia backed away, nearly colliding with a press of people guarding her back. Rover? But of course, she was wearing their garb. And by their expression and harsh tone, they did not like rovers.

"Don't think you're going anywhere," one woman in a dark gray gown said.

Faeblood . . . this is how the people saw Reina. "I've . . . I'm looking for flyers," Aunia said. "I flew with them over the Grashbear. Mathias. Keston. Fallo. You've had to have seen them. This is Dalin, isn't it?"

The scowls of the people deepened. They shuffled closer. People in front of her and behind her, but the alleyway . . . could she flee with that pig in the way? Pig. She blinked. It had a quilted cloth saddle fastened around its girth with knotted cloth straps. And stitched cloth saddlebags hung along the pig's side. Who would be riding a pig?

"Look alive," a raspy voice sounded.

Aunia squinted. Amongst the broken wooden boxes and broken jars, two little men, shin-high, drank from a clay jar over half the size they were. Clurichauns with their rosy, weathered faces. They were solitary beings generally. The last time she saw one was in Gaitha's basement lapping up a bit of spilled apple brandy.

Someone, the taller red-cloak, grabbed Aunia's upper arm and a raw thrill, like a sharp nail, rose through her throat. "Leave me be."

She yanked. He held her firm, his fingers pressing into her flesh like a vise.

The adrenaline spike landed against the pit of her stomach like a stone. Mygul. She sucked in a breath, squeezed her eyes shut, hoping to coax a pinching sensation in her temples. Nothing. Her mouth turned to dry paper. Did she even have her glowing blue globefire anymore? She hadn't seen it since the Boggleman's veil tendril lodged itself in her gut when she stood on Hebsolum's palm. Did that mean Hebsolum had it? Hebsolum, the thief who took her mother's amulet. The only good thing he had done was to help her cage the roiling blue storm cloud made of Edvaras' magic . . . but her bit of magic . . . the one that caused mischief, made her an outcast, kept her safe. He must have taken it, too.

She squeezed her eyes shut. Prison. Was that where they were sending her? How would Mathias even find her? A soft mew escaped her and Aunia shook her head. She couldn't show weakness. And there were clurichauns.

She turned her head to the alleyway where the clurichauns swilled leftover booze from broken crockery. "Help me."

One of the clurichauns looked her way, bright eyes going wide. "She sees us." His voice, gravelly and sing-song, sounded over the clamor of human voices.

"She don't." The blonder of the two clapped the auburn one's shoulder. "She do. Drat it. On our way, Sharpish." He pointed to the pig.

"She be the one Mara made mention."

"We can't be making the Boggles mad now, can we, you know," the blonde one said. "We go."

The Boggles? Did he mean the Boggleman? Aunia struggled against her restraint. "I want to, too."

"Want to what?" the red-cloaked man sneered.

"Want you to let go," Aunia said between her teeth. "You're hurting me."

The man tightened his grip. "I'm barely holding you."

Aunia struggled toward the alleyway. Saying please would cause possible faery aid to disappear but what poem could she utter? Aunia groaned. "Help me now it's good folk fashion. Aid to for those who seek compassion."

"You call that a poem," the blonde clurichaun said. He shook his head then made a running jump onto the pig's back. His green pants contrasted with the wine-stained saddle. "Come on, brother."

"Brandy. I'll bring you brandy," Aunia yelled.

"No one bribes the guard." The stinging heat from his slap rang into her cheekbones. "Where's that Davis? Cuff her good and she can blubber whatever nonsense with the other lobheads.

"Don't know," the shorter of the red-cloaked men said. He still clutched the boy's arm. "But that face is sweet even with your handprint."

"Ah, that's done it," Sharply said. "Dismount, Gargle. Now."

Gargle patted the saddle. "There's another tavern where—"

"Certain things don't get done. Now off brother, lest you go for a ride."

The two clurichauns glared at each other while some of the townsfolk shuffled aside and a thin man with iron cuffs jogged forward.

Gargle dismounted. "It's on you if this is a bad decision."

"I'm always the one you blame." Sharply scooped up the neck of a broken bottle, drew his arm back and made a mighty throw at the pig's backside. It hit with a thunk and the pig gave a squeal. People standing at the mouth of the alleyway fell back as the pig pelted straight for Aunia and the red-cloaked man.

"Doxy-churl," the guardsmen swore. He staggered back, pulling Aunia with him out of the way but Aunia yanked with everything she had in the other direction. The man's fingers slid over her upper arm painfully. There was the sharp rip of fabric. And then she was free.

Aunia ran.

Chapter Eighteen

BARNABAS AND BREAKFAST

If anything, action more than intent ripples the fabric of human interaction. — Ferris Runoldi of Bellatine

Mathias rubbed his face, wishing the bellowing vendors behind their small stands, wooden constructions covered in beige canvas, would quiet. A line had formed in front of the bakery since the Da Vennen had wandered off. The 'where' they went bothered him.

People pressed in too close. Too loud. Or they glared from a short distance. And the stench of unwashed bodies mingled with burned undertones.

"Not too crowded today," Keston said. Probably an attempt to ease the conversation between them.

"There's too many of the wrong kind," Mathias answered. They passed a produce stall with spring cabbages, radishes, and fresh peas. Eatable, yes, but where were the stalls for smoked meats and sausages?

"Whaddya mean?"

"There's not a faeblood in sight."

Keston nodded at a bearded merchant who sat behind a stall of farming goods. "We've already heard. The lord rounded them up."

"What about the ones with iron cuffs?" Mathias returned a wave at a passing shopper who, like most of the Dalinian population, kept his sleeves rolled to mid-arm. "They've a legal right to walk about."

"Would you be out this day if so many like you've been arrested?"

Mathias slowed, trying to ignore the disapproving looks being thrown their way. "I want to talk with one or two. Get their take. Your golden friend is nearby enough to deal with any magic."

Keston lowered his voice. "Talking to us might be dangerous for them."

"Zeller always said if you can't learn from what you hear, learn by what's not said."

"I miss him."

Keston's sympathetic glance made Mathias' chest hurt. Six months, almost, from Zeller's death. And it still made no sense. But today that wasn't the focus. The focus had to be their missing unit and to keep their eyes open regarding the Da Vennen. But what Mathias wouldn't give to prove Arch Vicar Bibb had been on the Bellow sands. Mathias' fist knew it. He just wished everyone else did.

"Are you hoping to connect here to the Cold Festival?" Keston guessed.

"I just want to learn the truth. Save our unit. Or avenge them. And Nyrissa . . ."

"You'd like her to stop blaming you."

Mathias slowed more. Coming along the line of stalls from the east side walked a Da Vennen soldier with a skinny fellow in a crushed blue velvet doublet and matching cap. With the ledger clasped in the thin man's arms, he probably was a representative of the merchant guild. "She needs to be told what's happening."

"Fallo—"

"I fear he's not giving her reports."

They stopped at the end of the bakery line.

Taf, Mathias sent, *anything more with Brinsaber?*

Do not frighten him away. Tafiriel's voice inside Mathias' mind sounded more tinny than silver.

Frightened? Did he mean Brinsaber could hear the telepathic chatter between them?

"Hey," Keston cried out. He bolted from the line back to the stall rows.

Mathias hurried after him. Grasped Keston's upper arm in front of the leather goods stall. "What are you doing?"

A vendor, a woman stitching a leather glove, followed Keston's line-of-sight. She cursed and ducked from sight.

"That's Barnabas Gearhart." Keston pointed to a bear of a man with fluffy blonde hair and a short, curled beard who stood in front of a weapons stall with the merchant guild representative and the Da Vennen guard. Keston pulled away. "He's worked with my father."

"We . . . Keston. We can't."

But Keston walked steadily forward.

"I told you. I paid my half." The big blonde man transferred double-edged fighting daggers from stand into a broad wooden box. "Look to my partner."

"He's holed up in jail." The guildsman set his open ledger on the corner of the vendor's stall and sunk his hand, with its too many rings, into his cross-body satchel. He pulled out a pot of ink and a quill. "Fifteen copper coins. Hand it over."

The blonde man dropped the last knife in the box and brushed his hands over his long orange tunic, taking in the Da Vennen soldier. "No."

The guildsman snapped his fingers in the blonde man's face. "I've too much to do to be waiting."

"So be on your way, fancy-pants," Barnabas said.

The Da Vennen guard pulled his shoulders back, making his bear-cloak part in the front and exposing a wide sword buckled at his side. "Watch your tone with the guildsman."

Keston came to a halt and leaned toward Mathias. "You know that insignia?"

The pen-and-pouch stitched emblem on the guildsman's blue velvet doublet was ordinary. "You take another blow to the head?"

"No. The mud-cloak's."

Mathias narrowed his gaze on the Da Vennen's beige linen tunic where a figure eight with a line severing the two circles was stitched on the right breast.

"If you can't get it from my dear partner, then consider donating the space. He did help save all our skins." Barnabas picked up the box and turned toward them, shooting Keston a toothy grin. "Unless o' course you preferred those walking mouths?"

"Shut it," said the guildsman. "My cousin was ripped to pieces by 'em."

"Mine as well." Barnabas set the box down on the table again. "Though I didna care much for mine. But I take living serious. It's why both of us sold me long blades below cost when those beasties came."

The guildsman shook. "You'll be paying. I've enough Da Vennen here to—"

"My dear flyers." Barnabas waved at Keston and Mathias. "Would ye care to settle a disagreement?"

Great, just what they needed. Mathias stepped in front of Keston, forcing himself not to grab the hilt of his sword. "What assistance do you need?"

"For you to turn around." The Da Vennen, nearly a head taller than Mathias, glared at them with a broken-tooth smile. "We've the situation firm in hand."

The guildsman flipped pages of his ledger. "I'd listen to him. Best take a merry hop-skip back to the bakery line."

"I've asked for help," Keston muttered to Mathias.

"Oy!" A cry rang out from the eastern side of the square. Mathias took a step backwards before risking a glimpse. Two Da Vennen soldiers and five guardsmen waved from the street leading to the blacksmith and warehouse district. "Escaped faeblood near the Forged Tankard."

"On your own, McNarish," the Da Vennen guard said. And he strolled past them slamming his shoulder into Mathias' on the way through.

The skinny guildsman glowered, snapped his ledger shut, and stalked off.

An escaped faeblood. Mathias rapped a fist against his thigh. What he could learn from him.

"It's the pubs where you find gossip and knowledge," Keston said with a wink. He then hurried forward to Barnabas, and the two exchanged a slapped-back hug.

"Good to see you, lad." Barnabas held Keston at arm's length. "Your dad—"

"In Adar, working on commission for his Dominus Titus Valerian."

"That windbag?" Barnabas laughed.

Keston shrugged. "Deep pockets and a want of new statuary, you know how it goes."

"Well, he can't do no better than Jayden Pendar, sculptor extraordinaire." Barnabas' features turned solemn. "How long you here for?"

Mathias stepped forward. "How'd you come about having a faeblood as a partner."

Barnabas shrugged. "Met Ned on the road and we decided to split the cost of a stand."

"He was by himself?"

"Oh, heck no. But his caravan had business in one of those villages near Vraelsfork."

Mathias frowned. "What kind of business?"

"We're not looking to get anyone in trouble," Keston said. "Just trying . . . well, there's this thing that happened."

Barnabas covered the wooden box of fighting knives with an oiled black cloth and drew a seven-pointed star on his forehead with a forefinger. "Understand. Ned didn't cause a lick of harm and he helped save scores of these fine townies. But as soon as the sky lost its storm clouds, the lord came with his new Da Vennen help and grabbed him and a bunch of others. I can't stay here to watch a hero be executed."

"Do you know anything about the flyer who fell?" Mathias asked.

"Sympathy is in short supply," Barnabas muttered, then he straightened. "I don't rightly know. Heard he was shoved."

Mathias closed his eyes. "What about the other two? There were three here."

Looking into the sky, Barnabas rapped at the stall table three times. "You're the one with the wild pegasus, ain't you?"

"Yes, but what has that to do with anything?" asked Mathias.

"You're not going to like it."

"We don't like not knowing," Keston said softly.

"Fine." The blonde man motioned them to come closer. "I won't repeat this and if you look for me, I'll vanish. The short of it is I end up in places I ought not. Like the barracks two nights back when I saw the Da Vennen driving a cart in the dead of night with a pair of docile pegasi tied and following along."

"Da Vennen with pegasi," Barnabas continued. "That don't seem right, I said to myself. And it wasn't. They get into the barracks and pour two of your flyers from the cart. Stumbling drunk and belligerent they are. Never saw a pair of boys get so riled up by foolish commands."

"Who was commanding them?" Mathias asked tightly.

"That the rub, init? It was the Da Vennen themselves. Told these flyers to fight each other, and they did. I . . . I wasn't expecting it. I mean, how could anyone? But the one curly top boy drew a knife across the neck of the other boy's pegasus. . A lethal blow, only the beast vanished . . . and I ran."

Mathias' entire body went cold. "Dark curls?"

Barnabas nodded. "The other boy had straight hair, darker than mine."

Garret and Patrick.

Keston and Mathias shared a horrified glance. No flyer would kill a pegasus.

We return to faery, Tafiriel sent. His silvery voice sounded cold.

Mathias swallowed hard. "What about the third flyer?"

"Him I haven't seen," Barnabas said, "but like I said, some of the townies tell it that he fell from the wall."

"When did they tell you that?"

"When they were crowded around my stand looking to buy swords." Barnabas rapped a fist against the right-side of his chest. "I am sorry for your loss."

Mathias closed his eyes. "Who did they say pushed him?"

"Story keeps changing, and I didn't see it. But I tell you, I wouldn't be much surprised to hear the Da Vennen glamored themselves to muddle the show."

Mathias stiffened. "The Da Vennen hate magic."

"Keep telling yourself but if yer not too busy consider why the mud-cloaks want the guildhall so bad. Or why the lord insists on having faeblood accompany his miners. Something is brewing here. Something nasty and evil. I'm leaving Dalin. I suggest you might do the same."

And with that the large blonde man scooped up the broad box of knives and headed west toward the street that led to the gate.

Disbelief hollowed out Mathias' insides and locked his feet in place until Barnabas disappeared between a blue-painted tailor's shop and a woodcarver's shop with carved columns.

"I have no appetite," Keston said.

"I don't either." Mathias straightened, desperate to grab a hold of anything that made sense. "But we'll eat, nonetheless."

After stopping for a loaf of bread and a small wheel of cheese from the bakery's adjoining cheese shop, Mathias and Keston made for the raised platform on the eastern side of the square between Lords Way and the road leading to the warehouse and blacksmith district. Mathias climbed the two broad, shallow steps.

Keston hesitated. "Isn't this where the lord addresses the people?"

"Aye." Mathias waved him up. "But there's no one using it now. And we're flyers."

Grimacing, Keston joined him, stepping over a handful of violets that had pushed their way through stone blocks and then, setting a jug of apple cider down. Both sat, resting their backs against the cold limestone wall.

Mathias shifted into a cross-legged position, balanced his food on his knee, and tore off a bite-sized hunk of bread. "Just how trustworthy is this Barnabas?"

"My family trusts him completely." Keston bit into a chunk of cheese. "And they've known him longer than I've been alive."

Mathias frowned and rolled the bread between his fingers. "I just—"

"Can't imagine with Garrett and Patrick?"

"They fought, yes. But they were cousins. Friends. They wouldn't have."

"I don't know what to tell you, Matty. Barnabas saw something and if it wasn't the truth, then it was a spell-glamor."

"Spell. Glamor." Mathias flicked the bread away. Having someone use illusion magic . . . that would explain quite a bit. The next question, of course, would be who. Faebloods? He doubted faebloods would have gone into the barracks. Those iron-laced places would be too much of a danger. And for what purpose showing Barnabas one thing and then later, showing all the townsfolk something else. It made more sense that Barnabas hadn't been seen but that would mean no spell glamor in the barracks. But how could flyers do what he described?

Being drunk wouldn't explain it. Especially with Brinsaber hiding in the Grashbear and no one knowing where Jules was. Had Jules and Brinsaber gone into hiding because someone was targeting flyers?

A flyer wouldn't stay hidden by normal threats and no magic affected a pegasus except for Chandarion magic... A sheet of snow-coldness slithered down Mathias' back. There was a flower that Edvaras had made that took away free will.

Mathias leaned forward. "There was a moment during the wyvern battle when Aunia tried to dismount off of Tafiriel while we were high up."

Keston choked on a bit of bread. "You must be mistaken."

"No," replied Mathias. "I'm not. There was that cloying soapy rose smell in the smoke from the wererat fire. And before that, I saw scorched petals inside the wererat's fire ring. Blue petals in Tafiriel's feed at the Cold Festival. I think we're being poisoned with one of Edvaras' flowers."

"It *was* a strange smelling fire," Keston said, frowning.

"I go over the battle in my mind and it feels like there're pieces gone, like I'm supposed to forget," Mathias said. "I do remember your fall and Aunia being on Hebsolum's palm—"

"Aunia was—"

"There's a lot you missed." Mathias pressed himself harder against the wall and fidgeted with the caged necklace under his shirt. The bit of Chand crystal that helped augment his telepathic connection with Tafiriel. Do not frighten Brinsaber away. That was what Taf sent last. Mathias pushed that nagging worry aside.

So many questions. With every answer they learned, it only led to more questions.

"We know that Basil's wererats have Navenra. And they are wererats. They helped us but who knows what their ultimate intentions are," Mathias said. "Or what if . . . what if someone discovered Navenra and is using it."

"You might think this is stupid, but Matty, what is Navenra?"

Mathias quickly told Keston about Edvaras' three flowers: Jaia for the faery repellent which Keston knew about, then also Leiaphae which caused invisibility, and Navenra which was supposed to give long life but instead took away clear thought. "You can see all three flowers in that Chand ice stone that Fallo stole."

"Wouldn't affect us," Keston said in a low voice. "We're immune to magic."

"We're not immune to Chandarion or Eaburrain magic . . . because our pegasi aren't either."

"So, you think there's a nefari-ess wererat infestation."

"Nefarious," Mathias corrected. "And maybe. It could explain what Barnabas was saying. If he said true. But he also said barracks. I don't know. It makes more sense for some of it but not for it all."

Mathias tapped at one of the violet's purple petals and thought of Aunia. She probably knew by now that he had gone. He hoped she wasn't too angry with him. But she was far safer there than here. Aunia with her steadfast assurance of knowing what to do, like her insistence of gathering all of Edvaras' flower to capture Edvaras' light.

He leaned back again. All three of Edvaras flowers.

Mathias handed Keston the rest of his bread and leaned his head back. He had reason to be grateful to the Mystic rover. Basil saved Aunia's life by slowing her fall after the marble giant had pitched her into the sky. And Basil's wererats . . . they had taken care of Keston after he and Revellie had also fallen.

"Whaddya thinking?"

"Still thinking about Basil and his band of wererats. Whether they're truly different from other packs of wererats. And I'm hoping the girl is alright."

"It's possible there is more than one type of wererat, I suppose. The ones on the Grashbear seemed to be decent folk." Keston folded a chunk of bread around a large piece of cheese. "So, what's the story between you and Aunia?"

"She was exiled. I couldn't leave her all alone—"

"Oh, come on. You are all lovey-eyed over that intriguing little peasant girl."

"She's not intriguing." Mathias' face heated at that lie. "She's just . . . unsolved."

Keston choked on another mouthful of food. "Unsolved?"

"Shut up." Mathias said, hooking the apple cider jug. "Fallo and Basil both want her identity hidden. Doesn't that make you wonder?"

"How do you know that?"

"I eavesdropped."

"You?" Keston's eyes turned wide and then he laughed. "I take it our new rebel Matty won't stay behind at the tower anymore writing weekly love letters to her highness."

Mathias drew his knees up. "My father expects me—"

"I know. We all know." Keston readjusted the knit cap. "I just thought with you eavesdropping you might be having second thoughts on doing what your family tells you. I mean Aunia . . . she is quite breathtaking."

"You leave her alone."

Keston pulled himself onto his knees. "So, you telling me that you neither want to pursue her or allow her to be pursued?"

"Keston," Mathias growled.

"It's just . . . she's quite fetching in rover garb." Keston pointed just beyond Tradewind Road.

Aunia sauntered by them, a circle skirt flirting around her ankles and a loose blouse sliding over a bare shoulder.

Her appearance hit Mathias' heart, but he scanned for more rovers. There weren't any.

"I'll go escort our lovely charge," Keston said.

"No. I'll go."

Chapter Nineteen

FLUTTERBYS

Perhaps I should be grateful for it but I'll never love the smell of patchouli and orange, particularly when it bears the undernote of wet fur. — Jayden Pendar, sculptor extraordinaire

Hiding and moving through shadows had kept Aunia from the men dressed in both red and furry cloaks but it was only after Jennium had appeared and thrown a faery glamor over Aunia that she breathed easier. Who knew that her little faery friend could extend her faery glamor to make Aunia . . . if not invisible, unnoticed. It would have been handy while she had still been at the village.

Aunia kicked a stone in the road and sent for a third time a visual image of finding Mathias. If this was Dalin, he had to be here.

Jennium jingled as an open place appeared and the dense buildings on either side of the cobble street, faded back. The space was lined with tables filled with metal, glass, and foodstuff items and people sitting or standing beside them yelling at passerbyers. And beyond them, tall, mismatched buildings with wooden beams and stone facades cast short shadows.

Aunia hesitated, uncertain to venture forward in such an open place. She'd be leaving the possible shadows inside narrow alleyways. She had only taken her first few steps forward when Mathias appeared in front of her.

With a cry, she threw herself at him, wrapped her arms around his neck, and the sensation of being utterly alone receded. She had found him. And Keston . . . he stood just beyond Mathias.

Mathias squeezed her once, warm hands against her back. But then he pulled away before she was ready to let go.

"I didn't think I'd find you," she said, and then hesitated. Mathias' spring green glow with flares of soft pink had flickered like sunlight through storm clouds. But now. It had dimmed with gray shadows and his expression turned unwelcoming.

The air pulled away from her lungs and she stepped back. "You meant to leave me."

Mathias' brow furrowed and the grayness of his glow contracted around his skin. "Oh, for Yasendra's sake, we were coming back." He whipped his head toward Keston. "Can you spot a cloak for sale up there?"

The clamor of the square dulled and Aunia bit her lip. She had traveled all this way, yet he didn't want to see her. She need not have left her village to feel this way . . . if anything, this was worse.

He turned back to her. "Why on the Harp are you wearing rover clothes?"

The furrow at his brow deepened. "Wait. You came from the warehouse district, didn't you?" He groaned. "You're the faeblood that the guards are after."

She stepped toward him, needing him to understand. "I didn't do anything wrong. Just talked to a pair of clurichauns."

"Clurichauns?"

"Revellie says they're leprechaun cousins. Drunkards. They sound interesting." Keston's voice faded under Mathias' glare.

Mathias pointed at her clothing.

"I had to," Aunia said. "You had my knapsack and my clothes were—"

"No, I didn't—"

"Mathias," Keston interrupted. "Her blouse is ripped."

Mathias' expression softened, and he lifted the torn fabric at her neckline.

She stiffened, willing herself not to cry. "Taya said big cities were dangerous and I—"

"What did they do?" he demanded.

She shook her head, blinking back tears. "This big oaf grabbed me. And they had this child. They wanted to give us . . . iron bracelets. And they have his mother in prison."

Mathias rubbed his forehead. "Please tell me you didn't do magic. You didn't send out that globefire of yours, right?"

"Globefire?" Keston asked, "Velli was serious about that? What else can you do?"

Aunia gripped her neckline and her father's amulet, which lay under it. "I didn't do anything."

"Then why would they think you're a faeblood?" Mathias leaned forward toward her and lowered his voice. "Exactly how'd you get here?"

Aunia curled her fists. "I wanted to be where you were and the rovers were lying to me. Making me think you were with us, so I ran out of Lena's vardo and then, well . . . I was here."

"Here. Dressed like a rover. And with no shoes."

"Wait," Keston said, "You skipped? You knew she could 'skip?'"

"Did you skip here?" Mathias asked.

"I guess," replied Aunia. Had she? She had been lifted out of the dirt after she jumped down from Lena's vardo and she hadn't done anything. But what other explanation could there be?

"Look, more questions later," Mathias said. "We'll buy you a cloak, some shoes, and—"

"Does Fallo know she can skip?" Keston asked.

"No." Mathias whipped around. "And I don't want him to. Not until I know what he's doing. Cloak. We need a cloak."

Aunia crossed her arms. She might have skipped herself. Things always happened when she was angry. And she had been very angry. She was getting angry now.

Mathias placed a hand on her shoulder blade attempting to steer her further into the market square. She dug in her heels.

"We have to hide you. You've put yourself in harm's way," he growled.

Harm's way? Well, if she could skip to Dalin. She could skip away. Why did she need anyone anyway? All it created was pain. She bit her lip. But to where? Back to the rovers? The Grashbear? Tatia?

"Oh, horse poop," Keston said.

"Horse poop nothing," replied Mathias. "You know about the whisperers and if the guards—"

"No." Keston pointed further up the Lords Way. "Your dear friend, Arch Vicar Bibb, is barreling down on us."

About twenty yards away, a tall man with black hair streaked in white and wearing a beige-colored robe leaned toward three men dressed in the bear-fur cloaks. The man was agitated. It was easy to tell by his staccato hand gestures and the reddening to the man's thin, hooked-nose face. All the men had a burnished red glow with a sticky black thread running through. Aunia stepped back. The man in the robe had the moistest, tangled one of them all.

Mathias' glow, muddy yellow, pulsed like a guttering candle. "Keston. Get her out of here. I'll waylay him."

Concern shoved away her hurt and anger. "Mathias?"

"Come on," Keston said. "We need to get you to safety."

But there were four of them. "No," she said. "Let's all leave. He's . . . they have evil in them."

"We can't. Aunia, please," Mathias pleaded. "It's dangerous. Go."

Keston tugged on her arm and Aunia stiffened. But what could she do? Jennium's glamor made her unnoticeable. Not invisible. She learned that when someone had bumped into her and then screamed with wide eyes. She let Keston draw her away.

They walked briskly along the perimeter of the item-laden small tables while Mathias strode to face the men, meeting them beside the raised platform. The robed man steepled his hands and looked pleased.

"Aunia, watch." Keston pulled her close to him as a townswoman in swirling blue skirts pounded past them. He leaned close. "Revellie says you're partially glamored."

Aunia nodded. "Because of Jennium."

Keston cocked his head.

"She's a garden faery. A friend." Aunia bit her lip. And Jennium used to belong to her father. Though how any faery belonged to anyone . . . Still, if this faery had been a friend of her father's what exactly did she do to help him? And why had she abandoned him for Basil? And why befriend her instead of going back to her dad.

"So, that's how you escaped notice when the mudcloaks went after you," Keston said.

Aunia startled. "Mudcloaks?"

"The Da Vennen."

"Who or what is a Da Vennen?"

Keston pulled her between a line of vendor stalls. "Arch Vicar Bibb is the head of the Da Caladorian Vennen order. It's a soldier religion predating our fair realm. I'd also wager the second biggest pain there is."

Beside them atop the closest table were thin metal rings etched with swirling vines and thin brass bracelets, all gleaming in soft hues from the afternoon sun. Aunia wrapped her arms around herself, remembering the iron bracelet threat. Iron. Something faeries abhorred. "Second biggest?"

"Too early of a morning after festival would rank first, don't you think?"

She peered over her shoulder where Mathias, shoulders hunched and his hand near his sword, stood with the robed man. The other bear-fur cloaked men, the Da Vennen, had left. "Mathias doesn't like him."

"Can't blame Mathias. His excellency puts a real bear claw in most honey hives."

"I don't like him either," she said.

"He's a love 'em or hate 'em kind of man. But then so is the entire Da Vennen faction. Bibb's taken it a step further though. Five years in leadership and he's expanded the order past the Wythrindle River. Busy converting the average Jills and Johns and sometimes a lord or lady, like Spatelly."

"What do you mean converting?"

"They get others to join their cult and then they enjoy an ill-conceived edict that grants them immunity from the crown in perpetuity."

"I don't understand."

Keston rolled his eyes. "Our first king Uriah—"

"Uriah and Yasendra." Aunia paused by the stall with hanging bunches of lavender and chamomile.

An elderly woman with nimble hands looked up from measuring out ground red powder from an earthen wear jar and the young woman standing across from her, basket in hand, shot Keston a frown.

"Keep walking," Keston murmured. They came to a halt by an empty table. "Anyway, our first king issued an edict giving the Da Vennen immunity. It's said it was a political move to placate the soldiers of the former kingdom when Tamore came into existence. And to allow them to continue on with their religion as the augurite order came into being. I suppose I understand the why but . . ."

Keston shook his head. "It causes so much problems and unless the crime is . . . how does Mathias put it . . . unduly grievous, there's little to be done."

Aunia shuffled about to face Mathias' direction.

"Don't worry," assured Keston. "He's dealt with Bibb before."

"He reminds me of Sigmus. How long will they talk?"

"Oh, long enough to make Mathias feel completely horrid. C'mon, there's no sense making ourselves miserable, too."

"But why does he want to make Mathias feel horrid?"

"I'd wager because Mathias accused him of something." Keston folded her arm over his. "I think I remember a stand with hair sticks. They'd be pretty enough for your wheat-gold and I wouldn't mind you having a fang."

Aunia dug her heels in. "What did Mathias accuse him of?"

"That probably should come from Matty. He gets rather peeved when I'm too free with my yap, and it's his story. Not mine." Keston patted her arm. "But he'll be happy if we can bring him some pleasant news, like you enjoying your first time at a market. Come on. There's more to see."

The crowd thinned and without needing to be mindful so she wasn't run over, Aunia slowed her pace, holding the side of her circle skirt up to keep from walking on it and lightly fingering the variety of trinkets. Her fingers paused at a dark blue bowl with painted flowers.

Nehla loved throwing pottery. However, she had never found a glaze to create this dusk-sky color. Aunia thought about asking what was used when a sun-yellow flutterby zipped past her. Eight-winged. Transparent body. It would have tiny but soft deer-like eyes if Aunia could coax it to land on her finger.

She rotated, keeping it in sight as it bobbed and weaved over the stalls. They weren't known to come into human communities, but they were sparkle-seeking faeries. Quite a few gravitated on the north bank of the little stream near her village where they'd flutter over the cache of false gold.

She turned a little further to the sight of Mathias surrounded by a crowd. The remaining heat of hurt-anger vanished, replaced by a tightening in her throat. She did not like him being surrounded.

"It's okay. He's a flyer," Keston said tightly. "And I'm sure Rev can sleep all of them if she must. But even with you glamored . . . we ought to hide a bit better. There's a fabric place over there."

Aunia pulled her attention from the off-white plastered building with banners, reds, blues and greens snapping from its awning back to the flutterby.

The faery flitted over the stalls and then was joined by a large orange one with a glow like dried blood and snow. Unease sunk into her body. It was only a dream in Taya's vardo, wasn't it? The Boggleman had fallen from the sky. She set the bowl down, knocking over several small wooden figurines. Keston could sleep the crowd if need be. But if this really was the Boggleman . . .

"Careful." Keston stooped to pick the items up.

Both flutterbys flew to the elaborately decorated stone well in front of a fallen down gray building. Aunia followed them.

Chapter Twenty

THE PLOW AND THE SWORD

Oh yes, your enemies will be a resource for treasure —
Gabryella ni Brier Reach, sorceress of the Fireling Order

"If it isn't Danalissa's young man. What a merry surprise." Arch Vicar Bibb of the Da Caladorian Vennen soldier order said. He waved toward the fallen merchant guild building, not looking at Mathias.

The three Da Vennen soldiers, fluffing out their furry bear cloaks and scowling, walked away. Each one gave Mathias a sneer as they passed.

Mathias forced himself to unclench his jaw. Still mindful of how fast he could draw his rapier. Mindful of the needle-like blade at the robed man's side and how fast he could draw his. Bibb would outreach him blade-for-blade. "You've always preferred more cosmopolitan areas. What brings you here?"

Bibb crossed his arms. "My congregation is anywhere valor and bravery live. But I suppose that would be unfamiliar to you and your unit."

Mathias stiffened. Unfamiliar? The question of how Bibb had unbroken his nose danced on his tongue.

He seeks to unfoot you, Tafiriel sent, his silvery voice a little more than a whisper.

I know. Mathias rubbed a thumb against his curled fingers and glared at the curve of Bibb's long nose drooping downward to its bulbous point. If his fist struck there . . . *You've found Brinsaber.*

Circumstances blows tattered speech upwind.

Mathias fought to erase the confusion he was sure appeared on his face. Meanwhile, Bibb leaned forward, head tilted as if he were listening in. But on what?

What are you talking about? Mathias sent.

Vibrations in your voice-box, not the only way to eavesdrop.

Mathias thumped his fist against his thigh. There was no way someone who wasn't a flyer could listen in, except for Aunia. And Taf wouldn't mind her. So, who? Da Vennen didn't play with magic. "I'll ask again. What brings you here?"

"My business is my own," Bibb said. "But gossip runs before yours. Banished, I hear, and by your good friend, the new Dar-Elect. She blames you for her father's death. Is that not true?"

Those words struck hard and Mathias' knees quaked at the memory of Dar Zeller's last moments. It was followed by the image of Nyrissa, thin lips twisted in a grimace and her usual freckled and sun-kissed complexion pale. She wouldn't even look at him when she banished him to Eddac Tower.

"But if you must know . . ." Bibb raised his voice and nodded at the gathering townsfolk. "Rhugante's Bear led me here to offer aid to these fine people."

When had they arrived? Men in simple tunics and worn boots glared at Mathias with their arms folded defensively, while women in long skirts and aprons frowned with fists clutched to their hearts. Even a few merchants joined near the crowd's back in their more vibrantly dyed doublets and gowns.

"But do let me offer condolences for your poor dead flyer," Bibb continued. He took another step closer to Mathias and the smell of citrus mixed with a balsamic earthiness and rotten meat permeated the air. "There's not much of him left, I understand, though Lord Emmet may have scraped enough for you to bury. A pepper pot perhaps."

Mathias gripped his fist ready to punch Bibb in the face but that smell . . . his stomach did a slow roll. He had smelled it at the Bellows.

Withdraw, Tafiriel sent.

Mathias tightened his fists with a pulse-like beat. He wanted to breathe the rising panic away but he couldn't risk another brush of that scent. Or tear Bibb apart. Or throw him bodily from the wall. What he needed to keep Bibb's eye from Aunia. *Not an easy feat. Bespeak Revellie and—*

Plans shouted come as no surprise.

Mathias stiffened more. Behind him, the crowd murmured. Someone made a sharp guttural noise and a wet splat hit the cobblestones.

"It's a pity for your flyer but you've no one to blame but yourselves. Provoking these fey beasts. And now with those wyverns and exploding our mountains." Bibb spread his arms wide, stretching the fabric of his robe across his chest. Something lay hidden under the woolen fabric at the center of his breastbone. Something thick, circular, and palm-sized. Too shallow for a whisperer bowl, not that a Da Vennen would be using one. But what if . . .

Mathias shook his head at the memory of one of Bibb's wererats accusing Bibb of leading other wererats. For a hot moment, Mathias wished he had silver.

"You're to blame for bringing down these walking mouths," a woman said.

"Indeed," Bibb answered. "And other fey things, too. Consider my dear townsfolk, what other dangers will these flyers bring to you?"

An ugly hiss went through the growing crowd.

He wants you to hit him, Tafiriel sent. *As soon as you do—*

I know. The crowd attacks. Mathias sent and clenched his jaw against the icy waves beating on his chest. Focus, he told himself. If whisperers or others with magical means were listening in, Mathias had no element of surprise. "We're protectors of this land."

"You?" Bibb said with a laugh. "You bring wererats, wyverns, and walking mouths to these people. What are lowlanders to you but faery food? Next, I assume you'll be sending the Mockmen trolls."

Boos and hisses overlapped the crowd's voices. It siphoned the very air away.

Reassure them and move out, Tafiriel sent.

Mathias swallowed. "We are charged by royal decree to keep the peace. We protect—"

"My order has a royal decree as well." Bibb stepped nose-to-nose with Mathias.

Mathias flinched, then cursed himself for the reaction. The stench that emanated from that man . . . he took a step backwards toward the growing crowd.

"It was signed and sealed by King Uriah himself," Bibb continued. "It guarantees my soldiers enjoy sole autonomy within this realm. It is we who are the higher servants for our populace. We who eliminate ineptness and corruption."

Bibb's face was so close. Mathias wouldn't even have to take a step to punch him. He sucked in tainted air through his teeth.

"These people know we are not made for magic," Bibb continued. "We are made for plow and sword. We were meant to live as we did once when we were Rhugante."

Some in the crowd repeated the ancient kingdom's name.

"There's reason why Rhugante is no more," Mathias projected. His voice sounded thin.

"Because our forebears were tricked by a faery," Bibb quipped. "One who subjugated our people to serve a brain-sick faery-blooded family."

The orange and myrrh caught in his teeth and Mathias couldn't help but shake his head in stunned amazement. Bibb dared to spew such heresy against the royal line and the Eaburrai Court.

The crowd didn't recoil. So not a good sign.

"Rhugante's heir was the Dagel," Mathias reminded them. "He shattered the Dama's heart with his greed and jealousy. It's why we live under this great doom and if it were not for Uriah—"

"It's been an age since that sorry story was made up," Bibb interrupted. "And since then we've had centuries of rampant faery attacks made worse by flyer provocation. We'd thrive but we're continually infested with faery and faeblood filth."

"Rhugante." The whisper crept through the crowd.

Bibb raised his hands into the air. "Rhugante. Free from faeries."

"Flyers have pledged to safeguard the realm and all its lawful citizenry," Mathias yelled over the crowd. "One of our own made the ultimate sacrifice to defend this town."

"Kill the bleeding faeries!" someone yelled.

"Down with flyers!"

The crowd pushed forward.

"We have a deterrent. A repellent. Something to keep these . . . walking mouths away," Mathias yelled. *Taf, I need you here.*

"But even an individual flyer could join our cause." Bibb snapped his fingers and a furry wineskin was handed to him by a merchant in red silk.

"Thank you." Bibb took it, turned, and shook the purplish brown stitched sack in Mathias' face. "Show solidarity with us. Show you'd join us to bring peace. Show that your allegiance is to the people first and foremost."

"Drink. Drink," the crowd yelled.

Bibb pulled the stopper from the wineskin's narrow neck.

Drinking would give Mathias a few moments, a space to free himself, and his mouth was dry. But drinking this now would be traitorous. It would be showing he turned his back on the Queen.

All the Eaburrai, Keston had to be in hiding with Aunia by now.

"I'll be about my business," Mathias said. He took the first two steps to leave this crowd behind.

"You won't, oh enemy of the people." Bibb snapped his fingers again, and the crowd roared like a hungry bear.

They grabbed Mathias. Mathias pulled back. Hand on his sword. There were too many. Too many hands gripping his arms and then his legs. Hoisting him into the air.

"You will release him," a deep, authoritative voice bellowed over the crowd.

And then, trumpets blared.

CHAPTER TWENTY-ONE

PORTAL TILES

Earth and Winter, Terralium. Air and Spring, Pavari. Water and Summer, Cascadia. Fire and Autumn, Ember-fall. — Names of the elemental faery courts.

P art of Aunia cried out not to follow the orange flutterby but she couldn't help herself. She needed to know this wasn't the Boggle-man transformed into another form. Probably it was nothing. Others had the same glow as him. Reina did and she was just a little girl. And more honest than Taya or Lena.

Aunia clenched her fists and kept walking, bare feet padding over the dusty cobblestones toward the tumbled gray-brick building.

That orange flutterby couldn't be the Boggleman. Even with that unsettling dream, he was dead. But . . . if he did live . . . what would that mean for her father?

The thought made her stomach hurt. Her father would be in more danger. Even if he was a Mystic like Basil said, any magic he possessed was muted by that cage—iron bars wrapped in dark crystal and a covering similar to the Boggleman's cape.

Jennium tugged at her hair and threw a mind picture of Aunia following Keston into the fabric shop.

"They can't see me, Jennium," Aunia murmured. She tapped her father's amulet from under her ripped rover blouse. Mathias, after all, was facing down an entire crowd visible. She surely could learn what she needed to know with the glamor. That flutterby . . . if it was the Boggleman?

The Boggleman had feared her mother's amulet. She was sure of it. Why else would he have wanted it from her so bad? That, and with its help not only had Aunia boxed a Chandarion's magic, but she had used it to summon fire salamanders to her village to defeat the heebles. Surely her father's amulet was powerful, too.

The memory of Lena's monotone reading voice washed through her describing the gills and speckled tail a strange child had when they washed onto the beach. Washed onto the beach and was adopted. Taken in. She had seen no evidence of the Boggleman having any of that but he was a shape-shifter. She had seen him change into a wyvern. And then back to humanish form when he plummeted from the sky.

The flutterbys zipped over the well to the broken building and she picked up her pace to catch up. Hurried thuds of boots hitting the stone from behind her made her turn. Even glamored, she didn't want to be run over.

"Hold up," Keston said.

She stepped in front of the well before she turned to face him and pointed at the broken building. "There are flutterbys over there."

"Flutterbys? I've heard of them. They seek sparkly things." Keston's attention darted to the broken gray building. "Curious. Problem is there's mudcloaks over there."

"Mudcloaks?"

"The Da Vennen," clarified Keston. "Most use real bear fur but mud's the same color, right? Childish, yes . . . but they're aggravating. And they're dangerous. Come on, let's pop into that fabric shop."

"Yes, but there's something they're attracted to." Aunia pointed to the right-side of the demolished building where the men worked.

"Yeah, that's where the entrance to the basement would be. There was a locked door near the foot of the stairs, too. Seems odd all the places, and with the mudcloaks involved, that's where they're clearing."

Aunia bit her lip. Continuing to the building was dangerous. Men who wore red and also ones in bear fur cloaks had tried to put an iron cuff on her earlier and threatened prison. "Well, they can't see me. We could both fill our curiosity."

"Mathias would kill me if anything happened to you." Keston set his hands on the lip of the well and a rich blue swirl mingled with his golden glow. "But they are after something. And it's foolhardy. I try not to be that. Sometimes at least."

"Keston."

"We should stay no closer than here. And I don't know. I could tell you a story. Maybe one on Prince Elris and the rover lass since we've been with the rovers. Or maybe you'd like to hear an adventure of Lord Chance?"

Jennium jingled warningly from underneath Aunia's hair.

"What about the Blood Ball?" asked Aunia.

Keston shot her a surprised look, then shrugged. "I suppose but it'll be things that I've heard. I was a babe at the time and my parents were living in Adar then. There could be some inconsistencies."

Aunia nodded.

Keston flipped over his hands, palm up. "Some say the ball was meant to celebrate the betrothal of Princess Kylandra and Aeryk de Wyvert of New Berlin, the future king-consort. Others say it was in anticipation of the arrival of the betrothal stone."

"Betrothal stone?" Aunia said but her gaze was yet on the flutterbys.

"A magical item found in faery but sometimes the high gnomes from Terralium—"

"The faery court of earth and snow?" Aunia turned to Keston.

"You know the faery courts?" Keston shot her a bright grin. "They know them in Adar but not everyone knows them here."

"Caedmon would tell stories about them. But he never said anything about a betrothal stone."

"Well, like I said, it's magical. Sometimes one of the faery courts will transfer items over to Tatia. I believe the last time it came was during the rule of Didianne, the mad Queen. It was supposed to come during the Blood Ball but it never did."

"Somebody there talks to the faery courts," Aunia murmured and peeked back to the men working. "What does the thing do?"

"Tatia *is* on the threshold between the worlds," he said. "Anyway, this stone . . . it's child-size in height with a hole bore through. Supposedly if you stick your hand through, you cannot clasp anyone else's hand from the other side unless it be your true love."

"And Kylandra was supposed to stick her hand through."

"She was. The suitor games were, well, going poorly. But she never arrived in the throne room. And when the King and Queen sent guards to go fetch her, the capital was attacked. Not many of the royals survived."

"And they think Mystics did it," Aunia said flatly.

Keston rolled his eyes. "Yes. A Ferris Runoldi, I believe his name was. He had come months before and wriggled himself into the royal family's confidence and the court. But the thing that seems strange is why Mystics would attack with knives. Why not magic itself?"

"Then you don't think it was Mystics—"

A sharp clatter and thuds drew Aunia's attention back to the broken building near the rubble-filled alleyway. There a gritty cloud of dust rose over a man with a wheelbarrow and an entire cloud of flutterbys lifted up from the broken building. A high-pitched hiss hurt Aunia's ears and the eight-winged faeries scattered. Except for the suspicious orange flutterby who flew over the worker's head.

"Something's drawing those flutterbys." Aunia leaned forward.

"Something from that building's basement, I'd wager." Keston gave her a look from head to toe. "And you're glamored. Okay. Stay close."

They ventured out toward the broken building.

Jennium buzzed, yanked at the hair under Aunia's nape, and threw a mind-picture of Keston and Aunia hiding.

"Ouch. Stop that," Aunia hissed. She didn't slow down as they ventured toward the broken building. Neither did Keston.

The hair-pulling stopped.

The slipperiness of dust on the cobblestones changed to pain and Aunia gritted her teeth as the soles of her feet found the smaller pebbled chunks from destroyed gray bricks. She slowed as she threaded her way to the worksite where a dozen townsmen, young and old, worked with four Da Vennen soldiers.

Keston slowed as well and talked behind his hand. "Keep an eye out. There's been rumors of pirated portal tiles."

Aunia frowned. "Portal tiles?"

"Skipping for those who aren't faeblooded."

Portal tiles could be handy for the Boggleman if they allowed one to skip. And he wanted to go back to Nonderu, if her dream had been true. She hissed as another stone dug at the arch of her foot. "Are portal tiles shiny?"

"You do need shoes. And yes. They are."

Shiny. The orange one could just be a flutterby.

They were about ten steps away when the townsmen straightened from shoveling and pushing wheelbarrows. Their clattering noise died down and was replaced by an uneven crackle and heavy footfalls. A Da Vennen soldier, deep scars lining his face and his bearfur cloak draping heavily over his broad shoulders, stepped forward. A sword hilt protruded from the top of his belt. He cleared the broken building and stopped on the cobblestones, turning cold black eyes toward Keston.

The workers and the other three Da Vennen soldiers . . . were they looking at her? Their gaze didn't seem to be on Keston. Coldness poured through her body and she reached up under her hair. Jennium was gone.

"A faeblood with a flyer," the Da Vennen soldier drawled. "Kind of interesting."

Two of the other soldiers picked their way through the debris field while the last one remained behind piles of bricks in the alleyway. The orange flutterby circled around this one's head.

"Faeblood? No. Just a pretty rover girl." Keston waved at a workman with a wheelbarrow. "I wanted to show her how industrious the Dalian people are."

"Pretty?" the soldier said. "She looks used."

"That's very rude," replied Keston. "I'm sure these fine workmen could show you civility. You know, in addition to what real work looks like."

Almost in tandem, several of the workmen moved further back in the broken building, their glows quivering. The cloud of yellow flutterbys, however, surged forward. They regrouped, swarming back to the space behind the stacks of broken bricks, and beat the orange flutterby back with their wings.

Keston bespeaks to show bravery. That we've every right to be here, a high silvery voice sent. Revellie.

Bravery? Aunia pushed ahead of Keston and pointed to the spot where the last Da Vennen soldier and a workman stood. "What's sparkly over there?"

"Br—bricks," the workman stuttered. "Just bricks. We're doing clean . . . cleanup."

Several of the flutterbys dove behind the brick stacks and then flew over to Aunia and Keston. They dropped thin knuckle-sized tile squares at their feet. The tiles gleamed iridescently . . . ever-changing reds, greens, and blues.

Keston's voice turned raspy. "Portal tiles."

The Da Vennen drew their swords.

"Right." Keston grabbed Aunia's hand. "We should let you get back to things."

"Too late for that," the dark-eyed Da Vennen said.

In a fluid motion, Keston released her hand and drew, his sword whistling from its scabbard. "I'm still the Queen's envoy."

"Little flyer, we're not worried about that."

Chapter Twenty-Two
WITCH COMPASS

The mind is a forge, and each thought a hammer strike—shape the world, or be shaped by it. — Lothar Gildenstahl, from Eberwald province in Uttalo

Mathias fought against the squeeze of hands holding him high in the air. Tried to free his hands to grab his sword, or better, his dagger for tighter spots, but they held him tight in a rolling motion as if he were out to sea.

Jeers and shouts that had crashed over murmuring harsh voices lessened while other voices and running boot falls echoed to the left.

Mathias struggled for a better look between the many heads that formed the crowd. On the raised platform stood another crowd.

Distance is a problem, Taf sent. *But Rev—*

Fallo's here, Mathias interrupted. Six, no more than that, guardsmen. Also, archers and bannermen. And Fallo. The band around his ribs loosened for a second, then re-tightened.

Trumpets blared a second time and the crowd holding him swayed as if they would drop him. Grind him under the press of their feet.

"Make way for his Grace the Marquis Emmet Dalin, sixteenth in the line of Ice-steel," a deep voice boomed. "Protector of the free people dwelling within the Grashbear's shadow. Son of Marquis Charl Dalin, descendant of Grand Marquis de Idenweigh, son of—"

"The lord would be safer in his keep," Bibb's voice sounded. He had to be in the crowd closer to Mathias' feet.

Mathias lifted his chin high, gaining a better view of the platform.

Fallo stepped out in front of a shorter man wearing the lord's blue and brown tabard. "In the name of her majesty and your lord's, disperse."

Several archers pulled an arrow from quivers and notched them.

Mathias was lowered, though the hands remained clamped on his arms and wrists, keeping him from his weaponry. The crowd didn't look as thick. Some must have scattered.

"Empty words from our hopeful would-be Dar . . . but wait. Her majesty pushed you away, didn't she?" Bibb raised his arms high, allowing Mathias to locate him. "This flyer has no jurisdiction over any in the soldier faith. We are free from their hypocrisy."

"The lord of this community says different." Lord Emmet Dalin, with his boy-slight frame, stepped beside Fallo. Emmet was one of the younger lords. Barely twenty years with russet-gold skin, dark eyes, and a circlet fashioned like a bent sword adorning his curly-haired head.

From his periphery, Mathias noted more townsfolk scampering away before he was hauled forward to be held beside the arch vicar.

"Yes, yes. Hail the lord." Bibb said, his cheeks turning red. "But pray tell, your people would love for the lord to tell us all about his most recent whereabouts. We've heard the rumors of him pushing a flyer from the wall."

The guards on the platform drew their swords and drummer boys, partially hidden in the back, played a solemn doom-doom warning.

Emmet waved his herald over, bent, and murmured something. And then, the short nondescript man projected out. "The lord commands you release the flyer and for all to disperse from the market square at once."

Tafiriel's silvery voice sounded flat. *Cat is coming and as soon as she's in sight, we go.*

Bespeak Cat and—

Don't, Taf sent.

Bibb turned his head. Gave Mathias a narrowed glance.

Mathias kept his features blank. It couldn't be Bibb listening in on telepathic conversations. The only way he'd be able to would be by magic. And Cat? They had to vacate before the Stanz commander arrived. When she found them, she'd probably arrest them. And who knew what would happen to Aunia. Hopefully she was holed up with Keston in one of the stores.

Fallo moved to the end of the platform. "Release my man and we'll be on our way."

"Arch Vicar," a cry rang out. Mathias and the crowd looked to the town's northwestern square and anxiety pierced his heart. In front of the broken merchant guild building stood Aunia and Keston surrounded by Da Vennen soldiers.

"Oh my, our rover faeblood who's been eluding capture." Bibb turned back to the platform and smiled at Fallo. "I suppose I owe our flyers a favor."

"That one is meant for the Queen's justice," Fallo yelled.

Some in the crowd turned back to the platform, muttering angrily. More than one eyed the archers.

"She's not a faeblood." Mathias yanked his right arm loose. *Taf, how soon?*

Half bell at best.

"That's a lie." A thick-bodied man pushed his way to the arch vicar. "She skipped in front of the Forged Tankard. I saw her do it. And when the guard tried to bracelet her, she spelled a pig to attack."

"Protect us from faebloods," a woman to Mathias' right yelled and other voices joined hers.

"How interesting. I thought it strange for a rover to be here when no caravans have come in but this explains it, doesn't it?" Bibb said. "Flyers are in league with faebloods."

"We have her under our jurisdiction," Fallo responded. "Touch her and imprisonment will look like—"

Lord Emmet interrupted. "Arch Vicar. You will desist. If you do not, I cannot guarantee your safety."

"And here I thought you were sincere about keeping our lands from becoming the new Spatelly." Bibb turned his back to the lord said. "But you would subjugate us."

"That is ridiculous," Emmet said. "All the faebloods I've imprisoned. Used them to protect our miners."

"But you refuse to imprison that one. Counting on honest words of a flyer. Not a faeblood?" Bibb pivoted toward Mathias with an arched brow and signaled the others to back away. "Let's prove it."

Bibb dipped his hand under his robe and pulled out a metal disc. It didn't look like a weapon, more like a compass with little red crystals dotting its outer ridge. But its needle arrow didn't point north. Instead, it spun toward the broken guild building.

A witch compass, Taf sent.

Mathias blinked. He had heard of them. They were used in the neighboring northern kingdom in the time of Edvaras to eradicate any who held magic.

"That's enough." Emmet snapped his fingers and half his guard, about ten men with swords drawn, came down the platform steps.

Bibb, however, held the item high for all to see the needle pointing at Aunia. "I'm not the one lying."

"A Da Vennen using magic?" asked Fallo. "Where did you get that?"

"Our Lord forgot to tell you? He gave it to me . . . to round up the faebloods. And that one. . . " Bibb pointed at Aunia. "Is a powerful one. Why should we allow a powerful faeblood rover to go to a mad faeblood queen?"

Fallo drew his sword. "Do not speak ill of my Queen."

Bibb gave a loud whistle and the remaining townsfolk in the crowd grabbed Mathias.

"Let him go," Fallo barked.

At the broken building, a Da Vennen soldier lunged at Keston while a second man swept his sword wide. Keston sidestepped. Ducked. Swords clanged together.

Keston launched up, hitting a different Da Vennen in the face with his sword pummel.

Mathias and the man grunted. And then, Bibb was in front of him, hand hidden in his robe.

Behind Mathias came a wet sluicing sound like blade meeting flesh. Mathias stomped hard on a captor's shin and yanked free. And then Bibb was in front of him, pulling a fist from his robe pocket. Mathias clocked Bibb in the nose and blue flower petals scattered high.

Mathias ran for Aunia while Emmet's guardsmen fought a few of the more belligerent townsfolk. *Taf. Get Rev to sleep . . . sleep those Da Vennen. Taf!*

From the merchant stalls, half a dozen Da Vennen soldiers ran for the broken guild building. Mathias pumped his legs faster.

Aunia ran through a hole in the soldiers' defenses with Keston defending her retreat. Two Da Vennen pressed Keston. The third chased Aunia.

Mathias closed in but the Da Vennen would reach Aunia first. The man grabbed her. Threw her on the ground. Raised a sword over his head.

"No!" Mathias screamed.

She rolled. The sword struck the ground.

"Just grab her," a new Da Vennen hollered.

Aunia scrambled to her feet, keeping the well between her and the Da Vennen.

Mathias was almost at the well when bricks rained from the sky. One nearly hit his foot. And one hit a Da Vennen in the back of the head. The man's fingers had been a hair's breath from Aunia's shoulder when he fell heavily to the ground. But, more Da Vennen were coming.

"Look out!" Mathias yelled and threw his body between her and the soldiers.

"Keston," she shrieked.

Keston was on the ground yards away. Bladeless. With a Da Vennen straddling him, sword point a hand's breadth from Keston's chest. Keston fought, two hands against the flat of the blade, to keep the sword from piercing his body.

Mathias swallowed hard against the quake in his body. Protect Aunia. Save Keston.

"Run," he yelled at Aunia.

But before he moved, the air turned blistering hot and a piercing whoosh screamed by his ear. Aunia's blue globefire burst from nowhere, careening around her head. It surged forward at Keston and the Da Vennen.

It struck the soldier's head. For one long horrible moment, the headless body remained locked in combat. Then a deluge of red spurted, soaking Keston. The sword dropped. Keston pushed the body off him, face contorted in disgust.

A dull thud forced Mathias' attention back to Aunia. She dangled limply between two of the Da Vennen.

"Release her," Fallo ordered. His arms and tunic were blood smeared as were the two guardsmen who flanked him. Other than them, Bibb, and the bodies lying in the marketplace . . . everyone at the platform were gone. Bibb stepped forward as did more Da Vennen. Where had all of these men been hiding?

Bibb strode toward them. "I'll take her."

"Leave her be." Fallo raised his sword. He was now only ten paces away.

The Da Vennen holding Aunia's limp form pulled a dagger to her throat. "Stay back."

A deep resonant gong filled the air, reverberating off the buildings. A warning that prisoners were being moved. Or escaping.

A black-robed and hooded figure appeared out of nowhere beside the Da Vennen and before anyone could react, pale lightning jumped from the stranger's hand to the Da Vennen's throat. The soldier's muscles locked up. His teeth clacked.

The stranger yanked Aunia free and the Da Vennen fell onto the ground convulsing.

Bibb and his Da Vennen rushed forward. So did Mathias, but the hooded figure holding Aunia disappeared. Skipped.

CHAPTER TWENTY-THREE
THE WORLD SLID BY

Rumor abounds that wererats or faeries are kidnapping the people as they sleep. But there is also murmuring that someone is building an army to be used against us. — Nyrissa Rieson, flyer of Lydinairre, daughter of Dar Zeller Rieson

Dizziness swept the ground away, blurring light into darkness, and Aunia slid from the world—or would have thought if not for the throbbing at the back of her head. She kept her eyes squeezed shut. Felt arms wrapped around her. The scratch of fabric against her cheek. And the jolt of movement. She had been somewhere. Tall buildings that looked as if they'd fall. And burly men in furry cloaks. Scenery and faces melded behind her closed eyes, moving in a nonsensible manner.

Thudding booms rattled her bones and her belly pitched like a creek overflowing with flooding rains. She groaned at the wet queasy taste in her mouth. She'd been protecting . . . protecting someone. She had felt the pinching in her temples. And a whirling ball of blue.

Where are you? A silvery voice echoed in her skull. She groaned again.

"I've got you," a man's voice murmured.

The world shifted again like she was going under. Everything was moving. Rocking. The hands holding her disappeared. Everything shifted. And faded to black.

"Is she okay?"

That voice hit Aunia's heart with a rich sadness and anger. Betrayal. She fluttered her eyes open. She was lying in a narrow bed. An upper bunk in easy reach. An enclosed space. Vardo. Unfamiliar one. Carved decorations from cherry wood fixtures fragmenting around the two human figures. Taya. Basil.

Aunia struggled to sit up. Taya, the liar. "Keep that traitor from me."

"She's a concussion. Let me tend her," Taya said to Basil.

The moving vardo hit another pothole in the road and everything in the wagon bounced.

"I'll tend her," Basil said.

A sob punctured Aunia's ears, and she groaned, covering her head with her hands. "Be quiet."

The bed moved again. Taya sat beside her. "I was afraid for you. I didn't want to see you get hurt."

Hurt? Soldiers. And swords. And . . . terror streamed through her body. "Mathias. Where is he?"

"Taya, get Reina ready," Basil requested.

Taya remained fixed at Aunia's side. "Why? Where are you taking her?"

"Elsewhere. She can't stay here."

The door swung open with a cavernous echo. Tharon entered the vardo. Swung his tall, lanky frame around a short, square table. He stopped a hands-breath from Basil. "What have you done?"

Aunia blinked. Keston lying on the ground. And Mygul. She had conjured Mygul.

"The Da Vennen attacked the girl. Attacked the flyers, too," Basil said. "I had no choice but to—"

"You were seen?" Tharon asked.

"Go get Reina." Basil pulled Taya off the bed. No anger slept in Taya's tear-filled blue eyes. She didn't look like Limi at all. The rover girl trudged for the door, her head downcast.

"I wasn't seen." Basil stood sideways in front of the bed, blocking Aunia's view, and rattling something made of glass. "But Bibb has a witch compass. Who knows all he can see. And our dear Aunia is wearing the clothes of our people. They will be coming for us."

"A witch—" Tharon sat heavily on a stool near the bed.

"He means to add her to his collection. And Reina too if he discovers her." Holding a small green-glass bottle, Basil sat on the edge of the bed. "Aunia. I need you to drink this."

"You do not know that," Tharon said. "Da Vennen do not like—"

"Magic?" Basil pulled the stopper from the bottle. "A perfect hiding spot for someone who does."

"But witch compasses need to be powered," Tharon countered.

"I know. And we both know what's been missing since the Cold Festival. Come on, Aunia." Basil lifted her head. "I need you to drink up."

Aunia swallowed the earthy and bitter liquid. It coated the back of her throat and she coughed. She stiffened and groaned. "Basil, where's Mathias? And Keston?"

"That's a fair question," Tharon said, "Where are the flyers now?"

"Hopefully escaped. Bibb fired up a mob and Lord Emmet, if it was really Lord Emmet, tried to get them to disperse. Problem is the wrong people know a bit about our young lady's inheritance."

Tharon stood. "She's—"

"Injured by brick to the back of the head?" Basil interrupted. "Yes. You're going to need to ride hard and find a place to hide until the Da Vennen and whatever shadow force is out there making people disappear give up."

"That comes from the wererats," Tharon said.

"And who wants more wererats to be created? People are vanishing without an ounce of being attacked."

"You don't know—"

"Da," Basil said. "Believe me or not with this one thing but get our people to safety. If you're caught up, not having us here will help you cry innocent."

The men fell silent and Aunia closed her eyes, willing the fog to lift from her mind. Another thump and a jostle and within the midst of a groan, a rush of memories struck her. She had skipped to Dalin. On her own. And they had been attacked. And . . . Mygul. Another piece of memory gave her a sharp kick. Keston pinned to the ground. Sword point at his chest. A blue rush to the Da Vennen and . . . she had . . . she had killed.

Tharon's voice turned rough. "They'll be looking for her in any rover caravan."

"I'm afraid so," said Basil.

Aunia pulled her fists against her mouth in disbelief and disgust. What would Mathias think of her now? What did she think of herself?

The door swung open again. Lena, with brown-red hair and thick body, entered with a basket over an arm and Reina by the hand.

"Good," Basil said. "Put the basket on the table and go tell the others to lash down any fly-aways."

"We're making the horses run?" Lena asked Tharon.

"Make for Lyttelton," said Basil.

"There are highwaymen on that back road," Lena protested.

"Then stay near the scrag hills," Basil said. "Mama's pack—"

"Do not mention her," stated Tharon.

"Da, there's little choice. Like it or no. She'll help keep you and the others safe."

Tharon raised a hand in protest. "That's *my* job. Keeping our caravan safe. Your job is leading you elsewhere. Go."

"Don't wanna go anywhere," Reina cried out. She sidled close to Lena and gripped her small dirty hands around the woman's arm.

"I'm sorry, lovely, but you can't stay here." Basil crouched down to the girl's level.

"But I've been good!" Reina's voice broke. "I've been very good. I promise. Haven't done any no-no's."

Basil reached under the bed and pulled out Aunia's knapsack.

"It's okay little one." Taya's voice. When had she snuck back in?

Aunia sat up, gritting her teeth against the throbbing in her head. Her hair brushed the wagon's ceiling.

Taya moved from behind Lena and hunkered down beside Reina, taking the little girl in her arms. Her voice was a low reassuring murmur, mostly incoherent except for 'you'll always be my sister.'

Aunia shook her head and regretted it. "Mathias. He needs to find me."

Basil pulled her knapsack over his shoulder. "He would not be happy if you're captured. And Fallo can help lead him to you. Da, tell the flyers . . . when they come. Tell them I've taken Aunia where her parents lost each other. Where smoke remains."

"Where my parents . . . lost each other?" Aunia blinked. She would go somewhere that her parents had gone. Learn something about them. And Mathias would find her. She blinked back tears. And going . . . this wasn't a choice.

"Reina, lovely, come here," Basil called, "and Aunia, here, I'll help you stand."

With the basket in the crook of his arms and Reina's hand in his, Basil pulled Aunia close. "Keep safe Da."

And then the world slid by.

CHAPTER TWENTY-FOUR

INKY CLOUDS AND WERERATS

To depose a lordling and to swell our ranks? Follow the three 'E's': Draw the Enemy's Eyes Elsewhere. — Arch Vicar Bibb of Da Caledonian Vennen

Mathias' boots slid on the cobblestones.

Aunia was gone. And the two Da Vennen soldiers who had held her . . . one lay crumbled on the ground, his face hidden under his bear fur cloak and a smoking dagger at his side. The other, a wiry-framed chap, rolled onto his feet and raised his sword at Mathias. Mathias stepped back from the well to give his sword arm more room. He risked a glance to Keston.

Keston was standing, blood-soaked. Dead Da Vennen at his feet. Da Vennen soldiers were advancing on him, but so were Fallo and the two guardsmen.

With the slapping of leather on cobblestones, the soldier ran at Mathias with a roar, sword over his head. Mathias side-stepped the soldier and angled his own sword for a gut shot. Steel upon steel chimed. The soldier's momentum took him past Mathias and Mathias pivoted, his left-side now protected by the well and facing the guild hall.

He, Keston, Fallo and two of Emmet's guards could overcome seven Da Vennen but how would they deal with the additional dozen Da Vennen pouring into the market square without the use of magic. Bibb was a problem, too. He remained standing near the platform with the witch compass in his hands. It was like he was activating something.

The Da Vennen soldier whirled around and charged Mathias. Mathias deflected the blow.

Something's preventing a sleeping, Taf sent.

How far are you? Mathias parried another shot.

About two fingers' width as the sun sails.

Ten minutes. Ten minutes against a Da Vennen soldier. Mathias had fought before. Maimed. But he had never killed. It had never been necessary.

"Should have stayed in your tower, boy." The Da Vennen soldier threw another shot.

Mathias deflected with the flat of his sword, his hip grinding against the well's rough stones as the enemy pushed all his weight onto his blade. Pointing his wrist down, Mathias changed the angle of his weapon, forcing the man's sword to travel down the length of Mathias' blade. The Da Vennen's sword fell away and Mathias rolled his wrist, bringing the tip of his own sword from the man's navel to his chest.

A thin line emerged along the center of the soldier's shirt. Cut cloth and blood. And behind this opponent the back-up soldiers approached. They'd be here in less than a minute.

The Da Vennen grunted and swung wide. The tip came a hands-breadth from Mathias' face and a strange, sweet smell filled the air.

"Mathias," a bright tenor voice called. "Step in."

Mathias was dimly aware of a pocket of sticky fog materializing at his right.

The enemy pressed his advantage by closing in. He gripped Mathias' blade and Mathias struck the man's sword arm with his fist.

"Two of you?" The Da Vennen soldier panted. The sound of disgust was in his tone.

Mathias' twin stepped beside Mathias. Mathias frowned. He didn't have a twin.

"Hurry, hurry," more voices said. "The fog."

And several Da Vennen charged.

Mathias stepped into the fog.

Three figures stood inside the inky mist. They were dressed in ragged puffy pants and belted jerkins. Their features peeked out from black cloud shreds and it took Mathias a moment to realize what he was seeing. Two humanoid rat people and a boy maybe fifteen years of age with a pointy sharp nose.

"Wererats," Mathias breathed. He sank into a fighting stance.

They remained still except the boy. "Keeping you alive is a never-ending task."

"What did you do with Aunia?"

Outside the dark fog, yells and crashes sounded.

"Don't have her. Basil does and she's safe," said the wererat man to the boy's left.

"What do you want?" Mathias asked.

The wererat men shook their heads. The boy stepped closer. "Your pegasi . . . two of them anyway have flown over the city. We've kept them from being seen. But you need cover. There's archers waiting to shoot them down."

"More flyers are coming. Catiryna," said one of the wererats.

And she would probably see Fallo, Keston, and himself arrested . . . unless . . . Mathias straightened. "How long will this mist last?"

"Not long," the boy said. "We'll get you to the others."

"How are you doing this?"

"Too many questions. Not enough time. Come on," the wererat boy said. "We'll keep the fog on you."

With a firm grip on his sword hilt and with the black cloud moving with them, Mathias followed the wererats.

Footfalls and more slapping leather sounded off the cobblestones. The Da Vennen were too close by.

"You can't hide," they called.

Mathias clenched his jaw, eyes darting through the inky wisps of fog but he could see nothing past two arms-lengths.

A clattering of hooves told Mathias that a pegasus had landed and the brick debris at his feet told him they were near the merchant guild hall ruins.

The wererats halted.

"Keep going, flyer," the boy said. "You're almost there."

Swallowing hard, and hoping this wasn't a trap, Mathias continued on, passing from one fog pocket into another. Mist swirled around Keston and Revellie.

"Mathias," Keston said in a low voice. "Tafiriel?"

Mathias shook his head. Fallo's face pushed through the fog from Revellie's far side. "Have him meet us away from the city."

"You can ride with me," Keston rubbed his face with his sleeve with a tongue click and a 'gah.'

"They're here somewhere," Bibb's guttural voice yelled over the foot-falls and curses. He and his Da Vennen soldiers were close to the guild building, too.

"Cat's on her way," Mathias murmured.

Fallo raised a hand. "We leave."

Keston climbed up into Rev's saddle and held out an arm for Mathias. He took it and swung himself up. Revellie bunched her back muscles under him, her frame slighter than Tafiriel's, and she ran. They sailed out from the dark fog into the late afternoon sun.

Several thwacks sounded along with the whiz of arrows.

Revellie tipped sideways with Mathias clinging with his thighs and the back of Keston's saddle. One arrow went wide. Another sailed past Mathias' elbow.

"Shield spell isn't working," Keston gritted.

As they dodged arrows, wisps of dark fog lifted from below and dotted the sky.

Revellie gained more altitude. Fallo and Paderro climbed as well—nearly sixty feet above them.

Behind them, coming from the southwest, flew a steel-gray pegasus with a flyer with long fire-colored hair. Catiryna and Yantexio. And she flew with four other flyers, including Myles on his black mare. That was almost all the flyers from Stanz Tower with her. Not a good sign. But . . .

"She doesn't know our spells are being blocked," Mathias yelled. *Taf tell Fallo.*

Fallo bespeaks to shut your mouth, Taf sent. *You'll fly without her.*

Not warn her? Mathias blinked. That was unconscionable. Cat could help them arrest Bibb for attacking flyers.

Several more arrows flew. Wide. But still a danger. Keston directed Revellie toward another dark cloud.

She'll soon notice herself, Taf sent as they flew through another sticky cloud. *Cat bespeaks to set down. Fallo bespeaks we are to keep flying.*

The cloud erupted into thousands of smaller shadows. Each with twitching movement . . . bone-white . . . smaller than a finger. Whisperers. The acrid scent of melted wax and burning cloth filled Mathias' nose.

His throat. Clinging as if to suffocate him. And then tiny fingertips dug at Mathias' face.

With a sharp whinny, Revellie folded her wings tightly and dove. Mathias clung tighter. Helpless. Keston forced Revellie to swing upwards. Mathias flung an arm wide to shoo the whisperers back.

The whisperers flew past them, continuing downwards. Spread over the town.

Below and still a good distance away, Cat and her men circled. Probably trying to ascertain where these whisperers came from. Would Cat believe they had sent the whisperers? Mathias groaned. They could not set down for Cat. And it was entirely possible that Fallo had called the whisperers. But if he could do it without the whisperer bowl, it didn't seem likely that Paderro would still be Fallo's pegasus.

Revellie continued higher in a westerly direction following Fallo into a low nimbus cloud. A direction to make Cat think they were heading inland, away from Eddac Tower. Make her give chase. Revellie continued higher into the cold, hazy blanket and then turned sharply north.

I await you at the closest empty farm, Taf sent.

CHAPTER TWENTY-FIVE

WITHIN THE FOLD OF DARKNESS

Such sweet pain when I look upon my daughter's features...so like my beloved. Perhaps she'd regale me a hero if I could repair past harms. — Ferris Runoldi of Bellatine

The abrupt halt when skipping was the worst. Aunia crumpled over her knees, ready to vomit. Basil bent down and patted her back while Reina, presumably Reina, ran from them with the whisper of leaves crunching under her feet. Aunia slowly sat up.

Basil had skipped them to a forest glade where triangular fern fronds encircled moss-carpeted earth and three-petaled pink blooms grew under poplar and oak trees. Aunia swallowed down the wet taste in her mouth and wrinkled her nose. There was a faint reek of smoke and lightning, similar to the smell at Clavis Peak when they had encountered a lingering storm spell. But nothing looked burned under the wooded leafy canopy.

"What is that smell?" Aunia struggled to stand.

"Keep still." Basil flipped up a woven blue cloth that covered the top of the wicker basket. "We didn't have the time needed to treat you. And

I'm certainly not the healer that Taya is, but let's take a look at that . . . yes, goose egg. You took a nasty blow."

Aunia winced when Basil touched the lump. It felt like icy-cold seared against the headache. Made her stomach twist. "They hit me because—"

"Because they're mean," Reina finished. She must have run back from her short look-about.

They hit her because she had killed one of their own. Well, it was Mygul but . . . Aunia bit her lip. It was her fault.

Basil, beside her, rummaged through the basket and brought out a small glass vial with a thin neck. He unstopped it. "Here it is. Something to mend your head quicker."

"You gave me something already. What was it?" Aunia croaked. She cleared her throat.

"That was for pain." Basil forced her fingers around the vial. "Take it or no but a clear head will serve you better."

She balanced the potion between her fingers and on her knee. "Mathias. Will he be—"

"He's a flyer," Basil interrupted. "He'll be fine and we've left word. Fallo knows this place. It'll take them a bit to get here. This is further west toward Vraelsfork but probably by tomorrow. Mid-morning. Maybe afternoon. Reina, lovely, no further please."

The girl had returned to her look-about and stopped beside an ash tree many yards away. "It smells bad."

"Yes. Things that smell bad are typically dangerous," Basil said.

Aunia blinked. Jaia smelled bad but . . .

"Have you eaten since morning, Aunia?" Basil bent again to the basket. Such a normal question. But nothing was normal. "There's bread and jam, and a bit of ham. And that potion will do you better inside you, not in the bottle."

Aunia lightly touched the lump at the back of her head. Looked at the blood on her fingers. She did not feel hungry. She wasn't sure what she felt. But perhaps clear-headedness . . . She took the potion, then pointed to Reina. "Why couldn't she stay with the caravan?"

"Wouldn't have been safe."

"Why not?"

"Aunia," Basil said. "You're dressed like a rover. It wouldn't take much for the Da Vennen or even Lord Emmet's men to figure out where to look for you. And your magic has made you both a threat to those who fear magic and made you quite attractive to those seeking power. We needed to disappear."

Aunia fidgeted with the tear at the neckline of her blouse to keep from staring at Reina's small form curled under a tree. Her magic. Something that she had absolutely no control over. "That explains me, but what about her? They wouldn't know her."

"They would." Basil lowered his voice. "Our faeblood little dear made the mistake of letting someone see her change beans for honey cake and Duke Vrael's guards came to collect her. Bad in itself. Worse when her brother tried to defend her by flying the family's shoes."

Turning beans into pastries. That was why Lena had threatened Reina with bean porridge. "Where's her brother?"

Basil's expression turned tight and his glow tinged with the palest pink. He sat down beside her.

Aunia leaned forward. "Her parents?"

"Dead, too, I imagine."

Aunia pulled her arms across her chest.

"She's a faeblood," Basil continued. "With what happened in Dalin, if the Da Vennen or Emmet's men found us housing her, she would not be the only one imprisoned, used, or killed."

Aunia shut her eyes and rocked. Reina's displacement. This was her fault, too. "I hate your lands."

"There's plenty to hate. But there's more to protect. Aunia, open your eyes." Basil held a steaming clay-fired cup. It smelled of willow bark tea and its bitter earthiness—something Gaitha would have given her.

She swallowed a lump from her throat, accepted it, and took a sip.

"Pie?" Reina stood over Aunia with a fistful of pink trillium flowers. Her glow had changed to a dim dandelion yellow mixed with twinkling starlight—an iridescence that came from her faeblood. "Don't want ham. And this place feels weird."

Basil reached out, brushed Reina's hair from her face. He then flicked a flourish with his wrist. A thick-crusted pastry, two-hands width, on a wooden plate appeared in his hand. "Apple. Your favorite, I believe."

"How did you do that?" Aunia asked, then blinked. "And my tea. Did you just pluck it out of thin air?"

"Energy courtesy of leylines. There's a thick one that runs through here. But if anyone asks, I've got a couple of crystals in my pocket spelled to produce food." Basil pulled a knife out of nowhere and cut the pie in three. "But your magic . . . how do you think you do it?"

"I . . . I don't know."

"Well, that blue fireball of yours. That is a force to be reckoned with." Basil handed Reina a small plate with a third of the pie.

"Mygul," Aunia muttered.

"Mygul," Basil repeated and handed her a plate. "I'm surprised you didn't summon it earlier."

"I don't control that. It's . . . I don't know. Gaitha always said it was a piece of Edvaras' light that attached itself to me. But Edvaras' light went into . . ." Aunia fixed her gaze on a maple branch three paces behind Basil. She didn't want to talk about her mother's amulet. "Well, Hebsolum has it."

"Edvaras?" Reina had a smear of apple syrup on the side of her face. "He crumpled a coastline up north. A lot of people are mad about that."

Aunia frowned. "Mathias told me about that. But Edvaras also did a lot of good things. And the bad things? Well, he was trying to escape with Naoma."

Reina cocked her head. "Who's Naoma?"

"His one love," Aunia focused back on Basil. "But you said leylines. I don't understand."

Mouth full of pie, Basil hurriedly chewed, then rubbed a finger against his lip. "Almost anyone could do magic. If they have the will that is, and can figure out how to pull the energy."

Aunia set her plate on the ground. It certainly had not been her desire to kill. She had only wanted Keston to live.

"We've leylines all around us. Mostly," Basil continued, "Think of them like oil pools and our desire can be the spark which lights it. But, it's also knowing just the right amount of energy to use. After all, blowing ourselves up, not a happy thing."

"Make me another?" Reina held up her empty plate.

Aunia handed the girl her uneaten slice.

"And Aunia, my dear, you have magic," Basil said. "Skipping and that blue light of yours. You'll need to learn how to use it. Control it."

Aunia covered her ears. How could she ever call on Mygul again? She had to make sure she never got angry. Things always happened when she was angry.

"Hey," Basil pulled her hands down. "What you did wasn't wrong. It was necessary."

"Necessary? Maybe I could have changed that soldier's sword into flowers. Or I could have skipped Keston away like you did with us." Aunia wrapped her arms around herself. She had skipped herself to Dalin.

Why not somewhere else? "But I get mad and strange stuff happens. Bad stuff. Sigmus is right. I am like a Dagel demon."

"Aunia, you saved a life. That Da Vennen soldier would have killed Keston otherwise. There is no mercy in them. What they see is either or. There is no in-between." Basil held up his empty plate and it vanished only to be replaced with two striped wool blankets. He handed one to Reina and one to Aunia. "And with you . . . what you have is a training issue. I believe I'm taking Reina to Q'thonos tomorrow. Maybe I should take you there as well."

"Mathias." She ached to see him. But he had never told her where they would go from here. She wanted to save her father. Go to Tatia. She had told Mathias that. He'd help her, wouldn't he? Of course he would. But he had also left her behind when he went to Dalin.

"Who's Wootonis?" Reina asked.

"Q'thonos," Basil said. "An earth-mage. Respectable legal magic is what he's known for. He lives off the Pardonway."

Aunia leaned forward. "You said Mathias and the others will come here."

"Yes. Yes." Basil drummed his forefinger against his knee in quick succession. "We'll wait till they come . . . at least—"

"Can I have a story?" Reina asked. She wrapped the blanket around herself. "Maybe a story of why this place smells bad."

"I'd like to know that one, too," Aunia added.

Basil frowned and looked left toward the darkening shadows. "There's a remnant of a death spell in a nearby clearing. A magic meant to chase away the Boggleman. We're safe where we are, provided we don't get too near, but the good thing is our enemies tend to avoid this place."

Aunia chewed her lip. She had dreamed of the Boggleman. Just a bad dream, surely. Then she straightened. Forced words from a throat gone dry. "This is where my father left my mother to die."

"That's a story for when the sun isn't leaving the sky," Basil said.

He didn't look at her.

"My mommy's dead, too." Reina curled tighter under her blanket. "I miss her. And Taya. I want Taya to be my new mommy."

Bleakness wrapped itself around Aunia's heart.

"Sadness," Basil spoke. "My nana told me this the day my sister went away that in every life the heaviness of sadness will rest upon our chests, choking away all sunny thoughts. But it need not last. Nightfall disappears at the dawn. However, know that within the fold of darkness . . . this is where it's easiest to see wisdom's spark. Gather this light about you and when the time comes, use them to light your way and chart your best past."

Aunia pulled the blanket over her shoulders. She did not need sunny platitudes like Gaitha would give. She needed a distraction like Caedmon would have offered. "What story will you tell us?"

Chapter Twenty-Six

One Worry at a Time

There's something hidden in the dark. An enemy. I am quite sure of it. The problem is are they also known as allies or not
— Wendalin Mensani, apprentice dar to Dar Syrick

Tafiriel's wings brushed the pre-twilight sky. The sun was at the horizon and the waning gibbous moon faintly gleamed over the distant Grashbear Mountains. Mathias, fingers laced through Taf's mane, leaned over his saddle while they flew over Baxter's Way beside the Brainhedge Row. They were many miles away from the Brainhedge Tree jutting up from the hedgerow where the caravan had camped the night before. Other than tracks in the grass showing that they headed north away from Dalin, it was like the caravan had disappeared. They were even checking the byways and barely-there goat paths, which connected to the north-south trade route. The caravan, even starting out on their journey minutes after the flyers left for Dalin, could have only gone sixty miles at best. Where were they?

How can you not sense her? Mathias gripped Taf's mane tighter. *You did when she passed into the Birchwoods miles from her village.*

There's magic keeping her hidden, Taf sent.

Like with Brinsaber? Mathias snapped.

He's—

Holed up in a blade-cave. You said so. And too cowardly not to go looking for Jules.

Tafiriel's wing flaps stuttered, and they fell a few feet.

Keston and Revellie pulled up beside them and Mathias raised his thumb in a 'we're fine' gesture.

I'm sorry, Taf. I'm just—

Anxious and worried. I understand.

Mathias rapped the top of his thigh with his fist. He wanted to ask more about Brinsaber and Jules. But this ache of not knowing where Aunia was made it impossible to concentrate. He wanted to feel her back against his chest and her flower-scented hair tickling his nose.

One worry at a time suffices, Taf sent.

Basil must be keeping her hidden. Mathias leaned back in the saddle. Not only was Aunia dressed in rover clothing, drawing negative attention for all rovers everywhere, but her globefire had killed a Da Vennen soldier. *But where are they hiding?*

Mathias glanced at Keston who still flew on his right-hand side. He'd be dead if Aunia hadn't intervened, but had she sent her globefire to kill deliberately? He didn't think she did. He had seen her flush, hands over her mouth in his periphery. And then a different Da Vennen soldier knocked her out.

They'd be looking for her—the Da Vennen soldiers—and Lord Emmet too with his men. Scouring for any rover caravans around.

Basil has magic enough to hide her, Taf sent. *But Arch Vicar Bibb has—*

A witch compass. Mathias finished. No Da Vennen would use anything that was magical but Bibb did . . . and none of the Da Vennen soldiers objected. Mathias' confidence in his fractured memories about the Cold Festival on the Bellows sand grew. Bibb had indeed been there. But then, wererats had been there, too.

Power seems to be more luring for the Arch Vicar than his herd's doctrine, Taf sent.

Mathias shrugged. Taf's statement rang true. And that made Bibb more dangerous. What other magic would he be willing to use? *The rovers . . . they couldn't have skipped away, could they?*

They passed over where the road narrowed between the brainhedge and a sharp outcropping of rock.

A whole caravan? Taf sent back. *People, maybe. Horses, unlikely. Wagons, no.*

Then where could they be? It isn't like they could tiptoe through the brainhedge. Mathias straightened. *The paths through the gates are all too tight, aren't they?*

Taf flicked his ears. *Fallo bespeaks. He wants to set down on the next resting ground.*

Mathias drummed his fingers against his thigh. *Lift higher over the trees first. I want to see if any wagon could travel through the brainhedge from a water gate.*

Taf rose over the brainhedge to where the last bit of daylight retreated from the hedgerow's twisted branches and shadowy green leaves. There were places, yawning dark shadows peeking from under the canopy. Places that maybe a wagon could hunker down and hide but all the water gates to get there were only a person-wide. How could they pass through? Unless maybe they hacked their way through.

Mathias directed Taf to speed ahead to an approaching clearing that Fallo wanted them to land at. It was where the road pulled further from the hedgerow and a rough-hewn cottage sat. The grounds around the structure allowed space for about a half-dozen wagons.

They landed and Mathias dismounted, running for the living wood and ironwork gate.

"Great idea getting water." Fallo dismounted and reached for the ties to his blanket roll from the back of his saddle. "I've got the key though."

"Commander," Mathias hurried back. "The caravan. I think—"

Fallo held up his hand. "Tell me after we've settled in for the night."

"We can't settle in," Mathias said. "We need to—"

"Stop." Fallo pulled the blanket roll into his arms. "Just who do you think you are? I'm commander. Not you. You think I want Cat and her crew to find us? Where do you think they'll go after they've been to Eddac Tower? We flew like we were going there before we jumped a cloud."

Mathias curled his fists. "And when she finds us? You're going to what? Direct more whisperers to attack?"

Fallo hit Mathias in the center of the chest with his bedroll.

Mathias staggered back, breath stolen, feet and momentum uneven. He landed hard on his rump.

"I did not conjure whisperers." Spittle flew from Fallo's mouth and he glared at Mathias with narrowed eyes.

"Apologies." Mathias held his hands out. The last thing he needed was for Fallo to realize he had seen him with a whisperer inside the brainhedge. "It's just . . . I think the caravan passed through a water gate into Froidelune."

Fallo turned toward the hedgerow. "It's too tight a fit."

"Maybe not everywhere," Mathias said.

Fallo shook his head. "We'll find her come morning."

"And if Commander Catiryna Pemble finds us?"

"We have a crown card. Those seeds of yours and making a faery repellant. The Queen will appreciate a weapon."

"But," Mathias started. "Aunia is the only one who knows how to make the repellant."

"Commander." Keston, already dismounted, walked over. "I owe her."

"It's dark," Fallo said. "None of us here have night vision."

"But it isn't night yet," Keston countered.

Mathias got to his feet. *Taf, if you can't sense Aunia . . . can you sense the rovers?*

Fallo lowered his bedroll in his hands. "You're splitting hairs, bucko."

People are people. Taf, who still stood by the road, faced the outcropping in the near distance.

What about the young girl who helped stitch Keston's head?

Taf stepped onto the road and halted. He then looked over his shoulder. *Paderro sends they are a little further north.*

Mathias blinked. *Paderro?*

The commander's pegasus stood, head down and ears drooping. Fallo closed his eyes for a moment, re-tied his bedroll, and clamored back on Paderro's back. "Lead on, old friend."

They took to the sky.

Nearly an hour later, and traveling north, Paderro and Fallo swung past the first hedgerow overlooking the Brainmere and landed in the contested land. Mathias with Taf, and Keston with Rev followed suit.

The rovers had set up a fireless camp against the other side of the hedgerow. Two figures rose from Tharon's driver boards and jumped down from the crimson wagon. Except for the two, it appeared all other rovers were inside.

Still mounted, Mathias followed Fallo and Paderro to the caravan. They intercepted Tharon and Besnik less than a stone's throw away. Neither of them looked terribly happy.

Fallo dismounted and held out his hands in a no-harm gesture. "We're not here to hurt or arrest. We're just looking for the girl."

"She isn't here," Besnik said.

Tharon jabbed the boy with an elbow.

Mathias dismounted. "We appreciate you keeping her safe and—"

"Here." Fallo stepped forward, pulled a wine sack over his head which had rested cross-body on him, and held it out. "Can we agree that you know where she is?"

Mathias frowned. The skin was new and he hadn't noticed it before. Must have been a gift from Emmet.

"Just tell them she's too great a risk to keep with us." Besnik took a wide step away from Tharon. "Or tell them to search the wagons if they don't believe us."

"Then where is she?" Mathias asked, dread sinking into his belly. "Aunia was attacked in Dalin and someone skipped away with her. Are you telling us it wasn't Basil?"

Tharon kept his hands at his side, refusing to take Fallo's offer of wine. "She was saved, yes."

"Then where is she?" Mathias repeated, then paused. "Basil didn't take her to the wererats, did he?"

"Not all wererats are evil," Besnik said.

"I'm sure they have their agenda," Tharon said tightly.

Mathias completely agreed with Tharon on that. Yes, wererats had saved the flyers twice in as many days but they were also there the day that Zeller died.

"He did not take her to the wererats. But perhaps that might have been preferable." Tharon centered his gaze on Fallo who still held out the wineskin. "He took her to where the smoke never dies."

Fallo paled or at least his body language, with his sinking shoulders, suggested he did. He swiveled to face Mathias and Keston. "Head back to Eddac Tower."

"Eddac? No. I'm going with you wherever this place is," Mathias said.

"You will not," Fallo ordered.

"Fallo—"

"Mathias, it don't matter what you think," the commander said. "You'll obey orders or I swear I'll have you banished to Uttalo itself."

Paderro will make sure she comes back to us, Taf sent.

We have to go with him, Mathias replied.

No. Both Paderro and I agree with Aunia's faery. We need to be sure Eddac Tower remains safe before Fallo brings her there.

Mathias curled his fists and Keston approached him from his left side, tugging his arm. No pegasus worth his oats betrayed his flyer. All flyers knew that but it seemed like Paderro was working behind Fallo's back.

"Come on, Matty. We'll await them at the tower with a hot meal." Keston looked at Fallo. "Around when should we expect you?"

The stars twinkled like distant fireflies as Mathias and Keston flew southerly toward Eddac Tower, while below them, farmlands and meadows gave up their daytime colors. Wheat stalks swayed in the light breeze with shimmery silver from the luminous moon while oat plants, with their blade-like leaves, ruffled with gray-blue.

They swooped lower to the velvety meadows dotted with gray-white wildflowers. It was unlikely that any other flyer would be out at this time of night.

Mathias rocked in the saddle as they flew. Nothing was happening the way he thought it should. How could he trust Fallo to do what he said? How could he leave Aunia like this? And what choice did he have? *Ask Keston if he's ever heard of this place where smoke never dies.*

Keston sat up in the saddle and patted Rev's neck.

Taf flicked his ears. *Keston bespeaks that before the king-consort wed he sought the Mystic who killed the royal family, and he found him in a glade in Fallo's lands.*

Vraelsfork? Mathias frowned. *Sorry. Go on.*

Seconds ticked by before Tafiriel continued. *Some say the king-consort interrupted the Boggleman from bestowing riches upon the killer. Others say he interrupted the Boggleman from taking the Mystic's captive. Either way, Keston bespeaks, one of them—mystic or Boggleman—summoned a storm spell.*

And what happened?

Revellie broadened her wing strokes until she flew beside Taf.

Lightning struck the Mystic and incinerated him, Taf sent. *But something still feeds that spell and the fire that it caused continues.*

Keston slumped back in his saddle as if something bothered him.

That's where Basil took her, Taf? Mathias sent.

Keston bespeaks while it's a haunted place it's doubtful anyone would bother them near there.

And Fallo knows this place because it's on his lands? Mathias sent.

Under the moonlight, Keston's hands turned upwards in an expression of 'I don't know.'

I do not trust Fallo, Mathias sent. *Even if Paderro is helping us.*

Do you wish me to bespeak that to Keston?

Yes . . . no. Mathias leaned into the saddle. Another half hour before they reached Eddac Tower and come morning they'd apprise the servants, have them prepare a chamber for Aunia, and figure out the proposal to give Fallo on what their next course of action should be.

Keston bespeaks, Taf sent. *He and Revellie have been waiting long enough to learn about Brinsaber and Jules.*

Tell them what you told me. Mathias bowed against the lip of his saddle. Taf had reported that Brinsaber had flown away to hide. An order he received from Jules before his flyer lost consciousness. Jules had been kidnapped. And who ever the kidnapper was, they were able to listen in on pegasi/flyer conversations. All pegasi-to-flyer conversations could be eavesdropped on if there were many miles between them.

Keston straightened in the saddle. Below them, fields drew back, and they flew over the village of Berrydell with its thin roads crisscrossing between fifty-some houses with their wooden and thatched rooftops.

Mathias clenched a fist. The news Taf had shared screamed that a flyer had betrayed them. How else would anyone know what a pegasi could do and how it worked?

I told Keston your worries as well, Taf sent.

I didn't bespeak those.

Taf tossed his head. *Yes, but I heard them. Keston bespeaks . . . have you told Fallo about the knight-sons. They're kin for him.*

When would I have told him? Mathias sent.

Revellie bespeaks not to fret about the knight-sons' pegasi. Tafiriel's ears perked. *They'd have crossed back to Faery if a flyer threatened them.*

Hatred poured through Mathias' chest. Even if the knight-sons had been poisoned, how could they possibly harm a pegasus. *That . . . that is good. They did not deserve to die.*

Mathias leaned forward, awaiting the sight of Eddac Tower and its compound breaking over the wide copse of yew and hornbeam trees. And it came. Crenelated parapet emerging like a circle of sentinels with its merlons casting long shadows over the rough-hewn blocks of limestone. One of the pegasus barn doors gracing the tower's sides, which stood three stories up, stood wide open and beckoned with the promise of lodging and food.

Mathias tipped his head, awaiting the peal of bells announcing a flyer's arrival. No deep rings came. Only the murmur of soft roars and dull clanging.

Keston bespeaks that sounds like mischief, Taf sent.

They flew over the compound's wall toward the courtyard lined with wooden and stone blocked workshops, kitchens, storehouses, and servant homes. The ring of metal against metal grew louder, along with grunts, cries, and screams.

Bespeak, veer, Mathias sent. *Eastern side.*

Both pegasi swooped toward the darker side of the compound and Mathias' breath caught.

Under the moonlight, bear-cloaked soldiers with long swords pressed ragged-dressed humanoid wererats with daggers while fully transformed beasts hamstrung soldiers with teeth.

There're more attackers, Taf sent.

And with Taf's help, Mathias made out dozens of chest-high and knobby-shouldered faeries with elongated faces and sharp teeth. Kobolds. Unseen by the others below, they attacked both Da Vennen soldiers and wererats.

There was no sight of Eddac Tower's population.

CHAPTER TWENTY-SEVEN

DREAMWALKING

Know that to spiritwalk means you retain sovereignty of your own desires but a walkabout while sleeping? The Eaburrai have come and kidnapped you to where they choose. Oh, you think that's not bad? What if they will not protect you or allow you to leave? — Thalindra Archon, Arcanis Primis of the Mystic Court

Aunia jarred awake, blinking. She tilted her head. There it was again, a high-pitched scratchy sound and then an unfamiliar voice. A murmur.

An amber glow from a campfire, built after she must have fallen asleep, showed a sleeping Reina wrapped in her blanket and Basil's dark form sitting apart, back against the nearest tree.

That thin whine scraped at Aunia's ears again but the murmur . . .

"You need to find him," said a woman's voice. Its timbre came flat and resonant.

Aunia rose. That voice sounded as if it came from Basil.

But then, the next voice was his. "I'll do what I can."

She walked toward the fire—to Basil—noiselessly and stood over him. She expected a greeting. But Basil acted as if he was unaware of her presence.

"But you freed them all, didn't you?" the woman's voice asked. It emanated from Basil's hands. Hands that held one of Taya's cards. Aunia kneeled beside Basil. The card glowed with a pale silver light. Silver. Like the one Taya had snatched from Aunia during the reading inside her vardo.

"That was the plan," Basil responded, "but not what happened. Someone else sprung the faebloods."

A woman's face, olive-tinged and beautiful, pressed against the card's shimmery sheen, like someone trapped inside a misted-over mirror. "Who?"

Aunia reached to steady herself with a hand on Basil's shoulder. And her hand went through him. She caught herself before she fell face-first on the ground.

Basil shuddered and hunched into himself. "That is the question, isn't it?"

Aunia looked back to where she came from. There was a sleeping figure barely visible in the ring of darkness outside the fire's light.

"Basil," the woman gritted. "Surely, you have an idea."

An idea? Aunia was dreamwalking. Spiritwalking came from conscious design. And something Gaitha did semi-regularly but dreamwalking . . . that was rare and the little she had heard of it . . . dangerous.

"Bibb has a witch compass," Basil said. "And he was in Dalin."

Aunia jarred back to the surrounding conversation.

"The Da Vennen hate—"

"The love of power can corrupt any doctrine," said Basil. "He could be behind the missing people, too."

The woman brushed her long dark hair back. "I'll check with my contact at Lunacanto."

"In case firelings are involved? You sure you can trust Gabryella?"

Aunia frowned. That name sounded familiar.

The woman composed her features serenely. "I'll do what I must to protect the faebloods."

"I'll watch for them too, like I promised, after I get Reina to safety." Basil crossed a leg underneath himself. "You haven't answered my question yet."

"You can't bring her here."

"Wendalin, what choice do we have?"

Wendalin. Basil's sister. The one in Tatia where the Darra chamber was. Aunia's heart fluttered over her sternum . . . where she could go to rescue her father. She needed to talk more about her plan with Mathias. Get him and maybe Keston to help her so she didn't face the Mockmen trolls alone. But her Mygul . . . Aunia bit her lip . . . it could handle defense. If she could control it.

"She is the daughter," Basil said. "She's going to need to be trained up."

"You could do that yourself."

"She has Rune's star book."

Aunia startled. They knew about her dad's star book? Did Basil look through it?

"You have any idea what I'm dealing with?" Wendalin asked. "Catiryna Pemble's been bespeaking Nyrissa here practically all night, and she's bent on conquest.

"Wendalin."

"Oh, Nyrissa's not believing Fallo and his men attacked Dalin with whisperers but she is angry with them leaving their post and losing men because of it. And these walking mouths . . . are they real?"

"Yes. They are at that. They came out of the Grashbear. And as for Fallo and his men, they've been protecting Aunia. If not for them, the Boggleman would have claimed her. She says he got her father."

"Good."

Aunia's mouth dropped. Good? She was not liking Basil's sister.

Basil's jaw tightened. "She knows how to make a faery repellent."

"Does she now? Can she find lost items too or whatever I wish?"

Basil rolled his eyes and quietly said, "Did you misplace something?"

"My amulet is missing."

Aunia wrapped her hand around the small Chand ice orb which lay a hands-breadth from her collarbone. Her father's amulet was still there despite her being in a dreamwalking state. She fingered the silver chain, tapped at the knuckle-length silver hand, and wondered where Jennium had found it.

"I am sorry to hear that," Basil said.

The pitched whine squealed, hurting Aunia's ears, and she reflexively reached out to push the card back. A wriggling and a buzzing made her feel as if she had touched an angry hive of angry bees. The sensation moved up her arm. Her torso. Her entire body thrummed.

She fell—or it felt like falling. And then, a dull clunk rang through her body and all vibrations ceased.

Light brighter than candles or lanterns danced beside black shadows on high ceilings. Aunia blinked. She stood once again behind a wooden room divider with narrow, evenly spaced slats. Her heart lodged in her throat. She was in the same spacious room she had seen in her nightmare in Taya's vardo.

"Yes, you've done well, my lovelies," said a high-pitched lyrical voice.

Curling her arms inwards, Aunia tiptoed to the slats and peered out.

In the center of the spacious room stood the Boggleman, long white hair disheveled, and a few dozen miniature skeletons wrapped in smoke, twirled around his head.

"Master, I am trying to work here," said a low melodious voice. The woman from before sat, back turned, in front of the long table between two tall windows. A brilliant yellow light gleamed around her. Not her personal glow, that was more a steely gray, but some sort of light source.

The Boggleman shooed the whisperers off with a hand wave and they flew, curving toward the woman, before flying out the window. Some yanked her mahogany-brown hair before they left.

"Must you work with them?" She turned, full lips twisted into a scowl. "And what have they done well? Weren't they supposed to bring your girl back with them?"

Aunia's chest tightened, heart hammering. She sucked in a long, slow breath.

In front of the woman on the worktable lay stacks of glass tubes. Many glowed with a brilliant yellow light.

"They did most adequately." The Boggleman walked to the bed with its decorated headboard and lifted a shadowy slip of fabric. He swung it over his shoulders and it flared around him, taking on his dirty snow and dried blood glow.

"Your cloak won't get you back to Nonderu." The woman stood, bending slightly to accentuate her low-cut gown. Hisses and screeches erupted from a large stone box near her feet. "And right now you only have energy to shift into . . . what, a flutterby?"

"Don't patronize me, Gabryella. I can easily have my cloak eat you."

"Perhaps, and then what?" Gabryella lifted a thin slab of rock from the floor and set it as a lid on the stone box. "Something made of the veil will only hold its shape for so long in our mortal world. Look how thin it is now."

"It will be fine now that it's with me." The Boggleman walked toward her. "I require some of those fire salamanders."

"Master. Please. I need these. But ... why don't you allow me to gather up something tasty for consumption. Something better than that tribe of kobolds."

"Those kobolds will help me get the girl." The Boggleman, stopping in front of Gabryella, ran a forefinger along her cheek. "And then, I return home."

"But if you return home and entice the girl from there? You said you have her father."

Aunia had her confirmation. The Boggleman had been the orange flutterby at Dalin and he still meant to capture her. She pulled her arms in against her chest. She needed to wake up. Get herself out of danger. But how?

The Boggleman slid the rock lid back on the box and more hisses and shrieks poured out. What were they keeping captive in there? One stack of yellow glass lights clattered and rolled across the tabletop.

"Master. They're part of the plan." Gabryella grabbed at the tubes to keep them from smashing on the floor. "Get our foothold in Worley. Take their portal. You travel back to your home and—"

"You have plenty." The Boggleman reached into the box and pulled out a black and yellow fire salamander. The creature, a little larger than the twisted-fingered hand that held him, began to grow. "Oh yes, by all means, grow. You'll plump up my cloak nicely."

The fire salamander shuddered, wisps of smoke curling from its tail. "Please Master, no. Cyndrix be good. Promise. Listen all words of Cromis Boggleman."

The Boggleman's lip twisted into a dark grin. "Oh, you will be good."

No. Aunia didn't want to witness another faery being eaten by the Boggleman's cloak. Her heart seared for the moss gnomes from the birchwoods. For Teezo Popkin who had helped when she'd run away from home. She wanted to look away but she couldn't. That cloak needed to be destroyed.

Her anger from the horribleness of it rolled through her like a dark storm, searing through her body. Vibrating, making Aunia shake. Anger turned to rage, and she hunched into herself. Fear crept in but not in time. The rage exploded past the container of her dreamwalking form and the force of it shoved her backwards. She fell and the wooden divider tumbled over with a clatter and thud.

The Boggleman's cape lowered, and he turned, fire salamander still in his hand.

Aunia raised her fists while Mygul circled her head.

"You can dreamwalk in the mortal world, too?" The Boggleman's grin widened, and he stepped toward her. "How delicious. Not squeezed out like your father thought. But what exactly are you? Potential like Zevara and that little garden faery of yours have been making or . . ."

As if she'd been called, Jennium appeared midair in the center of the room.

"Excellent." The Boggleman's focus left Aunia and centered on her faery friend. "I can ask you directly. Or my cloak can."

The Boggleman's cloak flared around his body.

Jennium darted to Aunia. Zipped by her head. Yanked her hair. Threw a mind picture of Aunia sitting up, yawning, and stretching.

She had to wake up. Biting her lip and near tears, Aunia pinched her own arm.

The Boggleman stepped closer.

Jennium yanked. Aunia pinched.

The edge of the Boggleman's cloak reached for her. Aunia stepped back. And back. Until she hit the wall.

She woke, tangled in a blanket, in the glade. The fire was near dead except for embers. Reina and Basil lay nearby asleep and her poppet lay across her chest. Her poppet that her dad and Nehla had made her. She hugged it against her body and sat up.

Chapter Twenty-Eight
BATTLE AT EDDAC TOWER

And it came to be that during the War between the Worlds that the Eldarghast bit into a mortal and created the first wererat. He also bit into several faeries but humans forgot what they became. — Teachings of the Mystic Court

S inewy wererat bodies, thirty-five Mathias counted in the courtyard, twisted below. Writhed. Hissing and growling. They sprang toward and away from the thirty bear-fur cloaked soldiers. Swords flashed in silver arcs and rang against daggers wielded by rag-wearing humanoid wererats. And unseen by the combatants, close to the tower's shadow and near the kitchen garden, kobolds bounced on clawed feet. Dashed into the fray, short blades gleaming. They predominately attacked Da Vennen soldiers who had their backs to the pegasus tower. The men fell screaming, grasping the backs of their knees.

Keston bespeaks, the Da Vennen are getting what they deserve, Taf sent.

Does he see any of our foot soldiers? Mathias leaned forward, hoping the pressure from the high-bucket saddle lip would ease his stomach.

No. Not foot soldiers nor servants.

Darts whistled through the air. Another soldier went down. And two wererats.

Another Da Vennen cried out. The soldier beside him whirled toward the kobold mob but he did not see the dozen surrounding them. He too screamed. And then his limbs bent in impossible angles.

The kobolds backed away as the soldier's face elongated. Clothes ripped and his cloak fell away as he came down on four legs. He charged the shadows and kobolds scattered.

Mathias leaned back in surprise.

Keston bespeaks if you are seeing that some of the Da Vennen are wererats, Taf sent.

Yes, I am but... One of Basil's wererats told Catiryna that another tribe of wererats belonged to the Da Vennen. Mathias had thought it a lie. Obviously, there was truth in it.

One of the Da Vennen soldiers broke rank and ran at the new wererat. Plunged his sword into its back. The wererat raised onto its back legs in an arc, swiped at the soldier, and fell over with a groan.

Mathias swallowed hard. He was getting his head around the dynamics that there was more than one type of wererat. And while he knew the Da Vennen's agenda, he didn't know what the wererats' motivation was. One side would win. And more forces might come. They needed to call for help.

Remember Brinsaber's warning, Taf sent. *And there are kobolds down there, too.*

I see them. Mathias shut his eyes, not caring that Taf eavesdropped into his more private thoughts. Someone had betrayed them. A flyer.

Another wererat fell, its body blending into the muddy soil. He counted the remaining ones. *Their numbers aren't decreasing.*

There are only ten. The rest are illusions, Taf sent.

Keston and Revellie swung lower, flying over the store house and barracks.

Ten against twenty-three? We can't let the Da Vennen have the upper hand. Mathias rubbed his forehead. A part of him considered bespeaking Fallo to warn him but who knew what information Fallo would reveal to a possible eavesdropper.

We should assume the worst when it comes to Fallo's discrepancy, Taf sent. *And Keston bespeaks. Do we wait this out?*

I should have warned Fallo before we flew off.

Perhaps. But you helped to draw attention away from Aunia. What is your reply to Keston?

I don't know. Protocol says to contact Stanz Tower but that would bring Cat.

Cat would certainly show up to help and afterwards she'd arrest him and Keston. And that would leave Aunia alone with Fallo until he was also arrested.

Keston bespeaks, Taf sent. *Tavish and a few others are lying in the mud. Dead.*

Mathias sought Thuroes' Harp constellation in the southern sky but it had already set. Three of their foot soldiers gone. But where were the rest? And their servants? Elowen, the head stable keeper. Sorrel, the steward. Briar, the cook. *Bespeak Cat. Tell her we need aid.*

I think between Revellie and I, we can sleep them, Taf sent.

But Revellie couldn't sleep anyone in Dalin.

Do you recall the magic item in play there?

Mathias blinked. *The witch compass? They're not that powerful. Unless* …

Two wererats in animal form rushed the soldier's flank while others in humanoid form faced the soldiers' line, waving daggers and throwing rocks. The Da Vennen line split in two. A half-dozen pivoted to become a new line while the first line rushed the humanoid wererats.

I will not bespeak the miles, Taf sent. *Not at this time.*

A Da Vennen soldier in the first line fell with a cry, curling his body around his left leg. Behind him, a kobold scampered off.

Then sleep them. Sleep them all! Including those kobolds.

The kobolds didn't sleep. They did, however, run out of the compound and Mathias lost sight of them. The Da Vennen, after staggering a bit, went down snoring as did the wererats.

The sky lightened into a pre-dawn dimness when Mathias and Keston landed in the blood-spilled mud, swords out. The first step would be to go body-to-body, removing weaponry. They also had to figure out where to put their prisoners. There were two small cells in the tower's basement—too small of a space for two dozen Da Vennens and wererats.

"Too bad we can't just kill them." Keston paused in front of a lean soldier and pulled throwing knives from the loops stitched onto the man's chest bandolier. "They'd do the same to us."

"You don't have the stomach for cold murder," Mathias said. "Neither do I."

"I used to think that." Keston pointed across the compound to the brown-stoned barracks. "But not only did they try to kill me, they killed our own."

"There's three there." Mathias removed two boot daggers from a shorter man and added them to the pile beside Taf and Rev. "But where are the rest of our men?"

"I hope they're fine. We storing this lot in the bull pens?"

Mathias looked up. "That might work."

"Oh, it'll work," Keston said. "Cramped, but no more than these mudcloaks deserve."

A heavy wooden creak drew Mathias' attention across the way to the barracks. Its iron-banded wooden door swung open. Mathias rose, sword in his hand. Men and women filtered into the yard. Many wringing their hands. The servants.

"Masters," Sorrel rubbed at his arm. "They came on us unaware. And we . . . I'm sorry we hid."

Briar, the cook, stepped forward. She reached her calloused hand out and stroked Keston's cheek. "How did you put them all to sleep?"

After a quick glance to Rev, Keston grinned and tugged at his belt with a wink. "Had spelled crystals stitched into me belt, don't ya know. But yeah . . . they're all used up now. Have to visit that hedge witch and see if she'll trade me for some new ones."

"Sorrel, where's the rest of our men?" Mathias wrinkled his nose against a wafting musty orange smell.

"It's Founder's Day at Berrydale. Most of the men have families there. I told them they could go. It's been quiet here . . . until now." Sorrel bowed his head and rubbed his wrist. "It's my fault. I've let you down."

Mathias shook his head. "No one could have known."

Sorrel glanced to his left to their dead men. "The three that stayed . . . they bought our way to safety. Thought the Da Vennen would break their way in but then those wererats and other men came. We were certain our fates would be short-lived."

"Well, your fate now is to help us load these Da Vennen into the bull pens," Mathias said. "They're spelled asleep but who knows how long that'll last."

"Of course." Sorrel snapped his fingers and the other servants scurried forward. "Strip them of weapons and Bario, fetch the cart. We'll haul these bagga-buffoons into the bull pen."

The servants disarmed the men as Sorrel went through their clothing, pocketing small pouches inside his brown wool vest. Probably coinage. Maybe written orders. Mathias planned on asking to see the loot afterwards.

Shortly after the cart arrived, they lifted each Da Vennen onto the short-bedded supply cart and drove off for the cattle barn. The soldiers' boots, hanging out from the cart, bounced with every bump.

After several trips, Sorrel and two older lads stood over a grouping of sleeping wererats with daggers drawn. Eight wererats slept on the ground. Almost the same amount lay dead. The others were either projections or they had fled with the kobolds.

"What are you doing?" Mathias called, trying to project his voice but not too much.

"We don't have resources to imprison these villains." Sorrell drew his dagger away from the wererat's throat. "And they're a plague on all humankind. Look away, young master."

"That's murder." Mathias crossed the yard, stopping an arms-length from the servants.

"Master Habrett," Sorrel said, addressing Mathias by his last name. "They're not human."

"Don't." Mathias raised his hand in a command. *Taf? I could use backup.*

Sorrel stood and both he and the lads lowered their daggers. They did not put them away.

Taf stamped a foot before walking over from the pile of Da Vennen weaponry. *These seem to be the same as the wererats that helped us on the Grashbear.*

Mathias swiveled. *Dalin, too?*

That I don't know.

Of course, Taf didn't. He hadn't been in Dalin during the attack.

The sun peeked over the horizon, bringing better light. Mathias could see the resemblance to the slighter build wererat atop the Grashbear. *Yes. This one helped Keston.*

Mathias turned back to Sorrel. "We'll take this one—all of them—to the cells in the tower's basement."

"You cannot be offering us such insult," Sorrel said stiffly. "We bled for you and you're taking in one of these?"

"Yes, you heard me right. There's information we can get from them."

"Master," Sorrel protested.

Mathias ran a hand through his hair. These servants had been through an awful scare. He hated to make heavy with his station, but he also couldn't allow these wererats to be killed. A strange development seeing that he hated wererats, but he was also indebted to them thrice. "Sorrel. I mean what I say."

The lads looked back and forth between themselves as if they didn't know what to do but Sorrel stepped back. "Then I regret . . . I cannot serve while they are here."

"That is your choice." Mathias held out his hand. "But I'll need the pouches you took off the Da Vennen soldiers."

Sorrel took another step backwards.

"Sorrel," Mathias stepped forward and caught a stronger whiff from that musty orange smell. It smelled like the cologne Arch Vicar Bibb wore. "That is not a request."

Sorrel turned to flee, but Keston stepped in the way, sword tip inches from the man's chest. "I'd do what he asked."

Sorrel knocked Keston's blade aside at the same time Mathias pulled his dagger from his belt. He slammed the pommeled hilt at the back of Sorrel's head and the man went down. The lads ran. The other servants stopped working, watching Mathias and Keston with stunned amazement.

"Check his wrist," Keston said.

Mathias nodded and pulled Sorrel's sleeve back. A Da Vennen figure eight tattoo with a dividing line, nearly scored, marred their steward's wrist. He turned to the remaining servants. "You are all dismissed. Get out. Get out now!"

The only servant that hesitated was Briar. She shook her graying blonde hair and with a hurt expression, followed the others out.

"We need to barricade ourselves in the tower after we take this one wererat," Mathias said as he went through Sorrel's pockets. One pouch felt weighty but not with coins.

"Barricade for how long?"

CHAPTER TWENTY-NINE
SCORCHED EARTH

It's been at least three months since they discovered land which will always burn. It does not impede our holdings. And it is more than time for Fallo to return to his happy gambling self. — Drake Vrael, Lord of Vraelfork, brother of Fallo Vrael

Aunia folded her body around the poppet and rocked until her heart slowed and the birds sang at dawn's light. The Boggleman was indeed here on the mortal side of the worlds and with his cloak. And now . . . did she need to be afraid of sleeping? But being awake wasn't much better. He had plotted to capture her with whisperers.

She shivered at the memory of his scarred face and his ominous grin when he said, 'Not squeezed out like your father thought.' What did that even mean?

She sucked in a slow, even breath. Traveling with Mathias to Tamore, she had decided that her mother must have been like Olivia. And that would have made Aunia similar to Gaitha, the village's magically powerful Eldest Daughter. But now, Aunia considered that she could be wrong. Maybe the Boggleman only chased after her mother to get her amulet. An idea hovered just out of reach but she couldn't touch it.

She frowned, wondering what he meant when he said, 'a potential like Zevara and that little garden faery of yours have been making.' Aunia sat up, glancing about for Jennium. She wanted to throw a mind-picture at her and ask but the faery had disappeared. She was disappointed yet also not. Talking wasn't something she wanted to do either. She felt so alone but she was also grateful that Reina and Basil still slept and near the fire.

Obviously, if her dreamwalking was real, then so was seeing Basil talk to his sister via Taya's silver card. Aunia had questions to ask Basil, but they'd keep for now. If anything, what she wanted was to feel Mathias' arms wrap around her and hold her tight, like he had at the ruins the day he had kissed her.

Her cheeks heated and then her stomach sank. He had pulled away after that . . . but only for a little while . . . and he had tried to protect her in Dalin.

Aunia rubbed at the poppet's button eyes. Zevara was the Lady of the Pavari Faery Court, the court of air and spring. Why would she have anything to do with making someone like Olivia? And how? Could it be something her father contemplated during his hours of research when she wasn't allowed to touch his star book?

Aunia blinked. She had her dad's star book in her knapsack. And he certainly wasn't here to forbid her from looking at it. She leaned toward its open flap and yanked it over. A moment later, she had the blue leather book in her lap, flipping through crackling pages.

She scooted to a growing patch of morning light and frowned. Many of these pages were written in a language she didn't understand, though she recognized her dad's large loopy handwriting. She turned to another page, and a keening lodged in the back of her throat. A black memory.

It's been almost thirteen years, my darling, and there's an-
other who would take my heart. I don't think she understands
that a heart cannot be given when a heart never was given
back. I miss you. I will miss you until my dying day.

Thirteen years ago, Nehla had gone on a boar hunt with her father to gain the annual boar-tusk wish allowing for a second joining. She would have officially gained Limi's mom as her own. But there had been an accident and Nehla had died saving her dad. Because her dad refused to kill anything. And he had let her own mother die as well. Those were the words that Fallo gave when he and the flyers arrived in her village. She always knew without being told that her father never loved Nehla but to write this before he took that hunting jaunt . . .

They both could have stayed in the village, forgoing the ruse, and Nehla would be alive. Did her father even deserve to be rescued from Nonderu? Aunia balled her fists and then, her shoulders drooped. Did she deserve to make that choice?

Aunia continued scanning down the page, hoping to read her mother's name. It wasn't there.

She flipped the page, and the next one. Surely her father must have written something about why the Boggleman had been after her mother and why he was now after her. She paused at another page, running a finger over his uneven lettering.

Chandarions are imbued with almost limitless power. Some-
thing Olivia did not have. But if she would've had this
amulet, the one that the mission from the ocean gave me, I
am confident that the Boggleman would not have abducted
her.

Aunia stirred uneasily. She had heard that phrase before, mission from the ocean, but she couldn't place it. Shaking her head, she continued reading.

Such an enormous help with connecting magics that my faery familiar cannot or will not do. Simply by holding onto the amulet's fingers, I've been able to see images from a person's past. Quite handy since I need to sift out the truth to find the Darra Chamber.

Images from a person's past?

Basil mumbled something, drawing Aunia's attention with a sharp jolt. He rolled over. Sleeping. How long would he and Reina sleep?

Aunia returned to the book and Jennium blinked, appearing in front of her face. Aunia jumped and her fingers slid. She lost her placement on the page and nearly dropped the book. "Jennium," she growled.

Aunia tried shuffling back to where she had been but the faery halted Aunia's page flipping, by hovering over a densely written page. The lettering was a lot smaller and some of the ink was smeared. She leaned forward, squinting.

Finding and releasing Olivia will restart the flow of the seven. I am certain Edvaras knew this. The story about the star-charts is only meant to discover where the missing Nymers went. And they will be needed before the end.

Olivia. A potential. Aunia bit her lip. "Jennium, the Boggleman said you and Zevara are making potentials. Like Olivia. How?"

Jennium jingled and projected an image of soot and ash.

"Yes, the fire is almost out but . . ." Aunia sat up. The burning smell, acrid and charred, wasn't coming from the campfire. She swiveled to face the clearing behind her. The clearing Basil made mention was dangerous to go.

Jennium threw another mind-picture, one where Aunia walked to the forbidden clearing and her parents stood beside it. They looked to be her own age . . . like they had when she had a vision of them in the Birchwoods. Her mother was so beautiful.

Aunia's breath caught. "Basil says it's dangerous there."

Jennium rose, circling around Aunia's head, and then darted toward the clearing.

Her parents lost themselves there and there were answers she'd be able to find. Aunia stood and walked to the clearing. She needed to know more.

The reek of lightning and smoke became stronger, and the amulet under her clothing warmed against her skin. Aunia dipped her hand under her torn blouse and gripped the milky-white stone.

Ash, oak, and black walnut trees grew closer together as she walked and the boughs spread out like a natural archway. Taking a deep breath, she hurried forward and halted. The clearing ahead—if it was a clearing—was full of dense gray fog. There was a hazy flickering as well. It looked as if things were ready to emerge from the murk. Aunia stepped backwards.

A ghostly form, a woman, stepped out of the mist, in various shades of gray. Her eyes, a light-color, were wide as if she were in shock. She lifted her hand imploringly.

The amulet could play the past. This had to be the past, didn't it? A memory? Or was it a haunting? Aunia swallowed hard. "If you're real. Show me. Show me what happened."

The ghost-woman disappeared, but the fog grew thinner. There was a figure within it . . . a male figure, holding a baby. He looked like he was arguing with . . . the woman who had just greeted Aunia but no words reached Aunia's ears.

At the man's feet lay a little girl, unmoving in the grass.

Was this her father? The woman who greeted her . . . had that been her mother? And who was the girl in the grass?

Without thinking, Aunia stepped inside the murk and the wash of sound cascaded over her.

"What were you thinking?" the woman yelled over the wailing baby in the man's arms. "You've broken every rule of hospitality there is and—"

"I had to," a younger version of her dad said as he shifted and bounced to calm the infant. "It's for our daughter."

"There has to be another way!" her mother screamed.

The baby. Aunia blinked. That had to be her.

"What way is there, Leia?"

The wind picked up, swirling the woman's long, thick hair around her head and a crack of lightning flashed.

"Run," Leia, Aunia's mom cried. "He's found us."

And like the time in the Birchwoods, the Boggleman stepped out from a glimmering, a hole, in the air.

Aunia stepped backwards, hand at her throat. He had two eyes. Not one with an empty eye socket. It was the same smirk, though, that he gave her father, and he waved his twisted fingers in a 'come-hither' motion. Her dad raised his hand and pulled his fist violently down. Lightning struck a foot away from the Boggleman.

Her dad ran at her mother, threw the crying baby into her arms, and yanked a curved knife from his belt. The Boggleman pivoted to her mother, pushing a hand out, and a gale of wind smacked at her father. It should have been strong enough to make Aunia's hair fly. It did not. But it did push her father back.

Her mother, baby held tightly against her body and one hand out, cried, "I command you to desist. Return to the underside from where you belong."

The Boggleman laughed and her father launched himself forward. The tip of his knife caught the Boggleman in the eye and trailed across his face. The Boggleman screamed and punched.

Her father fell onto the ground, tucked and rolled to his feet.

The Boggleman was hunched over, holding onto his face.

Her dad waved Leia to him. Took the baby. "Take my hand."

Another gust of wind struck the couple.

Her dad clenched his fist as if he would pull down another bolt of lightning. The Boggleman made the same gesture at the same time. Lightning flared, striking the ground where he stood with the baby. Dad and baby disappeared, leaving a pile of ash behind.

Her mother screamed and fire caught in the clearing with a fierce roar.

"I see her," said another voice. One that was outside the clearing. "She's here."

Another burst of fire filled the clearing and Aunia closed her eyes against her mother's final scream.

Her father had tried to save her mother. He must have . . . Aunia swallowed hard. Rocked on her feet. He must have skipped away. Just him and baby her. But he could have . . . he could have just skipped a bit . . .just skipped to her mother and all three of them away.

Her lips quavered. She kept rocking. Only dimly aware that the fog had vanished. Ash and soot covered the forest floor here while blackened and skeletal trees twisted in charcoal heaps.

In the center of the clearing stood a man-high monument stone with four smooth sides tapering to a point. Her mother's stone.

Chapter Thirty
THE UNFINISHED LETTER

All life is a cycle of beginnings, middles, and endings. We've all been taught this but perhaps they are not as cyclical as we've been led to believe. In the most simplistic form, the unfinished can lead to a new beginning or a speedy end. —
Dar Syrick of Tatia, advisor to the queen

Hauling the injured wererat down the last stone steps with Mathias, Keston panted, "How can someone so thin . . . be so heavy?"

"Not as heavy as Sorrel." Mathias readjusted his grip under the young wererat's muddy arms and shoulders. He was a thin lad with a scrawny light brown beard. Probably wasn't even as old as they were. They stepped down onto the grease-marked stone basement floor. "Come on. We're almost to the cell. Watch your head."

They turned from their low-ceiling kitchen with its large open hearth and a roughly hewn butcher's block to an open door, thick oak and iron-bound. Not a pantry, but a small prison with two holding cells, each about ten by six feet with a narrow cot and two buckets a piece inside.

They went to the cell with the open iron-bar door and laid the wererat onto the bedding. Sorrel, still unconscious, lay on his side, head close to the cot's edge and a strand of drool forming at the corner of his mouth.

Mathias felt the side of the lad's neck, grateful to feel a steady pulse, then felt the lump at the back of the head. Someone had thumped this wererat good. Odd. Now he was standing up for wererats. His father would believe he'd taken leave of his wits.

"If you want," Keston rubbed his hands against his pants. "We could get maybe two more in . . . a piece . . . though Sorrel will complain."

Mathias frowned and looked at the floor. Would it be worth going outside once more?

"And we're going to have to take care of them, and our Da Vennen prisoners. Won't the Arch Vicar be stabbing his plate when he hears this, eh?"

Mathias looked up. "Then they shouldn't have attacked us."

"Just saying, maybe you shouldn't have dismissed all our servants."

"You wanted to decide which ones we could trust?"

"The cook. I would've trusted the cook." Keston lowered his folded arms. "Matty, we're going to need help. We should bespeak Fallo and—"

"Stop," Mathias interrupted. He stepped out of the cell and after Keston exited, he closed its door and locked it. They were up the basement stairs, past the armory, and into the great hall. "There are several problems with bespeaking Fallo."

"I know the warning from Brinsaber."

"That's only the first thing."

Keston stopped. "You fear that Fallo's trying to overthrow Nyrissa's chance of replacing her father as Dar?"

Mathias slowed. He had almost forgotten about Fallo's failed attempt to meet up with other tower commanders and show them the way back to Aunia's village. He was after the Chand crystal that Naoma Sacella's wall was made from. And the reason why the village had shrouded themselves with magical invisibility. "Fallo's consorting with whisperers and their summoners. I saw him. He's plotting something . . . something to do with the marble from our moving giant. And Emmet's involved somehow, too."

Keston frowned. "It could be for our own good."

"Whisperers? Yes, they allow messaging for over miles, but they are evil. Evil waiting for a chance to strike. That lesson should have been learned if it has not . . . I cannot—will not—believe it's for good."

"And you think us leaving Dalin when that cloud of whisperers came . . ." Keston furrowed his brow. "Matty, I don't think Fallo has the brain-strength to control an entire whisperer cloud. A fae creature maybe. Or a fireling."

"Fireling?" The last thing they needed was that Adarian magical cult involved. They'd been banned from Tamore before Mathias had been born. Part of Dar Syrick's border spell had been fashioned to keep them from entering their lands. Or it had. The battle over the Grashbear with the wyverns had weakened it. Mathias hoped Cat had communicated that through the proper channels so the Queen would know. Mathias doubted that Fallo had.

They stepped outside into the yard.

"You don't think Fallo was talking to a fireling," Keston questioned, "do you?"

Mathias gripped his sword hilt. "There are fewer bodies out here."

The wererats woke and scattered, Taf sent.

Mathias repeated Taf's words while both pegasi flew down from the top of the barracks' roof.

"Then we're done hauling the living." Keston crossed the few steps to Rev and patted her golden neck. "We just have the dead to consider."

Mathias ran a hand through his hair. Tavish. Cyril. Oswald. The Da Vennen bodies and wererats. But he saw no kobolds.

They had no death. And no kobolds succumbed to our sleep spell, Taf sent.

Mathias nodded. "We'll bury our men and then the others after we've got Taf and Rev settled. And after we've had a sleep. In shifts."

Rev bespeaks. Taf threw his head back with a whinny. *She wants Keston to take first sleep to help him heal.*

Rev was a fine pegasus with great intuitive instinct, but unlike Taf, she nor any other pegasus could heal their flyers as fast. "I'll take first watch," Mathias said.

They went back inside, shut the tower's front door, thick oak banded with iron, and dropped the crossbar in place. Neither of them spoke while they crossed the main hall with its long hanging tapestries.

Mathias frowned at the one nearest to the cavernous and cold central hearth. It depicted the first Mockmen troll wars with dozens of pegasi flyers wheeling over the Grashbear and shooting arrows at Mockmen trolls who attacked the gray-stone city of Idenweigh. All the glory of battle with no dead littering the ground like what was outside their door. The real thing was so much different than glorified stories. Even the aftermath was different. Without all the servants and foot soldiers bantering and bustling over the flagstone floors, the tower felt and sounded desolate and hollow . . . like the crypt where Zeller lay.

They passed the metal door leading into the armory and continued toward the back of the tower.

"Mathias, whether you trust him or not, Fallo's going to need to know our tower's been compromised." Keston ducked through the arch within the circular interior wall and climbed the clockwise stone staircase which encircled the tower's main chimney and hearth. "And we should be prepared on what you'll think he'll have us do."

Mathias followed with a frown. "He wanted to make faery repellant. Thinks it'll help get us out of our bind."

Keston paused on the steps and turned. "We're going to grow it here? How long is its season and—"

"It's not really safe here, is it?" Mathias pushed past Keston, stomping up the stairs until he reached the third landing and exited through a side arch into a curved hallway. The storage door holding pegasi feed and water was immediately on his right at the southwest while the dorm room door where he, Keston, and Jules bunked was to the left and more toward the south.

He marched down the hallway and flung open the oak door with its blackened iron hinges into their dorm room. So much had changed since he had been here last. He stepped inside, cringing at the unfinished letter laying on his bed, one he had been writing before Jules and Keston talked him into going to Britchway for the Besmarion festival.

He crossed the room and pulled his feather-stuffed pillow over the letter a bare moment before Keston stepped into the room. One of the two windows, which allowed natural light within, had its shutters wide-open. Not exactly the wisest course. That entry point could have been breached if the Da Vennen had had grappling hooks. But, until today, Mathias had always felt secure that this tower and its compound would never be compromised. Mathias shut and latched the window, plunging the cheery room into gloom.

He moved away from the six beds in the dorm room to the westerly door and the pegasi stable. Stepping inside the spacious stable with its familiar hay scent and open-door stalls drew another pang within Mathias' chest. Would they ever be able to bring Brinsaber home?

Keston's footfalls sounded behind him, a padding slow gait as Mathias crossed the stable to the double barn doors, reddish-brown elm, a lighter wood than oak, but still fastened with thick iron hinges. He pulled the first door open, then the second.

"I'll grab fresh feed," Keston said from inside Revellie's stall, the middle one on the left-hand side.

"I'll handle the water."

Tafiriel, and then Revellie flew inside the stable as Mathias and Keston stepped into the adjoining storeroom. Mathias grabbed a bucket and crossed to the gravity-fed watering pipes. He twisted a copper valve and water rushed into the pail. It didn't take long to get the pegasi situated and to close the barn doors. Taf and Rev would probably get a good snooze, along with Keston—and he'd have time to contemplate.

"Keston, go get some sleep," Mathias said as they re-entered the dorm.

"You'll be able to stay awake?"

"I'll have plenty to do."

Keston nodded and walked over to his bunk, the closest to the window. "You know if it isn't safe here, there's always the greenhouses at Worley."

He didn't wait for Mathias' reply but fell onto his bed, without bothering with any covers. He was asleep in no time.

Worley. Mathias had considered that city before. The lord was friendly to his father. Mathias shut his eyes. And a big mouth when it came to talking with his father. One suspicious phrase that made Lyle think Mathias wasn't participating in the suitor games and he'd inform his father. Mathias returned to his bed, the one closest to the door, and grabbed the letter from under the pillow. He didn't bother reading it. It more than likely started with 'My dearest Keira, how much I miss you,' or something like that.

Instead, he folded the paper into quarters and stashed it in his footlocker with several other letters. Everything had changed with him deciding not to finish the letter but if he had stayed instead of going to the festival . . . something worse would have happened.

Mathias sat down. Keston nor Jules could be blamed for what happened. They had been their own jovial selves. They didn't cause Britchway to be burned down. And how could they know some wererats were evil, like the ones at the Bellows. Mathias clenched a fist. And others had provided them aid. He hoped to get answers from their captive wererat. Get answers too of why Sorrel had betrayed them.

He crossed the room and took a seat at one of the desks which had a small bookcase beside it and let his mind wander. Of course, led him back to Aunia. Everything came back to Aunia. What was he going to do with her? He was not the best one to provide her with protection. Who knew how long he'd be free.

You're a flyer of a wild one. You really think they're going to put you in jail? Taf sent sleepily.

They could. And where would that leave you?

If they're stupid enough to do that, I'd fly you away.

That pulled a smile from the corners of Mathias' mouth. It was extremely unlikely they'd try to shoot them down. The smile fell. But where could he take Aunia if that happened? Or even if the worst didn't occur? Her magic. Her magic was dangerous. Lethal. He began to understand why Gaitha had that tattle-book . . . why those villagers had been so afraid of her. *I'm not sure where you could take us where she'd be safe.*

The most important thing right now is for her to be found.

Agreed.

After a few more minutes stewing in his own pessimism, Mathias stood and stretched. The pouches Sorrel had taken from the Da Vennen . . . that thought sent Mathias from the dorm room back down to the ground floor to a small table in the great hall where he had tossed them while they carted Sorrel and the wererat into the basement cells.

He collected them, ten in total, and carried the rough-spun and leather pouches into the dining hall where the pegasi flyers, servants and soldiers would all join for a meal. He took a seat at his usual spot at the smaller head table at the back of the room, second seat on the right from Fallo's carved cherry-wood chair.

Sorrel. Mathias shook his head and dumped out the first pouch. A handful of copper coins softly clanged against the tabletop. He had only known the tower's steward for almost six months, since he accepted banishment and journeyed with Fallo to Eddac. But Sorrel had always given the appearance of being utterly devoted to the flyers.

More coins dropped out of the second pouch. And maybe Sorrel had been. The tattoo on the man's wrist was new. Mathias lifted and shook several of the pouches. He paused at a weighty one that made a strange tinkling rattle, non-coin-like. Mathias dumped the contents on the table and then pushed his chair back.

Portal tiles. The Da Vennen had the makings of creating a transportation pad for traveling over miles like the transportation room in Tatia. Like many of the lords and ladies once had, but they had been confiscated after the king-consort's rebellion. How could Da Vennen be in possession of portal tiles? Not just because they'd be hard to come by, but they were magic. Da Vennen hated magic, but then Bibb had that witch compass.

Mathias ran a hand through his wavy, dark hair. Riddling out what the Da Vennen were truly up to . . . taking care of prisoners . . . waiting to see if Aunia arrived safely. And needing to bury the dead before she got there. An old ditty crept into Mathias' head:

> *When ghouls emerge from shadows*
> *deep*
> *And in the night, through graves they*
> *creep*
> *The world itself begins to weep*
> *For time has come a world must*

sleep.

A sleep that never wakes.

Ghouls. They were another sign of the augury coming forth. But no one had seen any ghouls. Why was he thinking this stuff? Mathias stood up. He was tired. Hungry. Frustrated and angry. Of course he'd be thinking every dark thought. He needed to keep himself busy, and if he couldn't sleep, then maybe that wererat shouldn't be able to either.

Mathias headed toward the basement.

CHAPTER THIRTY-ONE

MEMORIAL STONE AND NARVIS

Some will say a broken heart is an honest heart and we are strong in broken places but not all bends in the road lead to good places. — Mollie Mae, estranged wife of Tharon Mensani

Jennium, her silky yellow dress swirling about her, landed on the blue-gray memorial stone with a soft jingle.

A keening lodged in Aunia's throat. Where my mother died. Where my parents lost themselves. She pinned her shoulders back and strode through piles of charred ash—powdery with chunks of splintery wood pressing on her feet.

Where my dad left my mother . . . because of the Boggleman. She kept her gaze fixed on the man-high object, easier to see than the patch of ground where her mother had screamed.

My dad skipped away. He took me to live a life in Naoma Sacella and he didn't talk about her mother because he was ashamed. He had left her to face her doom alone as Fallo had said. But what choice did he have? If he hadn't skipped, both she and her father would have been seared with lightning. And her mother would still be dead. Unless . . .

Aunia slowed her pace. The stone, square in width and appearing blurry, stood only a few steps now. If her father would have thought to have skipped to her mother's side and then skip all of them away. . . And there was a little girl, too. Asleep? Dead? Aunia wasn't sure.

"Jennium. This is . . . this is horrible." Aunia covered her broken voice with a hand over her mouth.

"The stone . . . is for your mother," Basil's voice came from the mouth of the clearing. "You're safe to see it for now but if the fog comes back . . ."

Aunia took that final step. Raised her hand. Fingertips dipping into crevices that made up etched but worn words. She curled her bare toes into the ground, and then her knees folded. They struck the ground, surprisingly damp, moisture soaking into her rover skirt. She shivered.

> *Magia Sequarie 22, 1050*
> *For my Leia*
> *Love's sweet truth I sought to find*
> *relinquishing our heart to shudder*
> *— — — — —duty*
> *sought you back again*
> *and tore your life asund—*
> *Ash and scorch were what I found*
> *when I come to rescue thee*
> *Others laid a claim too broad*
> *— —death forsaking me*

"Sir Nicolas Mimsey. Third century, I believe," Basil readjusted his orange bandana on his head. "Though some of the lines are changed."

"I . . . I can't make out all the . . ." A jagged well filled her throat. Made it nearly impossible to breathe. She stared at the date. Reread the words she could make out. Lingered on her mother's name. She reached up and caressed the grooves from the lettering. 'Love's sweet truth I sought to find.'

Sweet words could not make up for leaving her behind.

And then, realization slapped Aunia's cheeks with heat. This was not her father who had left the memorial stone. Not unless he came back. She punched her own thigh with the side of her fist. She turned her head toward Basil. "Why was the Boggleman after us?"

"At first, it's because he knew your da was looking to call the other Chandarions into the world and restart the augury. The Boggleman doesn't want that. He's been working on having the choice be Endynia, the Faery world."

Aunia shook her head. "There's something more."

"You," Basil started, "You were born in the Faery world. It gave you a magic that can't be explained. And it's why, dear Aunia, you must take on your father's quest."

The Boggleman, not her father, had killed her mother. She could see her dad in her mind's eye. Light brown eyes and wayward dark hair. Smiling with a fish on his fishing line. Stooped over and repairing a book. Drinking apple beer 'til he couldn't walk straight. She could feel his gentle hands brushing the snarls from her hair. Stroking her forehead to chase nightmares away. And he had left her mother to die.

Aunia leaned her forehead against the cool stone to steady herself.

"Aunia," Basil called. "Maybe you should come back."

"Just . . . stop." She turned her head so he wouldn't see the tears swimming in her eyes. He had let her mother die and Fallo came and set up this memorial stone. Who else could have done it?

"Aunia, please." Basil's voice sounded sharp. "You've a bit of a Chandarion's nymer about you. And where you stand, it's a place tainted with strong feeling and evil intent. You must come back from the clearing."

Around her, wisps of mist rose from the stone's base and she felt anger bubble inside her chest. "My father let her die."

"Your father tried to do right. You can succeed in doing right. But right and wrong sometimes look the same. Your father tried to do a spell. One he shouldn't have. It attracted the Boggleman and bad things happened . . . but you can make it right. All you need do is take on your father's quest. You want to go to Tatia, anyway. Come out. We'll talk about how to find the Darra Chamber. Free Olivia from Nonderu and—"

Aunia pulled her attention from the memorial stone to Basil's swarthy-skinned face. "I didn't tell you that Olivia was in Nonderu." But she had told Taya.

"Your father told me he had seen her when you were a babe. That Edvaras and Naoma are there, too."

Aunia leaned her head against her mother's stone. Inside she was screaming. Couldn't Basil see she was standing in front of her mother's . . . Her mother lived. Had. But no more. And instead of kindness, she was being told what to do.

"Aunia, I . . . will help you."

Basil needed to stop talking. It was making her head roar. She dropped her forehead into her hand, trying to press away the memories which poured out. Fallo talking to her nicely before discovering her father was there in the stable. The sword being drawn. The accusations. Fallo had recognized that Aunia looked like her mother. Knew it because he knew her mother. Loved her mother. "I can't trust any of you."

"Trust?" Reina's high-pitched voice carried. The girl appeared at Basil's side, and lunged forward, only to have Basil grab her by the shoulder. "Your parents protected you. Even if they died, they protected you. Mine just died and left me all alone."

Aunia rose to her feet, shaking.

"Reina, perhaps you should be quiet." Basil murmured. "Aunia please. Come back to us."

Whiffs of fog threads floated up to chest level, which shook Aunia. They reminded her too much of the Boggleman's veil tendrils. Aunia shuffled across the clearing and stepped back onto the hard-packed dirt.

She held herself stiffly. Getting to Tatia and rescuing her dad. These were all things that she wanted to do. She tightened her jaw. What she wanted to do right now was to find a quiet spot in the wilderness, throw herself on the ground and cry but she couldn't. She clenched her fists. "How soon until Mathias gets here?"

"Mathias?" Basil wrung his hands. "He's making sure Eddac Tower is safe. Fallo is on his way to collect you."

"He left me to be picked up by Fallo?" She turned her back on Basil and stormed to her sleeping area. Mathias left her. How could he? She slammed the book back into her knapsack and buckled the flap. Well, if he could leave her alone to her own defenses then she could get to Tatia all by herself. She jumped to Dalin after all. The amulet would provide her with the power she needed. She scooped up her cloak.

"Fallo is going to take you straight to Eddac Tower. You'll have time to freshen up before they decide where to take you. Or you could come with me. I'm taking Reina to Q'thonos first and then—"

"I don't need any of you." Aunia sucked in a breath, embracing the pinching in her temples, and grabbed the amulet stone from under her rover blouse. Mathias' face surfaced in her mind and she shoved it down with a shuddered sob. He had abandoned her and she could get herself to Tatia on her own.

Jennium jingled from somewhere and Basil's eyes widened. He hurried forward. "Aunia, we all need each—"

He disappeared. Everything disappeared. And she was encased in velvety black . . .

Until the sky beat on her with brilliant blue and the ground raced toward her.

She landed with an oomph in the tall grass and laid still for a long moment while pain pulsed through her body. And then there was nothing.

Warbles and trills mixed with chattering chirps and the rustling of grass drew her consciousness back and Aunia groaned. The western sun was lowering toward a hill with a gray pillar peeking out from over distant trees. She shook her head. Obviously, she was not in Tatia with its gleaming white castle, silvery stone walkways and gardens, nor its cloud-top surfaces. That was where she had wanted to go.

A piece of switch grass tickled her nose, and she sat up. There was nothing around and she had no idea where she was.

The thought of her mother dead surfaced again as Aunia touched the dried tears on her cheeks. This was an old hurt. She knew her mother was dead. This was only confirmation. And she'd be dead next if she didn't pull herself together. If only it had been Mathias who had come to fetch her. She had been so angry at the thought of Fallo. She pushed his bristled bearded face out of her head and pulled her bent legs against her body so she could rest her chin on her knees. A broken sob escaped her, and she wrapped her arms around herself. She wanted to be alone so she could cry. And cry she did.

Her father had skipped her away and all this time she had thought it had been her mother who gave her magical ability. That her mother had been a potential Chandarion. But she wasn't. It was her father with the magic. And he had performed a spell that attracted the Boggleman's attention. But what spell? She sniffled. It could have been to save that young girl that had been lying on the ground but . . . she would have also died when her mother did.

Did her dad really deserve to be rescued? Mad at him or not, her father was her father. She could save him and then make him go back to fulfilling this stupid quest of saving both worlds. And she could find Mathias and they could find a place where they could live. Maybe just the two of them in a little house. Maybe by a creek and a meadow. She closed her eyes. She needed to get to Tatia . . . alone , or find Mathias. And how would she do either?

She didn't see any faeries about. She chewed on her bottom lip. And she wasn't sure she could even trust them anymore. Who knew which faeries were allies to the Boggleman?

"Nia girl sad," said a crackly sing-song voice.

Aunia skittered back on her knees. "Narvis."

The fire salamander, waist-high and bipedal, with yellow and gray markings, long claws and a lizard-like chin shot her a closed-mouth smile.

"What are you doing here, Narvis?"

"Escaped from Cromis Boggleman I did."

Shivers crept along the backs of Aunia's arms. She had no doubt anymore that she had dreamwalked to where the Boggleman was. And she was relieved that Jennium helped bring her back before that cloak of his tried to suck her in.

"He's not in Nonderu."

Narvis' gaze lowered. "Agreed. Not in Nonderu."

"Where is he, Narvis?"

"With fireling."

"Fireling? What . . . who are they?"

"They bad. Capture Narvis kin. Put in stone box then put in glass tubes. Maybe Narvis, too. Poor, poor Narvis."

Aunia's chest tightened with the thought of stacks of glass tubes on the desk and how the woman, Gabryella, put a stone lid on the box while cries emerged. And the Boggleman . . . Aunia closed her eyes. He planned on having his cloak eat some of those fire salamanders. That cloak of his . . . it needed to be destroyed.

"I'm glad you escaped, Narvis." Aunia stood up. "Maybe you can help me."

"Help? Help how?"

"I need to—" Aunia paused. Did she need to find Mathias or just go to Tatia? Her stomach rolled at the thought of going alone. Didn't Fallo say the Queen was mad? Sooner to behead her than to help. She shook her head. He was only saying that to scare her. And it was working. But Mathias came from there. He'd be able to help her. And Basil said he went to Eddac Tower to make it safe for her arrival. Stupid excuse. Why wouldn't it be safe?

"I need to know what is around me. I can't stay here in the middle of nowhere."

"How you get here?" Narvis asked.

Aunia curled her fists. "I tried to skip."

"You wanted skip here?"

"No, I didn't want to skip here. I wanted to skip to Tatia."

"You only think of Tatia. One-thing. Yes?"

One-thing? She had not been thinking of only one thing. She was thinking about her mother. And Fallo. And Basil's yammering. And the pinching in her temples and if she hadn't skipped when she did . . . "I may have erred."

"Travel by rocks." Narvis pointed to the stone outcropping.

"What?"

"Mortal not know? Outcropping spell like mountain blade-cave."

Aunia frowned. The outcropping of rocks were just rocks. A jingle above Aunia's head brought her awareness to Jennium circling around her head. "Where have you been?"

Narvis leaped into the air, claws out, and Jennium danced back from the fire salamander.

"What are you doing?" Aunia barked.

"Get her." Narvis pointed to Jennium. "She traitor. Bring her to Cromis Boggleman and Cromis Boggleman forgive. Forgive Narvis. Forgive Narvis kin."

CHAPTER THIRTY-TWO

DEATH DUTY ON TURNIPS

Death cannot be fooled simply because you've carved a face in a turnip. — Wendalin Mensani, apprentice dar to Dar Syrick

"Hey, you. Wererat," Mathias poked a broom through the iron bars and skimmed the straw bristles against the lad's short-bearded face. "Wake up."

The lad rolled over on the narrow cot, throwing an arm over his head.

Mathias nudged him again with the broom.

"Jovaryn," he said groggily and waved away the bristles.

"Guess again." Mathias pulled the broom back and leaned it against the stone brick wall. "I need some questions answered."

The wererat sat up, set his ragged shoes onto the stone floor and hung his head over his knees for a long moment. "Am I your prisoner?"

"My guest but . . ." The candle flame sputtered in the wall sconce near the door as Mathias pulled a short stool from the jail room corner. He set it in front of the cell. "I'm not really sure if you're friend or foe."

The wererat stood up, walked to the other side of the cell and peered into the neighboring cell. "I see I get the same accommodations as your servant. This must be the nice dungeon."

"What do you know about my servant?"

The wererat touched the side of his head with a wince, straightened, and took the three steps back to his cot. He sat down. "I know he hid Da Vennen soldiers in your storerooms before he talked most of your garrison into leaving for your nearby village. Tried to talk to some of the servants too but most of them seemed to know their place here. I'm Ryver, by the way."

"Ryver?" Mathias knotted his fists. Sorrel's betrayal was like a punch in the gut. "Why did you come here?"

"Well, it wasn't to be captured for my trouble, that's for sure. But Basil's been wanting us to keep you and yours safe since you protect the girl."

"And you knew the Da Vennen were coming? Saw them hiding? Knew my servant had been turned?"

Ryver held up a hand. "Knowing they were coming was last minute. And I happen to be my company's scout. That's why I saw what I saw. I know how to keep my head down. Unless I get kicked in it, of course. You got any water?"

"I do. And I'll get you some after our chat."

Ryver leaned back against the wall. "Then please. Ask away."

Mathias tightened his jaw, pulled the heavy Da Vennen pouch from his jerkin's inside pocket, and poured portal tiles into his hand. They glowed with a faint iridescent hue. "Maybe you know why the Da Vennen might have these."

Ryver walked over to the bars. Mathias shuffled his seat back.

"Portal tiles. Was wondering how they were traveling so fast." Ryver shook his head. "I can tell you the dynamics of the soldier religion certainly have changed."

"What do you know?"

"How do I tell you this . . ." Ryver leaned his head against the bars. "It's not something believable, and yet it's true."

"Just spit it out."

Ryver gripped the bars. "Bibb is in the business of making wererats."

Mathias slowly placed each portal tile, one by one back in the pouch. How could a Da Vennen—the leader of the Da Vennen—be in league with wererats?

"How do you think I became a wererat? I was minding my own business learning a craft when the Da Vennens came along to recruit. I knew to keep my head down but Bibb, he has this witch compass that can pinpoint any faeblood and it pointed me out."

"That's a lie," another voice, crisp and mid-tone, sounded. Sorrel struggled to his feet from the neighboring cot and shivered.

"You can hold your tongue until I give you leave to talk," Mathias growled. It made him angry to think of all the bits of advice he asked from this betrayer. How many requests he had made for special foods and gifts to send to the heir princess. Sorrel was a man who had sympathized with the Da Vennen. Listened in on private conversations. Knew that the Da Vennen had portal tiles. Probably sought to free the Da Vennen as soon as Mathias and Keston would have turned in for the night and would have laughed at them being killed in their beds.

Sorrel gave Mathias a bewildered look before sitting again on his cot and grabbing the thin blanket to wrap around himself.

"Continue Ryver," Mathias murmured.

The wererat gave Sorrel the side-eye. "I was going to take you on this involved story of how I almost escaped capture but I didn't. I got bitten by wererats. Wererats that look to Bibb and given a choice. To become part of his army and travel to Spatelly or face the consequence of being both faeblood and a wererat. I'd be executed for sure."

"You expect me to believe . . ." Mathias stood. Paced. He knew Bibb was domineering and manipulative, but turning faebloods into wererats?

"I said it would be hard to believe but Bibb gave me and others like me a home and a community. It's a nice way of saying I was a prisoner." Ryver tapped at the bars. "Without, of course, the bars. But you must know, too. Even with this servant of yours in a cell with me, more Da Vennen will be back."

Sorrel leaped from his cot and dropped before the waste bucket. He became noisily sick.

"Oh, you worried of your punishment for being caught?" Ryver asked Sorrel.

Mathias crossed his arms. "Why are they coming? To free our prisoners?"

Ryver wrapped his arms around himself. "They want the girl. Her magic will be Bibb's crowning glory. And if she dies, those soldiers aren't going to care."

"And you. You want to keep her safe?" Mathias stepped to the side for a better view to Sorrel's cell. The man rotated between dry heaves and shivering.

"Yes. We do. And well . . ." Ryver dropped his voice to a whisper. "She wants to return to Nonderu. I'd like to go with her so I can save one of my friends. The Boggleman took him when we were running away after Britchway."

Mathias turned his back, fingers tapping at his cheek. A part of him was curious what the Da Vennen would do to Sorrel for him to become so ill. And another part considered Ryver's words.

I think he's telling the truth, Taf sent. He was yet in the third story stable, not yet sleeping. *You're not sleeping, either.*

"Think I can get that drink of water now?" Ryver asked. "And maybe something to eat. I mean the ambiance isn't too pleasing, but my stomach's not minding . . . provided there's no turnip."

Mathias held up a finger, a gesture to wait. If Bibb was turning faebloods into wererats, then it made sense that they were there with Bibb at the Bellows . . . but there was another riddle he wanted an answer to. "Your pack was burning blue flowers. Why?"

"We learned that both the Boggleman and firelings want the border spell to drop and one of them has been sending wyverns to beat at the spell. And wyverns . . . after so many times banging against that spell . . . Hebsolum was sure it would drop, so he gave us magical flowers to burn. They allow us to talk the wyverns into going back to their dens and sleeping."

"So, it's a flower to drug the mind. How long have you had it?"

Ryver huffed a bit of his light brown hair back. "If you think we were trying to control you, we weren't. Like I said, it was for the wyverns."

"Was it? The Boggleman used it against Aunia."

Ryver raised his hands, palm out. "That was never the intent. We would lay down our lives to protect her."

Mathias stepped closer to the cell. Stared into Ryver's brown-hazel eyes. "Why?"

"Because the choice is coming, and she is the path through. And flyer? If you decide to go after Bibb, me and my pack stand with you."

Mathias shared a long look with the wererat and he could find no lie in the boy's face. He held his hand through the bars. "The name's Mathias."

"Yes, that's what the wererat said." Mathias dug his shovel deeper into the ground. "The Da Vennen are using them to travel."

Keston, at his side, helped to dig out the last of the three graves for their foot soldiers. "Disconcerting, ain't it? I liked it better when they wouldn't use magic. But it makes sense now, all their attention to that fallen guild building."

"What do you mean?"

"They were pulling up portal tiles there."

Mathias paused from chopping at the soil, the shovel tip against the loosened earth. "You never said—"

"Lots of things happened between then and now. Didn't it? And believing all the lords and ladies handed in their portal tiles is a bit naïve." Keston dug another shovelful. "Think this is deep enough? Or you want the full six feet?"

Mathias wiped dirt from his face with his wrist. Be hard to crawl out of a pit with just the two of them. And so much to do yet. "I think we can have our men rest here."

Keston nodded, threw his shovel over the lip of the grave and climbed out. Mathias also climbed out of the waist-high hole. When flyers returned to bring the tower back to a full living condition, they could consider reburying their men. Give them a full ceremony to pay tribute to their sacrifice.

They lowered their men into their respective graves and covered them over. After, they sat on a wooden bench, a treated log split in half with feet, in front of the brown-stone barracks. The rest of the dead lay before them. Da Vennen soldiers.

"You don't think the dead wererats became ghouls, do you?" Keston asked. He lifted the back of his head from against the building's rough stone facade.

"That's a peasant tale."

"You said that about the Boggleman once."

"My mother used to threaten me with him." Mathias flexed his sore hands open and shut. The best way to get over the fear his mother had instilled had been to deny it. However, he couldn't deny it now. "But we've other things to worry about. Like the Da Vennen coming back. Ryver said—"

"What is this Ryver like?"

Mathias leaned forward. "He's a lot like you. Flippant. But I think truthful. If the Da Vennen are changing faebloods into wererats, the Queen needs to know."

"If? I think we've seen quite a few wererats who are faeblood." Keston tapped at his knees. "And he finds them all because of that witch compass. It boggles the mind what he's supposedly doing. And I certainly don't like that Bibb could use his witch compass across the square."

"What do you mean?"

"Witch compasses—or magic detectors as they call 'em in Uttalo—usually only work when you're right overtop of someone and by using a charged Chand crystal."

Mathias swiveled to better face Keston. "What do you know of magical devices?"

"My dad's a sculptor. He's received many commissions over the years. Was in Uttalo at least once before I was born."

"Then what would be your guess on how it's powered?" Mathias jolted as soon as the words left his mouth. He already knew.

"Matty?"

Hate exploded through Mathias with blinding intensity and he jumped to his feet. He wanted nothing so desperately but to fly back to Dalin and gut Arch Vicar Bibb with his sword. "He's using Dar Zeller's amulet."

"Matty. Matty," Keston called. "Do not be thinking of leaving me here alone with death duty and figuring out how we're feeding prisoners."

Mathias fixed Keston with a glare.

Keston did not shrink back. "Aunia's coming here with Fallo and we need to be thinking of our plan."

"Bibb is targeting flyers." Mathias' fists shook. "He's targeted Jules. With Patrick and Garret. And he killed Dar Zeller to get his amulet. He's looking to kill or change us into wererats. And the Da Vennen are coming back here."

"Then we need to figure out the why. Hey, how about I have Rev give the area nearby a scout before we drag all these Da Vennen out through the gate. Make me feel better."

Mathias nodded.

Keston stood. "And then after . . . you thinking we should risk ghouls and just leave the bodies for the Da Vennen to dispose of?"

The door to the third floor stable swung open. Revellie stood in front of the doors.

Mathias reseated himself and wished he could talk to Nyrissa, Zeller's daughter. Tell her he knew why Bibb had been on the Bellows sands. That was why she hadn't believed him before. She had said there was no motive. And no physical evidence. But if Bibb was using magic, then he easily could have used magic to fix his broken nose. Mathias swore he'd give him more than a broken nose next time.

A gold flash caught his eye. Revellie. And then motion. Tafiriel's blue nearly blended with the late afternoon sky.

Taf. What are you doing?

CHAPTER THIRTY-THREE
SECRETS EXPOSED

The sweet lies when two souls melt together in openness and trust. And poetry can give you multiple answers depending on how you read it. — Lady Danalissa Habrett, wife of Wallace Habrett of Wolfe's Eye

Aunia stepped in front of the fire salamander. "You cannot have her. We're going to stop the Boggleman, Narvis. Free your kin. But you need to work with me, not against."

Narvis erupted into fire. Flames soared over Aunia's head and a tarry smoke filled her nose. She raised her hand defensively, stepping back. "Narvis, stop this."

Narvis stepped forward as a living torch, his voice a crackling whisper. "Narvis cannot. Narvis takes garden faery . . . or Narvis . . ." The fire salamander's face appeared beneath the flames. "Regret Narvis feel. But still take Nia girl to Cromis Boggleman."

Aunia took another step back. "You are not my friend."

The Narvis-fire paused. "I not friend. I not because I scared."

"You're scared? I need to save two whole worlds," Aunia yelled. "I command you to go away. I've salt in my bag."

"You no salt."

Jennium twirled above Narvis and Aunia's heads with several sharp jingles and then a long bell chimed. A rumble sounded, shaking the ground and a spout of water fizzed inches from Aunia's foot into Narvis' face. The fire salamander halted, all flames dying down. He looked at her with wide saucer eyes. And then he disappeared. The spout of water did, too.

Jennium landed on her shoulder and Aunia, with shaking hands, transferred the garden faery onto her open palm. She dipped her knees and touched the ground where the little spring had been. The ground was dry. "Have you learned to make illusion glamours now, too?"

Jennium sank cross-legged on Aunia's palm and pointed toward the sinking afternoon sun. And a moving whiff of sky . . . no, not moving sky. Tafiriel. Relief spread through her core, down her limbs. She ran across the open field of grasses, arms waving over her head.

Tafiriel landed with a churning of galloping legs and came to a stop less than a child's throw away. Aunia slowed her pace to a fast walk and upon reaching him, threw her arms around the pegasus and buried her face against his soft neck. He smelled like salt and wind from a summer's day.

You found me, she sent. *Can you bespeak Mathias and—*

The enemy can listen into our conversations unless we are close together but Mathias and Eddac Tower are only a few miles away.

Aunia stepped back and the sting of tears hit her. *Mathias didn't reach out earlier because—*

It wasn't safe. Climb Aunia. I'll take you to him.

But why didn't he come with Fallo? Or instead of Fallo. Basil said—

Mathias wanted to come. But I advised no. Your Jennium told me we needed to be sure Eddac was safe.

You told him? Aunia took a step away from the pegasus.

The tower won't be safe for long but it is safe for now. Climb up.

She fastened her cloak, retrieved her knapsack, and climbed up on Tafiriel's bare back. They flew over a sprinkling of trees and grasses and minutes later soared up a large hill, moving over a well-worn road with deep wheel groves. Halfway up they passed a horse-drawn cart heading down the hill. Tafiriel raised into the sky before Aunia could make out what the stack of furry things were in the cart bed.

Up ahead, at the hill's crown, stood a brown-stone wall encircling a complex. In its center, a silver-gray tower jutted out like a boar spear. Other buildings, brown stone like the wall, surrounded the tower, along with wide spaces and small plots of greenery.

Trepidation mingled with the pang to see Mathias' face. She sat straighter on Tafiriel's bare back. *This is Eddac Tower?*

It is. Tafiriel circled over the complex. *Mathias is with that cart below. He'll return shortly.*

What is he doing?

There was a battle here. He and Keston are removing the dead. Taf landed between the tower and a line of other buildings.

Aunia dismounted, shoulders tight, and placed her palm on Tafiriel's neck for comfort. She could hear the murmur of Tafiriel bespeaking but not the words. It was obvious he bespoke to Mathias and there was nothing she could do but wait.

She walked over the courtyard's flagstones up to the tower where large barn-sized doors gaped open above. Stepping closer, she tapped at one of the thin glass windows which ringed the tower. They had a strange dimension. Each was about the width of her palm and about as long as the space between her elbow and fingertips. And the space between them was perhaps the breadth of three people standing shoulder-to-shoulder.

She peeked within the dark interior until a barked yell caught her attention. It came from a three-story building directly across from the tower. She walked toward it and Tafiriel hurried to block her way.

Do not go in there, he sent.

Why?

"Aunia?" Mathias stood yards away from her near the compound's gate. He ran toward her.

Relief, sorrow, home . . . it came flooding through her. She ran toward him, hair flying behind her.

Mathias caught her into a tight hug, arms pressed against her back, cheek against hers. He spun her around. When he set her on her feet, she felt dizzy but he didn't release her, and she didn't loosen her grip either.

"You're here. Thank all the Eaburrai Court, you're here." He leaned in and he kissed her. Drew back with wide eyes and then held onto her tight again.

Keston walked toward them both, head tilted and with a broad grin.

Aunia moved her hands from around Mathias' neck and gripped the front panels of his jerkin. "You left me to be picked up by Fallo."

"I . . . I'm sorry. I didn't have much choice and it would have been dangerous to bring you here first without someone reconning."

Aunia tightened her grip. "What do you mean?"

"The Da Vennen are still looking for you," Keston said. He stood a little off to the side and squeezed her shoulder. "And I'm glad we got you back safe. I do hear you skipped away before Fallo got to you?"

Aunia pulled back from Mathias. "Tafiriel?"

"I believe he's been speaking with your faery friend. I think they've become friends of a sort," Mathias said.

"I did not want to be flying anywhere with Fallo. He wanted to kill my father."

Mathias grimaced and Keston stepped forward.

"Where did Basil take you?" asked Keston.

Her mouth quavered, and she bit her lip. "I saw my mother's grave."

Mathias and Keston shared a look before Mathias plucked a leaf out of her hair. And then a second one. "We should get you inside," Mathias said. "We've running water in the tower. Heated even. I think a bath and then some food would do you good."

A bath. And food. They both sounded wonderful. She nodded. She could talk to Mathias about taking her to Tatia afterward.

Aunia fidgeted with her fingers while she walked up the tower's circular stone staircase. The steps felt cold against her bare feet.

"It gets quite warm here when the fires are all lit," Mathias said. "In fact, I think I saw Keston once grabbing his pillow to sleep on a landing over the winter."

Aunia breathed out a long puff of air, wondering how many stairs they would climb. Wondering what she was going to do next.

"I'm . . . I don't know what you need to hear about seeing your mother's grave," Mathias said. "I mean, I think it would be something I'd want to know but it would be hard."

His words struck a soft place in her heart and she paused on the steps. "It was. I knew but—"

"It's different seeing."

Her eyes stung.

"I am very sorry." Mathias put an arm around her. "She must have been remarkable if she was your mother."

"I don't know much about her at all." She swallowed hard and leaned into his warmth. "But I know her name now."

"First and last?"

Aunia pulled away. "Last?"

Mathias closed his eyes and exhaled slowly. "What name do you have?"

"Leia."

Mathias furrowed his brows and motioned her to climb. "I don't know anyone by that name but I've only been around other nobles and flyers."

Another archway was coming up. "Taya thinks she's noble born."

"Well, there's a Domesday in Worley," Mathias said.

"Not Tatia?"

"Worley is closer. And we are going to need to grow your stinky flowers. If heebles are in Tamore . . ." Mathias motioned for her to go through the archway first. "Worley has greenhouses. We should make for there soon."

She followed him along the curved hallway to a pale wooden door with a cast iron handle. The door opened without barely a squeak and they entered a small bedroom with a shuttered window and a narrow bed.

"You can put your things here. And do you have a change of clothes?" Mathias asked.

Aunia nodded. She walked over a multi-colored oval rug and set both knapsack and cloak atop the crimson-colored blanket. Mathias stepped to the other side of the room and pulled his fire-making kit from his pouch before opening another pale wood door. He stepped inside the second room and after several sharp clicks, the glow of candlelight spilled into the bedroom. Aunia followed.

Instead of stone-bricks, mosaic panels of pegasi flying over forests and waterfalls graced the walls. And in the center of the room stood a large, oval-shaped bath made from dark, polished stone. It was deep enough to sit in and have the water come mid-chest. Much bigger than the metal tub that Gaitha had. When she was younger, Gaitha would warm water and she and Limi would take turns taking a very shallow bath in front of the hearth. But mostly, full baths meant going to the creek.

"Do you see this valve?" Mathias turned the round copper dial and water gushed out of a copper pipe at the front of the tub. "You dial it this way and the deeper the turn, the hotter the water."

Aunia put her hand under the water and gasped.

"Too hot?"

She shook her head.

"Turn it back the other way when you want to turn it off and I'll fetch you a bathing sheet." Mathias flashed her a grin and went to the corner of the room where a large chest stood. From there, he pulled out a thin, beige-colored blanket and set it on a ladder-back chair near the door. "I'll leave you to it. I'm heading for the kitchens downstairs in the upper basement. And I'll be trying to make us food."

"Mathias?" Aunia called as he stepped into the bedroom. "I heard a noise in the other building."

"Right. You need to stay away from there. We had a battle before you got here. Da Vennen, wererats, and even some kobolds."

"Kobolds?" She wasn't sure that was what he said over the water.

"Yes. I don't know why but they scattered afterwards. The Da Vennen however." Mathias grimaced. "The ones who survived the battle, we made prisoners. They're in bullpens. Not the most secure but it's the best we can do. Anyway, Keston is barricading the tower door and getting our pegasi stabled for the night. We'll be leaving in the morning."

"You were in the cart earlier."

Mathias stepped back into the bathing room. "We've dead to handle. Do you need anything for now?"

Aunia shook her head, but she also clutched at Mathias' hand. He laced his fingers through hers and brought the back of her hand to his lips. His mouth felt warm against her knuckles and it sent her heart aflutter, pushing away all bad thoughts.

"Bathe." He plucked another leaf from her hair near her ear. "You've got quite a few brambles through that glorious hair of yours."

She stayed submerged in the water until the bath turned cool and the pillar candle had shrunk before she stepped out and dried herself off. It felt good to be clean, and after she had food in her belly, she could turn her thoughts back to what she needed to do. Like how to get to Tatia. Basil was right that no one person did everything alone.

Aunia dressed in her dark blue pants and a long mid-blue tunic. She couldn't find any candles in the bedroom so she confiscated the one in the bathing room and sat on her bed, flipping through her father's star book. She paused when she found an odd drawing in the center of the book spanning both pages. A map of sorts. The curve of the Grashbear looked the same as the one on Edvaras' map back at her village, but there were other things drawn overtop . . .

She pulled the book closer to the burning candle stump . . . strange symbols written in red and gold ink with delicate dotted lines connecting them. And tiny numbers scrawled along the page edges. It looked sort of like a star map.

Aunia flinched and lost her page placement. This couldn't be something like the starcharts that Mathias had hunted for, could it be? She knew her father had been after the same information that Mathias had. She had recently learned that Edvaras' starcharts were meant to discover the missing nymers of the Chandarions and she wanted to show all of this to Mathias.

She stood up and bounced on her toes. This was what Mathias needed to hear. To get him excited about restarting the augury again and to save both of their worlds. Yes, they could definitely go to this Worley place and start the Jaia flowers growing. Then they could continue to Tatia. She could free her father and he could help with the starcharts to help save both of their worlds. And after . . . she and Mathias could go off to start a life together.

All they had against them was . . . Aunia stopped dancing. The Da Vennen soldiers. The Boggleman, which Mathias needed to hear about, and Narvis . . . yes, the fire salamander was scared but turning on her and Jennium. How could she forgive Narvis for that?

The candle flickered. There wasn't much candle left. Yes, she could see by the dim light to leave this room but not enough to read by. *Tafiriel, do you know where there're more candles?*

Mathias keeps some at his desk in his room, Tafiriel sent back.

And where would that be?

Tafiriel gave instructions and Aunia returned to the curved hallway turning left toward the arch and an oak door with its blackened iron hinges. She entered the dorm room, candle in hand. There were several shuttered windows in this much larger room with six beds lining the wall on the left-hand side. Box-shaped wooden chests sat at the foot of each bed, and across the room along the interior wall near the door sat one long wooden desk with drawers instead of legs. The stool-chairs were all pushed in but one.

Aunia took a seat, set the candle on the smooth wooden surface, and rummaged through drawers beside the chair. Between two stacked drawers, she found three small books written in tiny, cramped handwriting along with quills, ink pots, parchment, a penknife and a small bottle of sand. And several pouches. Some were light with crinkly paper inside. Some jingled. No candle to be found.

She walked to the first footlocker at the end of a bed and opened its lid. Clothing lay within and also a smooth red-brown wooden box that smelled strongly of woodsy sweetness. It was big enough to hold a couple of candles, provided they weren't too tall.

Aunia opened the box to find many folded pieces of parchment within. Notes of some kind? Aunia bit her lip. She knew she should put them away unread but . . . she picked one up and unfolded it.

My dearest,

The distance between us is great but no vastness of land or sky can dim the fire which burns a heart with desire. And I pray when I return, you will look my way. See, my hands tremble—not from the chill of the wind as I soar upon my pegasus, but from the weight of words that can scarcely express the somber need I have for when my eyes next meet yours.

Aunia blushed. She must have discovered Keston's cache of love letters. Limi had told her of sweet rhymes that Kron had made up for her when they were courting. And Aunia wondered if Mathias would ever write something like this for her. She went to refold it and return it to its box when her glance caught the signature. And it started with an "M."

Frost and fire and salted tears exploded together and Aunia threw the box across the room. She stood, fist clenched, shaking . . . and then stomped to the box and the spilled contents. She opened letter after letter looking for a name. For this person that Mathias was writing. At the fifth letter she found it. Princess Keira.

She dropped the letter. Mathias was in love with the Queen's daughter? Was it ever a wonder why he never answered her directly when she said about going to Tatia.

She sat on the floor, gripped a strand of her wet hair, and folded over her knees with a broken sob. Two sobs. Then she straightened. Forced herself to swallow any other tears. She would not, could not allow herself to be diminished. She had important things to address. Far more important than have worry about a broken heart. A fat tear hit her cheek and rolled off her chin. She brushed it off with her sleeve. She could go to Tatia by herself. Why did he not tell her?

It is not advisable to leave this tower near dark, Tafiriel sent. *The Da Vennen are looking for you.*

Pressure built against Aunia's temples. The pegasus was right. She did not want any dealings with them. But she could make Mathias explain all this to her.

A low murmuring rang against her ear. *Don't you dare warn him, Tafiriel. I deserve for him to explain himself before he comes up with some . . . answer.*

There is much you do not know, Tafiriel sent.

"Yeah. I get that," she said through clenched teeth. And she headed for the door.

CHAPTER THIRTY-FOUR

A BOILING OF WHISPERERS

Yes, I have heard that the smallest of faeries can only feel one thing at a time and if that is true then whisperers, while helpful at times, feel malice for any who do not have full faery blood. — a lecture of Dar Syrick, advisor to the Tamorian queen, to his dar apprentice, Wendalin Mensani

"Is that boiling yet?" Mathias carved another slice of bacon from a cold slab while candle scones along the wall helped fill the underground high-beamed kitchen with shadow and light.

Keston pulled the iron pot rack from the kitchen's walk-in hearth and peered into a mid-sized cast iron cauldron. "Close enough. Wanna grab that pitcher of grain?"

Mathias set his kitchen knife on the heavy worktable and two-handed a massive clay pitcher over. "Do you know how much?"

"Think because I'm common-born I've cooked?"

"I'll put all of it in." Mathias poured dry oval-shaped grain into the cauldron, shaking the pitcher periodically. "And cook it down for a bit, but I've bacon sliced and with the bread—"

"It's stale."

"We'll toast it . . . but we can have our supper before we feed the prisoners. Aunia should be done with her bath, I imagine at some point and—"

"Maybe. But I know *I* like sitting in the tub till my hands look like shriveled apples."

"Stop that." Mathias returned the empty clay pitcher to the prep table, wiped his hands on a small towel, and pulled a bread knife from a wooden knife block. "You can start with frying up that bacon I sliced."

"You like her. Aunia, I mean."

"Of course I do." Mathias opened a wooden bread box and pulled two baked loaves out. Aunia challenged him. Reminded him of his heartbeat and that there was joy in the world. But she also frightened him. How could he even think of being with her when he couldn't provide a life for either of them? And he and Keston would be brought up on abandonment charges with Fallo despite coming back to Eddac Tower. Unless maybe they pleaded only following orders.

Mathias sawed into the first loaf. "Worley is the best plan of all. Get Aunia there and in Lord Lyle's safekeeping. Then reconning what's happening at Spatelly."

"What if Fallo says no to Worley?"

"Do you see him here? I don't, and if he isn't here by morning, I say we take matters in our own hands. We leave."

"And our prisoners?"

"We're not jailers. Ryver said more Da Vennen are coming. Let them break them free."

"And the wererat?" Keston asked.

Mathias pulled his hand back a bare second before he nicked himself. "Do you mind? I've enough to think on without all the questions."

"Like why you would keep this a secret?" Aunia's voice rattled off the pots and pans hanging on hooks by the hearth.

She stood in the center of the kitchen with a fistful of letters. His letters to Keira. The air left the room and Mathias set the knife down.

Keston turned on him with an incredulous look. "You didn't tell her?"

Mathias brushed crumbs from his hands. "I wanted to. Aunia, I . . . you have to understand. I never loved her.

Aunia stamped closer and threw the letters onto the butcher's block. "That's supposed to make it better?"

"No." Mathias tugged at the hem of his jerkin. "My family insisted I do this. To make up for—"

"People keep secrets because they are ashamed." Her cheeks flushed an angrier red.

"Or because things are unforgivable," Keston murmured.

Mathias shot Keston a glare. "You're not helping here."

Keston walked back to the hearth and picked up a long wooden spoon. "All you have to do is be forthright. I'm a flirt. I admit it but if you ask any of the girls—"

"I don't have any of the girls," Mathias snapped. He took a step toward Aunia, palms out. If only he could make her see . . . she had saved him from a miserable existence. She had. Or had she only confused the situation? She had. Or had she only confused the situation? "Aunia, I'm sorry. I should have said. I just—"

"Didn't know what you want to do? You think I haven't seen the conflict you've had?"

Heat grazed Mathias' face. "Tafiriel shouldn't have—"

"Your glow gives you away. Every time you think you are so good with a lie or an omission. Whenever you have doubts, I can see it. You like me. You might even love me. But you don't want it."

Her words sliced open his heart. He wanted to argue but what she said was true.

A clatter of wood against stone drew Mathias' attention to the hearth where Keston stood, spoon on the floor, with one hand out and the other with a forefinger bumped against his lip. He whispered, "What's that sound?"

"I do not need an assist," Mathias said hoarsely.

"I hear glass breaking and whispery laughs," replied Keston.

Mathias. There are whisperers in the tower, Taf sent.

"Whisperers," Mathias repeated. He waved both Keston and Aunia over. "Taf says they're here."

"Revellie, too." Keston hurried over. "She says they're breaking through the murderslots."

Aunia folded her arms. "Murder slots?"

"The narrow glass windows," Mathias clenched his fists. "But what can they do but spy on us?"

Scraping sounded on the floor above them and Aunia hurried over to stand by Keston. "They come from the Boggleman."

"He's dead," Mathias said.

"He's alive. I saw him. I dreamwalked. He's somewhere with a woman in a house in the mountains. She's making fire salamander lights."

"All they can do is report that we're here," Mathias said.

"No." Aunia stepped closer to Keston. "He said he wants them to carry me off to him."

Mathias reached for her. "That would take an awful lot of—"

There are an awful lot of them, Taf sent. *They've found the passage to the cellar. Hide.*

"Cell room," Mathias said. "Go."

Keston caught Aunia's hand and the two of them hurried out of the kitchen to the iron-bound door.

Mathias ran for the hearth, pulled the cross bar away from the fire, and followed them, closing the cell door room behind them. "We can't lock it from the inside."

"They can open doors," Aunia said. She stood under the sole light scone flickering on the wall.

"Is this the girl?" Ryver stood against his cell bars, all of his attention on Aunia.

"Keep quiet." Mathias patted his empty scabbard. "I left my sword behind."

"As did I but I'm not sure how much damage we'd do to whisperers." Keston took position at Mathias' side.

"Whisperers are nasty things," Ryver said. "If they're looking for you—"

"They won't give up until they find you," Mathias finished. "I know."

"Open the cell," Ryver said.

"What?" Mathias whispered. "I'm not doing that."

Sorrel rolled off his bed. "Open mine or I'll yell."

Taf, sleep Sorrel, would you?

Sorrel slumped back on his bed.

"It'll be hard for you to follow me if you don't open my door."

"What are you talking about?" Keston padded over to the cell.

Ryver pointed to the wall and then held up a small stone . . . no, a tile. A portal tile. "That is stone. Born in the mountains and it can be made to open a door."

Mathias walked to Ryver's cell. That tile must have fallen out of the pouch when Mathias had interrogated Ryver. "You can open a blade-cave door from a portal tile?"

Ryver tugged on his short scruffy beard. "I'm a faeblood. Course I can. Now, you joining me or not?"

"Keston, unlock the door," Mathias said. *Taf, I need you to bespeak Nyrissa.*

Brinsaber's warning—

I think the danger is already here, Mathias sent as Keston pulled the key from a hook by the door.

Tell Nyrissa that we must flee Eddac Tower. Tell her we have Da Vennen prisoners within. That they attacked our tower, and we had to defend as flyers. They're imprisoned in the bullpens and one is in the basement cells. After, bespeak Fallo and tell him Eddac is overrun.

Keston set the key into the keyhole and with a click, opened the cell door. On the other side of the room, a low creak came from the cell room door.

"Come on." Mathias herded Aunia and Keston into the cell. "They're breaking in."

Ryver held the portal tile to the stone wall. "Where's your nearest outcropping of rocks?"

"What do you mean by outcropping?" Mathias asked.

Ryver cocked his head. "You know, a pile of rocks. Boulders. Crags. The bigger the better."

"There's one at the bottom of this hill. In the valley," Aunia said. "Near a copse of trees."

"Then that's the one we'll try for." Ryver caught Aunia's hand. "Picture it in your head."

Mathias stepped forward to put his body between the wererat and Aunia but stopped when Aunia glared at him.

Keston shook his head, barely perceptible. A warning to give Aunia space. But he still had to protect her, didn't he?

Outside of the cell room, something crashed in the kitchen.

Mathias curled his fists. "Any time is good."

Ryver murmured a string of unfamiliar sounds. Some might have been words. But others sounded like the trill of bird notes.

If this works, can you and Rev meet us at the bottom of the hill? Mathias sent.

Where she was found, yes. Nyrissa bespeaks you are to meet Catiryna at Stanz Tower.

I acknowledge you spoke.

The dark gray stone rippled as if it were turning into water and a black hole emerged in the center of the wall. It looked like an untethered blade-cave entrance. Ryver waved them forward.

"We need light," Aunia whispered.

Taf, light please, Mathias sent. A second later, an egg-shaped white light appeared in the entrance of the cave. All of them entered—except Sorrel, who was in the adjoining cell and still sleeping. Nyrissa knew about the prisoners and that the Da Vennen soldiers would be back. Someone would free him.

The narrow passageway was full of stalagmites and stalactites. It twisted and turned and they followed it in single file for some time with Taf's light spell shining over their heads. Ryver in the front, followed by Keston, then Aunia. Mathias guarded the rear and cringed each time Aunia curled her feet against the jagged floor. They needed to get shoes for her. In the distance, water dripped, and it almost sounded like the passageway sighed. Mathias swallowed down his anxiety, counted the seconds as he stepped. And then, the moon, larger than half, lit the exit point with pale silver.

They came out in a field covered in tall grass with a cluster of elm, oak, and ash trees nearby.

"There," Keston said pointing in the sky toward the tower. Tafiriel and Revellie flew toward them in the night sky with a dark cloud following them.

"Whisperers are following," Mathias said.

"And no tack. No saddle. This won't be a pleasant ride," Keston added.

Mathias stiffened. He remembered too well Aunia nearly falling during the wyvern battle and then again when Hebsolum threw her. They'd be chased by enemies. And he couldn't risk her falling. He turned back to the rock cropping. The blade-cave opening was narrow, yes, but not too narrow for a pegasus. And if they watched their wings in the narrowest places . . .

"You can direct the blade-caves," Mathias asked. "How?"

Ryver pulled his curled fingertips from his mouth. "Think of what you want."

"Like one-thing?" she asked.

Tafiriel and Revellie landed heavily on the field.

Keston ran for Revellie. "Come on."

"No, back in the cave," Mathias said. "We can think of the out-cropping near where we found the rover caravan."

The cloud of whisperers grew closer and slips of bone-white shone through the smoky fog.

"Go," Mathias yelled.

Keston and Aunia ran for the cave. Ryver stayed still, gawking at the dark moving whisperer cloud.

Mathias, Tafiriel called.

"Come on." Mathias grabbed Ryver by the arm.

"There's danger overusing a blade-cave." The wererat's eyes had gone wide.

"We'll worry about that later."

Mathias and Ryver rushed into the cave with Rev and then Taf entering last. The cave entrance closed. Darkness enveloped them.

"Well, we can hope," Ryver said. "Can you describe this outcropping near the caravan?"

Chapter Thirty-Five

SUCH IS THE WAY OF MORTALS

Yasendra the youngest of the Eaburrai Court loved to race over green grasses at the foot of the Lu-Aequorath Falls but that love was shoved aside when a mortal brought his doom.
— Part of the Histories of the Eaburrai Court written by Hebsolum, high guardian of the Eaburrai Court

Aunia curled her icy toes from another sharp stone and reached for the cold, damp rock face.

"Here." Mathias extended his hand to her bent elbow to steady her.

Aunia jerked her arm away and glared at Mathias' bit of light hovering over her head. "Keston, can you change spots with me?"

"Um . . . that would be a no," Keston said, "Sorry love. File rotation is a serious bit."

"I wouldn't harm her," Ryver, who was in the lead, said.

Keston shrugged. "Didn't say you would."

They continued through other twists and turns while the wan magic light made rock faces appear like creatures ready to leap from the walls. Water dripped. The air grew stale.

"How much longer?" Mathias asked.

"Can't quite say," replied Ryver. "Re-using a blade-cave so soon is tricky business. I'm just hoping this won't lead us out somewhere bad."

I can help, Tafiriel sent.

You, Taf? Have another secret you're keeping? Aunia sent. Tafiriel had known about Princess Keira and Mathias and he hadn't said a word either.

"This is not my pegasus' fault, it's mine," Mathias said in a low voice. *What can you help with, Taf?*

I can lead us out.

Aunia stopped. "How?"

"Why do I feel like I'm missing most of this conversation?" asked Ryver.

"Hand me that portal tile," Mathias said.

"If you think it'll help," said Ryver. He handed the portal tile to Keston and Keston handed it to her.

The tile sparkled with a fiery tinge and felt warm in her hand. But handing it to Mathias . . . She sucked in a breath and threw it at him.

Mathias caught the portal tile with an expression like a bewildered calf. He then faced Tafiriel. *How do you—*

Set it against my nose.

Mathias did so and Tafiriel shut his eyes.

The tunnel filled with a sun-yellow light, and a cracking snapped with the ground shaking. After that, the underground vanished, and they stood in front of a squat three-story tower made of smooth gray-blue stone. Vines clung around broad windows with glowing flowers of pale lavender. And on the lush grass at their feet, flowers the shape and color of blue bells jingled, and delicate star-shaped daisies ruffled in the slight breeze.

In the teal sky overhead, a figure streaked toward them.

A tall woman, a sylph with long silver hair, pale skin, and large gray falcon-like wings, landed beside the tower. She looked at each of them with wide gray eyes. Wasp-riding ruork faeries appeared next . . . from where, Aunia wasn't sure, but they circled the sylph. After that, hand-sized breezling fairies with large purple eyes and translucent silver wings fluttered down from the sky.

These breezlings rushed to Aunia and swirled around her head. "Nia. Nia. Nia."

Keston leaned to Aunia's ear and whispered, "I see faeries. And they're calling you Nia."

The sylph woman laughed and said with a rich silvery voice, an octave higher than Taf's and close to Revellie's. "Most do in the faery world. But welcome to the floating island of Aeryth. Aunia. Mathias. Tafiriel."

Tafiriel stepped forward and bent his forelegs, resting a knee on the ground, in a bow before the sylph. *My lady, Zevara.*

The sylph nodded once and turned to Mathias. "We meet again."

Another thing he did not tell me, Aunia fumed. There had been a sylph on the Grashbear but it had not been this sylph.

Tafiriel rose, his wings unfurling slightly.

Mathias shifted on his feet, his fingers fidgeting with the hem of his jerkin. "I do not recollect you."

Zevara's smooth face broke into a wide smile. "Do you not? I told you once that you are a living candle imbued with magic's spark. But it would appear heart and soul have disengaged again. Such is the way of mortals, I suppose."

Aunia crossed her arms. "When did you meet a sylph?"

Not a sylph. The high sylph herself, Taf sent.

"It's quite alright, Tafiriel. Our Aunia . . ." Zevara curled a long finger along her smooth cheek. "She is quite the mystery, is she not? But to answer your question, I met this flyer when you were lost within the confines of Nonderu."

Nonderu. Keeping her breath even, Aunia stepped toward the sylph. They were in Endynia, in Faery. Faeries could not lie. But they could mislead. "I was seeking to rescue my father. Do you know what's become of him?"

"You were seeking a way to capture Edvaras' Nymer. If you found your father, it was quite by accident. But keeping you out of the Bogleman's grasp is a worthy task." Zevara turned to Mathias' pegasus. "Tafiriel, I do not fault you for bringing them here, but they cannot stay."

"Agreed," Mathias said.

Aunia shot Mathias a glare then returned her attention to Zevara. "I seek to rescue my dad. If I cannot stay, send me to Nonderu."

The breezlings gasped and drew back to Zevara causing the wind to ruffle the sylph's long white gown.

"My father is being held captive there," added Aunia.

Zevara laced her hands together. "My lands do not abut Nonderu for good reason."

Keston bit back a chuckle and Mathias shot Keston a glare.

"I know, I know." Keston flipped his palms over in apology. "Abut means two things leaning against each other."

Aunia rolled her eyes, unwilling to be amused by either flyer. She kept her attention on the sylph. "But you could help skip us there."

"I cannot," Zevara said. "Nonderu is between the worlds—in the betwixt—neither Faery nor Mortal worlds."

"What does that matter? I got to Nonderu through a betwixting tunnel before," Aunia said.

"Betwixting tunnel?" Ryver's voice sounded from behind her.

"Another name for blade-cave," Mathias whispered.

"You were dreamwalking, an incredible ability to be sure, but quite limited in what you can do," Zevara said. "And dangerous. The Boggleman's cloak can reach you when you dreamwalk."

"The Boggleman's cloak?" asked Keston. "What can a cloak do but keep you warm?"

"It eats faeries," Aunia snapped. "But the Boggleman isn't in Nonderu right now. He is in—"

"The Fireling kingdom in the Adarian mountains," Zevara interrupted. "And looking for a way back."

"Jennium told you that," Aunia said.

Aunia, this is high Sylph of the Pavari Court, Taf sent in a soft silvery voice.

"But I need to free my father while the Boggleman's gone," Aunia cried.

Keston, on her right side, shuffled closer to Revellie.

"And the best way to do that would be through Yasendra's Darra Chamber in Tatia." Zevara turned back to Mathias and crinkled her brow. "And you. What is it that you desire?"

Before Mathias answered, a hardwood door to the tower swung open.

"My Queen, I did not expect you." Another woman, a zephyr with soft, almost translucent golden skin, stepped outside. Her voluminous red silk gown whispered as she walked and her wide violet eyes stayed fastened on Aunia's face. "My master, he's gone for now but for how long, I do not know."

"Sheavine, all of Pavari is mine, including where the veil is thin. He will endure me." Zevara said.

Sheavine the zephyr also laced her thin fingers together and nodded.

"Mathias," said Zevara. "You did not give me your answer."

Aunia balled her fists. What did it matter what he wanted?

"To be returned to Tamore . . . near Worley and Spatelly. Our lands are in danger."

"And Aunia's quest? The two of you are stronger together than—"

"I have another question," Aunia interrupted.

Zevara straightened and whatever smile she had disappeared. "Ask."

Aunia reached for something to say. She did not want to be paired up with Mathias. "I would like to know what I am. What you know of me."

Zevara's falcon wings drooped, and she turned her back on the tower. "For some time, we have felt the pull of Chandarion magic in your world on both sides of your Grashbear Mountains. And this was even before the releasing of Edvaras' Nymer, though much has been set in place with that event."

Aunia stiffened. "Yes, but what do you know of me? And what is your involvement in the augury? The Boggleman said when I was dreamwalking that you and Jennium are making potentials. What are potentials? Why are you doing it? And my dad's star book says Chandarions are imbued with limitless power—something Olivia didn't have. Did you do something to her?"

Keston slid beside her and hoarsely whispered in her ear, "Perhaps tempering your words with a faery ruler might be a good idea."

Aunia whirled on Keston and then noted the paleness under his complexion. She was familiar with faery lies by omission but perhaps Keston was right. She clenched her teeth and set her hand over her heart. Faeries did not like human apologies but . . . "I regret my boldness. My anxiety to reach my father in time are shortening my words."

"I did not find your words short but rather long," Zevara said. "I can tell you that your father learned much from me during your parents' time in Pavari and I'm not surprised he wrote much of it down. The way of the Chandarions had been broken—"

"Since Edvaras," Aunia said.

"No, dear child, that augury has been twisted and pulled since the time of its conception. Perhaps it would have been different if Uriah and Yasendra would have done what they ought, but the human heart . . . it provides a great deal of complication. And the want of forgiveness will play its part."

"Forgiveness?" Aunia bit.

Mathias stepped forward. "What do you mean?"

Zevara raised her hand. "You will learn in good time. But for now, Aunia, I will tell you this. . Your father was given a gift from the ocean . . . one that he tried to spend away with forgetfulness and need. There is much to be done to set that right."

Prickles ran along Aunia's spine. A gift from the ocean. Aunia frowned. "I don't understand what that means."

The zephyr woman hurried toward Zevara and pointed to a glimmering in the air. Aunia shifted closer to Mathias and Hebsolum the dwarf stepped through.

"Zevara, I did not know you sought to visit," Hebsolum dwarf said in a squeaky voice and hurried forward, kicking at the jingling bluebells with his thick black boots. He slowed when he spotted Aunia. "You. How dare you be here."

"Hebsolum," Zevara warned.

Aunia huddled by Mathias, feeling his body heat touch her skin. It had been no accident when Hebsolum had thrown her in the air. He meant for her to plunge to her death. "Why do you hate me?"

"You and your ilk have destroyed my lady—"

"This girl has no blame in that," Zevara's silvery voice plunged into gale-like ferocity.

Keston and Ryver stepped in front of Aunia and Mathias remained at her side.

"You've taken one of mine?" Hebsolum roared.

"I am still yours, mi'lord," Ryver said. "But like we've said, we mortals work with a lot of conflicts. I've sworn to see her to no harm and I've sworn to serve you."

Zevara's breezlings rushed toward the navel-high dwarf and swirled his curling red-brown hair and beard over his eyes.

"You have Edvaras' Nymer. And my mother's amulet," Aunia called from behind her friends.

Zevara gave Aunia a scowl and raised her hand, commanding silently to be quiet. "Hebsolum. I will call on the Eaburrai Court here and now and they can extract you back to your regular duties—"

"I submit to your leadership." Hebsolum wiped his hair from his eyes. "And I give all of you leave to go—save the wererat."

Zevara raised an eyebrow. "And you will—"

"I'll not harm him. He's mine," Hebsolum said.

"Very well but later you and I will discuss that Nymer," Zevara said.

Chapter Thirty-Six

A Consensus

I will give over these lands to my sister's children before I see your murderous son with my title. — Lord Wallace Habrett of Wolfe's Eye

Ryver waved the party off after Aunia climbed on Revellie's back and he retreated into the tower with the zephyr and Hebsolum. Hebsolum as a dwarf. Mathias scratched his cheek, perplexed. It made no sense. He had seen the marble giant on the Grashbear during the wyvern fight. Was he a shapeshifter? Mathias planned on getting answers after they landed at Pavari's crown lands.

Tafiriel, with Mathias, and Revellie with Keston and Aunia, flew behind Zevara in a westerly direction—or at least Mathias thought it was west if the sun followed the same pathway as the mortal world.

The landscape beneath them stretched out to the horizon in a series of floating islands. Most were carpeted in lush grass and colorful flowers but some were covered in water and others in tall, bare mountains. All were connected with shimmering bridges formed from silver chains. It looked like never-ending sky beneath the mountains.

Mathias kept his fingers laced through Tafiriel's mane and his knees pressed against his pegasus' sides. They needed to have saddles before they returned to Tamore or be set somewhere where they easily could acquire them, along with weaponry. It was stupid he didn't have his sword on him when he fled the whisperers. He cast a glance back at Revellie and frowned at the sight of Aunia's arms wrapped around Keston's middle.

One cloud, two clouds . . .

Really? Counting clouds? Taf sent.

What would you have me do? Mathias swallowed down the lump in his throat. He had meant to tell Aunia about Keira when they had eaten supper with the rovers. That seemed so long ago now. And Keston . . . he better not try anything.

Off in the distance, robust creatures wheeled over the floating islands stacked with mountains. They had the front end of a bird of prey, an eagle or a hawk. Some had the back end of horses. Others with the back end of lions.

They passed an island shaded in mist and cliff faces and another where man-size bats spiraled over swishing tall grasses. Mathias gulped at the wind pressing in on his face. Everything felt like it was closing in despite the wide-open space.

Well, Nyrissa nor Catiryna would find him while he was in Endynia. Mathias closed his eyes against the tumble of worries. Bibb and his witch compass. Faebloods and wererats. He needed to get back to Tamore and save his lands. See whether Jules had been turned and was now in Spatelly.

They approached an island made of black basalt mountains and standing near the peak of the tallest mountain in contrast stood a bright-white stone castle. Mathias blinked against the stones' reflection but still drank in the delicate spires stretching unbelievably high under the white sun. Bright blue banners flapped in the breeze while air currents whistled through arches and open windows.

Zevara made for a wide balcony that set about midway up the castle and landed amidst a frenzy of short rainbows. Mathias joined her as did Revellie and her passengers.

"Welcome to Aetherwind." Zevara walked to a pair of crystal-lined double doors. "Come join me in my throne room."

They walked through a broad hallway lined with seven-foot-high ravens wearing amethyst-colored baldricks. Mathias slowed his pace to walk beside Aunia, keeping an eye on her nervous expression and the towering beaks. It did not come soon enough when they entered an enormous throne room.

The space was almost dizzying. A swirling mural of sunset colors occupied most of the exterior wall with a bank of windows overtop it. Several swings hung from the ceiling, presumably to perch and enjoy the outside view.

No one else was here, except for Zevara, who was walking toward a crystal throne at the other end of the room.

Aunia's gaze was on everything and her expression was filled with awe. He so wanted to caress her cheek. But she'd probably hit him.

It was a beautiful place, but it paled in her presence. He dug his fingernails into his palm. She could be safe here while he dealt with the wererats and Bibb. She had experience with faeries. Some of her friends were faeries. The only other option was to leave her in Worley and he doubted she'd stay put. *You'd be able to skip here again, wouldn't you, Taf?*

Zevara stopped in the center of her throne room with its shimmery tiled floor and snapped her fingers. Instantly four cushioned lounge chairs with cloud-patterned fabric appeared.

"Have a seat," Zevara commanded, "and Tafiriel, do lead your golden friend off to the courtyard. There are fresh apples there."

Mathias and Keston sat, and Tafiriel and Revellie exited back out the way they had come.

Aunia remained on her feet. "You said my father learned from you. How long were my parents' here?"

"Do you not know faerykind enough that interrogations do not bestow good-will?" Zevara sat on the chaise closest to her throne.

Aunia blushed. "I just—"

"Want to know everything while suffering a miserable headache with little food and little rest. I believe I have a solution."

Zevara snapped again and a willowy figure the color of twilight appeared. "Galeena, kindly take our young guest to a guest room. See that she has food and a soft bed. And Aunia, we will revisit your questions in the morning."

Keston rose. "But eating anything in this world—"

"That would be stealing food in this world and eating it. I am offering it, freely. And Aunia, do not fret about your companions. They will be off to bed for rest and slumber and a fresh morning."

Mathias frowned as Aunia left with the servant, surprised she hadn't protested.

Zevara can be very persuasive, Taf sent. *But she cannot make you do anything you truly do not wish to do.*

Keston sat back down.

"Sleep will be very good for her," Zevara said. "She's still healing from a blow to the head."

Mathias pulled his curled fists to his core and held them against his gut. It was only yesterday that she rescued Keston with that globefire of hers. And a Da Vennen had struck her hard. He would love to find that Da Vennen. "Your ladyship, might I ask a few questions of my own."

"Ladyship?" Zevara tapped her chin with her forefinger. "Yes, I suppose that would do. Ask away."

"How is that dwarf, Hebsolum?" Keston butted in.

Zevara turned her head to Keston. "That is simply his dreamwalking form."

"Dreamwalking?" Mathias said . . . like how Aunia dreamwalked. "Isn't it odd he doesn't look the same?"

"Why would that be odd? What we believe ourselves to be is not always what others see," Zevara responded.

"And his hostility to Aunia?" asked Mathias.

"Hebsolum has always had a fancy for Yasendra. He certainly never liked that she married Uriah, and he blames our first Chandarion hero." Zevara crossed her legs at the ankles. "Heb will aid any Chandarion or potential. He's compelled to, but it doesn't mean he likes it. And it doesn't mean that he will not take opportunity."

"Are you saying Aunia is a potential or a Chandarion?" Mathias asked.

Careful, Taf sent. *She will allow you three questions without cost. But after that she may decide to follow the faery guidelines.*

Mathias' heart sank. How many questions had Aunia asked so far? It certainly was more than three.

"Do you not recall your history," Zevara asked. "Of what happened to the children of Uriah and Yasendra?"

Mathias tugged at the bottom of his jerkin. "The Eldarghast cursed the children of Yasendra and saw them dispersed across many lands. It's the event the caused the War Between the Worlds."

"It was. And have you considered how many human generations have passed since that time?" Zevara raised an eyebrow. "How many generations must now possess at least a smidgeon of Yasendra's blood?"

"And Aunia possesses some of this blood?" Mathias crossed his arms. How many questions was that now?

"I believe you possess that as well, Mathias, son of Wallace and Danalissa," Zevara said. "Why else would my Tafiriel decide to select you?"

"But you said you feel the stirrings of a Chandarion on both sides of the Grashbear." Mathias leaned back. This sentence technically was not a question.

"I have at times. I do not understand it. Passageway perhaps through a betwixting tunnel or perhaps a potential using a significant portion of magic."

"Any magic?" Keston asked.

Mathias slid his foot over, making it look like he accidentally kicked Keston's boot. *Taf can you bespeak Keston?*

Zevara shrugged.

Keston, who had been leaning forward, fidgeted, knuckles knocking at his knees. He straightened. "Do you know what happened with Fallo?"

"Finally." Zevara's shoulders lowered, and she smiled. "Go to the mural and watch. It will not hurt you."

With trepidation, Mathias rose with Keston and they crossed the room to the mural.

"Why didn't you do what Revellie bespoke," Mathias whispered.

"Because we need to know this," Keston answered.

The mural swirled with color, creating what looked like a landscaped oil painting in progress. More brushstrokes appeared, layer upon layer, until it looked like Fallo had been painted on the wall. He sat in front of a fire, wineskin raised to his mouth, and the knight-sons at his side.

"They found your commander before he got to where some humans call Scorched Earth." Zevara walked up from behind them. "The answer to the question you did not ask Keston is no. You cannot trust him. He is bewitched like the others in your unit. This is all I will say and I give it freely but on the morrow I shall ask you what it is that you want and decisions will be made. Until then, you should get some rest."

Mathias slipped from a cloud-like bed nestled atop silver branches and walked across soft blue rugs which carpeted the floor in the guest suite he and Keston shared. Morning—if it was truly morning—had broken with white sunlight pouring through tall windows.

"I'm starving," Keston said from his bed. He stretched and joined Mathias at the window for the view of silver-leafed trees mixed with bluebells and gossamer star daisies. "The flowers . . . they look like the ones in Tatia, don't you think?"

Mathias tapped on a thin glass pane. "We need to get back to Tamore. Get to Spatelly."

"Find out what the wererats are doing and get ourselves out of trouble," Keston finished. "I know. But why not enjoy here while we're here. And I'm curious what sanctioned faery breakfast would taste like."

On cue, smells of freshly fried bacon and pancakes filled the room. Keston beelined to the frosted glass table and the polished silver chairs with their swirling twists and flares. Supper had appeared for them as well before they had retired for the night.

"I think I see the lady in the courtyard. We should go and—"

"Matty, eat first."

Mathias tugged on the soft neckline to the sleeping clothes they had been provided and joined Keston at the table. He raised an eyebrow at the assorted fruits offered, including small fruits with bumpy red-pink rinds. "Lychees. I haven't had these since I was little."

"Zevara does seem to know what our favorites might be."

"Keston?" Mathias broke the fruit's outer rind. "What do you think if we left Aunia here?"

Keston coughed and reached for one of the glasses of juice in the center of the table. "Leave her?"

"She'd be safe here. At least from the Da Vennen. We could leave her in Lord Lyle's safekeeping but I don't think she'd stay put."

"I don't think that's—"

"Bibb won't stop looking for her. He wants faebloods. The sort that can create storms. Can you imagine the prize Aunia would be to him?"

"Do you really believe she'd stay here? I think you just need to apologize to her. Talk to her. Explain things. Both with the letters and with what we need to do."

"She won't listen." Mathias pushed himself away from the table. "She's barely talking to me and when she does, it's with a snarl."

"Yes, and when she was scared, who did she huddle toward?"

"She rode with you here." Mathias snagged a piece of bacon, along with his fruit, and returned to the window. "She deserves someone better than me."

"Better? Yes." Keston shoved a large mouthful of pancakes in his mouth and spoke around his food. "But we all make mistakes. It's how we deal with our mistakes that's telling."

"Yeah, where did you hear that little treasure?"

Keston paused with a piece of bacon in his hand. "From my father. You have to understand, she's reacting the way she is because she's hurting."

Mathias bit into the fruit—a sweet burst of pear mixed with citrus fruit. "Wish that I had a father like yours. Mine will disown me and I don't know where I'd go."

"You're a flyer. You would always have a home."

"With Aunia."

"I think you're getting ahead of yourself."

They finished the rest of the meal in relative silence and headed to the courtyard where Zevara and Aunia strolled beside a flower garden, reed-like flowers with wide open rose-heads and black and gray seeds jutting from their centers. Mathias' heart fluttered with Aunia's glance but then she looked away toward Tafiriel and Revellie who dozed on their feet under an apple tree.

She looked paler, bringing out the light smattering of freckles across her nose and cheeks. Her dark blue pants and a long mid-blue tunic, previously torn and dirty were repaired and clean, like Mathias and Keston's clothing. And she had gold-colored sandals on her feet.

You must extend appreciation but faeries don't like thank you's, Taf sent. *They are false words that can mean little.*

"Your ladyship," Mathias approached Zevara and stopped ten feet away, dipping into a short bow. "I would convey my appreciation of our accommodations.

Well-done, Taf sent.

"Is that the betrothal stone over there?" Keston darted off to the right of the courtyard.

Mathias shot Keston a glare. As wise as Keston could sometimes be at his core, he was still the impulsive commoner who didn't think. Asking Zevara yet another question? And bringing up the betrothal stone when the suitor games were so large in Aunia's mind?

Zevara raised her eyebrow.

I'll bespeak Rev, Taf sent.

Keston went pale, raised his hands and headed back toward them. "Please forget I asked that."

Zevara turned toward Mathias while Aunia walked over to Keston.

"Betrothal stone?" Aunia asked. "The one you told me about in Dalin."

"I assume you enjoyed your favorite foods." Zevara hovered her long, graceful fingers over the red and purple grouping of reed-roses while Keston tried to distract Aunia with mention of other faery items.

"We did, your ladyship," Mathias said, "and as you said last night, the time is nigh to discuss us leaving."

"Yes to your own lands. There is a cost to that."

"You have us be prisoners?"

Zevara laughed, long and musically.

"Just allow Tafiriel to skip us back."

"Oh, Mathias, you do not understand. My Tafiriel using a portal tile was like a knock on the door. It was I who answered it. But going back . . . that is more problematic."

"Problematic in what way?" asked Keston.

Aunia rubbed at her arm, her complexion growing paler.

"Punching a hole through the veil . . ." Zevara said. "Well, that would risk the collapse of everything, something we don't want with Nonderu eating into the betwixt. And that means we must use a veil door and to use one of those means, a penalty must be made."

Mathias straightened. "What sort of penalty?"

"Something not easy, and something necessary." Zevara ran a finger over several petals. "The cost is . . . you must come to a consensus of what your plan is together and you cannot go back on your word without consent of the other. Otherwise, you will find yourself back here."

Aunia crossed her arms. "I want to save my father. Obviously, since I can't go to Nonderu from here, I need to go to Tatia. He's not going to take me. Not with 'his dearest' there."

"She is not my dearest," Mathias responded.

"Oh? That's not what your letter said."

"I told you that was my parents' idea."

"If you didn't have feelings for her, then a secret wouldn't have been necessary."

"How are we going to come to a consensus?" Mathias slid away from Aunia. "She is not going to forgive this."

"Sometimes there are things we don't understand," Zevara said, "and it might not be about forgiveness but enlightenment and understanding first."

You should have told me we wouldn't be able to escape from here, Mathias sent to Tafiriel.

Perhaps you could bend your pride and share your heart with the girl.

She won't listen.

Don't you think you should try?

Mathias turned to face Aunia. The highlights from her wheaten hair in the white sunlight . . . and pouty perfect bow mouth . . . those dark blue eyes staring off into the distance as if she were lost and always would be. It nailed his heart against his sternum with a sudden ache.

"Aunia." He walked over to her and took her hand. She, of course, pulled it away, but he did not step back. "There has been no suitor game for me since I found you. I did not know my heart still lived until you showed it to me."

She bit her lip and her voice came out harsh. "What about the princess?"

"What of her? She has dozens of other suitors." Mathias ran a hand through his hair. "Please understand. I stepped into this game not because I loved her but because I wanted my father to forgive me . . . for my part in my little brother's death. I should have been watching him. And this was a way my family wanted me to perform my duty."

Aunia crossed her arms. "I want to save my father."

"I will take you to save your father. I will go with you to save him as well all the way to Nonderu. But Aunia, please. Let me save my country first."

"How do you mean?"

"Worley is on the way. We'll plant Jaia in the lord's greenhouses, then spy on the wererats in Spatelly to get the intel we need. From there, we fly to Tatia."

"I'm really glad the two of you are getting on," Keston inserted, "but have either of you heard about the dangers of a veil door? If you don't follow instructions exactly, they will turn you to ash."

CHAPTER THIRTY-SEVEN

THE PRICE OF MAGIC

No leyline consumed and no herb or crystal upon her when that deadly fire hit. — Master Fallo Vrael, flyer of Paderro and commander of Eddac Tower

Aunia folded her arms while she listened to Mathias' plea. A day ago, she would have done anything for him. But now, in lands where her life could be taken, she needed to trust those around her from her toes to her heart. Mathias had hurt her. She couldn't trust him. But understanding . . . perhaps she had that within her.

"Aunia, I know you are mad at me," Mathias said, "but—"

"What if the Boggleman comes after me during your big plan?"

Mathias frowned and looked at his hands. "I will drop what I'm doing to protect you and after you're safe, we go back to my big plan."

"Even if he tries to devour me with his cloak?"

Mathias' glow flickered like it did when he didn't totally believe something. "I will stand between him and you."

Aunia glanced at Zevara, then Tafiriel who remained under the apple tree with Revellie. "We'll need provisions, saddles—"

"And weapons," Mathias interrupted.

"Then you are agreed," Zevara said.

"I suppose." Aunia squared up with Mathias. "Do you want to do the saddles?"

Mathias crinkled his face in a confused expression.

Aunia rolled her eyes and sent to Tafiriel. *Has Mathias forgot about manifesting?*

"Of course, I know humans can manifest in the faery world," Mathias snapped. "But I also know that anything manifested disappears when we leave this world.

"My amulet didn't." Aunia furrowed her brow. "Zevara, why didn't it?"

"No," Mathias said.

"Stars and piffle-faddle on a question's price." Aunia crossed her arms. "Here it be. Answer do, answer might. An answer would delight."

Zevara smiled. "Poetry for the faeries. A quaint little gift. This I will tell you. As manifestation comes from visualization and desire, the locking comes from the permanence of memory. A core memory with someone significant in your heart."

"Like my mother," Aunia said. "But I have no memory of her."

"What are memories but rich emotion painted in and by time?" asked Keston.

Aunia spun to face Keston who shrugged.

"That would be one of the best descriptions that I've ever heard from a mortal." Zevara stepped away from the red and purple reed roses.

Keston stood tall with a broad grin, though he looked a little stunned when Zevara grazed his cheek with her palm.

"And yes," Zevara said. "When you use a memory, real or imagined, that speaks to your very heart of heart. Then whatever you manifest lives not only in fluid thought here but also in physical form there."

Keston nodded. "Then, we manifest our belongings and see if we choose wisely. And Matty, don't put your heart of hearts where you think others want it. Put it where it actually goes."

It was a few hours later that they followed Zevara to a veil door by going through the lower levels of her castle to the ground floor and out a narrow door at the white-stone building's base. From there, Zevara hovered inches from the ground ahead of them on a white-stone road with an entourage of breezling and ruork faeries.

Aunia walked beside Tafiriel with his new saddle—high-lipped with double leather bucket seats. The pegasus provided a screen between her and Mathias, who walked on Tafiriel's other side. Keston and Revellie followed behind them.

On the third switch-backed turn and with a vista looking out over several floating sky islands, Zevara slowed. "Two more switches and we'll be at the base of the mountain and the veil door. But while we are walking, Mathias, I should tell you the black pegasus in your unit . . . he's quite unhappy."

"I'd imagine," Mathias said dryly. "He's joined up with wererats."

Aunia frowned. "What's so bad with that?"

Mathias leaned back so he could see around the saddle. "Are you serious? But yes, I suppose you've only seen Basil's merry band of wererat mercs swooping in to aid us. That's not what usually happens. Most of them will tear you apart—like they did for my mentor, Dar Zeller."

"And if they don't tear you apart," Keston added, "they'll try to turn you into one of them."

"Then why has Fallo joined up with wererats?" Aunia asked.

Mathias and Keston exchanged a glance as they pivoted again on a switch-back turn.

"I think some of our men may have been turned to wererats," revealed Mathias. "And two of them were kin to Fallo. Not Jules, but nephews of his, Patrick and Garret. Zevara helped us to see where Fallo is and he's with them. He may have been turned as well so we must do what we're going to do quickly and without being spotted."

Being turned. And without permission. The thought of that made Aunia shudder.

Minutes later, they were at the bottom of the black stone mountain, where another path curved along the edge of the island. They followed it until it opened to a flat basin where basalt columns with twisting dark green vines rose five man-heights tall. Past the columns, an interlocked basalt and alabaster archway stood.

Zevara stopped at the columns and landed, bare feet upon the path's white stone. The breezlings and ruorks continued buzzing over her head as she walked to Tafiriel and scratched his ear. "Tafiriel knows the way to go safely through a veil door. Follow him and remember . . . keep as quiet as you can as you move through your world."

Mathias and Keston both gave Zevara a bow before following Taf through the columns. Aunia nodded but Zevara merely gave her a long look and then flew away with her ruorks and breezlings following her. Aunia frowned, feeling a little hurt, and stepped through the columns to join Mathias and Keston at the veil door.

She startled at the darkness. It seemed as if night had come on this side of the arch. In the center of the black shadows stood a long rectangle that rippled as if it were made of water.

"I suppose it is door-shaped," Aunia said weakly. "Does it have a handle or anything?"

Tafiriel nickered. *All we do is stand before the door and—*

Give the pledge, Mathias finished.

Aunia tightened her fists. A compromise pledge. But what choice did she have but to accept? She was on the hook to help Mathias get the evidence about bad wererats. Then afterward, she could go to Tatia to save her dad.

Both she, Keston and Mathias said the pledge at the same time. That they would go to Worley first to get the Jaia seeds started, Spatelly next to get the information they needed, and then to Tatia and help Aunia save her dad.

The three of them along with the two pegasi walked through the veil door. It felt like crossing a field of stinging nettles.

They appeared into the mortal world wrapped in velvety darkness with a thick scattering of stars sprawling overtop of them as a cool night's breeze spread among them. They stood upon a long incline with a valley sprawling beneath them. Aunia squinted, trying to make out details, but all she could tell was there was a dark river curling like a black ribbon and embroidered with twinkling light on one side.

"Lumentago Valley." Mathias stepped beside her. "The island city of Worley is in the middle of the Whisp River there. It's where we're going but that's a lot of lights they have."

"Yep." Keston pointed slightly behind them. "And look."

Near the horizon where no trees grew, a thin fingernail of a moon shone.

"That's impossible. We should be seeing a gibbous moon not . . ." Mathias paused and ran a hand through his hair. "Time moves differently in Faery. And your parents were in Pavari."

"What does that have to do with my parents?"

Mathias turned to Keston. "This is Kankari Eve."

"I am here," Aunia wrapped her arms around herself.

"I'm sorry. You don't celebrate Kankari, do you?" Mathias asked.

She shook her head, and he explained how Tamorians celebrated a monthly festival at the dark of the moon by cavorting about like faeries. For cause. It was to entice the moon, which folklore said slid further and further into the other world, to return.

Aunia stepped back. "You celebrate faeries when your people despise them?"

"There will be so many people down there. Everyone in a ten-mile radius." Keston walked from Revellie to Mathias. "And I love the festival but maybe it might be better to hole up until it's done."

"No," Mathias said. "Bibb has that witch compass and who knows what its range is. Let's go mount up. We go in. Hide in plain sight."

Keston's boots whispered through the grass as he returned to Revellie and climbed into the saddle. "Well, high chance Lord Lyle will be in a good mood when we ask him our boon."

Mathias extended a hand to Aunia to help her climb into the back saddle bucket seat. "I told you; Lyle is my father's friend. He'll say yes."

Aunia didn't take Mathias' hand and his body posture deflated as she climbed up herself. He then climbed up as well.

The clamor of people roared in her ears even before they approached the river where crowds pushed as they awaited to be squeezed onto the arched stone bridge.

"Can't we fly over?" Aunia asked.

Golden yellow flickered at the edge of Mathias' glow. A color for when he felt understood.

"Could," replied Keston, "But it wouldn't be polite."

"And we have to appear polite," Mathias added.

They merged into the noisy crowd, at least three of her village's population, and Aunia cringed as strangers brushed against her legs despite the feel of the heady excitement pressing against her. Flickering torchlights marching atop the bridge's balustrades columns leeched glimpses of jeweled reds, blues, purples, and yellows into grays and blacks. They also made the bodies jumble together in furs and feathers, making the people appear like beasts.

Her knee bumped into Mathias', a familiar touch in a flood of strangers, and her breath caught. Was he counting? He did that when he felt pressed in. She did not move her knee away. The end of the bridge came and the pressure of the crowd eased. Conversation snippets became clearer and one had Mathias pressing the side of her knee with his palm.

"Yes, I'm quite serious. You won't find a rover for your mint potion here. They made off with the lord's daughter," said a woman in a heavy dress and a feather mask.

"I've heard they've caught them," a man dressed in a button-rich doublet said and he and his lady friend wriggled deeper into the crowd. "Executions? No, I haven't heard . . ."

"Mathias." Aunia leaned forward in the saddle. "You have to follow them."

"No, we have to keep our heads down."

They turned down a less traveled cobbled street where tall buildings loomed and slim stairs curved toward narrow doors. Painted signs swung in the slight breeze with its strands of distant music and chatter. Worley smelled like soap and sawdust, entirely different from the rotting and metal odor of Dalin. But pleasant or not, she wondered about the rovers who had been mentioned.

Another smell hit her nose, and she sat up. This was buttery and sweet and . . .

A pack of children ran by, heading toward that smell.

"Little ones and sweets, bad combination for us," Keston said. "We might want to hurry if we're attending the festivities."

"Then it's a good thing we're here." Mathias pointed through a dark iron fence at a four-story building that squatted on a large front yard.

Light flickered through the many windows . . . orange light which did not come from candles.

"This has to be the finest inn in all of Worley." Keston dismounted and tugged on the gate's bell pull. Above him, stone harpies glared from the top of the iron gate post columns. They looked almost alive.

"Finest except for The Diadem," Mathias corrected.

"And why are we not there?" asked Keston. "Wouldn't Lord Lyle welcome us with great regalia?"

"Regale," Mathias dismounted, his spring green glow fading into a dying yellow. He held out his hand to Aunia. "And it's better if we're not with his other guests."

Aunia accepted Mathias' help with dismounting. Felt she had to . . . his glow said he feared meeting his father's friend but more than that . . . he was holding onto a childhood pocket of pain. And she knew what that felt like. Knowing that you'd never matter.

"Is this Lord Lyle like the lord in Dalin when it comes to faebloods?" Aunia set her hand against Tafiriel's neck to draw on a bit of courage. She did not like those stone harpies.

"Lyle is much more tolerant." Mathias frowned. "But he's a stickler for rules."

"He did keep Aeyrk's policies as well until her majesty discovered—"

"We should keep this conversation for later," Mathias interrupted.

"Why?" Keston asked. "Will Worley's lord like me less?"

"We're getting company."

A boy, maybe ten years of age, scampered to the gate and stuck his hand between the bars. Mathias handed him a copper coin and the boy unlocked and swung open the gate doors.

As the boy led them to a brown stone stable at the complex's back, Aunia was too aware of Mathias walking at her side. He again was doing what he thought was right including ending a conversation she wanted to know more about. No. He didn't want others to hear it. She wasn't being fair. And then, she clenched her jaw. *She* never called anyone 'dearest.' How was she to forgive him?

Two stable boys appeared when they entered the stable . . . rows of hay-lined stalls, most of them occupied.

Mathias was brotherly to the lads. Rubbed Tafiriel down himself while food and water for the pegasi were brought. Messy dark hair. Movements deliberate and gentle. She ached to have Mathias' arms around her but she needed to stop that kind of thinking. She could work with him. And after he helped her rescue her father, she would leave to set up a life on her own. That thought made her want to hide in one of the heaps of hay.

"Aunia? Everything okay?" Mathias stood with Keston and the ten-year-old. Tafiriel and Revellie were unsaddled, groomed, fed, and watered.

She nodded and followed them to the inn's side door and through a dim hallway.

Giggles and glowing orange light spilled from doors left slightly ajar. Aunia slowed. Anxious to know what the light source was. Pivoted to push open a door.

Mathias clasped her hand and mouthed, "Keep up."

"How far are firelings from here?" she asked.

"They're in Adar. Why?" Mathias asked.

Aunia shook her head and followed the group. The hallway dumped them into a large dining room which could have seated all of her village but it was empty except for three separate tables with two and three people. These diners ignored them but a short furry man clearing dirty dishes paused in his chores.

"You looking for sup?" he asked.

Mathias shook his head. "We're looking for a suite with two bedrooms for lodgings."

"Then it's me you need. Name's Craymore." The man set the dishes down and yanked a large ring of keys from his apron pocket. "Be a silver piece each."

"Each?" Keston choked.

"Per night," Craymore clarified.

"Agreed," said Mathias.

"Excellent. Then you'll have the best rooms." Craymore led them through another set of double doors and through another hallway until they reached a shadowy curved staircase. "I'm quite pleased and proud of this next convenience. Makes all the difference in a noble's court let alone my humble abode."

The man clapped his hands and puttering orange light erupted overhead. Swinging glass tubes hung from the ceiling by iron poles.

Aunia's stomach recoiled to her spine. Fire salamander lights.

"Isn't this grand," the short furry man said. "Cost me a fair coin and then some but worth it, especially for Kankari dark."

Mathias touched Aunia's wrist, his brows furrowed, and then he looked back at the innkeeper. "Worley's having criminal problems?"

"When has riches and dark places not made chummy bedfellows?" Craymore led the way up the stairs. "But other than a few missing folks, the Harpy's only had one petty theft."

"Where'd you get the magic lights?" Keston asked.

"From a caravan of rovers, if you must know." Craymore scratched the back of his neck. "Course, it wasn't the merchandise's fault and that caravan's been taken care of."

"Taken care of?" Aunia asked.

Mathias grasped Aunia's wrist and gave it one quick, gentle squeeze. "Because of the kidnapping?"

"Indeed." Craymore smiled at Aunia. "So, I be wondering, will the young miss be joining us in the tasting? You'd be—"

"This one has business with her majesty," Keston said.

Mathias drew closer to her.

Craymore frowned, then nodded. "Of course."

They climbed the stairs and Aunia kept her gaze fixed on the paintings lining the wall—somber-faced people and unfamiliar landscapes—instead of the salamander lights overhead. It wasn't right imprisoning faeries. But Narvis had betrayed her the last time he saw her. She couldn't risk any more betrayal. And they might, if she freed them.

She came to a halt a few steps away from the top of the stairs and raised her fingers toward a canvas depicting a battle scene of the dead and dying. The painting's center featured an orange-haired woman and a white-haired man. Olivia. The Boggleman.

"Do you like the Capture of the Maid of Idenweigh?" Craymore asked. "It was one of the first paintings I ever bought."

"He doesn't have a scar across his face," Aunia said.

"Scar? I've never been told of no scar."

Aunia hugged herself. She supposed no one knew her father had carved his knife over the Boggleman's face. For the first time, she wondered what price her father had to pay to leave Pavari. And if it had anything to do with him never killing anything. "Is our room near?"

Craymore nodded, led them through another hallway and stopped at its end. He swung open the suite's door, stepped inside, and clapped. Orange light brightened the carpeted mid-sized room with its cushy chairs and a fireplace. A door on both the left and the right walls stood ajar to the bedrooms.

Aunia curled her fists. Gabryella had done wrong by coercing those fierce dragon-like faeries into glass tubes, imprisoning them for what could be forever.

They stepped inside and Mathias shut the door, nearly hitting the innkeeper's face.

"Aunia?" he asked. "Why don't you freshen up and then we can find where those pastries are."

She crossed the room, red carpet shuffling over the tops of her sandaled toes, and entered the bedroom, dropping her knapsack onto the quilt-covered bed. She padded to the room's only window, pulled aside the heavy red drapes, and set a knee on a carved wainscot chair.

This room too held a salamander light and a big part of her wanted to pluck the light down and throw it out the window so the glass could smash against the inn's front walk. But that would bring attention to them.

She turned to the low dresser with its carved 'bird' legs and made quick work with the room's water, basin, and herb-scented feather-shaped soap. She rummaged then for the chemise and a short sleeve gown she had manifested in Pavari. She had paid attention to some of the clothing in Dalin and knew that looking like she fitted in was important. Particularly if she ever needed to slip away. The gown caught onto something from the knapsack and her poppet fell out onto the floor.

Biting her lip, she scooped up the doll. She was doing everything now for her father. A father who had left her mother behind. Like she needed to leave Mathias behind. She breathed in the doll's rustling stale herbs while tears pressed against her burning eyes.

"Aunia?" Mathias tapped at the door. "You about ready?"

Chapter Thirty-Eight

THE DANCE

Dancing is the wheel on fire. High and low. Back and forth. And who knows what partner you'll end up with. — Dar Heyden, advisor to Tamore's queen, former Adarian Dance Master

Mathias turned from Aunia's door, fists tapping at the top of his thighs, and paced from the pale stone fireplace to a chaise lounge chair at the room's corner and back again. Getting to Lord Lyle could be problematic. He wondered if he was making the right choice by attending the festival, but ten days had already past. Bibb had time to implement more devilry. They couldn't delay.

Keston turned from the window and released the heavy drapes. His gaze held a question, but he simply sat on a cushioned window seat.

""In a way, the timing is better." Mathias drummed against the back of a green-and-gold stuffed couch with his knuckles. "Lord Lyle will be there with his family watching the festivities from his viewing stand. He's been known to entertain a few requests throughout Kankari eve. Going up should not generate suspicion."

"So, you go up and just ask."

"I am my father's son." Mathias shrugged, then swallowed hard. "And the sooner we get these Jaia seeds planted, the sooner the faery repellent can be made. I can also see if he knows of any activity around Spatelly. And we already know Lord Lyle is obsessively loyal to her majesty."

Keston leaned forward. "You believe the other nobles aren't?"

"I think Bibb used Navenra on the knight-sons and Jules. Same as what got used on me at the Bellows. If that little flower affects flyers . . . think, how will it affect those who aren't imprinted with a pegasus? Unless they have a strong core."

"Like Jules sending Brinsaber off to save him," Keston said.

Mathias nodded. "Lyle is unbendable in many cases."

The door to Aunia's room squealed open and Mathias' breath caught as she stepped out wearing a fitted blue gown over a snow-white chemise and her hair was freshly braided into one long plait. She looked beyond respectable, she looked every inch noble-born in a gown that nearly matched her eyes. Mathias walked to her on unsteady legs, and taking her hand, kissed the softness just below her knuckles.

Her eyes grew large and she bit the bottom of her lip, bringing a burgundy blush to that perfect bow. He barely resisted touching the wisps of wheaten hair curling behind her ear.

"You both ready to go?" Keston asked. "I'd like to get a few custard tartlets before they're gone."

Mathias released Aunia's hand.

When I toil, it doesn't mean I don't enjoy the sunset or the glory of wildflowers dancing in the breeze, Taf sent. *Do what you must but enjoy the evening.*

Agreed. Mathias exhaled and lavished the feel of his heart fluttering in his ribcage. *I can make amends with Aunia while we're at Kankari.*

Keston buckled his sword and scabbard around his waist.

"No, Keston," Mathias said. "Daggers only. It's a dungeon sentence to draw weapon in front of the lord.

The three of them left the inn. They walked past a candlestick shop, dress-making stores, and a toy maker shop all the while following the music until they reached an orange-lit and crowded square. Melodious lutes mixed with the drone of the hurdy-gurdys. Flutes soared. And drums vibrated against Mathias' bones. Aunia, walking beside him, paled. She probably hadn't seen so many people before. This had to be more people than she had ever seen. Her gaze, though, remained on the magic lights hanging from strung ropes. They gave the festival an almost day-like feel, so different from the flickering torchlights a Kankari festival would usually have.

"Do you like them?" Mathias pointed to the closest orange-glowing light.

"Salamander lights?" Aunia's voice came out as if she were close to tears.

"What's wrong?"

"I saw the Boggleman and a fireling woman shoving fire salamanders into glass tubes when I was dreamwalking. Those faeries are prisoners."

Mathias frowned. A part of him thought about saying giving faeries a purpose might not be a bad thing but he didn't. "Do you need to talk about it? Or maybe we could wait 'til we get the first part of our mission done?"

Aunia wrinkled her brow.

"We could go for those custard tartlets." Keston waved at the food vendor stalls. "Come on."

Tantalizing smells pulled Mathias' attention in different directions. Savory meat pies. Buttery shortbread. "There are quite a few choices."

"Custard tartlets first." Keston strode to a rustic wooden stall with a red and white striped canvas and plunked down a coin. "Six custard tartlets, please."

The vendor handed over six fist-sized golden crusted pastries and Keston scooped them up. He brought them over and handed Aunia two. Reluctantly, he handed Mathias two of them as well.

While they ate, Mathias turned his attention to Lyle's dark-wood viewing box, which stood not quite ten feet off the ground. The red drapes from its covered awning were drawn, meaning Lyle was probably in discussion with a current petitioner.

"These are even better than berry jams." Aunia licked a bit of filling from her index finger.

Mathias handed Aunia one of his custard tartlets as a half-dozen children thundered past them. "Keston, why don't you take Aunia to hear the storyteller. I need to get in line for Lyle."

Aunia held a tartlet in each hand. "I could go with—"

"No." Mathias stroked her hair. "It would be better if you stayed somewhat out of sight."

She frowned but nodded, allowing Keston to take her over to a beige-colored pavilion where the children gathered around an older man in patched clothing.

Mathias brushed his hands off and strode to the northern end of the square. Several salamander lights hung over a pair of guards who stood watch at the feet of the viewing box's stairs.

Hand on his heart, Mathias nodded at them.

"He's with someone," the first guard said.

"Will the interview be long?" Mathias asked. His gaze climbed the polished railing, admiring its resemblance to flowering vines.

"The discussion is on the execution. Come back later if you must," the second guard said.

"Yes, but can I get on his list?" Mathias asked.

"He isn't taking a list tonight. It'll be hit or miss."

"No one else is on his list?"

"There is no list," the guard repeated.

Mathias clenched his teeth and nodded. "I'll be back."

He trudged back to Aunia who sat on the cobbled stones with several of the children while Keston stood behind her.

"And they say a brilliant cloud of green erupted from his chest when he breathed his last breath," the storyteller said.

The man was telling a peasant tale about a possible Chandarion before Edvaras' time, but it was a myth. An agenda Adarians spoke of to make themselves feel important. He had heard this tale once when he was small and it had not gone over well when his father walked into its telling.

"Poems tell of this Nymer cascading into the sky . . . perhaps to the Dama herself. And it was this day that a darkness fell over Queen Didianne's mind. It is said this was when she hid the Darra Chamber away, never to be found."

Mathias exchanged a glance with Keston, who shrugged at him, and then pointed at a brunette near the square's circular fountain where musicians played and dancers spun.

"There's a girl by the dancing. Miriel's her name," Keston said. "I told her I'd give her a dance next time I was in Worley. You and Aunia should come."

"Dance?" Aunia asked.

Mathias extended a hand and pulled her to her feet.

The three of them walked to the fountain.

"Were you successful?" Keston asked.

Mathias shook his head.

Keston nodded and strode quicker to the girl.

Aunia tilted her head. "What is it between you and Lord Lyle?"

"I just need to wait till he isn't busy."

"No. Your glow shifts. It turns a dying yellow when you think of him. Why?"

Mathias closed his eyes. If she could see that he was hiding something, it was best to just be truthful. "He advised my father to get his mistress with child and proclaim him the heir. That I should be disinherited for who my mother is."

Aunia halted as did Mathias, causing other festival attendees to wriggle between them and the fountain.

"Who is your mother?"

"She comes from Adar," Mathias said.

"I don't understand why that's a problem."

"There's much about my father I don't understand."

The two of them padded closer to the edge of the dance square where a dozen or more couples glided with measured steps and rhythmic claps. Keston, now with a laughing Miriel, bounced along with the others in hops and spins. Beside Mathias, Aunia swayed to a hurdy-gurdy's counterpoint.

Hay bales had been placed along the square's perimeter in regular intervals. Some were occupied but not all. He should ask her to sit. No. He should ask her to dance. He sucked in his breath, wiped his palms against his trousers, and glanced at Lyle's viewing box many yards away. The drapes had been pulled open and a sharp jolt hit Mathias' stomach. His mouth turned dry. Even from this distance, he recognized Fallo's short broad-shouldered frame. "Do you see Keston?"

Aunia leaned back and forth. "No, but there are a lot of dancers out there."

Taf bespeak Keston. We must get back to the Green Harpy now. Mathias balled his fists. *Taf?*

Mathias grabbed Aunia's wrist and pulled her toward the dance floor. "We got to get Keston."

Aunia tugged back. "I don't know your dances."

"Mimic the best you can." Mathias pulled her hand up and put his other hand on her waist. "We got to get Keston and back to the inn. Before we're spotted."

They made one turn and a hop when he spotted Keston and the brunette a few dancers away at the dance floor's middle. Mathias slid himself and Aunia toward them. Aunia stepped on his foot.

"It's okay," Mathias murmured through a grimace. He then let go of her hand to grab Keston's shoulder.

Aunia cried out and Mathias' hand slid off her waist. He whirled. Another wave of adrenaline flooded his body. Aunia was in the grasp of one of the knight-sons.

CHAPTER THIRTY-NINE

FIRE AND GLASS

Determination is a singular force that if fueled can overcome nearly every obstacle. — Dar Syrick

The boy who had grabbed her off the dance floor had the same sticky black threading his glow as some of the Da Vennen in Dalin. He also had the beginning of a wispy beard and his dark blonde hair was cut bowl-shaped. Aunia fought to get free of him but he tightened his grip and pulled her in the direction of the tents set in the corner of the festival square. Tents that included the storyteller's tent. A dark curly-haired boy stepped beside them wearing the same red and gold doublet as the first one. He had a wine sack hanging crossbody over his middle.

"Release her," Mathias barked. Gray-yellow flooded his glow—his worry as he stepped forward.

Mathias loved her. She knew that. She hit the boy in the gut with her elbow.

The boy made an oomph sound and grabbed her by the neck, squeezing. "Don't try that again."

"Patrick," Mathias hurried forward.

"Ah-ah, not too close." Patrick said.

Mathias halted not quite a man's height away.

"Have to admit, Matty," Patrick said, "she *is* a beauty."

"Don't call me, Matty," Mathias growled.

"Patrick, come on. Manners," said the other boy. "Mathias, come join us in Lyle's viewing box. We can all be together again and catch up."

These had to be the knight-sons that Mathias and Keston had been looking for . . . in addition to their friend, Jules. But didn't they know getting her angry... Aunia glanced up at the salamander lights hanging overhead amidst red and yellow buntings. She did not want Mygul to show up and behead someone else.

The music from the dance floor continued though the closest towns-folk turned to watch her plight. And they whispered amongst themselves.

"Together? Yeah, we'll catch up, Garret, after your shadow releases her." Mathias' hand inched toward his dagger.

"So inhospitable," Patrick said. "Thought you'd be happy to see us. You've been looking for us, after all."

"And we've heard what you've done." Keston approached from Mathias' right side with the girl he had been dancing with. The girl took Aunia in, sandals to crown, and then wandered away.

"Heard?" Patrick said. "You know nothing."

"Nothing?" Aunia leaned from the grip Patrick had on her collarbone so she could see a glimpse of his face. "Like attempting to murder your pegasi?"

Smoky blue flooded Patrick's glow, pushing back the sticky black, and his grip loosened. "Attempted?"

Aunia sprang away and Mathias pushed her behind him.

"We know why you've not answered any . . . attempts for talk." Mathias glanced at the small crowd of people who had stopped to watch.

They remained a respectable distance back but all Aunia could see around them, besides people, was the fountain.

"But tell us," Mathias continued. "Where have you been?"

"How do you know we weren't ordered away?" asked Garret. "Maybe our Dar Elect—"

"You would hide behind a lie about Nyrissa?" Mathias interrupted.

Patrick crossed his arms, the smoky blue fading and the sticky black returning. "Says Nyrissa's favorite."

"Former favorite," Garrett amended. "Perhaps she gave us a secret mission."

A splash drew Aunia's attention. Several children had come up behind the fountain and were taking off their shoes and stockings. Aunia narrowed her eyes. Was that a long-limbed shadow climbing onto the fountain's edge? She looked for the source but the angle . . . it belonged to no townsfolk. She bit her lip. She had read about shadow fae from Gaitha's books in Naoma Sacella but she had never seen one before and she wasn't sure what it was capable of.

"Mathias." Aunia tugged his hand.

"She is rather cute." Garret tapped his chin. "But I thought she was a rover. Didn't Bibb say she was a rover?"

Aunia clutched her fists, remembering what she had heard about rovers and an execution, but then more faeries—dark faeries with stick-like limbs and others with saggy skins and with orbed eyes perched atop their heads—appeared at the fountain. Their glows, instead of colorful iridescence sheen, glimmered as if they were wrapped in oil-slicked tar.

"Why don't we start over." Garret tugged the wine sack free and pulled out its stopper. He held it out to Mathias. "Drink?"

Keston snagged the wineskin. "How about you tell us what happened in Dalin?"

"Careful that," Garret said. "It's a '23 Bacrae Noir."

Keston held the skin at eye-level. "Where'd you get it?"

"Mathias." Aunia tugged his hand again and mentally threw a command at the faeries to leave. A second long-limbed shadow joined the first, and they were creeping toward the splashing children.

Mathias gave her hand a squeeze and released it to grab the skin from Keston. "We don't care about wine. Answer the question."

Mathias was too busy to help. She was on her own. And there were no faeries but the dark ones at the fountain. They were so close to the children. She felt sick not knowing what they would do. She swallowed down anger. It was too risky for Mygul to show up.

Tafiriel? Aunia sent. Surely the pegasus could help her.

One of the shadows fell over a boy of about eight years and he cried out, falling from the fountain's lip onto the ground and out of sight.

Aunia gasped. Took a step toward the fountain. Mathias clutched her hand. He didn't understand. Thought he was keeping her safe but . . . where was Jennium? Any benevolent faery? Orange light swayed along the cobblestones and Aunia looked up again. Salamander lights. They had helped defeat the heebles in her village.

"Answer the question with something novel, like the truth. Where did you go?" Mathias snarled. "Where is Jules?"

"Jules? He didn't know what was good for him." Patrick looked at Garret. "Don't have a choice. They'll be too much like Zeller's nephew."

Mathias punched Patrick full in the face and his head knocked back.

Patrick straightened. Spat blood.

"What happened to Jules?" Mathias snarled.

Other children leaped from the fountain. It looked like they were kicking something but the fountain itself—stone and water—were in the way for seeing.

Salamanders weren't evil. Even with Narvis' betrayal.

"Look. We just want to talk about duty to more than the crown," Garrett said. "Duty to humankind."

"In other words," Patrick said. "The girl's coming with us."

Focus on desire and core emotion. Focus on one-thing. Not anger but determination. Nothing was happening. Aunia closed her eyes. Focus. One-thing. Not save the children. That was the goal but one-thing. Break the glass.

A pinching sensation—more of a tickling—pulled at her temples. The salamander lights overhead brightened. Dimmed. And brightened again with a fiery glow.

Focus. One-thing . . .

A boom shook the square. Fire and glass rained down.

CHAPTER FORTY

SLEEPING PEGASI

Nothing quite stirs terror in the heart as being stuck in a bad situation with nowhere to go. — Dar Heyden, advisor to Tamore's queen, former Adarian Dance Master

Bursts of flame landed on nearby hay bales, contrasting the now pitch-dark night. Fire caught like candle wicks on the colorful buntings. Sizzled. Sparked. Roared with smoky sweetness from the hay. Rope broke and flaming buntings floated to the ground. Dancers behind them screamed. The music stopped. Scrapes of boots and pounding feet ran by. Patrick and Garret may have exchanged a brief look. It was hard to tell in the lighting, and they turned tail.

"Aunia, stay here," Mathias barked and took off after them.

"Mathias, no!" Keston yelled.

But he had to get them. They knew what happened. And Mathias collided with a mid-framed body. He and the other nearly fell.

"Get out of my way," Mathias shouted.

"You'd leave her here?" Basil yelled. "You forget what hunts her?"

The mystic must have skipped here. And scanning over the crowd, it was near impossible to tell where between crackling fire and pushing townsfolk where the knight-sons went. Mathias shook his fists in frustration.

Keston pulled Aunia with him and stopped at Mathias. "Tents. Look. Da Vennen!"

Across the way, nearer to the lord's viewing box, flames licked the corners of several striped tents and thick smoke rose.

"You freed the fire salamanders," Mathias yelled at Aunia. How could she bring such destruction? Lyle would never agree to help them now.

"They were attacking children." She jabbed at a hand at the fountain. "You wouldn't—"

Keston interrupted in a sing-song voice. "Bear cloaked men coming out of the tents. We need to go."

A bell tolled and one voice cut through the clamor of the crowd. "By the lord's order, commence a bucket brigade."

"They'll be coming to the fountain," Keston said.

If enough people remained to help with a bucket brigade, they could save most of the square but . . . they'd also be seen by the Da Vennen. Patrick and Garret would lead the soldiers to them. "Back the way we came," Mathias said.

"Don't run," Basil snapped. "Walk fast. We don't need the attention."

They headed for the eastern road and the blockage of frightened people. The alleyway squeezed tighter. The air disappeared. Everyone pushed, making all motion feel like they'd sink like a wind-ravished boat in a storm. Mathias pulled Aunia behind him. Trying to shield her. Wanting to be shielded himself. Then the crowd broke away, spilling into other roadways, and the alleyway opened up.

Taf? Mathias gulped a breath, ran on trembling legs. They needed to leave Worley as soon as they made it back to the inn. It would be a quick 'put the tack on and grab their belongings.'

Taf didn't answer.

"They came down this way," said a gravelly voice a few yards back. "Find them."

"This way," Basil hoarsely whispered.

They turned left into a dead-end stacked with barrels.

"Back out," Mathias ordered.

"No," Basil said. "Give me your hands. We're skipping."

Mathias took Aunia and Basil's hands. Keston grabbed hold of Basil's arm.

For a moment, Mathias felt like he slid outside of himself, like everything was in motion though he didn't move. He felt weightless, and he stumbled to keep his footing. The barrels and the dead-end had vanished. They were in front of the candlestick shop.

"This wasn't a big jump," Keston said. "Shame you couldn't land us all the way to the Green Harpy."

"Definitely more ideal," Mathias said. He wanted to know why Taf wasn't answering. He tapped Keston's arm and then tapped his own ear. A silent question about bespeaking.

"Too many bodies to move for one Mystic," Basil said. "Let's not lose our head start."

They broke into a run, stars and the occasional candle in the window their only source of light.

"Mathias?" Keston's voice sounded strangled.

Well, that answered that. Keston obviously couldn't reach Revellie either.

Mathias' heart sank into his running knees. "I know. Me too."

They passed a crossroad with a drinking faucet and basin, and after that, they passed the toy maker's shop.

"What made the lights go?" Keston asked, a slight tremor to his voice.

"Dark fae," Basil panted. He was running beside Aunia and close to Keston.

"Faeries?" Keston asked.

"I tried to tell you," Aunia panted.

She spoke of dark shadows, saggy-skinned monstrosities, and creatures with eyes on the tops of their heads. What she didn't say was how she freed the fire salamanders.

"The Boggleman . . . he sent them," she revealed.

"I had hoped the Boggleman was dead," Mathias said.

"He isn't easily killed," said Basil.

They continued running, their footfalls nearly matching each other. It was a slight comfort having the murmuring voices coming from far away but worry still roiled Mathias' gut.

Mathias slowed and curved closer to Keston. Having a Mystic in their group kept them from speaking on their pegasi telepathic abilities. He leaned close to Keston's ear. "When did you hear her last?"

"Before we left the inn." Keston threw a look over his shoulder. "I hope these Da Vennen don't know where we're going."

They reached the inn's locked gates, shook the bars, and yanked on the bellpull. No answer. The torchlights on the gate columns were guttering and much of the lights inside the inn had gone out, though some orange hues still flickered from some of the windows. Obviously, not all salamander lights had been broken.

Keston jumped, grabbing the gate bars, his feet swinging from the ground.

"There are points at the top." Mathias turned to Basil. "Can't you unlock this?"

"Flyers encouraging crime?" Basil asked.

"Put up a good chase," projected the gravelly voice from earlier.

A black form, maybe thirty feet away, stood in front of a gang of six or seven others. How did they catch up so fast?

A sword whistled from a scabbard and the gang started walking toward them. Mathias and Keston only had daggers. And Aunia had her questionable magic source. It did not always come when it was called. And Basil?

Mathias pulled his dagger. "Any clever schemes in your pocket?"

A whoosh sounded behind the Da Vennen and a deeper patch of night lowered from the sky. Then a clatter . . . of hooves. Paderro. Fallo's pegasus put his body between Mathias and his party and the Da Vennen soldiers.

Keston, standing shoulder to shoulder with Mathias, dagger drawn, cocked his head. "Is Fallo the enemy, or no?"

Aunia rattled the gate rails behind them. "He says Fallo isn't himself. He's been drugged since leaving for Scorched Earth."

"Aunia," Mathias murmured, hoping she'd catch his tone. They couldn't have the Da Vennen or Basil know about the pegasi telepathy secret.

"They've Navenra'd Tafiriel and Revellie," Aunia continued. "Put it in their feed."

"Shut up, you," said a higher voice beside the gravelly hollow voiced one. "Surrender now or it'll go very bad for you."

Navenra. Taf and Rev had been drugged, and if it was like last time Taf had blue flowers in his feed, it would be hours before he shook it off.

"Fallo doesn't need his pegasus," the gravelly voice said. "Attack!"

The Da Vennen rushed forward and Paderro stamped a forefoot. The thump echoed through the air and the attacking men fell over. Skidded along the cobblestones. Snored where they stopped. Bear fur cloaks twisting around them.

"Hurray, Paderro," Keston cried.

Confused over what had just happened, Mathias shot Keston a glare, then turned to the Mystic. "Can you unlock the gate?"

The Mystic rover reached for the gate handle and tugged. A metallic rattle. Nothing more.

"Aunia, lovely, put your hand over mine, would you?" Basil said.

Mathias frowned. "Why do you need—"

"You think magic is limitless?" Basil snapped.

Aunia set her hand, small in comparison, over Basil's and they both tugged. The gate door gave with a snick and pushed open.

Mathias' heart raced as they ran across the yard, leaving the sleeping Da Vennen lie. Paderro ran ahead of them to the stables. His memory of being Navenra'd at the Bellow came in bits and pieces. Taf was sleeping and he couldn't leave his pegasus. They were stuck in this place. And who knew how long the Da Vennen would stay asleep outside the gate.

They reached the brown-stone stable's double doors. Mathias yanked open the right door and entered the lantern-lit and wide, central aisle. The ten-year-old, who had opened the gate for them earlier in the night, stood near the back of the stable in front of Revellie's stall with a bucket in his arms.

"Oy," Keston called and darted to the lad.

The boy dropped the bucket. It clunked against straw-covered flag-stones and the child darted off to a ladder at the stable's back and climbed to its loft.

Keston swore, ran, and climbed the ladder after him.

Mathias hurried to Tafiriel's stall; a space enclosed with wooden half-walls. His pegasus lay on his side in a pile of fresh hay, his side billowing. Pushing past the feed trough, Mathias dropped to his knees. "Tafiriel?"

He patted his pegasus' neck and shoulder. Called again.

Paderro, hooves clicking against the floor, paused by Tafiriel's stall and then moved to the adjoining stall to Revellie.

Aunia and Basil followed. Both passed Tafiriel's stall to Revellie's.

"There's Navenra here." Aunia walked into Taf's stall with a blue flower between her thumb and forefinger.

Paderro followed her, and Aunia, frowning, patted the black pegasus' neck. She entered Taf's stall. "He says he can't wake them."

"The wyverns that are drugged with this flower are only compliant for less than a day," Basil said. "It should be out of their systems in a few hours."

"We don't have a few hours," Mathias snapped. He continued calling Taf, scratching and patting his neck and shoulder.

Aunia dropped to her knees beside him, hands on his pegasus' blue hide, softly calling him.

Keston returned from the loft, panting. "The lad escaped through a loft hatch."

Mathias grunted, and Keston hurried to Revellie's stall and pushed past Paderro, crying her name. An anguished sound. It brought another lump of terror into Mathias' throat.

"Where'd the Da Vennen even get Navenra?" Mathias asked. "I've only heard of it not two weeks ago, and both your wererats and the Da Vennen are using it."

"I don't know how the Da Vennen got it," Basil said. "But my wererats got theirs from Hebsolum. Wanted to be sure the Boggleman's wyverns didn't break through Syrick's spell."

"Come on, Tafiriel," Aunia called. "Wake up."

"We can't stay here." Basil stood outside Taf's stall, an arm across the top of the half wall. "Or at least she can't. I'll skip her away and—"

"No," Aunia said.

"We're going to have to do what we did before." Mathias reluctantly pulled his fingers from Taf's blue coat and leaned forward to rise. "Tie up those soldiers, and cart them in. But where to stash them."

"Mathias," Aunia tugged on his wrist.

Tafiriel's eyes were fluttering open.

Taf? Mathias patted Taf's neck.

Tafiriel opened his dark blue eyes . . . blue almost the color of Aunia's, Mathias realized.

Taf blinked. Blinked again. *Why are you upset?*

You weren't answering. The band around Mathias' chest loosened mixed with another surge of anxiety.

I was asleep, Tafiriel sent.

Drugged you mean . . . with Navenra. Like on the Bellows.

Taf lifted his head with a soft nicker. He rose, legs shaking beneath him.

"Mathias," Basil said. "She cannot stay here. Your Tafiriel, as wondrous as he is, isn't in shape to fly and with two."

"We're stronger together," Aunia said. "Zevara told us that. And I have an idea."

"Idea?" Mathias stepped back, his gaze on Tafiriel who swayed unsteadily on his feet.

She nodded. "I have Leiaphae in my poppet upstairs."

"Leiaphae?" Basil moved to the stall's entrance.

"Another of Edvaras' flowers," Mathias said. "It shrouds as it'll make us invisible, but Aunia, do you know how to use it?"

"I think so," Aunia said. "We'll have to use a small space. There isn't much but if we can get Taf in Revellie's stall . . . I'll go in and get it."

"Go with her, Matty," Keston said. "I'll stay here."

"You don't even have a sword," Mathias said.

"Paderro has Fallo's." Aunia pointed to the black pegasus who hovered outside of Revellie's stall.

I can help, Taf sent. He stumbled as he took a step and huffed. *Go.*

Mathias gritted his teeth and took Aunia's hand. "We'll be right back."

Basil followed behind Mathias and Aunia as they ran for the inn. They entered the side door and hurried through dark hallways with their hands trailing along raised paneled walls. On either side of the hallway, drunken snores drifted from sitting rooms.

They passed through the double doors into the dining room where a few candles guttered on tables. Basil plucked one. The taper grew long in his hands. Basil shrugged. "Lead on."

They passed through another set of double doors to the stairwell.

"Basil, how did you find us?" Mathias asked.

"I've my ways," Basil said.

"Jennium." Aunia squeezed Mathias' hand. "He has faery sight, too."

"Hope you won't tell that to all," Basil added.

Every mystic has a faery familiar, Tafiriel sent, his tone almost dismissive.

"Your secrets are safe with me," Mathias said, "particularly if you keep ours."

"Of course," Basil said.

They got to their room and Mathias unlocked the door.

Keston's panicking, Taf sent, *Revellie isn't waking up. Paderro says she ate too much of those flowers.*

Too much of those flowers? Cold filled Mathias' gut. *We'll be there soon.*

He swung open the door. "We must hurry. Aunia, you grab your stuff. I'll grab mine and Keston's. Basil, you watch the door."

Aunia ran ahead of him to her bedroom and Mathias veered to the one he shared with Keston. He had taken two steps into the sleeping chamber with its two narrow beds when a door slammed and Aunia screamed.

Chapter Forty-One

THE BOGGLEMAN

Remain wary in your dealings with outsiders. Dark ones walk among them. — Edvaras, beloved of Naoma

The Boggleman lounged in the window chair, one leg thrown over its arms, and orange light from two swinging glass tubes dancing across his ruined face. He grinned widely. "What an enjoyable scream, my dearest Aunia."

Aunia, in her haste to grab her poppet and her knapsack, hadn't noticed him until she was alongside her bed. He grinned. She jumped, and her door slammed shut on its own.

She inched backwards toward the door while the Boggleman watched her. Her knapsack sat beside the dresser. Almost within his arm's reach . . . and with the star book inside. But she couldn't risk getting it. She needed to shroud the pegasi before the Da Vennen awoke but how could she now?

Even more terrifying was the wavy hole in the air beside the Boggleman, a glimmering like the one she had seen in the Birchwoods when the Boggleman dragged her father through. She swallowed hard. He imprisoned her father. He meant to imprison her. She well remembered the empty Chand ice column beside the other frozen figures . . . Olivia,

Edvaras, and his beloved, Naoma. He would attack and then he would hold her there frozen for all of time.

The door handle stung her fingers with coldness and she could feel vibrations through the metal . . . there was a voice on the other side of the door. A muffled voice. Mathias called her name. She leaned her ear against the wood. Straightening, she tugged again but the door wouldn't budge.

Acting like a frightened animal would not serve her but what could she do? She crept back alongside the bed . . . to her poppet laying against the pillow. Her sandal hit something with a high pitch clink and then a hollow ring. An empty salamander glass tube rolled under her bed. Several more lay around her bed. Her stomach caved in as she realized the Boggleman had probably released them—not for freedom, but to eat them with his cloak. The same cloak that billowed around his shoulders as if a breeze caught its fabric. But that was impossible. The window was shut.

She bit her lip wondering if she was safe from that cloak. But she wasn't dreamwalking and she wasn't faery . . . though she could have faeblood. She didn't know. And even if she was safe from the cloak, he could change shape into something more dangerous. And he had other tricks. She hadn't forgotten that he had pulled her forward by magic when she encountered him in the Birchwoods. It was that force holding her against the creek stones that had saved her. A force he had called mother.

The Boggleman continued staring at her, an index finger tapping at his scarred chin.

Mother. And water. She blinked. A fish widow had found the Boggleman from the ocean centuries ago, yes, but there was one Eaburrai who was attached to water. Kai-Marin. Kai-Marin had to be the core memory that the Boggleman used for the locking spell he had on his cloak. Would it be as simple as telling the Boggleman she knew what he used to make his cloak real in order to destroy it?

Aunia scooped the doll against her chest, and it crinkled with mustiness. Her father always said that doll would protect her—probably because of the Leiaphae inside. If she held it . . . its magic and hers mingling . . . Shroud me. Shroud me. If she were invisible for just a moment so she could think.

"How sweet. A parental love token." The Boggleman straightened on the chair. "You don't need that silly doll."

"I demand you return my father." Aunia gritted her teeth.

"I'll be the one making demands." The Boggleman waved a come-hither with his twisted fingers. "Come here."

Her hands went limp, and the poppet dropped to the floor. After that, the same phantom hooking sensation she had felt in the Birchwoods—and flying over the Grashbear too—grabbed her behind the navel. She took several steps forward, her body a stranger.

No. No. No. Aunia struggled. Tried to unfreeze her muscles to grab the bed. The dresser. Anything. Something to grab her like Kai-Marin had in the creek. Like Mathias had when they flew on Tafiriel's back. *Jennium. Jennium! Where are you!*

"Keep coming," he said, "Almost there."

She struggled to slide her foot backwards. To curl her fists. I'm not afraid. I'm not. I'm not going to obey some unwanted fish-widow's son. A burning sensation caught her just below her collarbone where the orb from her father's amulet touched her skin. Her muscles unfroze, and she came to a halt. "I'm not going anywhere with you."

An orange flame crown erupted around his head. "Such spirit," he crooned. "What if I give you an option? I give you what you want?"

He snapped his fingers and the glimmering beside him turned colorful like a soap bubble in the sun. And then, glowing coals dumped through the glimmering at the Boggleman's feet.

Steam wafted up as the coal heap lengthened and when the coals stopped pouring through, the ash-hot surface shifted. Moved like heated tree sap. She jumped as limbs sprouted from the molten goo. A head formed. Clothing appeared. Then, whatever it was, rose, facing the window and only inches away from the Boggleman.

Aunia's mouth went dry, and she gawked at the wavy brown hair. It slowly turned around. Took her in with its . . . his . . . light brown eyes. Her father stood there. But . . . it couldn't be her father. It was a trick. A torment. But could a part of that truly be her dad? She saw no brick-red glow around it, but its . . . his expression. The bruises and marks were the same as the last time Aunia had seen him in Nonderu.

"Say something, Runey the Oldy," the Boggleman said. "Your daughter misses you."

Her father lifted his arms wide as if he expected her to come running with a fierce hug.

Aunia's shoulders tightened. Why wasn't he yelling at her to run? Had he been broken during his imprisonment? Or was he finally showing the truth? That he really didn't care. That she was disposable, like her mother. Like that girl she had seen in her vision at Scorched Earth. That he never really cared.

"It looks like your daughter doesn't want you." The Boggleman held his hand up as if he'd snap his fingers again.

"Wait," Aunia said.

"Oh, you do want him? I'll make you a deal. He walks free if you come with me willingly. I swear it on my very existence."

Jennium's soft jingle rang against Aunia's ear and her tiny faery hands gripped Aunia's hair. She must have just blinked in. Faeries couldn't lie.

Aunia bit her lip and turned slightly toward the door. Mathias's voice calling for her drifted into the room. He sounded frantic, beating against the door. And Basil's voice was uttering poetic spells.

Basil. He had told her at Scorched Earth that the Boggleman feared her because she had a chance of stopping him like her father. Well, her father sure wasn't stopping him.

Jennium jingled again. Projected a memory in Aunia's head of her dad pushing the Boggleman through the glimmering first, telling her to run. Projected a series of images of her father protecting her. She then pushed an image of the coals as they first poured from the glimmering and buzzed.

"Shall I return him to his prison?" the Boggleman said.

Indignation flared in Aunia's heart. The Boggleman was lying to her. A faery lie to be sure but that thing was not her father. Broken or not, he wouldn't just stand there blinking at her. A sharp pinch grabbed her at the temples and she did not fight the sensation.

Mygul appeared in a glorious rage, curving upwards over her head like a miniature blue sun.

The Boggleman jumped sideways from the chair as Mygul curved upwards to Rune. It circled the Rune-being's head and his tan face turned shiny. The not-her-dad stumbled against the chair.

Rivulets of hot wax substance oozed from her father's reddened cheeks and plunked to the floor. Then his limbs lengthened, twisted, spilled out like deer guts.

This wasn't her father. Not her father. Aunia's knees shook.

Mygul expanded into a thin shell around the collapsing form. Pulsed with a boom. Blistering heat knocked her over and slammed the Boggleman against the wall. The basin and pitcher on the dresser crashed to the floor.

"I will stop you," Aunia screeched at the Boggleman as he pulled himself to his feet. "I will unlock that cloak of yours and—"

The Boggleman smiled and threw a corner of his cloak over Mygul.

Aunia screamed as gouging pain filled her. Parts of Mygul were siphoned into the cloak.

"Oh, so glad Hebsolum didn't get this," the Boggleman said. His voice sounded as if it came from the end of a tunnel.

"Mygul," Aunia croaked. "Door."

Mygul pulled away. Darted to the door in a wobbly line and crashed through it.

Jennium flew to Basil and landed on his head while Mathias raced in and pulled Aunia away from the Boggleman. Basil raised his hands and a pulse of yellow light flew from them. It hit the brass rod holding the heavy curtain up and it came crashing down. Aunia's mattress rose next.

The Boggleman snarled. And with two large steps, and over the hissing ash pile, plunged himself into the glimmering.

Mathias' arms wrapped tightly around Aunia and as much as she craved to be comforted, it was not the time. She pulled away.

"He has part of Mygul. I have to follow. Unlock that cloak before all of us are ruined." She turned to look at Mathias. "You promised."

"I'll go with you," he said. "Basil, help Keston."

"Are you sure, Mathias," Basil questioned. "What of Tafiriel?"

Mathias' grimaced as if he were in pain. "We are stronger together."

Chapter Forty-Two
FANNED WITH FLAME

When all has gone in smoke and you stand among the people who you do not trust for good or ill, it becomes imperative you trust your gut. — Dar Zeller Rieson, flyer of Startengo

The stinging nettle sensation faded from Mathias' skin and Aunia's upturned bedroom from his sight. Instead, he and Aunia hid between a heaping pile of shattered rocks and a rough cave wall while screams rang out and sandpaper shuffle of many feet dwindled. Above them, icicle stalactites hung. They were in Nonderu, the underground kingdom of the Boggleman and everything was bathed in a faint orange light

"I said, come back," the Boggleman said in his high-pitched musical voice.

Prickles ran down Mathias' back and he gripped his sword tighter, heart thudding. The Boggleman should have a rough voice, a voice like Bibb's. Not a voice like the Canthelark singers his mother employed during festivals. Especially not while the villain's cloak snapped up and devoured faeries . . . bat-winged creatures and squat, knee-high things with eyes atop their heads. It had even swallowed up two Mockmen trolls before the remaining troop fled.

Mathias peeked out. The Boggleman stood near the back wall in front of three ice columns with twisted-limbed people frozen inside and his cloak swirled around him. Backed up along the wall on the other side of the cavern was a boy near Mathias' age with disheveled light brown hair and a red ribbon tied around his neck.

"Listen," Aunia whispered. Her face looked pale in the orange otherworldly light. "Before he eats more of Olivia's energy—"

Aunia pointed toward the Boggleman and the frozen people. Realization struck Mathias like lightning rocking his core and spreading out to fill his chest. He stood in the presence of Chandarions. Olivia. Edvaras. And with Edvaras was his beloved Naoma. He blinked several times.

"Mathias," Aunia gripped his arm. "Pay attention. He's been feeding off her energy but she's near depleted and as for Edvaras, the Boggleman can't because his light is boxed."

The faint orange light filling the chamber . . . that came from Olivia. Mathias shook himself, nodded, then leaned against her ear. "He eats her energy with his cloak. Do you know what his core memory is to unlock that back into oblivion?"

"His desire to know his mother," Aunia murmured.

"His mother?"

Aunia leaned against Mathias. Whispered fast. "Kai-Marin abandoned him to be raised in a fishing village. She's an Eaburrai—"

"Wait. Kai-Marin is—"

"His mother. One he hasn't forgiven. That'll be his core memory. To make her suffer. I'll confront him. And I need you to save my dad."

"Your dad?"

"He's in that cage on the platform."

Mathias peeked out again in the direction of the boy. In the center of the chamber sat a raised platform and on that raised platform stood a large animal cage. A figure sat huddled within. "You sure that'll be his core memory?"

"I know because I know mine. I locked my mother's amulet in existence because of my desire to know her." Aunia gripped the neckline to her blue Tamorian gown. "Oh, and don't touch the cage bars. It'll be spelled to suck you in. Manifest a key instead and get the two of you back to the glimmering."

Powdery footfalls walked toward them.

"He's coming back," Mathias said.

Aunia balled her hands into fists and sucked in a breath. "You ready?"

A well of emotion erupted through Mathias and he squeezed her arm, preventing her from springing out of hiding. "No matter what. I love you."

He released her then, jumped out from behind the rocks, and sprinted to the raised platform and the cage.

"You," the Boggleman yelled.

If he could keep the Boggleman's eyes off Aunia until she unlocked that cloak . . . but he'd still be dangerous.

You're human, Tafiriel's silvery voice sounded faintly in Mathias' head.

I can manifest here. Manifest an entire army. An army of himself like the wererats had magicked in Dalin but his army would have substance.

Mathias leaped onto the platform beside Rune's cage.

"Oy," Aunia yelled, and she launched into verse:

> Your mother who've you've not forgiven
> Kai-Marin sails where stars are daring.
> In shadowed seas, but you're not caring.
> With whispered winds and tides unseen,
> She placed you beyond the worlds between.

The Boggleman's high-pitched laugh sounded startled and incredulous. "You'd dare? You've the wrong core thought. You'd be closer by imagining your entire world in flames."

The Boggleman's form rose, growing higher and towering over Aunia. Mathias gripped his sword. He had to help her.

"And to feel despair as you ought . . ." The Boggleman snapped his fingers. "Axe-pickle."

One lone mockman troll poked its tusked head through the cave maw that opened into this cavern. Surely a people, Mockmen trolls even, who had just fled to escape being consumed wouldn't return. Would they?

"Mathias," Rune croaked. His robust presence had withered to a husk. He was thin, bruised, haggard. "Manifest."

Mathias swallowed and dropped to his knees before the cage's locked door. Key or army. There was only one choice. Mathias closed his eyes and imagined an army of flyers. And knowing that he needed to add all details of the one-thing, he fashioned the men to look exactly like himself and with the purpose of keeping Aunia safe.

A symphony of thick-soled boots echoed off the stone floor with a mix of murmurs and metallic clinks of swords.

The Boggleman snarled and threw a corner of his cloak against the ice column where Olivia, long orange hair spread wide, permanently kneeled with a dagger held over her head.

"No," Aunia cried.

Rune screamed Aunia's name as a thundering rumble, grunts, and growls, erupted from behind.

Mathias swiveled on his knees. Raised his sword and caught a jagged slab of dark iron hacking downwards at his head. The beast-faced mockman troll gripped his mismatched leather-wrapped hilt and pressed his weight against it.

Mathias' arms shook. He rotated his arm as best as he could, changing the angle of his sword . . . horizontal to more vertical. The mockman's sword rode the sharp edge of Mathias' sword to the ground. And Mathias, lifting on his knees, angled his sword tip to greet the mockman's approaching face.

Mathias rolled, yanking his sword from the dying beast.

Inside the cage, Rune howled. Smoke curled from his fingers where he gripped the bars.

More Mockmen ran in from the cave entrance. Mathias staggered to his feet. Considered retreating to where the Boggleman tossed fireballs at Mathias' army. The army was smaller. Some were incinerated. Others drank in by the Boggleman's cloak.

Rune released the bars, fingers curled at his chest, and a bright light filled his cage.

Aunia had withdrawn back to the rock pile while his army was being decimated. He and Aunia had to retreat. Get back to the glimmering.

Two brown rats ran out from between the bars of Rune's cage and darted for Mathias. They shimmered as they ran, transforming into . . . Rune and the boy who had cowered along the side wall. Mathias raised his sword.

"Get to the glimmering. By the rocks," Mathias yelled.

Rune, however, raised his hand and a short, curved sword appeared within it. He also manifested a helm and a suit of light armor to cover his thin body. "Get to my daughter."

At least twenty Mockmen attacked. Retreating toward Aunia, Rune defended, knocking blades aside and Mathias took opportunities for killing blows. Several Mockmen fell.

Behind them, Aunia screamed as Mathias, pressed by enemies, couldn't look.

Rune took a large step backwards, leaving Mathias' side. He pointed at the lad huddled against the far wall. "Jovaryn, now."

The lad, no longer wearing a ribbon around his throat, raised both hands, while a third of the Mockmen split off toward him. A shimmer and a long table appeared laden down with foods and behind hanging on the cave wall was a long banner with all twelve Eaburrai. It was like the banner inside the blade-cave before Mathias and the others had been transported to the Dead Lands.

How would that help? Accidental conjuring. Had to be. Or the lad was very hungry. Mathias jumped back as a blade ran across his arm bringing a sick feel to his gut.

He continued fighting as did Rune. And behind them, the lad recited:

Hebsolum, I call your name
with every heartbeat, fanned with flame

The first mockman troll brought its sword down at Jovaryn's head. The lad dodged. Its iron sword rang against the cave floor. The beast lifted its weapon and ran at Jovaryn. The lad darted around the table and under.

A booming crack shook the cavern. And other creaks and cracks sounded. Along the far wall the three columns lay shattered, and the frozen people sprawled on the cave floor. The Boggleman pulled himself onto his feet as did the Mockmen trolls. And at Aunia's side stood the dwarf Hebsolum.

Chapter Forty-Three

THE RIPPING

It has been said that forgiveness is a gift. A gift that sometimes can have sharp edges. — Dar Syrick, advisor to the Tamorian queen

Time seemed to slow for Aunia. She stood near the pile of rocks that she and Mathias had hid behind. Mygul twirled around her head. Chand ice chunks scattered across the cavern floor, along with Olivia. Her orange hair spilled around her. Covered her face. And her body . . . she looked as if she were a life-sized rag doll.

"Aunia?" Dad pushed his way through the Mathias look-a-likes. They stood as if they were living statues as did the Boggleman and the mockman trolls.

The faintest wriggle of relief broke through Aunia's emotional numbness. Her father was free. But she neither shrank away from nor returned her father's hug. Instead, she stood blinking. Over and over, the Mathias soldiers had been blown apart by fireballs and sucked into the Boggleman's cloak. And now, her rover friends' dream of being reunited with Olivia was gone.

"Jovaryn, cavorting with Chandarions and the Boggleman." Hebsolum walked away from Aunia to the disheveled-haired lad. He halted.

Glared at Edvaras, who rose on shaky feet with Naoma, a pale woman with light brown hair. "You."

Edvaras' swarthy skin turned grayish.

"He is mine," the Boggleman snarled. His crossed arms lay pinned against his chest as if an invisible force crushed him. "And release me, statue."

Hebsolum. Fear crept back into Aunia's heart. She grabbed tight to her father's upper arm. The last time Aunia had seen the marble giant and his avatar, other than in Pavari, he had thrown her into the sky. He had meant to see her die. He was not a friend. Aunia stepped past Olivia's body. "You killed her."

Edvaras and Naoma, on unsteady legs, hobbled to the glimmering and passed through it.

"The Boggleman drained her nearly complete." The dwarf turned to face her. "She was useless."

"Use..." Aunia blinked. "Useless?"

"If you mean to finish him off, broken one, do it now." Hebsolum pointed at the Boggleman. "I won't stay here forever, keeping your adversary in place."

Dad moved to her side. Her dad who never killed. She needed him to retreat to a safer distance. If she killed the Boggleman . . . but that wasn't what she intended. The Boggleman deserved death. Didn't he? All the atrocities he had committed . . . but after she killed him, Hebsolum would kill her. Because he hated all who held any Chandarion magic.

She clenched her fists. And he had called *her* broken one. What was he thinking? That she was a potential who had gone wrong. Perhaps there had been bad things that had happened to him. Like losing Yasendra to another but he stood within his own pot of unforgiveness.

"You love Yasendra," Aunia said, her voice shaking. Anger flickered past the numbness. "You're in conflict because what you want and what you're supposed to do is different."

"Aunia," her dad warned.

"Dispatch him," Hebsolum's silver and purple glow flared, and he tugged at his red-brown beard. "Spill his life."

"Or what?" Aunia pinned her shoulders back. As soon as the Boggleman was dead, Hebsolum would turn on her. Like he had with Olivia. And killing wasn't what she had planned to do.

She glanced at her father. Killing was not an easy thing. Unmaking the Boggleman's cloak. That was her task. That was what she meant to do.

"I believe you need more incentive." Hebsolum looked past Aunia to where Mathias and a dozen Mockmen trolls stood in battle-ready poses. This Mathias, her Mathias, had a spring-green glow.

Muscles from several of the Mockmen twitched. They slumped forward from their stiff poses. Returned to fighting poses. One raised his sword to club Mathias, who still wasn't moving.

"Stop," Aunia yelled. She visualized Mygul beelining to the Mockmen and knocking their swords aside.

Her dad rushed to Mathias' side and interposed his body between the Mockmen and Mathias. He held his curved sword out at the same moment that Mygul clanged against the Mockman's sword and sent it flying.

Her dad parried another blade away from Mathias and sang:

> Lady of the ocean and the gifts you bring,
> With pearls of light and salt wind's sting.
> I call on thee to. . .

Her dad folded in a series of coughs.

"You will not finish that boon," Hebsolum growled.

Dad jumped back from a flurry of sword strikes. Several missed him by a hair's breadth. Dad kicked one Mockman back and swiveled to meet the next Mockman and his sword... His sword ran crossed the Mockman's neck. Dark blood gushed.

Dad stepped backwards, his eyes wide. "Aunia?"

Calling her dad's name, Jovaryn ran toward him.

Dad's body ruffled, like he was part of a current. Another loud sound. This time, a powdery squeal shook the cave ceiling. Dad's form rippled and broke apart. And then, he was gone.

"No!" Aunia glared at Hebsolum. Imagined Mygul blasting him in the head.

"You'd sacrifice your flyer, too?" Hebsolum asked. "Dispatch the Boggleman."

Aunia gritted her teeth, forcing herself not to behead Hebsolum.

"I can safely say my sister would not be happy with you," a female voice boomed around them. Her tone . . . her cadence . . . it was familiar, though Aunia could not place it. "She would not like it. Not at all, Hebsolum. You need to be sent home."

The dwarf disappeared as if he'd never been there.

Both the Boggleman and Mathias jolted from their statue-like stance. The Boggleman's cape swirled around him. "You have cost me dearly."

Aunia gulped back sobs. "I've cost *you*?"

The Mockmen held back, staring at the Boggleman while Mathias hurried to her side.

A tear spilled down Aunia's cheek. Her father was gone. She didn't know where. Or even if he yet lived. It was her fault. Hebsolum's fault. Did it really matter who's fault it was? He was gone. And she'd never be able to talk with him to see if she could forgive him.

"If I wasn't so angry, your tears would be amusing," the Boggleman said. His voice was no longer musical. "Instead, you'll stay in your father's cage until I have a new column for you."

"No," Aunia said. "You will not."

The Boggleman snapped his fingers for his Mockmen to grab her.

Mathias stepped beside her with his sword drawn and the Mockmen stayed still. Aunia took a step forward. This person before her with his Kai-Marin blood was Pogonias Cromis before he was the Boggleman. And he had once been loved. But how could she unlock his cloak into oblivion?

"By asking his mother," said a faint whisper.

Aunia paused. Of course. Dad's amulet had helped her see the past when she had stood near her mother's memorial stone. She slipped her hand under her chemise and took hold of the warm orb. Almost immediately, she could make out a faint ghost figure of a woman who stood at the left side of the Boggleman. A woman with tanned skin and rough hands, with a headscarf covering her hair and a back that was slightly bent. This had to be Ladonia, the woman that Lena had read about from Olivia's journal. The woman who stood up to protect Cromis when he was a boy. Who had sacrificed her own life to protect her son. And the Boggleman had destroyed the entire village when she died.

Aunia took another step forward.

"By all means, come," the Boggleman said. "My cloak is hungry."

"Your village killed your mother when all she wanted to do was protect you. You have not forgiven them . . . and quite likely, you have not forgiven yourself either."

The Boggleman recoiled. Straightened and reddened. "You will not speak on—"

"Unforgiven for the danger you put her in." Aunia pinned her shoulders back. "And the unforgiveable acts you've committed."

The Boggleman raised a fist.

"Each atrocity committed against you and on behalf of you strengthens your cloak. It is locked with your hate and your despair. But under all of that is your love for your mother, Ladonia."

"You do not know what you say," the Boggleman snarled.

"Ladonia, your adopted mom, is your lock."

The Boggleman rushed forward. Mathias stepped in front of Aunia.

And Aunia sidestepped Mathias and said:

> "Name is love and light and darkness bleak
> To fill the void is what you seek
> But in the world that you will find
> Forgiveness leaves you. You've left Ladonia behind."

"Tell him I forgive him," the ghost Ladonia said.

"She forgives you," repeated Aunia.

The Boggleman's eyes turned wide as his cloak spilled over his head. It looked like it would devour its wearer. He beat at it with his twisted hands while Ladonia hovered just out of reach.

Aunia frowned, then raised her hand. "And I forgive you, too."

The cloak twisted and shadow peeled from the fabric like thick dust. The Boggleman's skin had gone from palest white to a rug-burned red each place the cloak touched.

Aunia clenched both fists. "We forgive you, Cromis. Will you forgive yourself?"

"Shut up, shut up, shut up," the Boggleman screamed.

The cloak ripped in two and a pattering of what sounded like hail rattled against the cavern walls. All of Nonderu shook. The Mockmen trolls, who had stood waiting to see what would happen, bolted while the Boggleman screamed and clutched at wispy strands floating just out of reach.

"Come on, you two," Jovaryn said from behind them. He yanked Mathias' arm. "Before our way out closes."

Mathias and Aunia ran for the glimmering left by Edvaras while overhead laughter rang out from a myriad of different types of faeries. Faeries that escaped from the cloak. But they couldn't delay. As they ran to the glimmering, Aunia visualized a rucksack full of Leiaphae.

CHAPTER FORTY-FOUR

FALLING

One day they'll read the sacred text and maybe put together all the secrets. But will it be enough to save them? — Lady Danalissa Habrett, wife of Lord Wallace Habrett of Wolfe's Eye

Mathias followed Aunia through the glimmering and into bright light. They were within the Green Harpy stable with the morning sun pouring through its windows.

"Yasendra be blessed," said an unfamiliar voice.

Adrenaline squeezed his heart and Mathias stepped between Aunia and an entire unit of flyers. Flyers from Hauser Tower. "She's with me."

"A faeblood?" said one voice, and another said, "And what is that? That a skipping but . . ."

Mathias squinted. Six flyers—four male and two female, all near his age or slightly older—stood in the center aisle. Three of them raised swords as Jovaryn stepped from the glimmering.

"He's with us." Mathias re-sheathed his sword and held out his palms. "And we've been in Nonderu."

"Nonderu?" another unfamiliar voice said and a dark-haired man popped his head from Revellie's stall.

Mathias frowned. "Revellie. How is she?"

"Not good," Keston said from inside the pen.

She has colic, Taf sent. He lifted his head over the half-wall from his pen.

Taf, bespeak Aunia. Tell her to stay close to me.

I hear you, Aunia sent back. She moved to his side, and he wrapped an arm about her, grateful that she allowed the touch. He walked to Keston, keeping Aunia on the other side of the flyers. It had to be about mid-morning. How could so much time pass?

Time runs differently in faery and between the worlds than here, Taf sent as they passed his stall.

I'm sorry we were gone. Are you alright?

You had to go, Taf sent. *And it was I who asked for Hauser Tower.*

But Brinsaber's warning.

I'm fairly sure our eavesdropper knows where we are.

They reached Revellie's stall where fresh straw had been lay down. Fallo sat on his haunches, rubbing Revellie's abdomen with oiled hands. There were several fresh hoof-shaped indents on the half wall behind her.

"The Da Vennen soldiers said this girl by you robbed one of them. They wanted her for questioning," the Hauser Tower commander said. He was at Revellie's head trying to feed her peppermint.

Keston, pale and disheveled, kneeled in the hay patting Revellie's neck and crooning to her.

"She stole nothing from no one," Mathias said.

"But she does have the knowledge to make a faery repellent that'll save our lands," said Fallo.

Mathias kept his expression mild. He appreciated Fallo speaking up for Aunia but he did not trust him. *Taf, when did Fallo show up?*

Not long before you did. He was happy to find Paderro.

Mathias looked up. *And where is—*

He's in the back stall sleeping.

The Hauser Tower commander reached for a rag and wiped his hands. "Now Nonderu? You'd have us believe you crossed the veil to the Boggleman's lands?"

"You can have your pegasus bespeak mine," Mathias said.

"And the story with this fellow?" The Hauser Tower commander pointed at Jovaryn, who stood where the glimmering had been, hunched to be as small as possible.

"A prisoner of the Boggleman's," Mathias clarified. "We freed him."

The Hauser commander scratched his head. "And why were you in Nonderu?"

Mathias closed his eyes. "The Boggleman was after Aunia."

"After her? Why?

Fallo stepped forward. "That might be a question for her majesty."

Fallo bespeaks if you care for the girl, you are not to speak Rune's name aloud, Taf sent.

Aunia bit her lip.

The Hauser commander gave Fallo a serious look-over then shrugged. "The Queen you said. Well, you and your men, the ones you have left anyway, have a lot of explaining to do for Nyrissa. We were to leave for the upper lands soon as we found you but we'll wait until this precious girl is feeling better."

Mathias glanced at Rev. "How long will that—"

"Probably tomorrow or the day after."

Why do you have to explain to . . . Nyrissa? Aunia sent.

Maybe a formality, Mathias sent. *Though we should consider ourselves under arrest.*

Arrest?

Being held captive for wrongdoing. I was hoping we could have cleared our names first.

"Keston, we need to get her up. Get her walking. I'll join you. Murtagh. Breen. Escort Fallo, Mathias and his two friends to whatever suite they have in the inn." The commander pierced Mathias with a steady stare. "I'll assume you're agreeing to stay put?"

Mathias nodded. "Keston, you'll be, okay?"

"Frehn has been very helpful," Keston said. He made a gesture like he was adjusting a bandana on his head and then made a flickering gesture with his fingers. "Go get some sleep, Matty. One of us should."

Basil. Basil must have skipped before the Hauser unit could stop him. Or maybe before he was seen. Important, particularly since Lyle's daughter had been kidnapped by rovers and rescued by Da Vennen soldiers.

Fallo joined Mathias, Aunia, and Jovaryn, walking across the inn's yard to the side door accompanied by four of the Hauser unit.

We need to be careful here, Aunia. Mathias sent. *But we're safe from any of the Da Vennen for now.*

But there was still a wererat, Jovaryn, who'd be staying in their suite with them. Mathias planned on never leaving Aunia alone with him.

Aunia was happy with Mathias' help to pull the mattress of her bed back onto its frame. She had refrained from looking at the ash pile near the window, grateful when he cleaned that up as well. But there wasn't much they could do for the snapped off harpy leg from her dresser.

So many things had happened. Her dad had killed a Mockman troll. He had looked at her, dread in his eyes and his body rippling as if it was being unmade. He was gone. Olivia was dead. They were under arrest. But the Boggleman's cloak had been destroyed. And they had escaped

Nonderu. She should be happy about that part, but she had a hard time feeling anything.

"I'll stay here with you," Mathias said. "We should sleep. I'll take the floor."

Aunia looked at the grayish thread pulsing through Mathias' spring-green glow. "You do not feel comfortable with that decision."

Her voice sounded flat, but she didn't care. And then she felt guilty. He had created an entire army of himself to keep her safe and she had watched almost all of them die. He cared about her. But...

"You seeing glows...right. What you're seeing is my fear for your reputation. I plan on staying here in your room. I'll take the floor. But I don't want you unguarded with a wererat in the other room."

Aunia laughed, a high hiccup of one while her belly squeezed in knots. "Maybe he should fear me. I bring death."

"Aunia—"

"I saw you die, over and over again."

"They weren't real."

Aunia shook her head. To keep him safe, he needed to stay away from her. "You shouldn't be with me. Your people—"

"Hey. I told you in Nonderu and I stand by it . . . I love you." He reached for her hands. "And we're stronger together."

Her eyes filled. Maybe. Maybe together the two of them could do anything. But how? So much wrong had happened and how could they fix it? "Mathias, I should—"

He leaned forward, his face closing in on hers, and he was kissing her. The sweetness of it pulled the world away and she clung to him, feeling her heart flutter against his. For a moment, nothing mattered. He pulled away and ran a hand over her hair. "Come on, we both need sleep. Up into the covers."

She complied, crawling into bed, and he lowered himself to a bedroll on the floor near the broken door. They held hands for a few minutes. And then, under the flickering of candlelight, they drifted off to sleep.

AHNU-ENDYNIA GLOSSARY

Adar – (Ah-dar) – A country immediately south of Tamore and east of the island country of Bellatine.

Aetherwind – The island seat of the Pavari Court where Zevara rules. This island, along with all islands in the land hangs in the sky and is connected with silver chain bridges. Aetherwind is made of black basalt mountains and near its tallest peak stands Zevara's bright-white stone castle. This island also is home to a Veil Door.

Ahnu-Endynia – (AH-new EN-di-nya) – Conjoined worlds of both mortal and faery worlds. Ahnu is the mortal world and Endynia is the faery world. These twin worlds occupy the same space yet are separated by a thin veil made of ethereal material. Very little can pass through the veil without a specific entrance/exit, such as a Veil Door, as an example.

Aeryk de Wyvert (king-consort) – (Air-ick dee WHY-vert) – Deceased father of the heir princess Keira. He was born and raised in New Berlyn.

Ag-Haggy – A mountain on the Grashbear that looked like the wide tooth in a giant's mouth; however, it exploded at the climax of Faeries Don't Lie when the marble giant ripped through it.

Aiket – (Ah-KET) – One of the wererats from the blade-cave den who works with Basil.

Arensvald, Grand Duke of Uttalo - (AR-ens-val, Grand Duke of uh-TAY-low) – Naoma's father and historical figure. It is said he killed his own grandchildren.

Augury, the – The belief that if all seven Chandarions recreate the Heart Between the Worlds, then the lifeblood will beat through both worlds, saving both. But if the Chandarions do not succeed by a certain time, then the Dama Ximarae will have to choose which world will live and which one will die.

Aunia – (AH-nee-a) – Sixteen-year-old protagonist. Wheat-blond hair, dark blue eyes, heart-shaped face. This impulsive faery-friend is Rune's daughter.

Augurites – A para-religious order who believe in the augury (another word for prophecy) that one of the worlds, either mortal or faery, will die if the Chandarions don't all arrive to fix the Dama's shattered heart.

Axe-Pickle – A mockman troll leader.

Bacrae Noir – A type of red wine from Lambert's Vinyards. It is greatly sought after for its full-bodied wine and smooth, lingering finish. It has notes of blackberry jam and dark chocolate.

Barnabas Gearhart – Traveling blade merchant who is a family friend of Keston and his father, Jayden Pendar. He is a bear of a man with fluffy blonde hair and a short, curled beard.

Basil Mensani – (BAH-sill Men-SAW-knee) – Rover Mystic from Tamore.

Baxter's Way – Major Tamorian highway connecting Tamore to Adar and Bellatine.

Bearpaws – A landmark pair of tall hills near the ghost town of Idenweigh which is located near the Grashbear mountains.

Beggarfauns – (Beggar-fawns) – A gourd-like plant which grows near blade-caves. Sought after as an ingredient in spells. They can move on their own.

Bellatine – (Bell-ah-tine) – An island country south of Tamore. Home of the Mystic Court. It is also known for its naval shipping.

Berrydell (village of) – A village that is situated a few miles from the bottom of the hill where Eddac Tower stands. It has thin roads crisscrossing between fifty-some houses.

Besmarion – (Bes-MAR-ee-on) – A spring festival consisting of feasting, dancing and flirting.

Besnik – (BES-nick) – A short rover lad who is 14 years of age. He is a mischievous who has possession of a far-viewer.

Betrothal stone – A magical item that is sometimes sent from the gnomes of Terralium, the faery court of earth and snow to help determine who the heir of Tamore should wed.

Betwixt - The space between the worlds—a combination of both and yet neither. It is the undefined space between the worlds. Normally encompasses the veil. It can also mean an in-between place or time, such as dawn and dusk.

Betwixting Spell – A spell Edvaras cast which called all tunnels and caverns throughout the world to appear and create a passageway through the Grashbear Mountains. This tunnel allowed Edvaras and his followers to escape Tamore. It also created a spill-over side effect which remains in effect. For example, there are the sometimes-there and sometimes-not-there Blade-caves.

Bibb (Arch Vicar) – Leader of the Da Vennen cult, a soldier religion. The order's background dates to the time of Rhugante before the kingdom of Tamore came into existence. Bibb is a tall man with a thin hooked-nose face. He has black hair streaked in white.

Birchwoods – (Birch Woods) – A magical Betwixt place that is in between the worlds of Ahnu-Endynia. Magic runs unimpeded there and the unexpected—good or bad—can happen.

Blade-cave – A cave that is sometimes there and sometimes not. The villagers in Naoma Sacella call this the Betwixting tunnels. Some believe if the cave disappears while a person is inside then they are absorbed for all time. The sheep cave near Naoma Sacella is one of the blade-caves.

Bloodball – A past event which many of the royal family were slain.

Boggleman -(Bah-gil-man) – Antagonist. A slim white-haired man with a creepy musical voice and of indeterminate age. He has a scar running from an empty eye socket to his jaw. His fingers on his right hand are jutted out oddly as if they had been broken and left to heal badly. He intends to see the human world die.

Border Spell – A spell created by Dar Syrick which prevents firelings and dark fae from crossing into the kingdom of Tamore. Wyverns have been eating at the spell and have greatly weakened it.

Brainhedge – One of two hedges made of living brainhedge trees (looks similar to an osage orange hedge) which runs along much of Baxter's Way.

Brainhedge Tree – The largest tree in the Brainhedge. It is significantly taller than the others and at its foot stands a gate made of metal and living wood. It allows passage for those who possess a key to be able to partake of the water.

Brainmere – The grassy section between the two hedges of brainhedge trees which runs along the highway of Baxter's Way and separates the Marchlands of Froidelune and Dalin. A creek with waters with magical properties flows here.

Breanne – (BREE-ann) – Eighteen-year-old villager who is getting "beaded" (married) to Tinner. Limi's friend. Xissa's daughter.

Breezlings – A type of faery. They appear to be hand-sized with large purple eyes and translucent silver wings. They predominately live in the realm of Pavari.

Breen – A pegasus flyer stationed at Hauser Tower.

Briar – The cook at Eddac Tower.

Brinsaber – (brin-SA-ber) – Pegasus to Jules Mayrell. Brinsaber has been hiding somewhere in the Grashbear.

Britchway – A small town in the Dalin province and located north of both Dalin and Eddac Tower. This town was damaged severely by fire caused by fire salamanders and wererats during a Besmarion festival.

Caedmon - (KAYD-mon) – Chief, blacksmith and story teller of the isolated village of Naoma Sacella. He was like a second father to Aunia. Short cropped hair and corded muscles. He is of medium height.

Camlo – (Cam-lo) – A fifteen-year-old year old rover lad. Cousin to Besnik. He had dark eyes.

Canthelark singers – (CAN-the-lark singers) – A type of singer, who perform together with almost otherworldly beautiful and high-pitched voices.

Casmia – Rover woman from the Mensani caravan who dances.

Catiryna Pemble – (CA-tear-eena PEM-ball) – Commander of Stanz Tower. She is an outspoken woman who is maybe five feet tall with fire-colored hair. She rides a steel gray pegasus stallion named Yantexio.

Chand Crystal – This byproduct from Chandarion magic is greatly valued. Its uses include boosting the intensity of magic spells. Pegasi riders carry a tiny crumb of Chand crystal, usually in the form of a necklace or a ring, which helps their telepathic connection to their individual pegasi.

Chand Ice – Sometimes called Frostheart. This physical by-product of the shattered Heart of the Worlds can be used to store Nymers and can help boost the intensity of a magic spell.

Chandarions – Foretold in the augury that there will be seven in-dividuals who will be imbued with magic in the form of Nymers and they will recreate the Heart of the Worlds.

Clavis Peak – (Cla-vis Peak) – A sole mountain where Edvaras and his followers lived until the settlement was attacked, and then abandoned. The community was moved to Naoma Sacella. The villagers of Naoma Sacella believe this area to be taboo. It has also been glamored magically so it is invisible.

Clurichauns – (clear-ree CON) – A type of faery. They are typically depicted as small, wizened beings resembling older men, often with rosy cheeks and a mischievous twinkle in their eyes. They typically are drunkards or are prone to it. Some of the clurichauns living in Dalin include Mara, Sharpish and Gargle.

Cody Lambert – A faeblood who has been imprisoned in Dalin's prison. He is originally from Lambert's Vineyards.

Cold Festival – Annual festival with a variety of activities from balls to markets. This event takes place during the last five days of the Tamorian year.

Craymore – An innkeeper in Worley who runs the Green Harpy. He is a a short furry man who sometimes engages in unethical activities for profit.

Cyndrix – A fire salamander who was consumed by the Boggleman's cape.

Cyril – Footsoldier at Eddac Tower. Deceased.

Da Caladorian Vennen soldier order – (da CAL-a-door-ee-an VEN-ann) – Often known simply as the Da Vennen. They worship the Rhugante Bear and are loosely based on Mithraism from first century AD in Italy. They do not believe that humans should use magic. The sword and the plow is their motto. They also enjoy the privilege of Uriah's edict which allows them to be outside of Tamore jurisdiction, except for the most egregious crimes.

Dagel demons – Types of dark fae who have crossed into category of great evil.

Dalin – (Dah-lin) – The capital city of one of the marchlands in the kingdom of Tamore. It is known for its sword manufacturing. It has a bustling market due to its close location to the trade route between Tamore and Bellatine.

Dama Ximarae – (Dah-ma ZI-mah-ray) – The main deity and creator of the worlds of Ahnu-Endynia.

Danalissa Habrett – (Dan-na-LEE-sah Ha-brett) – Mathias' mother and Lord Wallace Habrett's wife. Originally from Adar. She was the queen's lady-in-waiting before her marriage.

Darra Chamber – A chamber that was said to once occupy the castle of Tatia where Chand ice and Nymers from Chandarions were stored. Inside the chamber is a window which looks into the Faery world and also the Eaburrai Court. It was created by Uriah to placate his wife, Yasendra.

Davis – A blacksmith from Dalin who fashions many of the iron bracelets that faebloods are required to wear.

Dead Lands – The land between the Grashbear Mountains and Naoma Sacella. A spell during Edvaras' escape from Tamore consumed all the leyline energy in this area causing most vegetation to die.

Diadem, the – The best inn within Worley.

Didianne (Queen) – (DIE-dee-ann) – A queen from centuries past who is known to have gone mad and she made the Darra Chamber disappear.

Domesday – (Dohms-day) – A written record which gives the names of all high-born families, along with their titles and lands. Updated every decade.

Dominus Titus Valerian – Adarian high ruler. Jayden Pendar, Keston's father, has been employed with commissions for him several times. The Dominus is know to be verbose and tiresome.

Drake Vrael (Lord) – Lord of Vraelfork and Fallo Vrael's brother.

Eaburrai – (Eh-BURR-ray) – Companions of the Dama. Minor deities.

Eddac Tower – (EH-deck Tower) – One of the tower forts which pegasi-flyers reside. Flyers watch over designated territory and towers are found throughout the kingdom of Tamore. Eddac is located in the Dalin province between the town of Britchway and the city of Dalin. Its complement include Fallo Vrael, Mathias Habrett, Keston Pendar, Jules Mayrell, and Patrick and Garrett. Patrick and Garrett are kin to Fallo and they are also known as the knightsons.

Edvaras – (ED-var-as) – Chandarion. Known as the rogue Chandarion who disrupted the augury. Edvaras ran off with his love, Naoma, along with their followers through the Grashbear Mountains and past the Dead Lands.

Edvaras stone – One of the two frostheart stones that Edvaras summoned. Both house the trio of flowers he made for his wife, Naoma. Gaitha avoids using the Edvaras stone for her spellwork as the outcomes are often unpredictable for her.

Eldarghast – (Elder-gast) – Uriah's elder brother who caused the Heart of the Worlds to shatter. This shattering caused him to be transformed into a monster and his birth name has been lost to antiquity. He is responsible for the children of Yasendra and Uriah to be dispersed across many lands, an event which caused the War Between the Worlds.

Ella – Taya's mother and the rover's lead fortune-teller. She and her husband, Karr, were killed when Taya was ten.

Elowen – The head stable keeper at Eddac Tower.

Elris (Prince) – A past Tamorian prince who married a rover. His descendant was Olivia.

Emmet Dalin (Marquis) – Lord of Dalin. This twenty year old lord holds the title of being sixteenth in the line of Ice-steel, and Protector of the free people dwelling within the Grashbear's shadow. He is the son of the deceased Marquis Charl Dalin, descendant of Grand Marquis de Idenweigh. He has a boy-slight frame, russet-gold skin, and dark eyes. He often wears a circlet fashioned like a bent sword adorning his curly-haired head.

Faery Courts – The four elemental faery courts include: Terralium, the court of earth and snow; Pavari, the court of spring and air; Cascadia, the court of water and summer; and Emberfall, the court of fire and autumn. There are three other faery courts.

Fallo Vrael – (FAH-low Vr-RAIL) – Commander of Eddac Tower and Mathias' superior. He is the brother of Lord Vrael from the Duchy of Vraelsfork. Fallo desperately wants to find the marble giant. He is a broad-shouldered man with a balding head. Paderro is his pegasus.

Fehn – Commander of Hauser Tower.

Ferris Runoldi – (fair-riss RUNE-oll-dee) – The Mystic believed to have committed the royal family murders during the Blood Ball.

Fire Keep – The university home of the firelings.

Fire salamanders – This type of faery can change its size, ranging from thumb-sized to that of a small horse. Generally, it has short limbs and cat-like eyes no matter what size it takes. Most of them have red skin.

Firelings – A magical order from in the southern country of Adar by the Boggleman. They used to be part of the Cragborns, people living in the terraced Tatian mountains. The order and its beliefs are generally in opposition to the Augurite order. They are known to dabble in many different types of magic. This order has attacked Tamore in the past and they are the primary reason why Dar Syrick erected a border spell around Tamore.

Forged Tankard – A tavern in Dalin between the warehouse and blacksmithy sections. The tavern owner is a woman named Brana.

Froidelune (Marchlands of) – (FROY-day-lune) – One of the Marchlands near the Grashbear. It has been separated from Dalin as the two marchlands fought over dominion of the Brainmere.

Gabin – (GAH-bin) – A baby from the Mensani caravan of rovers.

Gabryella ni Brier Reach – (GAB-ree-ella knee briar reach) – A fireling woman with mahogany-brown hair and a fondness of low-cut gowns. She has been working on imprisoning fire salamanders into glass tubes to make salamander lights.

Gaitha – (GAY-the) – Eldest Daughter of Naoma Sacella. She is Edvaras' true Dar and descendant of Edvaras. Petite woman with a bit of a limp. Dark skinned and graying hair.

Galeena – A faery attendant in Zevara's castle. She appears as a willowy figure the color of twilight.

Ganger – Foreman at the ruined merchant guild at Dalin.

Garrett – A cousin of Fallo and one of the sons to Lord Vrael's knights. He has dark curly hair.

Glevis – (GLEH-vis) – A small mining community close to the Grashbear Mountains. It provides iron and also rare materials to the city of Dalin for manufacturing swords.

Glows – An aura that surrounds a person or a faery. One of Aunia's abilities is to be able to see and read the glows of others.

Grashbear Mountains – A mountain range on the western side of Tamore which separates Tamore from the Dead Lands. This range is home to Mockmen trolls, wyverns, and other faery creatures. It is also riddled with blade-caves from the fallout from Edvaras' Betwixting spell.

Green Harpy, the – Second best inn in Worley. It is run by an innkeeper by the name of Craymore.

Gregwin – Healer who was tending Jules after his wererat bite. Gregwin is a portly man.

Harris – Twelve year-old villager from Naoma Sacella who Aunia's faery friends tease quite frequently. Velli's younger brother and Sigmus' nephew.

Hauser Tower – (HA-sir tower) – A pegasi tower located near Worley.

Hattie – Xissa's younger sister who resides most of the time out at the sheep cottage in the northern hills.

Heart of the Worlds – The Dama's exterior heart which beats lifeblood and magic through both worlds of Ahnu-Endynia until an accident shattered it.

Heavensfeet – A major city near the foothills of the Tatian Mountain range along Tamore's western border.

Hebsolum – The marble giant who lives under the Grashbear Mountains. This being, previous to Edvaras marbelizing him, was the guardian for the Eaburrai Court. He followed Yasendra into the mortal world after she married Uriah. There are rumors that he does not exist after centuries of searching for his marble hand and finding none. Fallo is obsessed with collecting some of this marble.

Heebles – This Dagel demon/faery looks like a moldy gourd with a wide mouth and sharp teeth. It has no other facial features. It has no differential between its head and body. It has two skeletal limbs which work as both arms and legs. Heebles attack in hordes and can strip the flesh off a cow in a matter of minutes. They communicate to each other in ratlike snarls and squeaks.

Heyden, (Dar) – (Dar Hay-den) – One of Tamore's royal magic-users who allegedly uses the stored and borrowed magic of Chandarions, particularly Edvaras'. He used to be a former Adarian dance master.

House of Nobles – A building complex above Heavensfeet where the nobility gather several times a year to help co-create laws with her majesty.

Idenweigh – One of the southern most towns along the Grashbear Mountains in Tamore. A pivotal battle was waged here in the year 996 (70 years earlier than the start of Faeries Don't Lie). The defense was led by Olivia. Currently, the town is mostly abandoned with rumors of it being overrun with ghosts.

Illysa – (Ill-Lys-SAH) – Second Chandarion. Her legacy includes creating the pegasi flyer troops after negotiating a truce with Zevara of the Pavari Court.

Jaia – (Jay-ah) – One of the flowers Edvaras created. This black, lily-like flower has a stench similar to skunk wrapped in honeysuckle. It is used as the main ingredient in making faery repellant.

Jarl – Rover man from the Mensani caravan. He is father to Besnik and a friend of Niall's.

Jayden Pendar – Keston's father. He is a sculptor.

Jennium – (Jen-nee-um) – Garden faery. Hand-sized and slender with dark curly hair, dark eyes, olive complexion, and iridescent wings. She has unusual abilities which includes a strong tolerance to iron.

Jovaryn – (Joe-VAR-n) – Wererat boy with disheveled hair and a red ribbon tied around his neck. A follower of Hebsolum. He has been taken by the Boggleman.

Jules Mayrell – One of the pegasi-flyers from Eddac Tower. Mathias' friend and nephew of Dar Zeller, Mathias' late mentor. Jules has a broad face and tousled auburn hair. Before the start of FAERIES DON'T LIE, Jules has been bitten by a wererat.

Kazik bird – (Kaa-zick bird) – An enormous bird who appears to be a cross between a flame-red peacock and a phoenix. He resides in the court of Pavari and his feathers, particularly the tail feathers, contain concentrated magic thanks to the Chandarion, Illysa. It significantly boosts the telepathic magic of pegasi and flyers. These tail feathers are in great demand. He does not shed feathers often.

Kai-Marin – (KI Mare-in) – One of the Eaburrai. Often known as the Sea Witch.

Kankari – A new moon festival celebrated each month in the mortal world as a way to entice the moon to return from the faery world into the human world.

Keston – One of the pegasi-flyers from Eddac Tower. Mathias' friend and sidekick. He is flirtatious and charming. He is tall with sandy brown hair and amber eyes.

Knight-sons (see Patrick and/or Garrett) – Cousins of Fallo and sons to Lord Vrael's highest knight. They are part of the Eddac Tower unit.

Kobolds – A type of faery. They are chest-high with knobby-shouldered, elongated faces, and sharp teeth.

Krissa – Eleven-year-old villager who helps out with healing duties after the heeble invasion.

Kron – One of the villagers. Limi's mate. Oskan's son.

Kylandra (Princess) – Former Tatian heir princess. She died during the blood ball.

Ladonia – (LA-dohn-knee-a) – Fish widow who adopted the Boggle-man when he was a small child.

Leia – Tamorian woman and Aunia's mother.

Leiaphae – (Lie-ah-FAY) – One of the three flowers Edvaras created. This yellow broccoli-stalked flower is used to cast the shrouding spell which will hide Naoma Sacella from all eyes.

Lena – Tharon's sister-in-law who helps to look after Taya and Reina. She is a woman with cinnamon-colored hair and high cheek bones.

Limi – Aunia's foster sister. Gaitha's granddaughter and heir to the title of Eldest Daughter. Limi does not want this position nor the magic that comes with it. Medium dark skin. Brown eyes. Wears her hair in many braids. 19-year-old and pregnant in the FAERIES DON'T LIE. Kron's mate.

Lord Chance – Hero in a book that Jules Mayrell reads and quotes from.

Lovari caravan – (Lah-VAR-ee) – One of the family caravan of rovers.

Lumentago Valley – River valley where the island city of Worley stands in the center of the Whisp River. It is also called Wythrindle River.

Lydinairre – (LE-din-air-ree) – Pegasus to Dar-Elect Nyrissa Rieson.

Lyle Worley (Lord) – Lord of the Worley.

Mathias Habrett – (MAH-thigh-as Hah-bret) – Secondary protagonist and Aunia's love interest. He is a pegasus flyer stationed at Eddac Tower after being exiled for six months for his unclear role in the death of Dar Zeller, his mentor. His pegasus is Tafiriel. Mathias has dark wavy hair, green eyes, and chiseled features. He is the surviving son of Lord and Lady Habrett.

McNarish – A merchant guildsman in Dalin. He is a skinny man who dresses in foppish attire.

Mensani caravan – (Men-SAW-knee caravan) – One of the family caravan of rovers. This one is home to Basil Mensani, his father, Tharon, and more.

Miriel – A pretty young woman from Worley who is a friend of Keston's.

Mockmen Trolls – (mock-men trolls) – Furry troll-like creatures. Most sport tusks. They consider themselves superior to humans, particularly when it comes to mining. While they are not intellectually superior, they are good at finding alternative solutions.

Mockmen Wars – During Olivia's time, there was several large scale battles between Tamore and Mockmen trolls. Olivia was integral to defeating them but she was taken by the Boggleman at the end of the war.

Mollie Mae – A wererat woman from the blade-cave den who works with Basil. Mollie Mae is Basil and Wendalin's mother and Tharon's estranged wife.

Moss-gnomes – Calf-high humanoid faeries who like to cavort under shady places and take naps on moss pads. They can dig through any ground as if it were "made of soft butter."

Mudcloaks – A derogatory name for Da Vennen soldiers.

Murtagh – One of the flyers stationed at Hauser Tower.

Mygul – (MY-gull) – The dark blue indigo globefire that follows Aunia around. It has been known to knock things over to create havoc.

Myles – (Miles) – Stanz Tower's second officer. He has auburn-colored hair and rides a black pegasus mare.

Mystic Court – An order located predominately in Bellatine, which monitors the augury. Its spell-casters tend to use musical spells and faery magic borrowed from their faery familiars.

Mystics – An order of magic-users who use faery familiars. Tamorians tend to distrust them as they believe the order is responsible for the Blood Ball.

Naoma – (NAY-oh-ma) – Edvaras' wife. She was born and raised in the northern country of Uttalo.

Naoma Sacella – (NAY-oh-ma SAW-cell-lah) – Edvaras' isolated village located past the Dead Lands. It is circled by a blue Chand crystal wall.

Naoma stone – One of the two frostheart stones that Edvaras summoned to house the trio of flowers he made for his wife, Naoma. Gaitha uses this stone to help her with more complicated spells as she has more affinity to this one than its brother, the Edvaras stone.

Narvis – A fire salamander in the Boggleman's court whose loyalties are conflicted. See fire salamander for physical description.

Navenra – (NAH-ven-rah) – One of the flowers Edvaras created. This lacy, blue flower was created to increase Naoma's lifespan but instead it restrains free will.

Ned – A faeblood in Dalin who was arrested after the walking mouth (heeble) attack.

Nehla – (NAY-la) – Limi's deceased mother. Aunia's mother figure.

Niall (Neal) – Taya's grandfather.

Nonderu – (NON-day-roo) – The underground kingdom of the Boggleman. It is located in the Betwixt.

Nymers – Pure energy heart shards which attach themselves to Chandarions and Chandarion potentials. Mygul would be an example of one.

Nyrissa Rieson (Dar-Elect) – (NAH-riss-ah REE-son) – One of Tamore's royal magic-users who should be able to use the borrowed magic of Chandarions, particularly Illysa. Acting general of Tamore's aerial troops since the death of her father, Dar Zeller.

Olivia – A Chandarion potential. Since Edvaras boxed his own Nymer (Chandarion magic) away, no full Chandarions have been born. Olivia is known in Tamore as the Maid of Idenweigh. She was integral to the victory against the Mockman Trolls in the year 996 (70 years earlier than Faeries Don't Lie). Rumors have it that she was abducted by the Boggleman.

Oomas – Dark faery creatures who are squat, calf-high, and have their eyes on top of their heads. They make good scouts.

Oskan – (AHS-can) – Large bear of a man with salt and pepper braids. Father-in-law to Gaitha's granddaughter, Limi. Father to Kron.

Oswald – Footsoldier at Eddac Tower. Deceased.

Q'thonos – (KA-THOUGH-knows) – An earth-mage who lives off the Pardonway, a road through the Pardownway woods between the cities of Worley and Heavensfeet.

Paderro – (Pah-DARE-oh) – Fallo's pegasus. Jet black stallion.

Pogonias Cromis – (PA-GO-knee-us CROW-miss) – The Boggleman's childhood name from when he was rescued as a child by a fish widow.

Patrick – A cousin of Fallo and one of the sons to Lord Vrael's knights. He has a wispy beard and his dark blonde hair is cut bowl-shaped.

Pavari, aka the Court of Spring and Air – One of the seven faery courts in Endynia. This court is ruled by Zevara and is populated with sylphs, windknots, the Kazik birk, and other air-type faeries.

Portal tiles – Magical knuckle-sized tiles that gleam iridescently with reds, greens, and blues. These give the ability of transportation across many miles.

Reina – (RAY-na) – Six-year-old faeblood child with dirty blonde hair who the Mensani caravan rovers took in. She is a fugitive because of her magical abilities.

Revellie – (REV-ah-lee) – Keston's pegasus. She is a golden mare who has a great sense of where she is at all times. Her telepathic voice is high and silvery.

Rhugante – (Rue-GONE-teh) – Previous to Tamore's existence, the land used to be called Rhugante. Uriah, the first Chandarion and husband to the Eaburria, Yasendra, originated from Rhugante and had been the second-born prince.

Rovers (Music People) – Traveling folk who live in horse-drawn wagons. They trade in hard-to-find items and usually have outstanding healing folk, along with fortune-tellers, and musicians. Ordinary folk usually consider them undesirable unless they need a healer or an item that they might have.

Royal Star – A seven-pointed star made of silver or other precious metals. The kingdom keeps track of who is in possession of one of these limitedly available items.

Rune – Aunia's father. Originally from Bellatine. He has medium brown hair and eyes, medium height and a muscular build. He's very graceful on his feet. He also is incredibly secretive, particularly of his and Aunia's origins before they arrived at Naoma Sacella. He is able to use power words, faery magic, and is able to 'skip.'

Ruork – Faery type. Refers to the buglike humanoid and the wasp it rides.

Ryver – A wererat from the Lord Chance band who has Mollie-Mae as its leader. Ryver is a 16 years of age, slender built, and has a wispy short cropped beard.

Salamander lights – A magical device that looks like an incandescent glass tube. It is powered by an imprisoned fire salamander.

Sheavine – (SHAY-vine) – She is a zephyr, a type of wind faery, who lives at Hebsolum's tower in the Pavari Court lands on the tiny island of Aeryth.

Sigmus – (Sig-muss) – Minor antagonist to Aunia, mainly due to jealousy as Sigmus considers Rune to be a father figure. Rune's friend. He is 29 years old, overweight with lanky dark hair.

Silvani (Queen) – The mother of Prince Elris. She gave him a royal star as a wedding gift.

Sir Nicolas Mims – Poet from the third century.

Skip (or skipping) – The magical ability to teleport from one place to another.

Sophia – One of the Eaburrai. Usually depicted as a scribe working on a scroll with twin cherubs tugging on her robes.

Sorrel – The steward at Eddac Tower.

Spatelly – A city on the outskirts of the Worley province and near the sea marshes.

Stanz Tower – Pegasi rider tower south of the city of Dalin. There is a rivalry between Stanz and Eddac towers. The troops within are commanded by Catryina Pemble.

Sylph – An air faery type. Human-sized with wings. Ethereal, beautiful, and resides mainly on the winds.

Syrick (Dar) – (Dar Sigh-rick) – One of Tamore's royal magic-users who uses stored and borrowed magic from Chandarions, particularly that of Uriah Galarue.

Tamore – The kingdom between the Grashbear and Tatian Mountains to the east and west; the Uttaloian Promise Bay to the north; and Adar and Bellatine to the south. Its capital city of Tatia is said to be in the doorway of the faery world and perched on clouds.

Tafiriel – Originally from Endynia, he is a wild-born pegasus, meaning he has crossed over through a blade-cave. He has imprinted with Mathias. His hide is the color of the noon sky and his mane and tail are pale blue.

Tatia – Tamore's capital which is located in the clouds above the city of Heavensfeet and near the western Tatian Mountains. This is one of the places in the world which is located in the Betwixt, or poetically said "on the threshold between the worlds." The city was created through magic by Uriah, the first Chandarion.

Tatia's Grove – A magical grove inside the lands of the Eaburrai Court.

Tatian Mountains – Western mountain range that marks the western boundary of the kingdom of Tamore.

Tavish – A foot soldier at Eddac Tower who was killed during a Da Vennen and wererat attack.

Taya – Twelve-year-old rover girl from the Mensani caravan. She has thick dark hair that she tends to wear in two braids and dark blue eyes.

After her mother's death, she became the caravan's healer and fortune teller.

Teezo Popkin – One of the mushroom sprites. He is stout with a short cropped beard and hay-color hair. Small enough to use a mushroom cap as a chair. He is a faery friend of Aunia's.

Thalindra Archon (Arcanis Primis of the Mystic Court) – (THE-lynn-dra AR-con) – Leader of the Mystic Court in the island country of Bellatine.

Tharon Mensani – (THERE-on Men-SAW-knee) – Leader of the Mensani rover caravan.

Thessalie – (This-ah-lee) – Adarian community which follows the more Mystic-centric holidays.

Thuroes – One of the Eaburrai. Depicted as a handsome man with a harp on his lap and with an ale mug toppled over. A river of beer flows from his ale mug with the stream transforming into the sea. Mathias believes he was born under this Eaburrai's watchful eye.

Tinner – Nineteen-year-old villager and Caedmon's blacksmith apprentice. He is to be beaded (wedded) to Breanne.

Tys – A mysterious type of faery who do not like to be forced into one shape. Their untampered shape is unknown.

Uriah Galarue – (YOU-rye-ah Gal-a-roo) – First Chandarion and beloved of Yasendra. Their love affair led to the breaking of the Heart between the Worlds, and created the need for a new Heart. The Dama Ximarae sentenced Uriah, along with his descendants to become Chandarions, destined to watch over and protect both worlds until a new heart is fashioned.

Veil Door – A magical entrance/exit that can cross between the worlds. The one in the Pavari Court looks like a black shadowed s stood a long rectangle that rippled as if it were made of water.

Velli – (VELL-ee) – Seventeen-year-old villager who is often antagonistic toward Aunia, mainly due to jealousy. She is an attractive and slender teen who is on the promiscuous side. Limi and Breanne's friend. Harris' older sister. Sigmus' neice.

Vraelsfork – (Ver-rails-forks) – A duchy in Tamore which stands near the kingdom's center. Fallo originates from here.

Wallace Habrett (Lord) – (WALL-is Ha-brett) – Mathias' father. Lord of Wulf's Eye.

Wendalin Mensani – (WHEN-da-lenn Men-SAW-knee) – Apprentice dar to Dar Syrick. Sister to Basil. Daughter to Tharon and Mollie Mae.

Wererats – Cursed humans who can assume the shape of common rats, human-sized rats, or rat men. A form of lycanthropy.

Whistling Teapot – A tavern in Dalin.

Willard – One of the guards at Dalin.

Wind-knots – A type of storm faery. Finger-sized. Generally they appear as thumb-sized grey-clad lads.

Witch compass – A magical device that points out magic-users with a needle arrow. They typically look like a compass. Bibb's is decorated with little red crystals dotting its outer ridge. Some witch compasses can also suppress other magic within its location.

Wylie – Rover man from the Mensani caravan. Father to the baby Gabin.

Wyvern – Dragon-like creature with two legs instead of four. It can exhale fireballs and sometimes toxic gas.

Xissa – One of the council leaders of Naoma Sacella. A no-nonsense woman who wears her greying hair in a bun. Breanne's mother. Head cook.

Yanna – A blacksmith in Dalin. His smithy is close to the Forged Tankard.

Yantexio – (Yan-TEX-ee-oh) – Catiryna Pemble's steel gray pegasus stallion.

Yasendra (Galarue) – (YA-sen-dra) – Youngest of the Eaburrai. Fell in love and married Uriah, the first Chandarion. Their love affair was directly involved in the breaking of the Heart of the Worlds. Her depiction as a blond girl running has not been seen on any recent murals.

Yasko Coates – (YAS-ko Coats) – Lena's younger brother. He's quite good with the violin.

Zeller Rieson (Dar) – (Zel-lar Ray-son) – One of Tamore's royal magic-users who uses stored and borrowed magic of Chandarions, particularly Illysa's. General of the Tamore's aerial troops until his death.

Zevara – (zee-VAR-ah) – The Great Sylph, leader of the Court of Air and Spring, also known as the Pavari Court. She is a tall fairy woman, with translucent skin that is paler than milk. She has long flowing silver hair and large delicate-appearing wings though sometimes her wings appear to be large, gray, and falcon-like. Her voice is a rich silvery voice similar to Revellie's.

ACKNOWLEDGEMENTS

Writing is such an isolating activity and despite having incredible ideas floating around in one's head, staying motivated can be problematic. I count myself fortunate that I've both had and have so many wonderful teachers, mentors and colleagues as I continue forward with the Heart of the World series. This story certainly has been shaped by the support, encouragement, and inspiration from many wonderful people.

I do have some special shout-outs:

First to my street team, the Fae Furies. It is exciting to watch our chat group blossom into a dynamic and magical group. Your enthusiasm, dedication, and support mean the world to me! From sharing posts to spreading the word about this story, your efforts are bringing this book into the hands of readers. Thank you for believing in me, in my stories, and in the magic of this world. You are certainly helping to make this dream possible.

To my Blue Pod group, particularly Lou Schlesinger and Elizabeth Burton. Your insights and enthusiasm are beyond invaluable! In fact, thanks to Elizabeth, this story has the right ending. Both of you make me feel so incredibly supported. I'm also looking to seeing your novels go out into the world!

To my Saturday Epic group, Brenda Carre, Bruce Paulik, Tyson Dutton, Valérie Leroyer, Pat Hauldrin . . . . and occasional visit from Ali Nouraei: We've been together . . . what, over four years now? I simply cannot imagine going on this authoring journey without any of you. From our time meeting up with David Farland every week for the Epic course and we have grown, learned, and supported each other. I look forward to our continued journey as we forge our authoring paths side by side.

M. Colin Alston and Leann Burke. Have I mentioned lately how much you two are my heroes? Having you by my side makes me believe I can do anything!

To Daryn Kirscht from Oak Valley Media. Thank you for helping me to polish this story and also, for asking excellent questions!

To Cristina Tanase. Everytime I see the cover of this book, it makes my heart happy. I'm so glad that the universe aligned and I found you to be on my team.

A special thanks to Apex-Writers. Working alongside David Farland's legacy writing group is an adventure everyday! I have built strong friendships with this group and the resources.... five years of multi-weekly lectures by industry leaders, plus courses. It's been a game-changer! Plus, hosting, scheduling, and providing marketing content has been and is an incredible opportunity.

To my tribe at Superstars, I can't wait to return in 2026 and with published books! Anytime I think I can't, I think of you and I know I can.

It certainly is an incredible journey running with Wulf Moon's Wulf Pack. This group of movers and shakers are taking the writing community by storm. If you want to learn how to get your short stories out into respectful markets, and more... well, this definitely is where you want to be.

To my Magic-Weaver sprint group: Day Leitao and Lusine Torossian. Not only do you ladies keep me motivated but our time sprinting and discussions are sheer magic!

A special shout-out to the Greater Lehigh Valley Writers Group (GLVWG). Without you, I would not be where I am. Thank you!

Also, to my beta readers and critique partners, particularly my Canadian critique partners: Wonnita Andrus, Merilyn Liddell, and Monica Sagle Zwikstra: your thoughtful feedback most definitely has helped shape this story into what it is today.

Additionally, to my family. Thank you for your patience as I spent countless hours lost in the worlds of faeries and prophecy. Your love and encouragement gave me the strength to keep going, even on the toughest days.

A special thanks to my readers. This book exists because of you. Your excitement for faeries, magic, and adventure fuels my inspiration every day. Thank you for diving into the *Heart of the Worlds* universe.

And last, to all my flickering lights out there who don't realize how wonderful you are. One of the things that I'm most passionate in getting across is the message that even if you feel like you don't belong, you belong first and foremost to yourself. AND like Aunia, you deserve to be celebrated for all the positive and creative things you bring into the world. You are enough. And I wish all good things for you!

With love, gratitude, and faerie dust,

TF Burke

ABOUT THE AUTHOR

TF Burke is a seasoned writer and passionate advocate for the authoring community. A former officer of the Greater Lehigh Valley Writers Group (GLVWG) from 2009 to 2013, she served as both president and chair of the record-breaking, sold-out Write Stuff conference, which featured pre-conference workshops and a bustling book fair.

Currently, she works with David Farland's Apex-Writers as an admin, where she coordinates an impressive multi-Zoom weekly schedule featuring industry leaders and emerging talents. In addition, she provides engaging content for social media, blogs, and more. Plus, she presents on authoring topics for various writing groups and hosts multiple writer-focused Zoom calls, including Apex's Strategy, Mindcraft & Wings, Midweekers, and others.

Her published works include hundreds of newspaper articles, blog posts, and fiction. Her books include bestseller, FAERIES DON'T LIE, Book 1 in the Heart of the World series; a collection of short stories, WHIRL OF THE FAE: MYTHS, LEGENDS AND SECRETS; and a short story, A FIREFLY'S CONSCIOUS AND THE PSYCHOPATH, featured in the MurderBugs anthology. The third book in her YA fantasy series, Faeries Don't Hide is slated for release in November 2025.

When she isn't writing or supporting fellow authors, she enjoys medieval-style fencing tournaments and melees—a pursuit she's embraced since 2010. She's equally at home exploring museums, libraries, and ancient ruins, often indulging her love for history and storytelling.

If you've enjoyed her work, please consider leaving a review on platforms like Amazon or Goodreads to help others discover these adventures too!

Also By

- FAERIES DON'T LIE – Book 1 of the Heart of the Worlds series

- WHIRL OF THE FAE

- A FIREFLY'S CONSCIENCE AND THE PSYCHOPATH, a short story in MurderBugs, the 2nd volume in the Unhelpful Encylopedia (available also in Audiobook)

Aunia's adventure continues!

Available on preorder & releases 11/25/25

Aunia is on a desperate quest to find the sea-witch who holds the secret whether her father yet lives and if he's lost within the more treacherous realms of Faery Lands.

At the same time, she is drawn into a dangerous conspiracy where the fate of Tamore hangs in the balance. Mathias needs her help not only to clear their names and avoid arrest, but to stop the Arch Vicar Bibb and his growing wererat army from wreaking havoc.

With every step, Aunia must navigate treacherous magic, fractured alliances, and deadly enemies while also uncovering intrigue that will change everything.